Ghosts of the Sahara

GHOSTS

of the

SAHARA

To Marty,

Enjoy —

Monique Williams

Monique Williams

This book is dedicated to Eddie Williams
who was my angel on earth
and who enriched my life in immeasurable ways.

ACKNOWLEDGEMENTS

This book took nearly two years to complete and I couldn't have written it without the love and support I received from my late husband, Eddie Williams. Kennedy Hunter, the journalist portrayed in this book, was part of our daily conversation at the dinner table and she became as real to him as she was to me.

I chose Morocco as part of the setting for this book because of its beauty and poetry. I have much affection for this beautiful country and its people. Like many who came before me—moviemakers, writers, painters—I find the country to be an endless source of fascination and inspiration.

All the characters created are the product of my imagination and I know of no conflict between Berbers and other Moroccans. The conflict was created for fictional and dramatic purposes only.

I'd like to thank my family and friends who supported me spiritually in this lonely endeavor called writing. You know who you are. And I'd also want to thank the staff at the various cafes I frequented who allowed me to use their space as my home away from home. You know who you are too.

GHOSTS
of the
SAHARA

PROLOGUE

The door onto the rooftop blew wide open as Kennedy Hunter stumbled out amid the laundry that hung to dry. Blinded by the brightness of the day, she held both hands out in front of her and moved to the edge of the rooftop and peered over it. The building stood five stories tall and was as nondescript as those surrounding it. It was the first time in days that she had inhaled fresh air and she took it all in, the sky, the air, the heat, the noise. She had been let out from her room on the rooftop, and she was free.

She eyed the city across and below her, the vast expanse of buildings that went for miles on end, and listened to the cacophony of sounds rising from the streets. A cumulus of clouds filled an otherwise unblemished sky as she listened to the wind dance on the rooftop.

She did not sense the ominous threat the Shergui presented.

The Shergui, a North African wind, hissed and hovered over the rooftop. It came from the Sahara, swept across the plains, and on the days it blew, people felt jittery and weary. It was hot and heavy and filled the air with fine desert sand that clung to your skin like fleas on a dog.

Suddenly, the skies turned dark and cries filled the air above her. She lifted her eyes to the horizon and saw a dense mass move towards her. She was puzzled, unsure of what it was when at once, and before she had time to identify it, the mass, a herd of locusts, pummeled her and threw her down to the floor.

The locusts had invaded the North African skies eating their way through everything they met. Like the biblical curse of the ancient pharaohs, they blanketed the skies and formed a tight lid on the city.

Buzzing like bees, they began their predatory feast on Kennedy Hunter. They entered the many cavities of her body as they crawled up her legs and gnawed at her eyes, her ears, the soft flesh of her earlobes, the tender skin above her lips.

They wrapped her like a mummy and then, suddenly, as if a telepathic message had traveled through them, they gave up on their meaty repast and took off like a flying carpet, away from her, in search of a more befitting vegetarian meal.

For hours, she had lain on the rooftop amid the countless locusts that perished. Then she crawled back to her room, closed her door, and fell into a large, dark abyss.

When she awoke, her eyes, shut tight as if glued, felt dry and sandy.

She heard noises in her room then smelled The Torch before she saw him. He smelled of North Africa: frankincense, turmeric, coriander, mint. His silhouette cut a sharp figure in the dim room. Clad in a billowing seroual topped with a djellabah, he squatted on the floor in front of a clay pot filled with burning coals on which he placed the locusts he had gathered from the rooftop.

The locusts sizzled and turned red. He snapped their heads, tore their legs, and bit into their flesh as she listened to the crisp and crunchy sounds he made. He placed a few locusts, red as blood, on a platter and shoved the platter towards her.

"Eat! Eat!" he said impatiently.

She pushed the platter away from her not wanting any of his offerings. He grunted in disapproval and stomped out of the room.

She dropped back on her cot, weary and fell into a deep sleep. That night, the abyss felt like a womb, it drew her deep inside enveloping her and in it, she felt nurtured and safe.

Days later—she doesn't know how many—he came back and again roasted the locusts that had perished on the rooftop and offered her a plate. This time, she was hungry and not about to refuse whatever he offered her. She had been without food for several days so she relented and ate the locusts that ate her.

He sat by her side, a smirk on his face, his piercing gaze observing every move she made. He handed her a glass of water. She grabbed it and swallowed its content in one gulp.

"You're going home today," he said.

"Thank you," she replied wondering why she was thanking him and feeling like an idiot for doing so. It is a crazy thing, a distortion of the mind that prisoners often sympathize with and thank their captors. She had just thanked him for holding her prisoner for over thirty days. She's had plenty of time to think about the reporters who came before her, those who just wanted to tell a story and were executed in front of cameras. And she's had plenty of time to think about her own death.

When he let her out onto the rooftop, he chose the day the locusts invaded Casablanca.

"You've learned your lesson, haven't you?" he said crisply.

She nodded.

"Good," he said. "Reporters have to learn their lessons. You'll serve as an example for all those who'll follow."

Wordlessly, she nodded her head in approval. She was afraid he wouldn't free her. She just wanted this to end, one way or another.

He threw his head back and chuckled. The tinny, silvery chuckle that she had grown accustomed to.

Then he opened the door and pushed her out onto the rooftop.

"Go, go," he said, "au revoir, Kennedy!"

CHAPTER ONE

Fifteen years later

From above, Casablanca spread for miles to the Atlantic, framed by the shoreline and harbor to the West, and the medina to the East. An indigo sky hovered, tarnished only by a cumulus of white clouds that floated above like so much cotton candy.

Below, at street level, the atmosphere was anything but restrained. The din rising from the streets shattered Kennedy Hunter's ears. The sounds, smells, and cries of the street overwhelmed her when she set foot in Casablanca. Peddlers shouted and taxi drivers blew their horns competing for every tourist's attention as pedestrians mingled with cars, scooters, and mules in a shoving contest that no one was winning. The smell of grilled kebabs and French bread combined with the sweet odor of almond pastries sold nearby by street vendors hit her nostrils reminding her that she had passed up on her airline food ration in favor of fruit she had packed in her carry-on.

She remembered that North Africa was not about order. Good form was reserved for indoors. Outdoors, Darwinism prevailed. Scream louder, push harder. Still, the brouhaha excited her and infused her with vigor in spite of her weary state. She was, at once, apprehensive about her upcoming work and aroused.

She walked out of the terminal into a day infused with winter brightness, her eyes scanning the crowd. Her gaze landed across the street where a thin, wiry man leaned on a Renault, legs crossed, a cigarette dangling from the side of his mouth. He wore jeans, an aviator leather jacket, and brown loafers. His face revealed the brutality of the North African sun. Mahogany skin burnished and leathered like the hides hanging in tanneries across town.

At the sight of Kennedy, he let his cigarette drop to the ground and dashed across the street. He grabbed her suitcases with the enthusiasm of someone expecting his pending tip to be generous.

"*Francais, Anglais, Espanol*?" he said reciting his linguistic menu.

"All three," she said, "have your pick."

He grinned. "Good, then we'll speak all three." He opened the door and bowed. She caught a strong odor of stale cigarettes as he shut the door behind her.

"*Mademoiselle*," he said, "which hotel?"

"The Riad Salam by the Corniche, please."

He nodded, flashed a toothy smile that reminded her of corn-on-the-cob and entered the car. He extricated himself from the mayhem around them with a natural agility and forged straight ahead.

Once on the road, he eyed her through the rearview mirror. "My name is Sami," he said, "and I'll be your runner during your stay." Runners were the most important asset a reporter could have in a foreign country. They were also called "fixers" or "spotters"—savvy individuals who knew the terrain, had connections, and knew when to grease the palms of officials.

She detected a regional inflection, a musical tone to his speech. There was complicity in his dark eyes and they shone like black olives. He was a man who could convey a lot with one glance and she liked that.

"Glad to meet you, Sami. Mine is Kennedy."

"Kennedy?" He appeared puzzled. "Like the president?"

"Yes, like the president," she said. He nodded his head in disbelief.

Kennedy leaned back and closed her eyes for the nineteen miles that separated the airport from the city. She was experiencing sensory overload and was glad he concentrated on his driving instead of assailing her with questions.

She lowered her window. Crisp air filled the vehicle as they passed rows upon rows of palm trees edging the road. Men and women in *djellabahs*. Mules loaded with fruits and vegetables. Women walking subserviently, heads bowed, baskets delicately balanced on their heads. Postcard image. Not much changes in these parts of the world, she thought. Here, life was like a river, it just flowed.

Images from the past drifted in her mind as they neared the city. The Torch. *The Atlanta Dispatch* had given her a picture of him, as if she needed one. He was in his forties now. Weather-beaten. Henna and leather. Khakis, head covered in a turban. So romantic, she thought. So Hollywood. She recalled he had a way of charming the international media, not by his omnipresence but by his reticence, by building a mystique that served him well. He was the valiant soldier, the rebel with a cause. Like a rose. Beautiful, velvety, fragrant. And everyone fell under his spell. Casting a blind eye to his thorns.

Then came September 11, 2001 and everything changed. The world changed. Terrorism became an international threat and the romance of the rebel went out the proverbial window.

But she didn't underestimate The Torch. He was a son-of-a-bitch then, and now everyone estimated he was the face of Al Qaeda in North Africa responsible for the Madrid bombing and various other ones in Casablanca and elsewhere.

She knew first hand of his sting. Felt it. Lived it. He had injured her with impunity. Wounding her at a time when she was neither ready nor mature enough to handle such an adversary. Yanking the chair from under her as she was getting ready to be seated.

From him she had learned about fear. And strangely enough, he had taught her something about fortitude. Yet, years later, the fear lingered, lived right below the surface of her skin. Resided in her cells, clinging to her like a leech she could not yank.

She wondered how other war reporters lived with trauma. No one she knew ever talked about it. They just lay in the dark and try to remember which war they are fighting. Bosnia? Kosovo? Pakistan? Iraq? Rockets falling in the middle of the night all sound alike.

She pushed those thoughts aside not wanting them to multiply, get out of control, like a mitosis gone mad. Here and now, life was real. The winter sun licked her face, lingered on her shoulders, and a cool wind whispered in her ears.

Sami woke her from her reverie when they reached the hotel.

"We're here!" he said.

She cast a glance his way and smiled. I'm going to like this guy, she thought. The irony of the situation was not lost on her, she wondered if—to borrow a great Hollywood line—this was the beginning of a great friendship. Then, she dismissed him for the remainder of the day, needing and wanting, a hot shower, a soft bed, and a working phone.

CHAPTER TWO

Fringed by an oasis of palm trees, bougainvillea, and evergreen, the American College was a stately Art Deco building on Casablanca's largest boulevard, Avenue Mohammed V. The stucco and wrought iron building, adorned with cupolas, balconies, and 1930's motives, occupied half a block. Its presence was, by all standards, an imposing one.

More than an educational facility, The American College was the cultural link between the United States and Morocco, and the only alternative to those wanting an American education.

Its director, Dr. David Stevens, a man with an impeccable Ivy League education, was the driving force behind the institution. A strong proponent of humanities and liberal arts education, he directed his educators and students to enrich their souls instead of their pockets. Computers are fine machines, he would tell them, but they possess a built-in obsolescence that eventually renders them useless. What survives is culture and history. He was certain that nations who do not know where they are coming from could not know where they are going. An appreciation for culture—dance, music, literature—and for civility will get you further in life. And technology without culture is tantamount to teaching an elephant ballet. He may master the *jete* and the *bourre* but he will—forever—remain an elephant.

Socrates, Plato, Camus, and Sartre were quoted in classes as if they were living entities. Philosophical discussions were not, in the director's opinion, an intellectual exercise. Culture, he thought, was what separated and differentiated us from animals. We thought, therefore, we existed.

In diplomatic circles, he was a man who enjoyed the trust and confidence of everyone. Contrary to the perceived image of the Ugly American, David Stevens projected an image of the cultured American, something many considered an oxymoron.

His friends included members of the diplomatic corps, the royal family, the foreign press and the who's-who on the Moroccan scene. He transcended the label of educator; he was a diplomat without a portfolio and a negotiator of cultural exchanges. He also possessed a can-do attitude and a sense of urgency that was, indeed, very American, and certainly appreciated by those needing his intervention. He understood local sensitivities, reserved his directness for other Americans and treaded lightly when needed. Rumors were that whatever was said to him would follow him to his grave.

Even before meeting the director, Kennedy was determined to obtain an interview with The Torch. She knew, however, that he never granted interviews and his whereabouts were revealed to few. And she felt that if anyone knew where he was, it would be Dr. Stevens. He knew a great deal about Berbers, was respectful of their culture, and was, probably, the only westerner who knew The Torch's location.

The director's office at the American College captured the local flavor. Leather hassocks and carpets in rich hues dominated the room. Clay pots adorned with intricate patterns filled the floors, and on the director's desk stood a small American flag. On the walls, there were headshots of several American presidents, dead and alive, and a picture of the Statue of Liberty. Behind him, on a credenza, pictures of his family. A smiling wife with two daughters. The wife in her early-forties, daughters in their late teens, fair-skinned and bright smiles. They were on a boat in a marina, wind in their hair. Pure Apple Pie.

Dr. Stevens introduced himself with a warm and friendly handshake. He was six-foot-three towering over most Mediterranean men. He had, still, a full head of hair but his temples were turning gray adding a distinguished look to his already polished image. Clad in a navy American-cut suit, crisp white shirt, red tie.

"A pleasure, Miss Hunter," he said, "I'm an aficionado of your paper and articles."

"Thank you," she replied, "didn't know anybody read them other than my friends."

He flashed a smile revealing American teeth, flossed after every meal. He motioned Kennedy towards a chair.

"Oh, I do," he said, "I get most American papers here. A bit late. . . but I still read them all."

"I'm particularly fond of your paper," he added. "Did you know that your managing editor and I went to college together?"

"I had no idea," she replied. "He kept it a secret."

He chuckled. "I see, Miss Hunter."

"By the way, I'd feel better if you'd just call me Kennedy."

"Sure. I'd prefer Kennedy, too. In fact, one of my favorite presidents, although his legacy has been questioned lately."

"Obviously, my parents' too."

"I was a young man when he died but my generation has been touched by him. His charisma. His looks. And then, of course, his untimely death." He grabbed a pen on his desk and leaned back in his chair. "All the elements to create a mythological figure. He ushered in a new era for

America and in this part of the world, people haven't forgotten him."

"Sometimes, his name can be a burden," she said. "A hell of an act to follow—like I have to live up to it, or something."

"I can imagine," he replied, a generous smile on his face. "I know a Spaniard named Jesus, an Italian named Caesar, and one named Hannibal."

They laughed simultaneously. The ice was broken. Charisma oozed from his pores.

"Well," she replied, "I once met an immigrant from Guatemala who named her daughter America."

"The ultimate act of patriotism," he said. "Now, what is it that I can I do for you?"

"Well," she shifted in her seat and leaned forward, "I'm here to meet The Torch."

He nodded. "O.K."

"I'd like to interview him."

He managed a smile.

"I was told you were my best chance to meet him."

"Miss Hunter," he reverted to a formal tone, "please understand that I'm in this country as a guest and as such I'm completely apolitical." He paused and gazed straight into her eyes. "The current conflict is one where I do not take sides. My host, the Moroccan government, is most gracious in allowing us to import our culture and also to subsidize us in the process."

"I understand your concern," she answered. "It would be presumptuous of me to ask you to take sides in this conflict. I'm only interested in reporting on what's happening. The world knows little—if anything—about The Torch. My goal is to tell a story."

The Torch, a north African rebel of Berber descent, had been hiding in the Sahara for over fifteen years and no one had interviewed him since Kennedy had.

He nodded. "Miss Hunter, I see your point. However, I

can't take a chance on even appearing partisan. Partisan-ship could mean the death of this college—and that," he added, "I can't let it happen."

She felt defeated but pressed. "I was the last one to in-terview him."

"Yes, I know. I remember."

She paused hoping for a reversal of heart but his face remained impenetrable. "The American media is clamoring for an interview with him. CNN and others are trying hard and they'll soon beam their lights on him and his people. It's just a matter of time."

"True," he said, "but I won't be the one starting this ava-lanche."

She persisted. "Could I ask you to give it a thought?"

"Sure. And I will. But I make no promises." He leaned forward. "The Berbers have been here long before the Ar-abs. They are Moslems and think of themselves as Arabs." He paused then resumed. "They have intermingled with Arabs for centuries. I don't know why The Torch thinks that they need a leader and a nation of their own. He also wants a return to Islamic values."

He scratched his head. "This attempt to raise their con-sciousness may be the craziest idea of them all. Look at what Arafat did to his people, there was no such thing as Palestinians until he invented them."

She pressed not giving up. "People are interested in hearing his story, his philosophy."

"The problem with telling the story of rebels is that in America we tend to Hollywood-ize them—permit me to make a verb out of it."

"Not anymore. Not since 9/11," she replied.

He shifted in his chair. " 9/11 changed everything."

There was a knock at his door. A young woman walked in, eyed Kennedy and the director. She looked pale and nervous.

"What is it?" he asked.

"Dr. Stevens, can I see you for a moment?"

"Can it wait?"

She eyed Kennedy apologetically.

"Well . . . it's urgent," she whispered.

He rose from his chair, apologized, and walked out of the room. Kennedy heard him talk outside the door. She caught only fragments of the conversation.

"*Emily . . . when . . . gone for four days? What do you mean?*" Momentary silence followed by more whispers, then, "*Oh, my God.*"

He walked back in, his composure had changed, and his face was ashen. He sat back behind his desk, eyelashes fluttering, unfocused.

"I'm sorry, Miss Hunter. We have a little emergency."

She got up, took her reporter's pad, and extended her hand to him. "In that case, I better leave. Thank you, Doctor."

He did not object. "My pleasure. And enjoy your stay in this beautiful country," he said, his voice straining. "If you ever need some recommendations for great restaurants, I'd be glad to recommend some."

------•◆•------

Outside the gates, Sami waited. He was in his favorite position, leaning against the car hood, cigarette dangling from his mouth. He hurried to open the door as she neared him then spat his cigarette on the sidewalk. Without a word, she got in.

"Everything O.K. *Mademoiselle*?"

"Not really. Unsuccessful meeting."

"Maybe I can help." He turned back to face her.

"The Torch," she said, "what do you know about him?"

He looked over his shoulder as if searching for something

or someone. His tone changed immediately and he lowered his voice to a murmur.

"Many, many stories. What does *Mademoiselle* want with The Torch?"

"An interview. I want to meet him. I need to write stories about Berbers."

"Not easy, Kennedy. *Pas facile*. He's hiding. Always hiding. Nobody knows where. Maybe the mountains, the High Atlas, or the Sahara."

Sami drove off, his foot heavy on the gas pedal.

"Tell me, Sami, are you a Berber?"

He looked through the rearview mirror; his eyes acquiesced, which did not surprise her. He possessed the delicate features of his race. Aquiline nose, almond eyes, high cheekbones, and thin lips.

"From the High Atlas, Miss. A *Shleuh*."

"How well do you know the Atlas Mountains, Sami? And the Sahara?"

"Very well, Mademoiselle. Both, very dangerous. Not good for woman alone. Mountains are cold, roads icy in winter. Snow." He paused. "The *Sah'ra*," he pronounced it like locals with emphasis on the first syllable "is very far and dangerous."

"You might need to take me out there."

He did not reply, just nodded, his dark eyes filled with doubt as he eyed her through his rearview mirror.

CHAPTER THREE

Stench rose from the city's dump but Mohamed trudged through the mountains of litter as if it was a treasure hunt. He was seeing opportunities, possibilities—not refuse. For most of his life, fourteen years in all, he had risen early and gotten there before other scavengers showed up. Territorial wars broke out consistently. Looters tore each other like carnivores in the wild. Rummaging through the heaps of things people threw away, he always found everything he needed for his survival. Perfectly edible food that needed little, if any, washing. Clothes. Old books. Shoes with miles to go. And a myriad of items he had no market for—a prosthetic leg, a black dildo, handcuffs, a set of false teeth.

His routine was set—dawn at the dump when trucks came in, and at dusk, tending to his secondary occupation, pimping for prostitutes. Either way, he felt he dealt with human refuse. He knew the city in ways no one else did—at dawn rising from its slumber and when it went to sleep, spent from excesses, debauchery and sin.

Suddenly, Mohamed saw a large mass under an uneven mount. He dug with both hands and pulled. It did not yield. He tried again. No luck either. He got on his knees and with both hands frantically cleared the spot. Finally, he saw it. It stuck out like a sore thumb. *It was a thumb!* The sight sent him scurrying. He broke out in a cold sweat, acid rising in his throat. He bent over and heaved it all out. Stench over stench.

He wiped his runny nose and mouth with his sleeve. Hands trembling and holding his breath, he removed all refuse around it. Minutes later, a body was in full view.

She was still. She rested amidst the garbage, curled up like a seahorse, her body bearing the language of sleep. Her face had acquired the ashen color of death and a crusty film had formed around her lips. Her sandy hair, dry and weathered from exposure, hung loosely on her shoulders. A hair strand had casually fallen on her face casting an accidental gentleness to her features. She wore a gossamer tunic and hip-hugging pants revealing a body that neither age nor nature had yet tarnished.

Mohamed looked away. He could not muster the courage to look at her face. His eyes, quick, sharp, and discerning, scanned her body. Then he saw a purse lying near the body. He grabbed it. Opened it. There was a wallet inside. He took out all the dirhams. Then he hit pay dirt—dollars. He leafed quickly through them. Jackson, Jackson, Jackson. No Lincolns, no Washingtons. Good. He loved Jacksons.

Quickly, he returned the wallet and emptied the purse from its contents filling his pockets.

He felt a stabbing pain in his heart. She was lovely and he wondered whether she was one of his girls. She was badly damaged, had lost some of her glow but he knew she had once been beautiful.

He stepped away still eyeing her with intensity feeling both mesmerized and disgusted by death. He wanted to touch her, turn her over to see the face, but he did not possess the sang-froid he needed for such task. Allah, he thought, *forgive me.* He felt a pang of guilt and knew he needed to do the right thing. *I'll call the cops,* he thought.

He fled away from the girl, his feet flying over the refuse, certain that her spirit, seeking revenge, would rise from the entrails of the dump and find him wherever he went.

CHAPTER FOUR

The three knocks at her door startled Kennedy. She had told Sami to take a day off; she was not expecting anyone. She needed time to find and connect with her sources, research her articles and map out a plan.

Two Arab men stood before her, thin, dark. One tall, one short. They wore gray suits, matching ties, dark sunglasses, and they reminded her of wise guys in Mafia movies.

"*Mademoiselle*," said the tall one, "we're here to pick you up," his voice as flat as stale beer.

She paused shortly, her eyes shifting from one to the other. "It must be a mistake, I haven't asked for anyone to pick me up," she said pushing the door back.

With his foot, he jammed the door. "No mistake," he said, "we're here to take you to your interview with The Torch."

Startled, she gazed back at them but all she met was their vacant faces.

"Please follow us," he said, a commanding tone in his voice.

"I need to gather a few things. My cell phone, my tape recorder, my notebook, my camera."

"You won't need any of it, Miss, nothing, *rien du tout*."

"Can I, at least, grab my bag?"

"No. Nothing. *Rien du tout*."

She felt apprehension but her journalist instincts told her to go along with it.

They walked to the elevator, their composure stony as they rode down. All three left the front door, entered a Peugeot parked at curbside, a driver already at the wheel, motor running.

When she slid in the back, the short one sat next to her, the tall one upfront.

"*Imshi! Imshi!*" He motioned to the driver to move. Kennedy waited until the driver had pulled into traffic.

"Where are we going?" she asked.

No one answered. The man at her side pulled something from his pocket. It was a red bandanna and he immediately wrapped it around Kennedy's eyes.

She fought back. "Wait a minute!" She screamed. "You're not going to blindfold me!" Her arms flew across his face.

He pulled back, his dark eyes piercing her face. "*Oui, Mademoiselle. C'est les conditions.* Those are the conditions. If you want your interview."

Anger rose in her throat and blood sped to her head at a dizzying rate. Her pulse quickened and the thumping of her heart resonated in her ears.

Still, she relented letting him blindfold her. His slender fingers tied a knot behind her head and as he brushed against her, she smelled him. He reeked rancid. Tobacco and sweat. She felt a loss of control and an uneasiness she did not like. He pulled a rope from his pocket and tied her hands in front of her.

"Damn you!"

He ignored her. They drove quietly and when they broke their silence, they spoke in short sentences and in a Berber dialect she did not understand.

She kept quiet but thoughts whirled in her head like a cork in an empty bottle.

For a while, they traversed the city. The blaring horns and the jerking movements continued and then suddenly, everything calmed down. They were out on a highway, away from the city, their ride interrupted only by an occasional clearing of the throat or a horn blaring in the countryside.

"How long is this gonna take?" Her impatience grew in the backseat.

"Not yet," said the man by her side. He did not explain.

She remained in her silence listening to her breathing, her heartbeat, and the few cars on the highway. Suddenly, she realized she could no longer hear other cars. It was as if they were the only ones traveling on a deserted road.

They rode a while longer. An hour? More? Perhaps less, but time seemed eternal in the backseat. How did I get myself into this, she thought, just for an interview.

Unexpectedly, the car stopped. She felt relief. The end of this unpleasant episode was near, she thought. Doors opened, a man grabbed her arm and pulled her out. More doors slammed. She stepped on an unpaved road, her feet stumbling on small pebbles and rocks. A man led her by her elbow and reluctantly, she followed.

"Can you take this thing off?"

"No. *Pas encore, Mademoiselle*. Not yet. *Avancez! Attention!* Steps, in front of you," he said, "go up steps!"

"This is ridiculous!" she yelled, "don't you think you're overreacting, you idiot! Take that damn thing off of me!"

"You take off, you go back!" he answered. She heard the silvery chuckle of the other two.

She walked up narrow metal steps and entered a door. The man guided her through the door inside a small place. She immediately knew she was inside a plane. He pushed her forward and into a seat. Like a blind man, she fingered the seats feeling their contour.

"*Continuez!*" he yelled. "*Asseyez-vous!* Sit down!"

She did and he sat next to her. She heard a rustle behind her as if they, too, were settling down.

More Berber talk. Animated conversation between them. This time there was an added voice, one she had not heard before and he sounded angry. Or perhaps it was just the way they talked, she wasn't sure. Some languages sound angry. Like German and Arabic. Guttural languages that made everyone sound mad. German, a man once told her, was the language you spoke to your horse. Right now, she thought, I would like to speak the language God can hear.

Someone cranked a motor. A whining noise filled the air while everyone sat quietly. Her heart nearly came to a full stop.

Although restrained by the cords around her wrists, she grabbed the man by the arm and dug her nails into him. "You sonofabitch!" She yelled breathlessly. She repeated it again, just in case he had not heard her the first time around.

"*Calmez-vous!*" he said yanking her hands off him. "Calm down!"

"Calm down? Are you out of your freakin' mind? What's this, some kind of a stupid joke?"

"No joke, *Mademoiselle*," he replied matter-of-factly.

"Don't Mademoiselle-me to death! Just tell me where the hell we're going!"

He did not reply, just leaned back in his seat, and sighed heavily.

The plane moved slowly across the runway then whirled forward and lifted off the ground. Her head filled with sounds, she leaned back and surrendered. Behind the bandanna, her eyes felt heavy. Soon, the droning sound of the motor was the only sound anyone heard. They flew for more than two hours. The men had nodded off and their breathing turned heavy. *That's it, you bastards, take your stupid naps.*

The temperatures inside the plane had plummeted and

she felt cold. She also had an urgent need to go to the bathroom. It would have to wait.

Then the plane began circling. She counted three full turns thinking they were going to land.

But they did not. They just kept flying.

Suddenly, the man grabbed her arm. "Get up!"

She slid out of her seat. "Take that damn thing off of me!" She reached for the bandanna and yanked it. He fought back and another man rose to the rescue. They placed it back on her eyes and held her tight.

Then he removed her shoes. She kept her foot rigid while he struggled to place boots on her feet.

"Damn American women!" he yelled.

Finally, he slid her feet in and tied the laces on hiking boots. Then he lifted her arms pulling straps around each shoulder.

"What's this?" She yelled raising her voice above the din of the plane.

He just grunted. Then he lifted her left leg and slid it through another strap. He did the same with her right one. It felt like a backpack. All right bastards, I guess we're going on a trek.

At last, the man removed her blindfold and untied her hands. Night had fallen and it was dark inside the Cessna. She was strapped to a parachute and standing by the door.

"Where am I going with this?" she yelled.

"Down," he said, a smirk on his face. "Down. The *Sah'ra*."

They held her tight. She kicked them in the shins in an attempt to free herself from their grasp.

Panic gripped her and she felt a tightening in her chest. She could not hear the sound of the plane, the thumping of her heart hammering in her chest. First signs of tachycardia. I'm going to have a coronary right here and right now, she thought.

He slid the door open and a gush of wind blew in the cabin. Kennedy's face contorted from fear.

"You're freakin' crazy!"

They shoved her upfront. A man took her right hand and placed it on the ripcord. "Count to ten before you pull this!"

She turned to look at him and saw the contempt on his face.

You sonofabitch.

Your face will be seared in my memory forever.

Her face beaten from the wind, she eyed the ocean of darkness below. Her blood pressure plummeted and her breathing became shallow. She felt as if life was being sucked from her.

"Jump or I'll push you!" he yelled. "You wanted an interview? You have it!" He chuckled. Metal against metal.

"You dirty sack of shit!" she yelled then summoned all of her strength and kneed him in the gonads. He doubled over. Held his crotch.

"*Putaine!*" Whore.

She grabbed the door. Looked out. A gust of wind blasted through blinding her. She shut her eyes. *Dear God, help me.*

She jumped into the thick of the night, her hold on life as thin as breath, knowing with certainty that neither the night nor the desert were forgiving.

CHAPTER FIVE

Detective Ahmed entered the double doors of the American College. Dealing with death was an aspect of his job he found very unpleasant. It was too unsettling. Particularly when the subject was a young woman. And more so if it was an American one. Murders were not commonplace in Casablanca. Robberies, yes, but murders were, in his opinion at least, an American mania. Americans, he thought, were some of the most educated people on this planet, yet, they tore each other up like rabid dogs. Just look at their movies, he thought. No one can outdo them in the many ways they kill.

Nonetheless, he liked them—*Les Amerloques*—for their generous characters, their big smiles, their carefree attitude. Yet, the few times he has had to deal with them on some investigations, he found them rigid. They went strictly by the book and made everything more difficult for him. They simply did not understand the ways of his country.

The detective was unable to shut off the dialogue inside his head. Should he tell The American College of the body found or should he just ignore it? It would certainly simplify his life if he did. No investigations. No media intervention. No headaches. The woman had taken off and simply vanished. It was common occurrence. Young adults seeking excitement in Casablanca or Tangier, succumbing to the allure

of drugs or prostitution often disappeared. He never understood why Americans, always overly cautious in their own
country, turned careless in his throwing all caution to the
wind. Well, too bad. They often get their comeuppance.

He did not know if he could handle the consequences of
a murder. It would be a public relations nightmare. He hated to see his fellow citizens portrayed as callous or cruel.
With Americans, things were never easy. Surely, there'll be
a price to pay.

He remembered the gutted body on ice-cold metal. How
could anyone turn such a beautiful girl into such a mess? He
thought of his daughter and his wife and a stab traversed his
heart. He shook his head to no one but himself and decided
that as a good Moslem, he would do the right thing.

Against his better judgment, he entered the College and
was now in Dr. Stevens' office, fists clenched, legs trembling wondering how to break the news to this gentle giant.

"Ahmed, my friend! *Salem!* How are you? Dr. Stevens
said as he embraced the detective.

"Good, *Merci*. Thank you, very much," answered the Arab. *"Et vous, Monsieur Le Directeur?"*

"Very good, thank you. Please sit down. Can I offer you
a cup of tea, with *nana*, of course?"

"Merci, merci," answered the Arab. He offered a shy
smile at the invitation. He found the notion of Americans
addicted to mint tea amusing.

Ahmed eyed the well-attired American. Instinctively he
reached and adjusted his own tie. He was conscientious of
his physical appearance and wore his finest uniform today.
It was important to him to make a good impression on the
American.

"What do I owe the pleasure of your visit to?" Dr. Stevens
said.

Ahmed cleared his throat. "How's your family, sir? *Madame*, your wife, *les enfants*, the children—everybody O.K.?"

he asked. He needed to warm up before he plunged into such an unpleasant subject.

"*Merci*," answered the director, "everyone is fine."

"*Monsieur*," said the Arab, "your students? O.K.?"

Dr. Stevens straightened up in his chair. His face turned somber.

"Why, Ahmed, are you asking?"

"Because . . . "

"Because why?"

"Do you. . .have a student missing, *Monsieur*?"

"Well," Dr. Stevens answered, "we have a young woman who went out hiking south of Marrakesh last weekend and she hasn't been back yet. She is a student of anthropology and does this frequently."

"*Monsieur* . . . ." The detective stalled.

"What do you have, Ahmed?" Stevens said. Arabs had a way of stalling without getting to the point. This is one time when American directness was required.

"A young woman . . . *h'ram* . . . shame . . . beautiful . . . ". He nodded, a look of incredulity on his face, then noticed the impatient face of the director. "Her name was in her small purse—Emily Carrington."

"Is she dead?" Stevens' impatience began to show. He wondered when Ahmed would get to the point.

"*Oui, Monsieur* . . . "

"Where was she found?"

"At the city's dump."

Blood drained from Dr. Stevens' face. The city's slums, the *bidonvilles*, were a site of wretchedness and squalor. He wondered how Emily Carrington, a child of privilege, could end up there.

"Oh, God. Oh, God." Dr. Stevens shivered.

"*Monsieur*, I'm sorry. Very sorry."

"What happened to her, Ahmed? Who did it? Do you know who did it, Ahmed?"

Ahmed hesitated. He did not want to describe the condition of the body. He knew that once this image inhabited the director's mind, erasing it would be nearly impossible.

"We don't know, yet. We just found the body. This morning."

"Where's the body?"

"At the city morgue, *Monsieur*."

"Do you need somebody to identify her?"

"Well, she doesn't look good. Nearly all decomposed. But we found this." He retrieved something from his jacket pocket. He handed it to Dr. Stevens. It was a student's identification card with Emily's photo.

Stevens' hands trembled as he held it. Jumbled thoughts whirled around in his head. He thought, how such thing could happen, here, in Casablanca where he felt safe. Such brutality did not exist here. Murder was very scarce. American parents entrusted their children to him and he felt he was their guardian and they were like his own offspring.

And now this.

He sat crushed by the news, too numb to react. He needed to notify the parents. He didn't know how to break the news to the family. He never had to do this before. He was searching his memory to try to remember where the parents were from. Then, he remembered. Atlanta. She was from an affluent family in Atlanta. Her father had been a diplomat in Morocco and his daughter had returned long after his death.

"*Monsieur*," Ahmed startled him. "We'll begin investigating immediately. We're going to need her dental chart from America and fingerprints. Then, we will know for sure."

"Of course, Ahmed. I will contact the family. Please leave that to me. That's something that I've to do." Dr. Stevens held his head between his hands. "Ahmed, can I ask you to keep this confidential? At least until we've notified the family in the States."

Ahmed bowed his head. *"Pas de probleme."* He rose to leave when the director motioned him to sit down.

"Ahmed," Dr. Stevens said—he was in command again and was thinking fast on his feet—"we do not want this to turn into an international incident or a diplomatic crisis."

"Oui, Monsieur," answered the Arab. *"Je comprends."* He understood all too well. Discretion was part of his job description.

"Good. Let's keep this from getting into the news and the diplomatic circles. It could trigger a quick departure of all foreigners."

"Bien sur, Monsieur." Sure, no problem. He was happy to keep it all under wraps. His office was neither capable nor ready to handle the international media. Experience told him that when it came to foreigners, it seemed as if their lives were of greater value. He could almost visualize American headlines, in capital letters. American Found in Dump in Casablanca. Certainly not the romantic image everyone had in mind. He dreaded the sensationalism of the tabloids. They would have a field day, he thought. Nothing they'd like more than a gory story with all the international intrigue that came with it.

He recalled, years earlier, the story of an older American man, a millionaire with a villa in Tangier. His sexual prowess and discriminating taste had garnered him a distinct clientele—young Arab boys, dark, handsome, and very accommodating. One clear summer day as the sun rose over the city, the millionaire was found naked and tied spreadeagle to his bedposts. Every young boy in Tangier was arrested, interrogated, and often, beaten up. After turning the city on its head, the authorities focused on his American lover who confessed that he had killed him in a jealous, uncontrollable fit of rage.

Ahmed rose to leave. He shook Dr. Stevens' hand and left, troubled by what the future would bring to him.

CHAPTER SIX

One thousand one . . . One thousand two . . . One thousand three . . .

At a thousand ten, Kennedy yanked the ripcord of her parachute. The canopy snapped, unfolded, then inflated like a balloon. Her hands tightened around the harnesses as she floated in a sea of darkness, seesawing, back and forth, back and forth.

She was as frightened as the day Harry Bernstein had taken her to an amusement park, insisting on her riding the roller coaster. Up at a 90-degree angle and down at more than 65 miles an hour. Up and down. Up and down. He was screaming and laughing like a kid while she clutched her stomach. Soon as they got off, she had thrown up all over the place. She was never good at this stuff, she thought. Only a kid as big as Harry could enjoy such a thing. In his life, Harry had substituted oxygen for adrenaline, living for the next thrill, his system continuously revved up.

She recalled the Vietnam stories he had often told her after a glass or two, when he'd loosen up, the words would gush out of him like an overflowing river. Now, as she floated between earth and heaven, Harry's words came back to her.

I had to bail out . . . and the enemy . . . all around, surrounded me. . . there was nothing but VC's . . . I was a shooting target for the enemy . . . .

She remembered his words and now they rose to the surface of her psyche.

She often thought of him when she was in trouble. He was older, more mature and knew how to survive under any circumstances. They had a relationship that had lasted for years and survived their geographical distance. He lived in Virginia Beach and she in Atlanta where she had moved to work for *The Atlanta Dispatch*. It was one of those relationships where no questions were asked after her long absences overseas.

The night was dark and thick as she slid through the dense air. She shivered and perspired simultaneously; her teeth shattered. Cold sweat slid down her sides traveling all the way down her legs.

I hit the ground, luckily, feet first . . . I snapped my harnesses and hid out . . . rolled up my canopy . . . and let it shield me . . . .

Thump. She hit the ground.

Sand. *Terra firma.*

Her heels dug deep into the soft sand. She stumbled and rolled across until she came to a full stop. The canopy followed trailing behind her. She was dizzy and disoriented but pulled the canopy towards her and snapped her harnesses off her body. She rolled up the canopy and pulled it around her shoulders.

She let her eyes adjust to the darkness. The silence that encircled her fell like drawn curtains. It was all so unreal. Dreamlike. Her eyes pierced the dark finding the night too black. Reluctantly, she advanced a few steps. Her heels sank into the slick, smooth sand, still hot from the sun. As slick and smooth as she remembered it to be.

She knew this desert. She knew it well. Temperatures in the summer rose as high as 170-degrees and plummeted at night. As vast as the United States, she could walk days without coming across any living matter. Not a tree, a shrub, or a flowing stream. The Sahara crossed ten North African countries—to the west, Morocco, to the east, the Red Sea and Egypt until it reached the green pastures of the Sudan Sahel one thousand miles south. All and all, some three million square miles of sand and gravel. Sand so perfect that even the gods could not improve on its beauty. Now and then, mountains chiseled out of stalagmites rose unexpectedly. Or an oasis nestled amidst palm trees and surrounded by lakes emanated like a mirage, a figment of one's mind.

The word Sahara itself—*Sah'ra*—meant wasteland. A land so barren that life retreated and water became its nectar, its soul, its king. In some places, it rained but once every forty years and when it did, it was like a biblical deluge, ambushing the animals and killing many that had never experienced any downpours.

Deep inside the earth, seeds resided for years, their tendrils routing deep and far for moisture, waiting for an avalanche to awaken them from their slumber. During the hottest time of the day, leaves rolled themselves like a carpet surviving only on a few droplets of humidity. *How long could I survive*, she questioned herself. Unlike the fauna and flora of the desert, she knew she could not endure but a few hours. She wondered, with trepidation, about her fate. What will happen at dawn and once the mercury climbed again?

She let go of her anger for The Torch—she could not allow herself to seethe for long. Survival was all she could think of.

She sat on the desert floor, pulled the canopy tightly around her, and watched the full moon cast its light on the dunes and slopes surrounding her.

She listened to the ubiquitous language of the desert, the

mystical idiom of the wind, plants, and creatures. She didn't want to think about the desert creatures hiding deep in the sand, the ones that came out only when the sun faded.

Nocturnal predators.

Black scorpions, scarabs, skinks, lizards, horned vipers. Long, slender creatures with shiny coats and glistening scales that crawled out in the night and slithered across the sand leaving behind delicate imprints as evidence of their existence. They moved in the desert with economy, knew how to preserve their strength, and behaved as if they possessed a thinking mind.

She wondered if she could learn a lesson from them. Learn to be parsimonious. To give of herself in minute amounts. To ration herself like an I.V in a drip-drip fashion. Could she do it?

She heard whistles, hisses, and cricket-like sounds. An owl hooted, its cries echoing in the night. Kennedy's eyes probed the dark seeking for moving shapes. She knew they would come for her. She was a prey. And there was a predator waiting for her. They could smell her. They had *already* smelled her. Fennec foxes with tiny bodies and oversized ears. Languedoc scorpions, swift, poisonous, deadly. Desert monitors, lizards with scissor-like jaws, strong and primitive.

She felt impotent, powerless, because she could neither hear them nor see them. Instinctively, she pulled the canopy tighter around her.

Suddenly, she heard laughter. A rolling sound she recognized followed by more rolling sounds. Then she heard grunts. She looked in the direction the sounds came from and saw large moving shapes. She saw their shining eyes first. A pack of hyenas were eyeing her, their bobbing heads moving in the dark. They formed a semi-circle, advancing carefully, a few steps each time as they sniffed the floor of the desert.

Hurriedly, she stood up and took off her pants. She tied

a knot at the bottom of one leg and began scooping sand with both hands all the while keeping an eye on the hyenas. She crammed sand a third of the way up the leg packing it tight, took off a shoelace from her boot and tied it around the pant leg forming a large tight ball of sand. A sand bat.

Then she waited.

She saw them near her. She had her pants ready in her hands, twisted, so that she could fling the leg up in the air.

They were just a few feet away. She lifted the leg up and with one cry flung it out.

"Go! Go away!"

Undaunted, they advanced farther. She took her weapon again and flung it again.

They backed off grunting.

Suddenly, a hyena split from the pack and ran forward attacking her from behind. Emboldened, the rest of them inched slowly.

She saw him, turned around and just in time, lifted the leg and swung it hard. She hit him right in the eye. He shrieked from pain and retrieved a few steps back. He was, temporarily at least, immobilized. She lifted her bat again and flung it hard. She hit him again. His shrill cries cut the night like a stiletto.

Wounded, he scurried away in the dark. The rest halted then grunted. Slowly, they turned around and moved away. Minutes later, the dark swallowed them and the night returned to its stillness. Still, the absence of sound did not make her feel any safer. Contrary. Her senses were on full alert, pupils dilated, epidermis thorny.

She probed the dark and listened to the music of the night.

Finally, she lay down, half-naked, her sand weapon by her side. She was cold and shivering, feeling the hypoglycemic drop that comes after an adrenaline rush.

And she felt small, tiny in this ocean of sand, as small as

the period at the end of a sentence. She recalled how Harry, the man that was the only constant in her life, had taught her to separate her mind from her body and how to make her body respond to her mind. He had learned it, years earlier, from a Navy Seal. He, himself, was a former Navy Seal and was now retired from the life he had once loved.

He taught her to close her eyes and visualized a bright sun inside her solar plexus. To make it grow big, then bigger, hot then hotter until it filled one's body and one melded with the sun. "Make it pulsate with energy, turn it into fire!" he had said. And she did now. She made the fire travel inside her body coursing through her veins like liquid gold. She let the golden liquid flow like lava from a volcano and she surrendered to its blistering spell. It spilled from the top of her head down to her limbs and her feet and finally, when she felt it had penetrated and permeated each of her cells, she formed a bubble of heat around her and locked the energy in. Slowly, she began to warm up.

Finally, she relaxed and thought of Harry in the desert. What would Harry do? He'd have a plan. He'd fight. Harry, she thought, would be ruled by the need for survival. "Don't succumb to weakness!" he'd say, "otherwise natural selection will take care of you. Be tough, be prepared." But then he'd also know when to let go and when to conserve his energy. Yes, she thought, he'd know. Finally, she dropped, spent by the force of sheer exhaustion.

She dreamt she was an eagle. She was large and powerful and she was flying high above the desert, wings fanned, eyes sharp as a laser. From above, she could see the sea of sand below her and the creatures moving in the desert. She spotted an agama lizard scurry and quickly disappear into the sand. His coat was bright orange and his hind legs and tail a glistening purple. She saw sand ripples like ocean waves and honeyed dates dangling from palm trees. In an oasis, she saw her reflection in shimmering and translucent

waters, a strong fearless eagle soaring through the firma-
ment. She saw a fox run wild and a snake bury itself in the
sand. She looked into the fox's eye and she read his mind.
The animals spoke to her, and she understood their idiom.
It was a silent tongue, yet, she understood it.

They told her they were ruled by fear and instinct, and
she felt a kinship to them. She felt they were part of her, not
separate from her and her connection to them was one that
brought her much joy and serenity. At that moment, as she
coasted over the skies, she felt bold and omnipotent.

Her dreams alternated between peaceful and conflicting
until the curtain of darkness rose from the desert.

CHAPTER SEVEN

Morning broke clear and for the first time Kennedy Hunter saw the desert across the filtering light. The sun hung liquid pale in the sky and its beauty filled her with awe. She squinted at the horizon and as far as her eyes could see, there was nothing but golden sand.

The grit in her mouth brought her back to the moment. She had been without water for many hours. She attempted to ignore her thirst but the more she pushed the gnawing thoughts aside, the more they invaded her mind. In the desert, men had gone mad without water. They had drunk their own urine. Camel carcasses littered the desert floor, their humps butchered open by men who believed they carried water in their backs. This myth was repeated to every generation of desert travelers with no one ever wanting to believe the truth—camels retrieved water from their cells, as they needed it. They were creatures genetically engineered to survive the desert.

She thought of her own urine. I need liquid she thought, but I also need the salt in my urine. In some cultures, it was therapeutic to drink your own urine. Gandhi did it. So did many mystics. She needed to overcome the fear and repulsion that came with drinking her own urine and by doing it, she'd be like coal walkers who step on smoldering embers to conquer their own fears. If I can drink my own urine, she thought,

I can drink or eat anything. She removed her pants and lowered her panties. She took her boot and squatted on the desert floor urinated inside her boots. She brought the boot to her nostrils, sniffed the rank odor mixed with sweat and suppressed the gagging reflex that overpowered her. She pinched her nose with one hand and with the other brought the boot to her mouth.

Hurriedly, she took a big swallow and dropped to the floor. She quivered and coughed for several minutes, sweat pouring from her, the lingering taste of urine still in her mouth. Her tongue traveled the length of her lips and she felt the dry parched skin. The urine had helped, but not completely. She still needed water. I have my mind, she thought, and I can create any fantasy.

Like she had done before when she was cold, she closed her eyes and surrendered to her wet fantasy. She let the fantasy take volume in her mind, her body, and her world. She saw herself immersed in cool running waters, in rivers, in springs, under cascades that came from the depths of the mountains and saw herself roll under and over ocean waves. She let the waters flow over her, saturate her face, breasts, arms and legs and enter every cavity in her body until she felt cooled, hydrated and quenched.

Finally, she rose and walked back to her canopy. She eyed her surroundings. The sand bore evidence of the nightlife in the desert. Invisible tendrils dressed the desert floor. Long, skinny ones. Three legged ones. The nocturnal ballet of creepy crawlers. Carefully, she examined her canopy in daylight noting that she had been wrapped in impenetrable nylon all night long.

———————•◆•———————

At a distance, somewhere between her and the end of her field of vision, she saw advancing silhouettes in the horizon.

They formed a blotchy picture, watercolors bleeding into a canvas. She stood on both her feet, her arms flailing. *Hey, I'm here!* She yelled. *I'm here!* But they weren't hearing her. She cried several more times. *Hello, here!* This time she did it for no other reason then to hear the sound of her own voice.

She ran across the sloping dunes, and each time she climbed another dune, she'd lose sight of them. Still, she kept running, her feet kicking sand in her face until she ran out of breath. Her boots weighed her down, and she thought of removing them. She staggered in the sand, her head, heart, and neck pounding. She had broken out in a sweat and sand had invaded her face, chest, and nostrils. She tumbled in the sand realizing that no matter how many sand dunes she'd climb, she wasn't going to reach them. They were too distant. How distant, she didn't know. *Hurry*, she thought. *Please hurry.*

The climb had made her hot. For a moment, she considered the certainty of her fate had she crossed the desert in the dog days of summer. That thought, fleeting as it was, made her uncomfortable. Surely, she thought, I'd have died.

She gazed upon the horizon and saw a dark blotchy form taking shape. She watched the figures grow larger as they neared her. They formed a caravan of men, women, and camels. Some rode on top of camels, others walked. They wore long flowing robes that swayed in the wind like wings on a bat. A Berber tribe of the desert or Touaregs, she wasn't sure. As they advanced, she felt no sense of desperation. Contrary, she felt resilient and suddenly renewed.

Awaiting their arrival, she began thinking like a reporter again. Her mind drifted. She started forming her article in her mind, constructing its elements one by one. All she had was the lead, the first paragraph every article begins with, the one that either hooks or loses the reader. The remainder of her story was yet to happen, yet to be told.

CHAPTER EIGHT

The autopsy room was arctic. Detective Ahmed was certain that somewhere in the backroom they were raising penguins.

Ahmed donned a white lab coat and a gas mask. The smell of formaldehyde assaulted him as soon as he entered the room. It filled his nostrils and imbued his being all the way to his molecular self. For days thereafter, he wouldn't be able to rid himself of the peculiar odor.

The room was sterile, antiseptic. There was a mobile cart for the transport of bodies and two stainless-steel autopsy tables fitted with holes to drain body fluids. A small-parts autopsy table sat aside. Scales to weigh organs hung over the tables.

The body had already been tagged, photographed, and put in a cooler and assistants were now wheeling it out.

The on-location report had stated that the body was found already invaded by spiders and millipedes—a sure sign the victim had been dead for more than forty-eight hours. Contrary to popular belief, time of death was not always easy to ascertain. Cold weather slowed down decomposition, while hot weather sped it up.

The head and neck of the victim were greenish-red and rigor mortis had already disappeared giving way to a softening of the tissues. Decomposition was well on its way and the swollen body made visual identification of the facial features nearly impossible.

The medical examiner, a wiry Frenchman with an ashen complexion and a long narrow face, was talking into a microphone. Ahmed thought the man had spent too many years with the dead, too many years looking at the dark side of life.

As is the protocol in all autopsies, the doctor began with the external examination of the body. He moved around the table making a visual inventory of all visible marks on the victim. Latex gloves in hand, he picked up a scalpel and pointed to the body.

"Look, detective. Blisters are forming on top of the skin."

"*Oui*," answered Ahmed as he neared the table. The bitter taste of bile rose in his throat and he swallowed hard.

"It explains the gases that have been forming," continued the doctor, "and the swelling of the body. She's been dead for about two to three days."

The doctor moved around the table and began probing the head. "There's a straight line around the neck. A ligature." He took his measuring tape and placed it against the neck. "Measuring approximately...thirty centimeters in diameter. The angle of the ligature suggests strangulation, not hanging. A rope, a string?" He lifted the head and viewed the back of the neck. "There's bruising at the base of the neck where the killer might have applied pressure."

He moved to the other side of the table and examined the lower parts of the body.

"She's had an appendectomy. There is a small incision on the lower right quadrant." He then lifted the body and examined its underside. Blood had settled on the back where the victim had been lying. "Present," he continued, "is fixed livor mortis on the dorsal aspect suggesting that she died in a different location then moved to the dump."

The detective was following the dictation when his eyes landed on the girl's feet. Geometric tattoos adorned her feet. The tattoos were the kind applied for Moroccan ceremonies—weddings and other occasions—certainly not the kind of adornment American women favored. This discovery puzzled him but he did not interfere with the doctor's concentration.

As if reading Ahmed's mind, the doctor resumed his dictation. "There're brown stains on the plant of the feet," he said, "tattoos. They are not permanent ones. They appeared to be made with *harqus*." *Harqus* was a paint made from nutgalls, ashes, and spices used to create tattoos on hands and feet.

Although the room was icy, sweat poured from under the detective's shirt, and his forehead was dotted with glistening beads. He detested this part of his job but he knew he had to be here. This case was important to him and his presence was imperative. He didn't want any friction with the Americans.

The doctor picked up a scalpel and with a sharp cut made a Y-incision from shoulder to shoulder down over the breasts all the way to the pubic area. He exposed the ribs and the heart where he took a sample of blood from the pericardial sac.

Ahmed muttered a small prayer under his breath. He was thinking about the sanctity of the body. Moslem law allowed for autopsies only in special cases. He liked that. Return to Allah the way Allah had created you.

The coroner removed the heart, lungs, and trachea in one solid chunk and laid them on the table. They'll all be weighed and examined separately.

Ahmed looked on, mute, too repulsed to utter a word.

The liver and spleen came next followed by the stomach, pancreas, and intestines. They, too, would be weighed and examined and samples of them would be sent to the lab for toxicological analysis.

The girl's abdominal cavity lay open, a vacant carcass, her body nothing more than a repository of bones. Ahmed thought that she looked more like a gutted deer than the beautiful girl she once had been.

The room was silent. Deadly silent. The doctor's voice reverberated throughout the room interrupted only by the rattle of surgical tools.

The head was examined last. The doctor was looking for signs of hemorrhaging behind the eyes and he found them. "I found it," he said, "petecchiae." He raised his eyes and forced a smile. Ahmed's face remained expressionless. "Strong evidence that strangulation occurred."

With calculated precision, the doctor slid his scalpel over the top of the head and made a cut from ear to ear. The scalp was peeled forward like a mask exposing a bare skull. An assistant holding a power saw cut into the skull and removed a slice of the skull. The sound of the power saw shattered the room leaving behind a deafening stillness. The assistant had done this with such casualness, Ahmed felt that his own viscera and its contents were going to end up on the table.

Through the created cranial hole, the brain was removed and weighed. The cavernous aperture lay open like an empty crater.

Finally, after what seemed to be an interminable amount of time, the doctor turned to the detective.

"Detective," he said, "my opinion is that this girl has been strangled. We're waiting for additional tests results and, of course, there're finger prints and dental records—all of which have been requested from the American Embassy." He stopped to catch his breath. "Initial findings, however, strongly suggest that strangulation is the cause of death."

Ahmed nodded. *"Merci,"* he said.

He walked outside the autopsy room to an office where a

phone sat on a desk. He picked up the phone and dialed the number of the American College.

He was immediately connected to the director.

"Yes, Ahmed. What news do you have for me?"

The Arab hesitated. "I'd like to stop by your office sometime soon. Could you arrange for me to meet with Emily's roommates?"

"Do you have anything for me? What are the autopsy results?" The director sounded nervous and anxious.

The detective remained guarded, not wanting to say too much.

"*Monsieur*," His tone was hesitant, "I can say that the girl here died from strangulation."

"No!"

"I'm sorry, *Monsieur*."

"I cannot believe this!"

Ahmed heard the distress in Stevens' voice.

"Why, Ahmed? *Why?* Why would anybody want to strangle such a beautiful girl?"

"*Monsieur*," he interjected, "I said, the girl we have. We do not know for sure. We're waiting for additional results. We have requested dentals, fingerprints…"

"Detective?"

"Yes, *Monsieur*."

Ahmed waited. He let the silence grow between them.

"Is there anything else you need to tell me?"

"*Monsieur*, did Emily wear henna tattoos on her feet and hands?"

"I wouldn't think so. Usually Moroccan women do, but not American ones." Stevens paused. "I could ask her roommate, Morgan Taylor. I can get you an answer immediately. Hold a moment. I'll call her on my other line."

The detective heard the director switch lines. He listened to him question Morgan Taylor, then immediately returned to him.

"Detective, Morgan said no. No tattoos of any kind on Emily Carrington."

"This girl has tattoos made with *harqus*."

"Does it mean, detective, that this isn't Emily?"

"Maybe not." He paused preoccupied. "Maybe not."

Ahmed felt deeply troubled by it all. He wanted to walk out of the morgue as fast as he could. He needed to see real people with real bodies. Not spare parts. Moreover, he wanted the sun to emit its rays on the whole of humanity. Beam its light on darkness.

There were many unanswered questions. The tattoos. The dental records. The fingerprints.

For now, all he knew was that Emily Carrington or whoever the girl was, had died from asphyxia. A cord or a string pulled tightly around her delicate neck.

Dying for air. The specter of death at her heels.

CHAPTER NINE

She finally saw them. Ten men, five women, fifteen camels and several girls of different ages, the oldest about ten years old. They were Berbers. The men, dark, slim, wore *burnooses*, a striped woolen cloth that covered their entire body. A muslin scarf called a *cheich* covered their heads and necks shielding them from sandstorms. The women wore long layers of white cloths under their *burnooses*, and hoods over their heads. Colorful yarns that held their hoods dangled to their shoulders. The colors of the yarns and the jewelry represented their tribes. Golden amber beads adorned their necks and large silver pendants dangled on their chests. They all wore silver *hamsas*, the hand symbol that warded off the evil eye. Large triangular clasps called *fibulas* held their burnooses together, their sizes and design symbolizing their tribal status.

The women went unveiled, their white cheeks painted crimson, their slanted eyes delineated with kohl, and their noses and chins dotted with black beauty dots. Tattooed lines descended from the middle of their bottom lip all the way down under their chins.

The girls, from the youngest to the oldest, wore round hoods signaling their virginity and readiness for marriage. Their faces and eyelids were painted the color of saffron

and they wore jewelry in the shape of salamanders and tur-
tles that were deemed to possess magical powers.

The oldest girl handed Kennedy a crude gourd shaped
like a canteen and filled with water. She rapidly gulped
down its content. The girls had formed a circle around her
and watched her. She returned the gourd to the girl who
had handed it to her and followed the caravan, trailed by
the women and all the girls. The women were timid, avoided direct eye contact but the girls continued their watch,
uttered words, and sentences she did not understand, and
giggled incessantly. The very young ones had frontal gaps
in their mouths where their teeth were missing, and when
they laughed, they shielded their mouths with their hands,
a gesture which endeared them to her.

They walked for hours, the yellow glow of the sun burning in their faces. Now and then, the women and girls gave
up on walking and mounted the camels. They didn't come
across any people, animals, or civilization of any sort. And
they saw nothing but miles and miles of sand and gravel.

Kennedy Hunter felt tired, dirty and hungry, and eager to
stop or reach a destination. At the head of the camel train
was their leader. He stood tall on his camel with the bearing
of a man in charge, his eyes roving over his people. She hurried along and accosted him. He descended from his camel.
His fingers and toes had crusted dirt nestled between the
crevices and he smelled of armpits. His skin, the color of
copper, formed deep creases around his mouth and hung on
his face like the flaps of a dog's ears. With her hands she gestured indicating to him that she wanted to mount his camel.
He nodded and grinned broadly revealing a gap in his
mouth where his two front teeth had once been.

"*La, La, La* . . . " he said in an angry tone. One could tell
he was accustomed to ordering his people.

"What you mean, no?" she yelled back, "I'm tired and I
need a camel!"

The women and girls had stopped and were now staring at her. He grabbed her by the arm and pushed her along.

"Let go of me!" she screamed while loosening herself from his grip.

"*Imshi! Imshi!*" he said. Go! Go!

She grabbed the talisman and the amulet he wore around his neck and yanked them. The talisman held the Kitab, sacred Koranic verses, and the amulet protected him from the evil eye.

"What are you wearing this for if you're not a man of God!" she yelled, "where's your Allah? *Allah! Allah! Allah!*"

He understood her words. Anger flared in his face, his nostrils quivered. She had shown disrespect for his Kitab. He reached and yanked it back from her.

She let him have it back, too weary for confrontation. She knew his mission was to take her to The Torch and he couldn't go back without her. Frustrated, she dropped on the hot desert floor.

He eyed her suspiciously. The rest of the camel train came to a full stop. The women gazed, the men argued in loud voices. He came forward, his eyes flashing with anger. In a heated tone he gesticulated and went into a tirade, none of which she understood. He pointed to the desert. "*Koum, koum . . . aji m'ana.*" Come, he said, come with us.

Suddenly, a woman spoke up then descended from her mount. He saw her, yelled back at her then withdrew a long whip from his side and flung it across her way. It slashed the air like a samurai's saber. The woman recoiled, her dark eyes filled with both anger and fear. Then, obsequiously, she remounted her camel. Finally, he waived Kennedy off in displeasure and walked away. Everyone followed obediently. The girls remained behind, timid and hesitant.

The girl who had trailed Kennedy since they met grabbed her hand and held on to it. Her honeyed eyes, rimmed in kohl, were begging Kennedy to come along.

"Aji, Aji!" Come, she said. Come. Kennedy was too depleted and did not respond.

The camel train left, the girl trailing behind. Now and then, she'd spin around to see if Kennedy was following. A few hundred yards later, Kennedy saw her make a quick run towards her. The girl removed her gourd and her hood and flung them at Kennedy. Then she ran behind the caravan, her robes flying beside her like wings on a butterfly.

Kennedy watched their silhouettes shrink and disappear behind sand dunes then resurface again until the little girl became a tiny black dot. And just as they had appeared, a dot in the horizon, they became one.

And when they were gone, she was one.

She lifted her eyes to the sky and saw the crisp, azure sky. The sun pulsated like a heart, its unrelenting beat offering no respite. Exhausted, she untied her laces and removed her boots. She let the sand run between her toes like diamonds flowing out of a pouch.

Now what?

She hadn't thought much about the consequences of her actions, except, of course, that she had acted impulsively. She didn't think they'd leave without her. Well, they did. Now, she was trying to justify, to herself at least, her actions. She refused to let fear control her. It was easy to succumb to fear and let it rule one's life. Still, she wasn't certain this was the time to take risks.

Her life, however, had always been a gamble and she had never been nor was she going to be a fence sitter. Fences, she felt, were emotional crutches that turned indecision into paralysis. Or worse. Into a crippling malaise. Playing it safe, they called it. There were plenty of idioms and metaphors for it. Not taking chances. Hedging your bets. She knew them all. To her, it meant you lived life as an observer, not a participant. You didn't jump into the waters with both feet, just dipped in your toes, and retrieved them as soon as it got uncomfortable.

She couldn't allow such a thing to happen. It wasn't part of her lexicon. *I will not swim with the current*, she thought, I *will* not. Now, in the middle of this desolate land, she wondered if she had perilously walked the tight rope without a net. Bungee-jumped without a cord.

She pushed all the negative thoughts aside. Right now, she had to remain strong. She shielded her head and face with the girl's hood, and lay down on the sand. Soon, she fell hard asleep, her body yielding to the fiery sun.

CHAPTER TEN

When she awoke, her skin burned and her throat felt dry and parched. She drank water from her gourd, wet her face with it, and placed her boots back on. She tied her shirt around her waist and walked, semi-nude, in the direction they had all disappeared. The sun was in the west now, its onslaught diminished, and she was traveling south. Her head covered with the hood, the gourd attached to her pants, she followed in the caravan's footsteps. She resisted the urge to drink all of her water allowing herself only an occasional wetting of the lips or a few sips.

After climbing countless dunes, she sighted an oasis. She stood on top of the dune wondering if she was experiencing visionary illusions. Rows of palms rose from the earth. Water flowed between the palms and the plots of planted corn, barley, and oats. The water came from a spring that traveled down the center of the oasis irrigating the date-bearing trees and houses that framed it.

From where she stood, it had been impossible to notice the oasis until now. She found the energy to punch the air with her fist and flung her shirt around like a lasso. Her march in the desert had seemed eternal. Happily, she donned her shirt and continued with renewed vigor towards her destination.

At the edge of the oasis, she saw a *ksar*, a flat-roofed square compound the color of red clay. Made of mud and rubble, the compound consisted of four fortified buildings and granaries. The buildings also served as a fortress against outsiders. Four crenellated towers adorned with lozenges and chevrons surrounded a massive outer wall pierced by arrow slits. The four towers, one in each corner of the structure, hid a covered alley where a well was located.

The massive wooden doors adorned with hook-shaped knockers were ajar. Livestock lived on the first floor of the *ksar*. Ladders led to the second floor granary, and on the third floor were the living quarters for the many families inhabiting the *ksar*. A single wooden pillar supported a ceiling made of thuja branches. The Berbers and their herd of animals had gathered in the center of the courtyard. The donkeys, goats, and camels had kneeled in a pious pose as if praying, their somnolent eyes barely open.

When Kennedy entered, the girls came running. Their leader, who hadn't noticed her, didn't seem surprised by her presence.

"*Salem*," he said, bowing respectfully, his eyes averting hers.

When he rose, their eyes met. She looked him hard and didn't bow in return. "*Salem A'leikoum*," she said. There was no submissiveness in her tone, just civility.

With a hand motion, he invited her in. There were several men, women and children, some of which she was seeing for the first time. The place was noisy with children playing and chasing one another. She found the women gathered around the well engaged in the preparation of food. They raised their heads acknowledging her presence, their dark brown eyes shone. Kennedy nodded and they responded. She joined them on the tiled floor. Immediately, a woman placed a pewter teapot filled with tea and mint leaves on the ground. She placed tiny glasses on a brass tray, raised the teapot to eye level, and poured her tea. On the tray, she placed almond and sesame pastries. Kennedy eyed the pastries and felt a stir in her stomach. She grabbed a pastry shaped like the horn of a gazelle and bit into it. It was crunchy outside, soft, and mellow inside. Then she sipped the mint tea finding it overwhelmingly sweet but not minding it at all.

She watched two girls lower a large aluminum container attached to a rope down a well. They giggled as they struggled to raise the filled container. On the ground, there were clay pots filled with smoldering coals. A dead sheep, her throat slashed, laid on a straw mat, its hide already partially removed around the throat.

A woman with the dexterity and zeal of a butcher removed the skin as another held its hind legs down. She removed the skin from the body by slipping it through as if she was removing pantyhoses.

She raised a hatchet above her head and with one big blow severed the animal's head. It rolled on the side, its eyes wide open as if caught by surprise. She picked it up, rinsed it with water poured from a kettle, placed it on the open fire then kindled the coals with a wooden stick. She returned to the animal and slid a knife down its middle. The entrails spilled on the mat and with both hands, she scooped the viscera out. She severed a leg at the joint and cut it into chunks. She rinsed the chunks with cold-water letting the bloody mess run on the floor then cut the chunks into smaller bites, which she placed in pots and on the fire.

Nearby stood a *tajine* filled with *harissa*, a spicy combination of pimentos, garlic, cumin, coriander, and olive oil. Plates flowed with dates, prunes, figs, olives, and grains. She scooped spices and dried fruits then added grains and vegetables she picked from mounds formed on the floor. The *ksar* smelled of freshly butchered animals and heavily spiced food.

The men, squatting, washed their hands and feet with water poured from kettles held by the girls. They cleaned their faces, their ears and slicked their hair back. The girls did not make eye contact with their elders and attended to their needs respectfully.

Outside, dusk showered the desert and palms stood tall and dark against the evening sky. The temperatures had fallen to a comfortable bearing and a peaceful aura bathed the ksar and its inhabitants.

A girl led Kennedy upstairs. She found soap and water in the *hamman*. Moorish *zellige* tiles covered both the floor and walls of the bathroom. A sieve in the center of the room allowed for drainage. There was little else: loofah, gourds, and Berber towels.

Kennedy disrobed immediately. She had worn the grit of the desert for too long. The girl looked away, embarrassed by Kennedy's nudity. She filled a gourd and poured it over Kennedy's head. Kennedy laughed and the girl, hesitant at first, brought her small hand to her mouth hiding her laughter and her missing front teeth. She rubbed soap on the loofah, worked up a lather then scrubbed her back until it turned red. With unrestrained enthusiasm, she attacked Kennedy's feet which sent Kennedy into a fit of giggles. Water was splashed all over the room. The girl's eyes glimmered.

Kennedy realized she did not know the girl's name. She decided to try the bit of Arabic she knew. "*Ishmeck?*" Kennedy asked.

The girl's eyes grew wide. "Nawal," she replied. She appeared startled Kennedy was able communicate with her.

Nawal brought towels and wrapped them around Kennedy. She then disappeared and came back with a loose Berber caftan and mules. Kennedy slipped into the caftan and mules and sat on a soft leather pillow Nawal had brought in for her. Holding a large ivory comb in her hands, Nawal combed Kennedy's russet hair. She worked the knots out and straightened her hair behind her back. She opened a delicate flask and poured rose water in Kennedy's hands.

From a boned box engraved with a floral motif, she retrieved a small stick filled with kohl and applied the black powder around Kennedy's eyes. For a moment, Kennedy forgot she was an American reporter on an assignment. The clothing and rituals transported her to a different time. Finally, Nawal held up a mirror. She was a transformed Western woman with all of her contradictions. Kennedy smiled at the transformation. She felt serene and let go of the combativeness she had grown accustomed to bearing. Aggressiveness, here and now, seemed as out of place as her gray Dockers and combat boots.

Downstairs, they had all moved from the courtyard to a large room carpeted with Berber rugs. Lining all four walls were sofas draped in tribal rugs. They had all changed into loose caftans and festive clothing. The men wore loose white tunics tied with richly embroidered belts, white turbans, and leather sandals.

Meanwhile, the women had placed brass and ceramic platters on the floor. The platters brimmed with *tajine* mutton, chicken, couscous, and vegetables. There were finger bowls filled with water near each plate but no utensils. The Berbers formed a circle around a large couscous tray set in the middle. They reached into the tray, filled their hands with couscous, packed it tight into a ball, and then flung it into their mouths. Their fingers moved swiftly as they combined balls of couscous, vegetables, and mutton.

They ate in silence, surreptitiously eyeing Kennedy as she, too, formed balls of couscous with her hands. She saw the surprise on their faces when she formed her first ball, packed it tight then flung it into her mouth. The girls exploded in laughter, the women amused by the girls' outbursts shushed them.

The roasted sheep's head sat on a large platter. A man grabbed it and with a small hammer busted it open. He cracked the skull open letting the cooked brains spill out of the cavity. He placed them on a plate, which he offered to Kennedy. She tore a chunk and placed it in her mouth savoring the soft and mellow tissue. She chewed slowly. Her absence from food had given her a colossal appetite and she enjoyed every bite, lingering as they all chewed in silence.

They spoke occasionally but mostly concentrated on eating. Dogs gathered around them, forming a second circle. Now and then, the girls threw food in their direction. A frenzy, ignored by all, ensued and the quiet meal would suddenly turn into a battle for morsels.

After the meal, the girls brought a kettle of water, went around the table, and poured it on everybody's fingers. The girls placed *sebsis*, water pipes, in front of the men who had settled into the large pillows behind them. The acrid smell of hashish filled the air as the men sucked the smoke out of their pipes. Bowls of ripened fruits filled the table and tiny cups of coffee sat in front of everyone.

The women hurried to clean up the table as the night descended on the *ksar*. They lit oil lamps and candles and placed them on tiny tables. The girls brought out musical instruments, which they distributed. They handed a *ghayta* to their leader, a wind instrument made with two cane tubes and a horn bell. To the rest they gave *ouds*, a lute-like instrument and *derboukas*, clay tambourines covered with sheepskins.

Kennedy Hunter leaned back against the pillows, closed her eyes and listened to the music. Ancient sounds wailed through the night.

Suddenly, a woman Kennedy had not seen before came out from one of the rooms. She wore dark, heavy make up and rows of coins adorned her head and hands. Her skin was like alabaster, soft, fleshy, and it glowed in the dim room. Her breasts were full and flowed out of her dress. Her whiteness stunned Kennedy. She looked as if she had never spent a day in the sun. She must be treated like a queen bee, Kennedy thought, kept in the dark, and well-fed.

The woman moved to the center of the room. Her eyes focused on some invisible mark, she swayed to the slow rhythm of the music. Her hands and feet, painted with delicate tattoos, moved in harmony with her undulating hips. She lowered herself to the floor, dancing on her knees to the beat of the *guedra*, a dance that originated in low tents.

Kennedy watched her, mesmerized by her performance. She thought the dancer was the most sensual woman she had ever seen. And she was fully clothed. Through a veil of hashish smoke, Kennedy eyed the men. There was a dangerous lust in their eyes, a wanting she recognized. It made the hair on her neck stand on end. The lust was coupled with a yielding of control, a surrendering exhibited in their bearing. Like a lion after a kill, resting under a shady tree.

No one paid attention to the man who, visibly aroused by the dancer's performance, fondled himself, his hand moving in slow strokes over his tunic.

Then the rhythm increased to a frantic pace, the musicians beating on their *derboukas*, the dancer moving at a dizzying pace, the man's strokes ever quicker. The music crescendoed as the dancer, in a visible trance, hurled her body around until she fainted and fell on the floor. Eyes shut, hands trembling, a moaning ignored by all followed the man's release. Suddenly everything came to a stop. Beating of drums, beating of flesh.

A second woman came in and lit a clay container filled with coals. She fanned the coals with a palm frond until they turned hot and red. She dropped a mixture of herbs, tiny pickled snakes, and animal hides in the clay pot. A crackling noise and dark smoke wafted into the air. She fanned the smoke towards her face as she whispered incantations. Then she carried the clay pot in front of Kennedy and held it close to her face. Kennedy leaned over and inhaled the acrid odor. She peered inside the pot; the mixture had sizzled into a black ball shaped like an eyeball. The evil eye. Kennedy winced. Inviting spells or warding them off was common practice with Berbers.

A curtain of smoke filled the room, thick, dense, and pungent. The girls had fallen asleep and Kennedy was fighting an increasing urge to do likewise. She felt a ceding of her body and leaned back on the pillows. Her eyelids felt heavy as if drapes had fallen over her eyes and she struggled to stay awake. At once, the colors in the room turned vibrant. The reds turned redder, yellows glimmered, and auras emanated from everybody and everything. Beams of light radiated from within the Berbers like light bulbs lit from the inside out. Their garments draped over in opulent folds taking on a Daliesque quality. The fruits on the table turned luscious, succulent, swelled with ripeness. The men's faces glistened to golden sienna, eyes shone like black onyx. The women looked fertile, voluptuous, their fingers, arms, and necks laden with jewelry. Alabaster and lava.

It was dreamlike. But she did not know whose dream she had inhabited. She was seeing their world in a way she hadn't before.

Suddenly, she saw their faces juxtaposed with the faces of the animals in the desert, the ones that were in her dreams. The fox, the snake, the lizard. The women morphed into snakes, the men into foxes, back and forth. Then she saw herself rise above it all, floating above the room, her etheric body eyeing her solid body. She was watching herself from above, wearing her clothes, seeing her identical self down below. With her consciousness ever present, Kennedy felt she had crossed over to a different world. A reality that existed only for a few. A fourth dimension.

The music resonated and vibrated. The notes, clean, lucid, sharp, flowed like crystal water over a creek. The string sounds of the *oud* echoed inside the room and outside into the darkness.

A woman scooped coarse salt from a brass pot and threw it at doorsteps and in corners of rooms as if she was inseminating a field. Seeds against evil. She was chasing and warding off the *djinoun*, desert ghosts that morph into people and entice them to cross over into their world.

A man rose and neared Kennedy. He kneeled down and she felt his hand reach out and touch her. She eyed him and saw a face she had seen years earlier. The Torch. Whether he was real or imaginary, she couldn't tell. His lips moved, articulating words she couldn't hear. When he touched her, she flinched, her body holding ancient memories.

Then he reached for her naked feet. He seized a foot and stroked it, ever gently, running his fingers on the plant, the heel, the toes, between the toes, lingering, pressing, releasing, pressing. He reached down and let his tongue travel the length of her foot, between the toes, between the folds of her skin, pushing, digging, releasing. A finger traveled up her leg under her dress following her inner thigh and her legs were gently parted. She felt a pressing of the flesh, a soft stroking, like a paintbrush on a canvas. Up and down. Back and forth.

Kennedy closed her eyes. Her body arched and shudders scaled her back. Then she let go, surrendering to the sweetness of the moment. The release was slow and long coming. It crescendoed inside her body as if a string had been pulled tight then released, its sound vibrating into the night. Then, gleaming colors and flashes exploded around her like shooting stars in the universe.

Somebody grabbed Kennedy's hand. "*Aji, Aji!*" the voice said. She rose and staggered, led upstairs by a hand she felt but couldn't see. The room was bare, just a narrow mattress on a naked floor. She fell on a mattress, the room spinning like a kaleidoscope. Faster and faster. Then, she saw nothing but blurred faces and scurrying shadows in the desert night.

CHAPTER ELEVEN

Detective Ahmed tossed copies of the local papers on his desk. His hands trembled, his blood gushed through his body like water through a busted dam. The headlines in both *L'Opinion* and *Le Matin* jarred him.

American Heiress Disappears. Feared Dead.

Someone had leaked the information to the press, for a price, of course, and he knew that. I will find out who the bastard is, he thought.

He eyed his assistant who was looking at him with accusatory eyes and shrugged as if saying I-am-not-responsible-for-this-mess.

Phones rang, the fax machine spewed message after message and the cop at the front desk of the station was ready to walk out.

Outside the building, on the boulevard, the foreign press had practically set up shop. Television cameras crews and their trucks, photographers, reporters, and lookers camped and settled in for the long haul.

The detective would have done anything to stop this avalanche but once it had started to roll, he knew there was no stopping it. If it had been up to him, he would have kept the whole story under cover. Forever. Freedom of the press was not a constitutional right here. He feared the worst. His office was not equipped for the onslaught of the international press and the phones, manned only by two secretaries, were already tied up for hours to come.

The detective eyed the mob outside his window. He told his secretary to lock herself inside her office, do whatever she wanted with the phones, and slipped through a back door. Today, he thought, the best place to be is away from this office. Today, I will begin my investigation in earnest.

He drove out of the station and went straight to the American College. A secretary ushered him in. Dr. Stevens stood up when Ahmed entered the room. The detective noted that the American's bearing had changed. His shoulders stooped and his large frame had nearly shrunk. His features were drawn, dark circles under his eyes.

There were two young people seated in the office. "Let me introduce you to two friends of Emily Carrington."

The two students rose from their chairs and shook the detective's hand.

"This is Morgan Taylor and Brent Seabrook," said Stevens "Morgan and Emily share the same apartment and Brent and Emily dated for while."

Morgan Taylor smiled faintly and Brent Seabrook blushed at the mention of his name and relationship with Emily.

Nineteen-year old Morgan had a fair complexion, curly short hair, and wire-rimmed glasses. She wore tight hip-huggers and a fitted cotton top that rode above her navel. She had no visible make-up on her face and her clean face was the face of the typical American teenager.

Brent Seabrook possessed an Aryan face and hair that betrayed his Germanic origins. He wore a generic long sleeved tee and baggy jeans.

"*Monsieur*," began the detective, "I'm sorry you had to learn from the headlines that the body we have at the morgue doesn't belong to the missing person. But we suspected it anyway."

"Yes, we know," answered Dr. Stevens. He turned around and eyed the two students.

The detective continued. "The question now *is*: Who is the girl we have and where is Emily Carrington? We found the body with the clothes Emily wore before her disappearance but the dental records and the fingerprints submitted by your embassy don't match." He paused shortly. "We have a switched identity. Somebody wanted us to think that Emily Carrington was dead—and *peut-etre*, maybe, she is—but the body we have, as I told you, doesn't belong to her."

The director nodded. Morgan Taylor and Brent Seabrook remained silent, listening intently to the detective as he explained his findings.

"Miss Taylor," the detective continued, "you're certain that Miss Carrington didn't wear henna on her hands and feet? For special occasions, or even if she was likely to do anything like it."

"No," answered Morgan. "She never did anything like that. Although, I'm sure she would have liked to do it sometimes. She was, maybe I should say is adventurous."

Brent Seabrook, who had remained silent, interjected. "Yeah, she would have tried something like that. She was very interested in local customs, tribal ones. Especially Berbers."

The detective, who had been taking notes, raised his eyes at the mention of Berbers. "Humm," he answered, "how much interest did she have in Berbers?"

"A lot," Brent replied, "she wanted to write about them. She was fascinated by their history and traditions."

"Do you know, *Monsieur* Seabrook, if Miss Carrington had any contacts with Berbers?"

Brent did not answer immediately. He held his hands in his lap and twisted his fingers. Finally, "well, she had tried to set up interviews but I'm not sure whether she succeeded or not."

"Who did she try to set up interviews with? Would you know?" interjected the director. He had been listening to the exchange between the detective and his students.

"I'm not sure," said Brent. He brushed a flock of hair that had fallen on his left eye with a nervous hand movement.

"I think she tried to contact the local tourism department," said Morgan. *"The Departement de Culture."*

"I see," answered the detective. "Why was she going to Marrakesh?" He cast a glance at Morgan for an answer.

"She was going for a long weekend trip. She loved Marrakesh. She said that she was going to visit the place, take pictures, take notes."

"Alone?" asked the detective.

"Yes, alone," answered Morgan. "She preferred going alone on those things. She told me it gave her an opportunity to study the place and take lots of notes."

"That's why we had not been worried," interjected the director, "we knew she was going for four days, so when she was found or at least her look-alike, we were shocked."

"Do you know of anybody who would want to see her harmed?" asked the detective.

All three eyed each other simultaneously. "No," they replied in unison.

"I can't think of anyone wanting to hurt her," said Morgan, "Emily is a sweet, wonderful person."

"What do we know about her family?" asked Ahmed.

"The family lives in Atlanta," replied the director.

"Any parents?"

"Her mother is alive. Sick but alive," said Morgan.

"Any sisters? Brothers?" asked the detective.

"Yes," answered Morgan. "She has an older married sister she's close too."

"Anybody else?" the director asked.

Morgan took the lead. "Never heard her talk of anybody else."

Ahmed picked his notebook and scribbled something. "Is her family wealthy?" he asked as he raised his head up.

"Very wealthy," answered the director. "As a matter of fact, one of the wealthiest families in Atlanta. Related to the Coca-Cola fortune."

"I understand," said Brent, "that if Emily never worked a day in her life, she would be fine. She had a trust fund established in her name."

"*Je comprends,*" said the detective. He understood.

"I've been keeping the family abreast of all developments," said the director, "and so does the embassy. I'm certain your office has been contacted too."

"Oh, yes," answered the detective, "the family has called several times."

Morgan stirred in her seat. "Detective Ahmed," she said as she spun around to face the detective. "I'd like to tell you that Emily kept a very low profile on the money thing. Few knew of her wealth and she didn't act at all like a rich kid."

The detective nodded.

"In fact," continued Morgan, "she was very leery of people who befriended her because of her money."

"I see," the detective said. "Miss Taylor, I'd like to visit your apartment and check on Miss Carrington's personal belongings."

"Sure," said Morgan, "you can come anytime."

The detective rose to leave. He shook hands with everyone. The detective noted Brent's moist hands and the sweat beads that gathered above his upper lip.

CHAPTER TWELVE

Kennedy awoke at dawn as light penetrated the room. She had slept like a dead man, remembering a night inexplicable by laws of nature. Her reality had been altered and her interpretation of it challenged. She felt she had met the Berbers on a different level, exposed to a dark and cryptic world she knew existed but never experienced.

Outside, the desert was shedding its night cloak for a gossamer veil of light.

She rose to the bare window and peered out. Down below, dozens of tents had set up camp around the compound. Sometime during the night, nomads from distant oases had gathered for their annual bridal fair. The market place was teeming with camels, horses, sheep, and donkeys. There were stalls with silver jewelry, carpets, and domestic goods spilled on the hard ground, a cornucopia of objects to buy and sell.

Behind the tents' walls, a bartering of a different kind took place. Girls, young, virgin, fresh like a spring breeze, willing and ready to be paired with the man who will buy them for a camel or the dowry their fathers brought to the table.

From above, Kennedy eyed the girls. They huddled together, their faces pale, their eyes lined in dark kohl, their cheeks crimson red. They giggled like the little girls they were, hiding their anxiety behind laughter, waiting for the man who will point his finger and say, *I want that one.*

At ground level, a brisk wind blew raising curtains of dust. Women and children clutched their *hendiras* tight under their chins as they went from vendor to vendor.

As she viewed the scene from her window, Kennedy thought that somewhere, in there, was The Torch.

Nawal came in with Berber clothes in her hands. Kennedy found a pail with water and a gourd. She rinsed her eyes, face, and slicked back her untamed hair. Then she removed her clothes and slid into khakis and a shirt.

"*La, La, La,*" Nawal said when she saw her in her khakis. She pointed to the Berber *hendira* she held. Kennedy did not understand the spoken words just the implied ones. Nawal was objecting to the change of clothes. Kennedy ignored her objections and stayed with her khakis on. They did not want her to be conspicuous—a western woman amongst tribal people. Kennedy had other motives. She wanted to meet with The Torch on her terms, like a western journalist, not a submissive tribal woman. Right now, right here, she thought, you are what you wear.

She followed Nawal downstairs and found the Berbers in the courtyard around trays of bread, jellies, oranges, and pomegranates.

A man bowed as she entered and invited her to join them. The women hurried to pour her tea and sat a dish of pastries in front of her. She ate in silence thinking about what the day would bring. She thought of her unusual circumstances. It was the first time in her career she's had to endure so much for an interview, to jump through so many hoops before meeting her subject. She couldn't recall ever hearing of a journalist parachuting out of an airplane for an interview. This may be the first in the annals of journalism, she thought. She recalled meetings in alleys, on boats, in parks, restaurants. Once even in the bedroom of a playboy actor who met her, sprawled on his animal print bedcover, dressed in nothing but silk shorts. A cheetah stalking his prey. An absolute gentleman, he had asked her to join him.

Never before had she been on an assignment without the tools of her trade—a camera, tape recorder, reporter's note-book and laptop. She felt naked without them and had to count on her keen sense of observation and memory to tell her story. In more than one way, this, indeed, was a first.

Strangely, there was no apprehension from her part. The more she endured, the tougher she became. Still, she need-ed to resist the urge to want to precipitate events, to hurry things up. Time, among tribal people, was of little im-portance. They worked and lived at their own rhythm. Try-ing to hurry things up was not only futile, but discourteous and ill-mannered—at least from their point of view.

Finally, Kennedy left the compound escorted by Nawal. Sandy grounds surrounded the compound and stalagmite mountains stemmed out of the earth into a cobalt sky. The cool breath of the desert hit Kennedy with such force she felt dizzy and light-headed. The sun, liquid gold, beamed above her. She shielded her eyes from its intensity.

They walked in silence. Kennedy dodged rocks and peb-bles laying down the trail while Nawal, barefoot and care-free, her soles protected by a thick layer of coarse skin, skipped over rocks as if dancing over soft velvet.

They walked past mud houses down to the market where tents and lean-tos had been pitched. As expected, Kennedy attracted undesired attention. Everywhere, Ber-bers halted to gaze at her. Children formed circles around her as Nawal attempted to keep them at bay. A boy tugged at Kennedy's pants but Nawal chased him away and threw a rock at him.

Minutes later, Nawal came to a full stop. They stood in front of a large white tent made of heavy canvas. The roof and awning were made of wool and hair sewn together, pegs and ropes hammered into the ground held the tent in place. A golden sphere, symbol of The Torch's tribal power, adorned the top of the roof.

Two Berbers in military fatigues and AK-47's stood by the entrance of the tent. Nawal walked in first through a flap in the tent. Kennedy followed. Inside, the tent was divided in two sections. Center place was the men's area, decorated with colorful wool mats and furnished with large cushions. A brass tray filled with small gold glasses and a teapot sat at the center of the room.

Separated from the men by a divider was the women's section. There were mattresses on the floor, small benches, and a loom. In a corner was a storage area with sacks of corn, barley, and wool. At the far corner, Kennedy heard the sounds of baby lambs. There was also a *mihrab*, a prayer niche, with bright red and green wool hangings dressing the walls.

Kennedy waited for her eyes to adjust to the dimness of the tent. Nawal squeezed her hand tightly. At that moment, The Torch stepped in. His silhouette loomed dark as he stood against the bright desert light.

"*Salam.*"

Nawal ran off immediately leaving the tent wide open.

He was dressed like the Blue Men of the Sahara. A *tagelmoust* wrapped his head. The blue cloth possessed a waxed and polished metallic shine. Since water is a scarcity in the desert, nomads beat the dye into the fabric. His skin was unevenly tinged with the blue dye like a canvas with many layers, each revealing a hint of color. Copper and cobalt. The cloth covered his mouth and the tip of his nose and his eyes were the only visible trait in his face. The veil was adorned with brass *tcherot*, inscribed decorative amulets that told of his tribal status. Over his veil, he wore a white turban wrapped around his head and down under his chin. His white robe covered his entire body and on one shoulder, he wore a matching white scarf flung casually over his other shoulder. He walked barefoot, his slim, bony ankles peeking under his billowing white robe.

Scumbag, she thought. You and your kind for turning the western world into turmoil. For your false piety, your subjugation of women, your hypocrisy, your fanaticism.

In spite of the rage she felt boiling inside of her, her legs trembled. She felt as if the bulk of her body was going to collapse, falling from under her like a house of cards. Many thoughts cluttered her head, past, present. This sudden burst of emotions made her wonder, for a fleeting moment, why she had accepted this assignment. Why did she think she could push aside all emotions, wipe the slate clean, and be an objective reporter. How could she? Too late for regrets. Now she was here and he was facing her, his right hand extended ready to shake hers.

"Miss Hunter," he said, "welcome to my place." The same voice. The same timber. Mellifluous and authoritative at the same time.

She nodded without responding not wanting him to notice her nervousness.

He gestured toward the large pillows on the floor inviting her to sit. She did, and he followed suit. He lowered himself on the carpet, placed a pillow behind his back, and crossed his legs, yoga style.

There was a pen, a pad and a tape recorder on the floor for her use.

"Forgive me," he said, "for all the inconveniences you've had to endure. We needed to be sure you were not followed. I'm sure you understand."

He uttered his apology but she doubted his sincerity.

"That was overkill," she replied, "I could have died in the desert."

He forced a smile. "I doubt it. You're tough. You had to earn this interview."

She did not reply. This was neither the time nor place to argue with him. Moreover, she did not want to squander this opportunity. Losing control would work to her disadvantage.

He leaned over a tray and poured tea in a glass. The aroma of verbena filled the air. He handed the glass to Kennedy. As she leaned over to grasp the glass from him, their fingers touched. She flinched and retreated as if touched by a bolt of lightning. He raised his eyes and in them, she recognized something, an uneasiness born of intimacy.

"It's been a long time," he said. He lifted his veil and looked her hard.

She studied his face. His face was beat by desert winds and marked by the passage of time but the aquiline nose, the chiseled face, and the knifelike gaze were still there. The hard sun had mummified the skin and vertical lines cut deep furrows into his face like erosions in a riverbed. Now he appeared to be one with the desert, not just from the desert, but also of the desert, like *drin*, the indestructible weed that grows sporadically in the Sahara.

"As you can see," he resumed, "I live among my people, far from the so-called civilized West." He had put emphasis on the word so-called.

Kennedy interjected. "I'd like to start taping this conversation, if you don't mind."

"The equipment is there for your personal use. Please, feel free to use it," he said.

Kennedy placed the tape recorder between them and pressed the Record button. She listened to its humming sound before she grabbed the pen and notebook. She always took notes and recorded simultaneously. She never completely trusted equipment or batteries for it would not be the first time she had relied on a tape recorder and ended up with a blank tape. Also, she would not have to look at him while she wrote.

He watched her fuss with the equipment. While she settled in, he held his steady gaze on her.

He had given her an opening by mentioning the West so she decided to continue this line of questioning.

"You just mentioned the West. Perhaps you care to elaborate about the things that you like or dislike about the West."

"Like, dislike, ah . . . " he answered, hesitating. "All those words. I prefer precise language, like, love or hate. They relay true emotions, not ambiguities."

She did not react but her mind reeled. *Here we go again*, she thought. He loves words, loves language, and loves manipulating both.

"And what is it that you love or hate about the West, sir? And aren't you a product of the West?" she shot back.

"You're right. I'm educated in the West. In America, as you already know." He moved against the pillows and readjusted himself. "The things I love about the West are the same things I hate. A dichotomy of sort."

He chuckled. Then his face hardened, his eyes spewed fire.

"I love your freedom. And I hate your permissiveness," he said. "Now, isn't that a contradiction in term? Your quest for individual freedom and self-expression is in itself absolutely admirable, yet, that same quest allows much too much individual freedom."

"Could you explain?"

He paused, took a sip of his tea.

"Take for example your first amendment right. Theoretically, a beautiful concept. The right to speak up, to express oneself. However, too many people abuse it with absolute impunity."

"Could you elaborate?"

"Sure. For instance, you have no fear of authority. Your leaders are consistently debased in public, in your media."

"The price we pay for democracy," she replied.

He ignored her comment. "Authority is essential in any society," he added. "You have to fear it before you can respect it."

She wanted to stop the pontificating but thought otherwise. Let him speak, she thought, I can always edit.

"Secondly, you belong to a corrupt society, Miss Hunter. Corruption of the highest degree. Insidious corruption. You create wants in people to enrich few at the top. You have turned materialism into your new religion. You profess to be a Christian nation but what you are is a nation of pagans. Your only God is money."

"I believe that most Arab nations are as driven by consumerism as we are," she replied. "They buy most of our goods and don't seem to reject any of the petrodollars we send their way."

"Export your goods but keep your values," he said his voice crisp as dead leaves.

"To say that your culture is superior to ours only because it shows more restraint is cultural arrogance," she fired back.

"I cannot think of a more arrogant culture than yours. You are exporting your Madonnas, your Baywatches and your McDonalds. You are turning youth everywhere into vapid, shallow, self-absorbed creatures whose only preoccupation is self-indulgence." He waved a hand in the air. "It's like masturbation—it's pleasurable, but it's only purpose is pleasure for the sake of pleasure."

She nearly erupted in laughter but he was deadly serious so she lowered her gaze and kept writing.

He continued. "The diet you're feeding the world comes from your cultural septic tank."

He waited for an answer. He wanted a mano-a-mano combat; she was not ready for it.

"I'm not here to condone or condemn the actions of my country, over which I have no control."

"Let me make another point then," he said raising his index finger. "Let's talk about your cherished second right amendment. Your absolute lunacy with guns. There are as many guns in your country as there are people. No civilized society should own guns. In fact, *that* is the hallmark of a civilized society. Imagine, if you will, a world as armed as the United States. *Imagine,*" he said, his voice rising, "the chaos that would cause."

She thought it odd that he would be condemning gun ownership. A case of the frog calling the pig ugly.

"Where do you get *your* guns from?"

He eyed her, a look of incredulity on his face. "From those who cherish your kind of freedom. People who believe that all people should fulfill their destiny of self-determination."

"How do you intend to fulfill your destiny?" she asked.

"Miss Hunter, my destiny was determined when I was born. I'm a fatalist. But, *In sha'Allah,* with God's will, I'll fulfill my destiny the way freedom fighters usually do."

"Freedom fighters are sometimes called terrorists," she said. "Which one are you?"

Angered, he rose at once and paced around her.

"I'm not a terrorist!" he hissed. "How dare you call me a terrorist? I'm a freedom fighter! Not a terrorist!"

She waited until he simmered down. She could hear his staccato breathing. Hard, shallow.

"Would you be wagging a war against your government or against the West?"

"No, not for the moment."

"Then when?" she pressed.

"At the right time. When all the other venues have been exhausted." He said this with a calculated pacing, weighing his words carefully.

"What would you do to get your message through?" Kennedy asked.

He shifted in his seat. "As I indicated, I'll use the usual channels to get my message heard. Meaning, the media, international diplomacy. The non-violent type of protest. Gandhi style."

"What if those don't work?"

His answer was quick in coming. "Then, we'll go to plan B."

"Plan B?"

"That's when we'll do whatever it takes to get ourselves heard."

He was so casual he could have been talking about the weather.

"Would you resort to violence?"

"As I said, Miss Hunter, whatever it takes. It is self-explanatory. Your conclusions."

"Tell me why," she asked, "you feel that your people have a right to self-determination, now at this moment in history when, in fact, Berbers are as much part of Morocco as Arabs are?"

"I'm certain that you know our history, Miss Hunter. I come from proud people, warriors. Fierce ones, as a matter of fact. Allah wants me to fulfill my people's destiny."

"Are you, in fact, conducting an Islamic revolution which has little or no support from your people?"

There was no expression on his face, but his body told her plenty. He shifted and sat erect directing his gaze towards her.

"Are you questioning my *raison d'etre*, Miss Hunter?"

"No," she said, "I'm questioning whether your people appreciate or need what you're doing for them or is this a one man crusade against a non-existing enemy?"

"The enemy is real, Miss Hunter. Not perceived, as you may think." He raised his hand to his veil and adjusted it around his nose and chin. "The enemy is time and time will convert all Berbers into Arabs. One day, there won't be any

Berbers. Like many other cultures, they'd merge with others, disappear forever. The Mayans, the Incas, the Romans, the ancient Egyptians. Name them."

She pressured him further. "Berbers don't seem to have any conflict with that."

He eyed her suspiciously. "Miss Hunter, the Jewish people have maintained their identity against all odds. For thousands of years, they have fought cultural integration. Their biggest mistake was to align themselves with the forces of Satan."

His voice rose in anger. "I'm here to save my people from total annihilation and from cultural imperialism."

He rose abruptly. He walked to a corner of the tent and picked up a document.

"Here. This is what I think." He handed it to her. Several pages written in a tightly scripted hand. "My philosophy. And where I'll take my people—should they choose to follow me."

He stood facing Kennedy. "Have you heard of the Manifest Destiny, Miss Hunter? It's a 19th century doctrine stating that the United States had the right and duty to expand throughout the North American continent." He stopped shortly as if waiting for her to absorb his words. "Imagine, Miss Hunter," he wagged a finger in the air, "imagine a country making a unilateral decision about expansion. Imagine the courage—and the audacity—it takes to make such a declaration. Now, surely you won't object to others wanting the same for their people, would you?"

He was turning the interview into a personal confrontation. She felt growing unease.

"I would like to ask you about the subjugation of women in the Islamic world."

"Subjugation?"

"Yes, the oppression of more than fifty percent of the Moslem world population in the name of Islam."

"Women are not supposed to rule the world, Miss Hunter. They are incapable of making rational decisions. They are volatile beings with no intellectual capacity."

Fuck you. She wanted to get up and pounce on him.

"Women give life, sir. A woman gave birth to you, not a man. Moreover, what do you call women like Madame Currie, Golda Meier, Margaret Thatcher, Indira Gandhi, and countless others. Even Benazir Bhutto, a Moslem woman."

"I call them insipid puppets. It's God's will that women should be inferior to men."

"Where does it say that women are inferior to men? You're seeking control of their bodies and souls. You want domination of the wind."

"It's God's will!"

"God's will isn't to own each other. God gave us free will so that we could own ourselves."

"Enough!"

He neared her and bridged the gap between them. "Well, Miss Hunter. This is my own manifesto. Read it." He flung the document on her lap. "I would expect you to publish it."

At that moment, there was a rustling behind them and the silhouette of a woman appeared. She stood directly behind him, frozen.

Surprised, he wheeled around. *"Im'shi! Im'shi!"* Angered, he ordered her to leave. The outside light shone on the woman's face and Kennedy caught her pale face and her Berber attire. She wore large golden amber beads around her neck, rows of bracelets dangled from her wrists and strings of silver coins adorned her head.

Hesitantly, the woman eyed Kennedy.

Suddenly, another woman came in the tent. This one was large, voluptuous and her ebony skin glistened. She was a black Berber, a Negro, a descendant of slaves imported from Mali decades earlier. She forcibly grabbed the standing girl's arm and led her out. The girl spun around, eyed Kennedy and as they exited Kennedy caught sight of her sheer blue eyes.

A moment of awkwardness fell between Kennedy and The Torch.

Kennedy broke the silence. "I still have many more questions for you."

"I'm certain that you'll find the answers in my manifesto," Miss Hunter.

"Sir," she said, "I'd prefer that you'd answer my questions."

"Anything you'd like to ask me is found in my manifesto. I'd expect you to read it and publish it," he repeated.

"I'm afraid that it won't do. I didn't ride two days in the desert to be your propaganda machine."

She heard the silvery chuckle. "The American media is nothing more than a whore," he said, his voice dripping with sarcasm, "it'll go to bed with anyone."

"Perhaps," she answered, "but I don't."

"You'd like us to believe that you're objective and neutral but, by the mere fact that you edit—you pick and choose the quotes that fit your story best—you're, in fact molding the story to fit your own personal bias."

"I'm afraid that you're mixing objective reporting with advocacy," she replied, "I'm not here to advocate anything."

He was a slippery eel sliding between her fingers. She was trying to hold on to him but she knew she had lost him.

"The only way to tell your readers what I think is by letting them read my own words, Miss Hunter."

"Sir, I'm the reporter and I do the writing."

"Good day, Miss Hunter. Have a safe trip back home," he said. He stood up and turned to leave.

Kennedy remained seated unable to control the rage she felt towards the man. He had pushed her to the edge promising an interview and delivered little.

"I have one more question for you," she yelled behind him. "Who are your heroes? Arafat? Idi Amin Dada? Pol Pot? Milosevic? Tell me, *who*?"

The Torch walked out.

Kennedy fought the urge to chase him. She reminded herself that she was his prisoner and that there was a fine line separating courage from stupidity. Instead, she lifted the tape from the recorder and placed it and the notebook inside her pants' pockets. She grabbed the manifesto and walked out to where Nawal waited for her.

She stood in the bright sun fighting the fury that filled her throat then quietly followed Nawal back to the compound.

CHAPTER THIRTEEN

He awakened in the dark, head thumping, heart pounding, sweating profusely, yet, shivering from the internal freeze that permeated his body. He thrashed the covers from his bed and sat in the darkened room listening to the howling winds on the Virginia Beach boardwalk.

Harry Bernstein knew he just had a nightmare. But this was not the kind of nightmare he usually experienced. There were no jungles. No helicopters. And no VC's chasing after him. There was only Kennedy and she was drowning. There was a lake. Deep, dark and covered with a sheet of ice. Kennedy had slid in it and he was trying to grab her. But he could not. She was screaming, *Harry! Harry! Help me!* But she was slipping from him. He reached for her hand and the closer he got, the further and deeper she went. He was losing control, his fingers gliding as if greased with oil.

In his dream he saw the fiery mahogany mane, fanned like a peacock go under, and the last thing he saw were the brilliant amber eyes, wide with fear, their gaze ever steady on him.

Kennedy! My God, he thought. *She's in deep trouble. Kennedy!*

He leaped out of bed, hit the cold wood floor, and dashed to the bathroom. The house was pitch-dark; he flipped the light switch on. He looked at his reflection and saw the face of a grown man having a panic attack. He reached for the bottle of Xanax—which is what he always did—then thought otherwise. Instead, he turned the faucet on and splashed his face with icy water.

Then he went to the kitchen, filled his coffee machine with water, and set it to brew. He sat at the little kitchen table wiping his face while attempting to steady himself.

He eyed the clock on the kitchen wall. Five a.m. His mind raced. Something happened to Kennedy. He knew it was real. It had happened before. The first time he met her, he knew she was a kindred spirit. She was like him. Made of the same fiber. He had always known the depth of their connection. There was energy between them and neither could control it. He recalled, once, not long after he had met her, she had dropped an earring and he had lifted it up from the floor and gingerly placed it back in her ear. When he had touched her skin, he had sensed a jolt that left him trembling. Since, their connection had been profound beyond words. Sometimes he knew what she was going to say before she said it. Sometimes she finished his sentences. Often he knew she was going to call and minutes later the phone would ring. Neither needed to talk about it. They just knew. It was what it was.

There were many more incidents when he knew of things happening before he was told. He recalled the first time it had happened, he had been riding in his SUV when suddenly he was overcome by a sense of dread and he had to pull his vehicle aside and stop. He had been thinking of her when his chest tightened. He didn't know why but all he knew was that she was in trouble. At the time, she'd been in Bosnia. He had gone to a phone booth and called Ty, her friend at the paper, and sure enough, Kennedy had been injured as a military jeep she was riding in toppled. She had survived, bruised like hell, but she had made it.

Now, he needed to talk to her. He needed to talk to somebody. He eyed the clock again. Only ten minutes had lapsed since the last time he had looked. He decided to call the paper in Atlanta. He dialed the number and all he got was a menu. If you want this, punch that. He was so frustrated. The world has been taken over by robots. Robots everywhere. He hung up and dialed again. Then he punched the extension for the news desk. Surely, somebody would be there. The night desk editor answered.

"Joe Harmond," the voice said.

Harry did not know any Joe Harmond although she had often mentioned the names of her colleagues. "Are you the night editor?"

"Yeah, that's me."

"Joe, listen. This is Harry Bernstein. I'm a friend of Kennedy Hunter. Have you heard anything from her lately?"

"Well, no. Nothing I can tell you. You need to talk to the managing editor and he ain't here."

"Ain't?" Great grammar from a newsie.

"Yeah. Ain't as in isn't."

"I see. When does he get in?"

"Depends."

"Depends on what?"

"Depends on whatever."

Great. This guy was a wise-ass and the last thing Harry wanted right now is to deal with a wise-ass.

"All right. Thanks for the great help."

"Hey, no problem man."

"Can you transfer me to Ty Johnson's desk?"

"What's his extension?"

"I don't have it."

"Well, I don't know it. I gotta look at the internal phone book and I don't have it right here on my desk."

Harry knew a few morons with high I.Q's and this one was definitely one of them. He hung up and dialed again.

Listened to the menu again until he heard the one listing reporters. Finally, he got Ty Johnson's desk. Ty and Kennedy had worked for a medium size newspaper in Virginia years earlier and they had remained friends and followed each other to Atlanta where they worked for *The Atlanta Dispatch*. Harry knew that Ty would not be in at that hour but left an urgent message to call him back. It would be at least two hours before Ty would get back to him.

He was pacing the floor when he decided that he needed to get out of the house. He slipped on jeans and a large parka and walked into the night. It was a thing he always did when he felt boxed in. Walk aimlessly into the night until his mind cleared and his body tired. Walk until his heart stopped pounding and logic sunk in.

The streets were desolate. Inside the beach bungalows that populated that side of town, lights went on. People starting their day. He put his hands inside his pockets and plunged into the thick of the night. The January wind was brutal but he didn't mind it. He even liked it. The pain it inflicted on him made him feel alive. Made him think of other things other than Kennedy. That's what's good about pain. It puts you in touch with your body distracting you from the demons that troubled you. Pain was good.

He walked down Arctic Avenue all the way to Laskin Road. He knew there were few businesses open at that hour. He knew of a little dive that was open all night, a local greasy spoon right at the corner of Laskin and Pacific. They served flapjacks the size of flying saucers and filled you up with so much coffee, it could awaken a dead man. He could use some of that right now.

He passed a myriad of hotels, restaurants and shops that were or should have been closed. Winter business was hardly worth the bother. He was sweating under his parka and his ears and the tip of his nose felt numb. A few blocks down the road, he saw the faint light of the restaurant and hurried along.

When he made it to the corner of Laskin, he dashed across the street and just at that moment a car came from nowhere rounding the corner. The driver broke so hard the car screeched and the smell of burning tires filled the early morning air. Harry jumped onto the curb as the car fled into the faint dawn.

"Hey, you asshole! Where did you learn to drive?"

Sonofabitch, Harry thought, I'm the only soul on the damn street and he nearly mowed me down.

He ran inside the restaurant. There were a few people seated around a counter and others in booths. All locals. None of that tourist crap in January.

He straddled a stool at the counter. A waitress, who obviously ate too many pancakes and molasses, sat an empty cup and without asking filled it up. She eyed Harry over her reading glasses while wiping her hands on her apron.

"Pretty nippy out there, eh?"

"Yep." Here we go, he thought, the weather bit. People loved talking about weather around there. Well, there was plenty of it. Before he moved to the area, somebody had bragged that Virginia Beach had all four seasons. Sure, he thought. All in one day.

He warmed his hands on the cup of coffee then rubbed his cold ears and nose. It felt good being inside.

"Anything to eat, cowboy?"

Cowboy? When was the last time anybody called him cowboy?

"Sailor or soldier," he said. "In this area, we're sailors or former sailors. Never cowpokes."

"Same to me."

"There's a difference between cattle ranches and Navy bases."

"Not to me," she said. "One and the same macho crap, if you ask me," she grinned a greasy grin.

He looked at her and for a moment, he felt he could ram

a fist into her smug mug. He decided to let it go and clam up. Ignorance coupled with stupidity were a deadly combination.

"I'll have breakfast. Ham and eggs, over easy. Pancakes. Go easy on the butter."

She looked at him as if saying you-ain't-in-no-fancy-restaurant but said nothing.

He looked outside the window. Dawn was breaking and he could hear the sound of more vehicles traveling the street.

He looked at his watch. Only six a.m. Time was slower than molasses in January when you're waiting.

Breakfast arrived so quickly, he wondered if the cook had the eggs ready to go before he even got there. She placed the plate in front of him, filled his cup and stood there, in his face, hands firmly planted on her hips.

He decided to call the paper again. Damn, I forgot the phone number.

He pulled his cell out of his front pocket. He noticed that it had run out of juice.

"Phone?"

"Right there." She pointed to the end of the counter never taking off her eyes from him.

He walked over to the counter and dialed the number.

"Newsroom."

"Who's this?"

"This is newsroom."

"Yeah, I know it's newsroom. Who's speaking?"

"Joe. Who do you want?"

Damn. The same friendly cretin. He had as much use for him as a bottle of cold piss.

"Is Ty in?"

"You again? What's his extension?"

Harry remembered it. He heard the transfer being made.

"Tyrone Johnson."

"Hey, Ty. Harry Bernstein here."

"Harry, my friend! You calling mighty early. I just placed a call to your house. Where are you?"

"In a greasy spoon in town. Staring back at two wide eyes in front of me."

"What's up, Harry?"

"You heard anything from Kennedy?"

"Why?"

"Well, I'm worrying about her. I have a hunch she's in trouble."

"How do you know that?"

"I don't. Just a feeling."

"As of last night, we know nothing. Desk has been trying to connect with her for three days. We left phone messages, e-mails and messages at the front desk of the hotel. No answer."

"What's going on?"

"We don't know. Last we heard from her she was trying to set up interview with subject. Then, *pouf*, vanished."

"Anybody there we can connect with?"

"Yeah," Ty said, hesitantly. "The American Embassy, but they know nothing."

"Who else?"

Ty paused. He sounded as if he was eager to say something but could not.

"Ty, what is it that you're not telling me?"

"Well..."

"Come on, Ty! We are like family. Don't hold back on me, man!"

"O.K. We had people at the hotel go check her room. Everything is there. Camera. Laptop. Recorder. Even bag and I.D. Press pass. Everything is there. Toothbrush. Clothes. Except Kennedy."

"Strange. Real strange."

"She left without her bag and press credentials. I don't like that," said Ty.

"I don't either."

"Don't sound like her. She wouldn't do that."

"Ty? Sounds like she was kidnapped or something."

"Yeah. The suits are worried. Martini was on the phone calling Casablanca last night. I heard him try some of his pseudo-French down there."

"Ty, I don't feel good about any of it. I know she can defend herself under many circumstances but there are situations she can't control."

"Yeah. I don't like the smell of it either."

"What's next, Ty?"

"I'm sure Martini is trying to find out what's happening. There are other reporters in the area. I wonder if he tried that angle."

"Hope so, Ty. Hope so." Harry was thinking. My God, she asked me to go with her and I turned her down. He could kick himself now for not doing so.

"Harry, you still there?"

"Yeah, I'm here. I was just thinking about what I could do. I'm confused."

"Listen, man. I'll keep my eyes open here and my ears pointed. I'll keep you posted on anything I hear." Ty paused. "And I mean anything."

"Thanks, Ty. Thanks. Call me anytime. Day or night."

Harry hung up and returned to the counter. He eyed the eggs in front of him, they looked even less appetizing than before. Right now, he had so much bottled up energy he could do anything. Run a marathon. Punch a bag. Jump out of a plane. Bungee jump. But what he really wanted was a cigarette. He wished he had one. Except that he had stopped smoking months ago. Damn. Moments like these, he could light one the size of his leg. Inhale it. Filter and all.

He eyed a man at the end of the counter. He was a worker and blue collar always smoked. His shirt pocket bulged. He turned to him.

"Could I bum a cig from you? I'll treat you for coffee."

The man reached inside his shirt pocket. "Here, have it man. No need to treat me." He offered a crooked smile then took a cigarette out of a pack and handed it to Harry.

Harry thanked him as he took a cigarette from him. He brought it to his nostrils and took a strong whiff. Damn, he thought, the bastards smell so good. Too bad they kill you. He kept sniffing it as if he had the elixir of life under his nose, debating whether to light it or not. He knew better. One puff and he would be back at it. That's all it took. Smoking two packs a day. Wheezing. Struggling to go up stairs. Smelling like . . . . Oh, well. He put the cigarette in his coat pocket and gulped the last of his coffee. He threw ten bucks on the counter and walked out the door.

"Bye, cowboy!" the fat lady sang.

He couldn't bother—he had other fish to fry. He placed his hands in his pocket while still holding on to the cig. Just in case.

Outside traffic had increased. The holistic and health food store next door was open and patrons were drifting in. Something about the people frequenting the place that was unsettling to him. Why did all of these people look so puny if they ate so healthy? Must be all the beige food in their diet. Beige tofu. Beige oats.

He walked inside the store just to burn time. He passed the organic food aisles and went to the book section. Racks of mags he'd never heard of. Past life regressions. Tantric sex. ESP. Reincarnations. Channeling. Shamanism.

What was that all about? Here was a world he had never known anything about. He picked a book by the Dalai Lama and read the cover. Finding inner peace. Finding your purpose in life. Interesting, he thought. I'll get that. Then he saw another by a Florida psychologist who dabbled in past lives and grabbed it too.

This stuff was for all the weirdoes that came to that Edgar Cayce Foundation, he thought. The holistic foundation was right down the street attracting those who believed in all that metaphysical crap. Locals did not hang out there.

Behind a counter, there was a young woman with spiked black hair and ghostly skin. She wore black clothes, had her nostrils pierced and purple nail polish.

"Mornin'," she said. "How you doin'?" When she smiled, he noticed her pierced tongue.

Ouch, he thought. "Good morning."

"Looking for something in particular?"

"No, not really." He was looking through the glass counter where stones, jewelry and various other accessories were displayed.

"I just received a gorgeous stone. An amethyst."

She took out a purple stone from the counter and handed it to him. "It's full of energy."

Reluctantly, he took it. "What do you do with it?"

"Massage it. Hold it. Feel it."

Massage it? Geez. He could think of a million things he would rather massage.

"I see." He looked at her and she was looking back at him but not really. Beyond him.

"Your aura is stressed today," she said.

"Excuse me?"

"Your aura is stressed today. Your colors are really off. Negative. Dark."

He couldn't help but smile. New Age hooey. Psycho babble.

"Well," he said, "I'm off. Completely off kilter."

"It shows," she replied. "You need to balance your energy and get rid of the negativity around you."

Yeah, right, he thought. What else is new?

"This stone should help you. It would restore your energy."

She's trying to sell me something. Typical sales clerk.

She was still smiling. "I have other things here that might help you."

By now, he was beginning to think that he needed to get away from her before she suckered him into buying some dumb shit. "Like what?"

She leaned, opened a display case and retrieved an object. It looked tribal, as if it came from a primitive society.

"This is an amulet," she said. "You know, a good luck charm. It's a good one."

"What is it?"

"It's called a *Hamsa*." She held her hand up and spread her fingers. "Five."

"Like a hi-five?"

She giggled. "Sort of."

"It's from Africa," she said.

"I see."

She looked at him, holding the amulet in her hand. It was made of wood, shaped like an open palm. Coarse in design. "It's against the Evil Eye."

He cracked a smile. "I didn't know there was such a thing."

"Sure," she said. "Everywhere. Evil forces. Negative energy."

She held it up by its leather strings. "This one is from North Africa. Morocco, to be exact."

He felt a frisson go through him. He could not believe what the kid was saying.

She was caressing the amulet. "Touch it," she said. "It feels good."

He grabbed it. Touched it. He felt nothing.

"You should buy it. It'll protect you and your loved ones."

He reached for his wallet. Pulled a twenty-dollar bill and handed it to her. She spun around, rung the cash register and handed him five back.

"You should wear it," she said. "Here, let me help you." She unlocked the clasp, leaned across the counter and placed it around his neck. Then she patted his chest. "There," she said. She stepped back admiring it. "It looks good."

"Thank you," he said then turned around to leave. He did not know what to make of this encounter.

"*Psst*" she called back. He wheeled around. "You need to do something about that aura of yours."

He nodded and forced a smile. He went to pay for the books under his arm.

"And," she said. He turned around again. "The girl. . . the one in Africa, she's all right. She'll be fine." She nodded batting eyelashes that moved like a broom sweeping a floor. "Don't worry," she said. "Be happy."

Harry hurried out of the place. This kid was weird. He needed to get away from her. She was starting to scare him. He paid for the books and ran out to the street.

A cold winter wind danced in the streets and an ocean mist had filled the air. He placed his hand in his pocket, found the cigarette, sniffed it, sniffed it again then tossed it out on the street. The books firmly planted inside his coat pocket, he hurried through the deserted beach. As he walked, he found himself reaching for the amulet around his neck.

CHAPTER FOURTEEN

They assembled under a clear and luminous sky. A camel train made of three camels, two Berbers and Kennedy. She was given a gourd, a head wrap, and sunglasses. The two Berbers were thin, wiry, with taut skin on lean bodies and copper-colored faces. Their eyes were hard, dead, like the landscape from where they spawned. She watched them as they loaded their camels with their sides bulging with water, food, tents. They threw woven rugs over the backs of the animals, and at last minute, as she watched them, they shoved two gleaming AK-47's, glazed mahogany and icy steel, into their oozing bags.

Kennedy wore khakis, boots, a *hendira* over her shoulders and back, and a white cotton head wrap tied around her head. Inside her pants' pocket, she held the only proof she had of The Torch's existence—her taped interview, her notes, the manifesto. She patted her pocket, following the contour of the tape, making sure that it was all there.

At her very core, she felt no satisfaction. Once more, he had led her to the well, let her wet her lips, but left her dry. Thirsty. He left her wanting more. But that's the way it was with him. He gave some but withheld, kept that leash tight. She was the dog at the end of his Pavlovian leash. Holding her back. And again, he had angered her. Again, she had let him anger her.

Now she was furious at herself for allowing him to control her, to dictate the terms of the interview, to dictate the tone of the interview. It was a control she didn't relish giving up. She liked the way it felt when she was in control. Not controlling, just in control, knowing that the exchange between her and her subject was balanced and fair. She did not like it when she was manipulated, turned into a pawn on a chessboard. All too often, she's had to remind those she interviewed she was writing articles, not advertisement. And if they wanted to control the content of the writing, they should just buy ad space and write their own copy.

Now, it happened again. Just like it happened before. With him. And she had vowed that she wouldn't let it happen. She had hoped that he had matured, mellowed. Of course, it was ridiculous to think that you could pierce the eye of a tornado, tame it, alter its course and lead it where you want. Its traits were inherent. Its sole purpose was to destroy. And destroy it will.

In retrospect, she thought, maybe I erred in my judgment. Time did not always mellow people. Sometimes, it hardened them even more, making them less penetrable. They built fortresses, carapaces, invisible bars, and divorce themselves from the rest of us.

Now, as she fell into the rhythm of the camel, rocking back and forth, she wondered where she'd go from here.

She eyed the two Berbers riding alongside and tried to imagine their lives. Who are these people? And what worries them? Her answer came fast. Survival, she thought. That's what worries them. Basic. Primitive. Darwinian. As simple as that. Food. Shelter. Protecting their families. No high-falutin notions of existentialism. At the bottom of Maslow's hierarchy of needs.

Their simplicity had awed her. It showed in their faces. An acceptance of life as it is. They owned little but seemed serene. Children played with polished cow bones. Adults derived joy from simple tasks. Butchering an animal. Cutting vegetables. Cooking with coals. Music. Dance. Weed.

She smiled when she realized the absurdity of life. How easy it was to lose sight of what was real. Of being swept up by expectations—real or imagined—and by the setting of unachievable goals. Here she was, denuded of all material possessions, things she thought she couldn't live without, and yet, she had not needed them. She had been reduced to her aloneness. Living with her *self* without the stuff that cluttered her life. And suddenly, she found it liberating. Liberating that she could own her *self* and not be owned by her *stuff*.

Yes, she thought, it's easy to be owned. To allow stuff to own you. Or people to own you. People, like stuff, can tug at you. They can drain you. Wanting, wanting, wanting. Emotional leeches that suck the life out of you. Never giving back. Only taking. And always wanting more.

The world was full of those. Mothers. Brothers. Sisters. Friends. Colleagues. Name it. They were there, hands out, grabbing, grabbing, grabbing.

How can anyone keep one's identity? Remain whole. Unfragmented. She didn't know if she had an answer. She didn't know if there was an answer. She knew—without any ambiguity—that she had learned a lesson in the last few days. The neon light in her head had been turned on, flooding the recesses of her mind, shining its light on what was important and what wasn't. Moments of enlightenment—epiphanies—happen when least expected. Under dire circumstances. Like right now, in a barren desert where her survival was as fragile as wings on a dragonfly. Thin, delicate, diaphanous.

She eyed the stretches of shimmering sand that stood before her and saw its awesome beauty. She probed its texture thinking, it's beautiful and ominous. Like people, beautiful and ominous at once. Millions, billions, trillions of grains clinging together to form waves of dunes. God's hands at work. It was a sampling of perfection and a scar on the earth. It inspired you or swallowed you. It lifted you or destroyed you. It nurtured you or killed you. Just like people.

I won't let it kill me. I will let it inspire me. Lift me. But not kill me.

She lifted her eyes to the sky and murmured a prayer for the road. Dear God, she said, give me the strength to accept your challenge. Illuminate my trail. Shine your light on me. Allow me to learn my lesson but spare me the pain.

The Sahara was going to test her willpower—she knew that. It tested the willpower of all those who ventured to cross it. It was unforgiving and it challenged those who thought of it as their equal. Its floor was littered with the bodies of those who belittled its nature, discounted its might and dismissed its wrath. It didn't allow for recklessness. Or slackening. It possessed but one weapon—the sweltering sun. Under its throes, everything surrendered. The land, its residents, all succumbed under its flames. Bleached, parched, seared. It was a world ruled by fire. And fire always won.

And when night fell, when the fire retreated, the desert opened its door to windstorms. Replacing the furnace for pandemonium. Millions of square miles of yang energy. No wonder, she thought, its inhabitants were so passive, accepting. You cannot fight fire with fire. You fight fire with water. You cool it. You fight yang with yin.

Perhaps that's what I should do with The Torch, she thought. Fight fire with water. She shrugged to herself. She wasn't sure. Sometimes you need to fight fire with fire.

She raised her eyes to the eastern sun and adjusted her sunglasses. The sun rose to her right and she was traveling north. Straight north. The sun would move from her right to straight above her head and finally would set to her left. She liked knowing where she was going. Directions, positions. Always cracked maps before any trip and analyzed her position. Always visualized maps and paid attention to land-marks. A thing she had learned from Harry who had taught map reading in the military and was fanatic about checking up maps for the shortest trip in the city. She kidded him about it since it never prevented him from getting lost. But at least he'd say, he could always stop and read a map. She mostly navigated according to some internal compass and visual clues. A grocery store to the left, a white building to the right. Harry had a passion for maps—he posted a world map on the walls of his bedroom. Liked to know where everything was. Countries. Oceans. People. She had once bought him a globe at a mall store catering to *National Geographic* fanatics. It was his favorite store at the mall. That and *Brookstone*, a gadget store where he found himself in the company of kindred spirits. A heaven where he could spend hours looking at tools, gripping them, testing them. Marveling at the design. Everything from carpentry tools to micrometers warranted his attention. He loved creating things with his hands. Carving. Chiseling. We're different but alike, she thought. I'm a carpenter of words. He is a carpenter of wood. I carved and chiseled words, molding stories. He carved and chiseled wood, molding shapes.

Now, as she prepared to cross the desert she found herself missing him and she wished he were there because if anybody knew about survival, he did. He'd know how to preserve his energy. He'd know what to do if he was under attack. And she'd trust him with her life. Something she was certain she couldn't do with the two men by her side. She glanced their way and thought, Who are you kidding. Trusting them would be tantamount to trusting a snake. You know that soon or later he will strike.

So she trailed behind them. Feeling safer as she watched their backs. She preferred it that way. Watching their backs instead of the other way around. Never allow them to surprise you. *Never be the point man.*

They followed the burning glow of the sun. There were no road signs, just endless miles of sand dunes filled with dreams and legends. Legends of those who had dreamed to conquer the Sahara. Arab nations to the north, Touaregs, Mauritanians and Legionnaires. They came in search of golden fortunes and saw their dreams disintegrate into dust. They left behind abandoned towns filled with their ghosts and remnants of the past. For to conquer the Sahara was to conquer the unconquerable. The indomitable. Like trying to grasp the wind. And like the wind, the Sahara belonged to no one. It allowed temporary passage or home to those who held their reverence in tow, who respectfully feared it. Like with obedient children, insolence was not tolerated and didn't go unpunished.

To Kennedy, the sun was neither a friend nor a foe. It was what it was. A hostile energy force, the embodiment of a universal power that exacted respect. Its scathing breath scorched the desert, but she knew that one foot above its floor, the temperatures were forty degrees cooler. She would stay on her camel as long as she could. The nasty beasts slobbered, grunted and bit, but were well suited for this task. They could travel more than thirty miles a day carrying as much as four hundred pounds of cargo and stay without water for as long as a month. Certainly, she thought, they'd outlive me.

———•◆•———

They had taken the road right after her encounter with The Torch and now she was beginning to feel weary and dry. The sun had moved straight above her head and she was longing for a stop.

They came across ruins that stood like shadows, fortresses built by Legionnaires, vestiges of a past. Embedded in their walls were petrified dragonflies, beetles, frogs and the writings of those who had wanted others to know of their existence. Testimonials. *I was here, remember me.* A lifeless world. A world that once was.

They rode inside the ruins of a courtyard, retreated into a shady spot and stepped off their camels. The animals were tied and supplies were taken off. The Berbers placed coarse rugs on the rocky floor, washed their hands and feet and kneeled to pray. Religious rituals were part of their daily life. They turned to Mecca and closed their eyes. *Bismil'lah . . . . In the Name of God the Merciful, the Compassionate.* They recited several *ayats* from the Koran as Kennedy looked on.

Finally, they rose and took out metal bowls from their bags. Kennedy sat on a rug stretching her legs and back. They walked away from her and she watched them cut and gather *drin*, a spiny grass that grew sporadically across the desert. They came back, their hands filled with shrub that they neatly stacked. They lit the shrub fanning it with their hands and placed over it a container with water. Then they retrieved goat cheese, dates, and pomegranates from their pouches and set them on the ground. They tore flat bread with their hands and handed a chunk to Kennedy. She bit into it and chased it with water from her gourd. They watched her and talked between themselves.

"*M'jiane, m'jiane*" said one, nodding in approval.

She nodded back. Then he opened a container filled with *khlii*, large strips of lamb that have been seasoned in *chermoula*, a marinade of coriander, cumin, garlic, oil and vinegar. The meat had been dried in the sun and except for its shape, it reminded her of beef jerky. He tore a large strip and handed it to her. "*La, la, la.*" She refused politely. What ensued was a dispute she didn't understand. They argued loudly, shoving the meat under her nostrils, not accepting her refusal.

"*Kol, kol!*" he insisted, pointing to the meat.

She didn't like lamb and she wasn't going to eat it. She pointed to the fruits and he went on a diatribe praising the merits of cured lamb. She maintained her position feeling as if she was in a bazaar negotiating when he finally relented, a grimace on his face. He turned around and spat on the ground, seemingly disgusted. Then he placed a finger on one nostril and blew its contents on the ground. He repeated the same with his other nostril. He wiped his nose with the palm of his hand then reached and grabbed a handful of dates, almonds and walnuts and handed the whole to Kennedy.

Kennedy nodded and accepted the food. His beady eyes never left her. She chewed quietly as they chewed on their *khlii*, pulling and tearing it with their hands.

The Berbers filled a teapot with boiling water, placed a handful of loose tea inside, another handful of sugar then added dried verbena. They drank their tea with pastries that they offered to Kennedy. The two men then leaned back on their mats and closed their eyes.

Kennedy went behind the walls surrounding them, squatted down and urinated. She had her pants down when she heard the sound of a trickle behind her back. She wheeled around and saw the Berber with his pants unzipped, his flaccid penis in his hand. Well, she thought, we're in total harmony. He was looking at her bare buttocks and began milking his organ. Their eyes met and she stared hard at him. There was a smirk on his face as he brandished his penis. His organ was large, erect and he fondled it furiously in sharp quick strokes never averting his eyes from her. She rose, pulled her pants up and walked back to her rug. When he returned she feigned indifference as they gathered their bags, rolled the rugs and mounted the camels.

They rode in silence, the sun claiming its rule over the sea of sand. They came across no one. Life had retreated finding shelter in sand. Even snakes disappeared, buried, for no snake and no lizard survived temperatures over one hundred and five degrees. The sole predator was the pounding sun.

Kennedy trailed behind the two men. Now and then, they'd disappear behind sand dunes but she was never far following the tracks they left behind. She was always aware of their presence. Suddenly, she heard a noise, *tatatatatata tata*, a rapid fire that broke the deadly silence. She immediately halted and listened. One of them had wheeled around and was coming back. He was a few yards away from her when she saw the fear on his face. The camel was as panicked as its rider.

She jumped off her mount and dove straight into the sand. The Berber took a hit and slumped over his camel. His camel emitted a distressing grunt and buckled under as they both fell into the sand.

Next, her camel was struck. He emitted a shriek followed by a grunt and fell down on its knees like an Arab when praying to Allah.

She scurried and hid behind the mass of her camel. He was heaving, his chest and belly rising in quick labored spasms. He was obviously hurt. His large moist eyes were turned to her and in them, she saw an awareness of things to come. Her own heart was pounding so hard she feared it would leap out of her chest.

She heard distant voices. Immediately she ran to the Berber's camel. She reached into the bags and pulled an AK-47 out of the pouch. She crouched near the camel, cocked the weapon, put a round in the chamber, and clicked the safety off. Then she slid low behind the camel and used him as a shield. She scanned her immediate surroundings but couldn't see the second Berber; he was way ahead of her.

She waited. Seconds later, she saw them, two men running down the dunes, sand kicking in their faces. They wore billowing white garments and their faces and heads were swathe in white turbans. They were darker than Berbers, nearly black, and the only naked features in their faces were their eyes. Touaregs, she thought, fierce, hostile, brutal. The lords of the desert. Their voices neared her and she heard them clearly. Feet away from her. They spoke loudly in a dialect she didn't comprehend. Enemies of The Torch? Robbers? It mattered little to her.

From their shoulders dangled two HK-G3 with bi-pods and scopes. They slowed down as they neared her, their roving eyes searching the ground. They eyed the dead Berber, kicked him in the sides, spit on him then moved to the camel and repeated their actions.

"*Shouf, shouf! Ha'da me'it*". Look, he said, he's dead.

Kennedy waited until they were in clear view. Her breathing was so labored she was certain they could hear her. At once, she rose from behind the camel and pulled the trigger. A spray of bullets went off blasting everything in its path. *Tatatata tatata*. Caught by surprise, they went soft at the knees then crumbled like an old detonated building.

Kennedy fell back on the ground, a stabbing pain in her chest. She waited until silence filled the air and slowly rose from behind her dead camel. Legs trembling, she approached the two dead Touaregs and the Berber who rode by her side.

She returned to his camel and grabbed another clip of ammunition. She replaced the clip and placed another round in the chamber. Painstakingly, she walked up a dune and down another one and found the first victims of the ambush. The point man was crushed, his camel toppled over him. The Berber's jet black eyes were open. The last time she had met them, they were golden, full of gleam and want. She closed her eyes, this last image still fresh in her memory, spun around and walked away.

Weapon in hand, she descended to where the Touaregs came from and found their camels hobbled and muzzled. She scanned the area but saw no one. She walked to the camels and released their ropes. She led them to where the carnage took place, emptied the load from the back of the dead animals, and placed it on the new camels. She found a compass, another AK-47, several rounds of ammunition, water, and food. She eyed the Touaregs that lay dead under the scorching sun wondering whether she needed to take their weapons or not. They'd load me down, she thought, but better take them then leave them for someone else. Never looking at their faces, she unclenched their already stiff fingers from the weapons. She split the load between the two camels, mounted one and rode away, never looking back.

Dear God, she thought, *I've just killed two men.*

She was hot, dirty and spent from the emotions but she needed to move on, place a distance between herself and the massacre she had just participated in and witnessed. She retrieved her gourd, drank from it, and then poured water she knew she needed to preserve over her head. She let the water run down her face and neck cooling her overheated scalp. She ran her tongue over her parched lips and tasted her salty tears mixed with the grit of the desert.

Aloud, she began a dialogue with herself. Hearing her voice felt good. It distracted her from thinking about what just happened. The dialogue was one she always had when stressed. Affirmations she often used. Pumping herself up. Not thinking about her circumstances. Rising above them. Which always ended with a conversation with God. Or with somebody. She wasn't sure. She had learned that from her French mother. Her mother was always negotiating with *God. If you do this for me, I'll do that for you.* Like a man on his deathbed. Most people, she thought, prayed to Santa Klaus. A mile long list of things they wanted. Let me win the lottery, give me a new car, a bigger house. Gimme, gimme, gimme. Well, she thought, I don't want any freebies from *You.* I want to make a deal: if you let me survive this, I'll make it my purpose in life to serve on this planet. Those who need more food, more compassion, an ear, a hand.

CHAPTER FIFTEEN

She lifted her imploring eyes to the sky and that's when she noticed that the sun was losing its strength. It had left the heart of the sky and was now moving west. The terrain, too, had changed. It was rockier and flatter. A barren plateau of sandstone and gravel. Here and there, summer grass and scrubs dotted the earth. And she could see ahead. No sand dunes blotting the horizon.

In the distance, she saw the remnants of yet another town. Like Sodom and Gomorra. Deserted, abandoned. Eroded by time and weather. She neared the ruins deciding that this was a good place for her to spend the night.

She approached the place weary but calm and filled only by the need to lie down and sleep.

Standing at a forty-five degree angle were two walls forming a natural shelter for her and the camels. She descended from her mount and tied them down. From her supplies, she retrieved a crawl-under canvas tent that she planted on the ground. She placed a rug on the rocky and uneven ground and retrieved some of the food left from the Berbers. Then she made a fire from the dry camel dung she had collected. There were wool blankets rolled up by the sides of the camels and she retrieved those too. She knew she was going to need them. Desert temperatures dropped more than a hundred degrees at night. She then crawled under the tent, placed the blankets by her side and stretched down, her body sore from the long hours on her camel. She took off her boots and her head wrap and with water from a gourd washed the grime from her face.

Outside, darkness fell heavy and the desert life was beginning to awaken. Snakes, lizards, foxes, lynxes would soon be out looking for prey.

For a while, she listened to the desert noises and the crackling embers by her tent. Then she fell hard asleep in a dreamless state, as hard as a dead man.

———•◆•———

She awoke in the dark by the sound of hollering winds. The billowed walls of her tent rattled as they inflated and deflated with each gust of wind. She rose and looked out. The moon poured silver and filled the sky's heart but she saw nothing but shadows. The camels were kneeled, their silhouettes a dark mass outside the tent.

Her senses now fully aroused, she listened to the wind, to its nocturnal dance. She knew that desert travelers and Berbers could identify the various winds of the region by their sound. They even had different names for wind. The Shergui, the Haboub, the Shahali, the Sheimoun, the Solano, the Hibli, the Aajej, the Hamsin. She couldn't distinguish between any of them. They were each capable of creating their own music, a variation on the same theme. They hissed, hollered, roared, danced, whistled, shrieked, whispered, murmured, or moaned. To desert people, they were like people, with character and personalities. The Aajej was mean, capricious. It twisted, turned, and swept everything in its wake. The Hamsin was hot, feverish, and grave. It whistled day and night until one went mad. The Harmatan, nicknamed the red wind, was undoubtedly the most feared.

When it blew, it was like blood pouring from the sky. God shaking his matador cape over our eyes.

The specter of doom loomed over Kennedy but she remained composed. It was something she wasn't able to comprehend about herself. The more critical or dire the situation was, the calmer she became, and the more lucid her thoughts were. There was no rushing of blood, no hammering of the heart, just a peaceful knowing. It was a sense of fatalism, an acceptance of her reality and a deep respect for the harmony that was and is.

There are rules, she thought. Rules in the universe, rules in the desert. She had followed the rules of the sun, went with the flow, swam with the current. But now, she was going to have to follow the rules of the night, the rules of the spirits—the *djinoun*. The desert spirits that all travelers feared.

They morphed into winds, humans, creatures. They were the ghosts lurking along the dunes, the seductress dancing in the wind, the predator sneaking under the sand. They were the gods of the night. Moody, volatile, fickle. They lured, enticed, deceived. Like magicians, they thrived on illusion and fakery then drove travelers to insanity.

She recalled how her mother, who was French but raised in North Africa when the region was under French Protectorate, had appeased the *djinoun*. She was respectful of them, even fearful. They weren't to be undermined. They needed coaxing, cajoling. She kept them at bay by keeping them out of her house. She prayed to them and begged for their benevolence. Raw, coarse salt was scattered around the house—at entries, around windows, anywhere golden light filtered. *Djinoun* weren't welcome. As a child, Kennedy was certain that they'd rise from the bowels of the earth and abduct her. Spirit her away to the miasma of evil that lived below the North African soil.

As they roared across the landscape, she listened to their deadly dance knowing that she was being put to a test.

She raised the flap of her tent, looked out and stuck her hand out. Sand blasted her hand and her face like razors. The moon hid behind a sheet of sand, its glow diminished as if it, somehow, it knew when to cede the stage to another player.

The camels moaned and grunted but their presence felt reassuring. Would the *djinoun* spare them? Would they spare me? She didn't know.

She dug into the bags of supplies opening packets of dried fruits and *khlii*. Then she found what she was looking for. A bag of salt wrapped in an Arabic newspaper. It wasn't raw or coarse, just plain table salt but decided that it would do. She scooped some with her hands and spread it around her tent. Cannot hurt, she thought. Better safe than sorry. Then she wrapped herself in a Berber blanket and closed her eyes. She thought of America. She visualized her life as it was. She visualized the newsroom and her editor, John Martini. Danced on the sand in Virginia Beach. Smelled the ocean. Tasted the salt on her lips. Felt the wind in her hair.

Shortly thereafter, she succumbed to the seduction of the dark and fell asleep.

———•◆•———

Sometime during the night, the restless spirits relented. At dawn, she awoke and raised the flap of her tent. Sand stood two feet tall blocking the entry, but she found the camels, unharmed, eyelids as tightly shut as a pair of clams.

With both hands, she shoved the sand aside and walked out to a dry and dusty day. The sun had taken its cue from the moon remaining ensconced behind a veil of dust. She wrapped a muslin scarf around her head and mouth leaving nothing but her eyes naked. Then, she gathered her tent, rugs and supplies, unleashed the camels and rode away.

CHAPTER SIXTEEN

Days later, wary and weary, Kennedy Hunter saw a quick movement in the horizon. It flashed before her eyes and for a moment, she thought that the desert's affliction was getting hold of her.

Visions of dancing ghosts.

Then, it happened again. Quick, transient, fleeting. She recognized the top of a passing car.

She rubbed her eyes, took a deep breath, then let go of the raw sobs that came out of her chest.

She patted her camel's neck. All right, camel, she said aloud, You've been good to me. We're almost home.

At once, the road became visible. There was only one road cutting across the desert, the one that would lead her out of it.

She descended from the camel and stood by the road. Soon, there would be trucks and cars passing by.

She heard the sound of a nearing car. Her heart pounded with anticipation as she held out her hand. The car came roaring but did not even slow down. He passed her and as she pivoted to see him, the driver honked and waved at her.

Sonofabitch.

Minutes later, there was another car. She leaned forward, nearly being run over, but he didn't stop either. Seeing her with two camels didn't help, certainly they thought she was a nomad.

Another car sped by, then another and another but no one stopped.

Suddenly she heard the sound of a larger vehicle. A truck or a bus, she wasn't sure.

She pushed the two camels to the side of the road, patted them, and whispered a thank you she was certain they understood. Then she pulled the AK-47 and waited. The vehicle was fast approaching. It was a large truck with an open back. She neared the side of the road and stuck her hand out. The driver noticed her. She could tell he didn't intend to slow down. She jumped to the middle of the road and as the truck approached, she aimed her weapon squarely at the driver's face. Then she fired a blast of bullets in the air high above the truck. *Tatatatatata tatatata tata.*

The truck screeched raising clouds of dust and stopped a few feet from her nearly mowing her down. She ran to the driver's side.

"Laayoune?"

The man's face was the color of death. Lips trembling, pupils dilated, he pointed to the back of the truck.

She jumped on the bed and found herself in the company of several goats, a donkey, and a few chickens. She made a spot for herself and stood on the truck holding on to its side. She watched the camels get smaller and thought, *There are angels on this planet and they don't always have wings.* She then took off her head wrap and let the wind run through her hair and face. I'm going to survive this, she thought, as the truck tore through the desert.

———•◆•———

Several hours later, they reached Laayoune. The sky was indigo, the air sharp, stabbing and furious. Kennedy pulled the hendira over her shoulders and placed the headwrap around her head and neck. The truck drove through town and stopped at the market place. The market teemed with Bedouins, Touaregs, and Berbers. It was a noisy place. She leaped out of the truck and walked to the front. She yanked open the passenger door and slid next to the driver. She had her weapon hidden under her hendira with the muzzle sticking out.

"I need money," she said. She put her thumb and index together and rubbed them. *"Flouss."*

Fear registered in his face when he noticed the weapon sticking under her garment.

She lifted the garment and showed him the weapon.

"Sh'al Ha'da?" How much for this.

His eyes widened when he realized she was trying to sell him the weapon. He burst out in laughter revealing a row of brown teeth. He turned around and spat out the window.

She repeated the question. *"Sha'hal Ha'da?"*

He eyed the gleaming AK-47, then her, then the weapon again. She could tell he really wanted it.

"Ana In'shouf". He brought his index to his eye. He wanted to check it out.

"La, la, la!" she said. No way. No touching.

"M'jiane." Good, he said. He nodded. *"Ham'sin."* Fifty dirhams.

"La," she said. Cheap sonofabitch. *"Me'iat."* One hundred dirhams.

He held both hands in the air then screamed looking positively pissed. *"La, la, la!"*

He was saying no but his eyes said yes. He really wanted the toy.

Well, she thought, let's split the difference. Seventy. *"Seb'in."*

He grinned. What a deal. She knew she was giving it away.

He retrieved a handful of bills from his shirt pocket and counted seventy dirhams which he held firmly in his hand. She opened her door and stepped out to his side.

"*Ya'Allah*, get out," she told him.

He walked out of the truck and she followed him right into the thick of the crowd. There were women and children walking through the market. She wanted to be surrounded by people. She held one hand out and he placed the money in her palm never taking his eyes from her. With the other, she handed him the weapon, which he immediately hid under his jacket. Soon as she grabbed the money, she wheeled around and ran into the crowd disappearing into a sea of bodies. He was too busy hiding the weapon. She knew he wasn't interested in her. He got what he wanted. At bargain basement price.

She hurried through town searching for the bus station. She immediately found it. There were plenty of passengers waiting. She found a ticket office and walked to its window.

"*Dar el'Beida*". Casablanca.

The cashier looked up and told her the bus was leaving in a few minutes. Then she handed Kennedy a ticket and pointed toward a platform where a bus awaited.

Kennedy searched for a public phone and found one on a nearby platform. She walked to it, dropped several coins inside, and waited anxiously.

Finally. "Hotel Riad Salam."

"Listen, this is Kennedy Hunter. I'm your guest. Please notify my driver Sami of my arrival."

"Yes, *Mademoiselle*. How're you doing?"

She cut him short, fearful that she was going to run out of coins. "Call Sami at this number," she proceeded to tell him Sami's number, "tell him to pick me up at the bus station in Casablanca. The next bus arriving from Laayoune."

"Sami? He's right here waiting for you. For days."

"Then tell him."

"Laayoune? It's far away."

"Yes, yes, yes. Hurry, please, don't forget."

"No, *Mademoiselle*, I won't forget," he said, *"bon voyage, Mademoiselle."*

No kidding.

She ran inside the bus, took a backseat, and watched a mob of people and livestock fill the bus.

Chapter Seventeen

American Heiress Missing, read the headlines of *The International Herald Tribune*.

Kennedy quickly shuffled through the week-old papers on her desk. Same headlines in every paper. Emily Carrington, student at the American College in Casablanca, missing for several days.

Kennedy realized that she needed to get caught up on worldly events for the time she'd been in the desert. Hard to believe, she thought, you can go somewhere where nothing happens and come back feeling as if a chasm has been created in your store of knowledge.

Quickly, she skimmed over the pages. Emily gone to Marrakesh. A short bio. Quotes from Dr. David Stevens. She recalled what a pleasant man he had been. How he had cut short their conversation. She remembered the nervous woman coming in and interrupting their conversation. Her journalistic ear ever pointed, she had heard the whispers behind the door. *Emily, when? Disappear? What do you mean?* And then, *Oh, my God.*

She had not asked any questions. Did not follow up. Just set it aside and left to meet The Torch. Now she remembered it all. The ashen face of the director after he heard the news—Emily had already been missing.

Suddenly she recalled another woman who had interrupted another conversation. The one who had walked into the tent when she was interviewing The Torch. And the second one who had followed grabbing her by the hand and lead her out. What was that all about? Her mind was racing but she pushed all thoughts aside knowing that she needed to concentrate on her article, the one about The Torch. First things first. She needed to call Martini.

The phone rang in Virginia Beach. She visualized the newsroom and its occupants.

"Where were you all this time? We searched heaven and earth for you," he said soon as he heard her voice.

"Well, if you had searched hell you would have found me there. I was meeting The Torch. Out in the Sahara."

"Well, did you get the interview?"

Typical newsman, she thought. The most important thing was the interview. "Yes, of course. I've got something for you."

"When would I see it?"

"Soon as I write it."

"And when would that be, if I may ask."

"Give me a couple of days."

"A couple of days? Are you nuts? I give you this afternoon. You have six hours to write it. I want it for our next edition. Get on with it."

"John, cut me some slack. I'm back from the lousiest week I have ever had and you want an article in six hours!"

"Kennedy, you can write an article in four hours. I know you can do it!"

"Listen to me, John. I'm not writing some seven-inch opinion shit where I show off how smart I'm! I need time and space."

He sighed. "How much space you need?"

"At least forty, fifty inches to start with—maybe more."

She visualized him nodding, a thin smile on his face.

"Damn!" he said, "you brought in the goods."

"Yeah, John, I guess so."

"Kennedy, you'll get the space. Whatever you need. Front page. As for the time . . . "

"Yeah?"

"Hurry up. Stay up all night if you have to."

"John, who is going to edit my piece?"

"I will. Nobody touches it."

She liked that. "Great, I don't want some pissy-ass kid right out of journalism school to carve up my stuff."

He erupted in laughter. "Reporter's ego."

"No. No ego involved. After all the pain I went through to get this interview, I want to see it treated with respect."

"It's a deal."

"John, there's something else you need to know."

"Yeah, and what's that?"

"He gave me a manifesto—some 5,000 words penned by him."

"And?"

"He wants us to publish it."

She heard him sigh. "Well, we don't publish anything on order, you know that."

"Of course, I do—I just wanted to run that through you. You need to know."

She was about to hang up when she heard his voice again.

"Kennedy? You know that friend of yours, Harry? The man has been pestering us to death. You need to call him ASAP. Before I become homicidal."

Now she was laughing. "Will do. Immediately. If not sooner."

She hung up then thought, How come he did not mention the missing girl in Casablanca? After all, I'm here. Then she realized it wasn't the kind of story Martini would be interested in. He loathed celebrity journalism. He would not even characterize it as journalism. Tabloids were, in his opinion, bottom feeders.

Chapter Eighteen

The Torch knelt, picked up a paper, then another and another, his eyes scanning the headlines like an X-ray machine. *The International Herald Tribune, The New York Times, Le Monde* and of course, *The Atlanta Dispatch*. He was everywhere. Kennedy's article had gone over the wires and every newspaper had picked it up. The Torch's picture was splashed over page one, in a prime location, right over the fold. *The Atlanta Dispatch* had used an old archive picture, one in which he wore his veil. *The Torch,* read the headline, *Is this the new face of terrorism?*

He felt ire rise in his throat. *A terrorist,* she called him. He was nothing like it. A terrorist. He was a freedom fighter, a man of conviction and labeling him a terrorist was condescending and insulting. Hands trembling, he opened the front page of *The International Herald Tribune* with much anticipation. It was the kind of exposure he always coveted—nothing but the best of the international press.

He went straight to the lead. *Although he wears a veil,* it read, *The Torch is anything but your average nomad.* The article went on to describe him in details—his early childhood, the family's wealth, the education at U.C.L.A and, notably, his famous dislike for westerners. It was all so well researched and detailed but it was not the manifesto he had given

Kennedy Hunter. They were not *his* words. They were the words of that American reporter, the one who had irritated him with her insolent behavior. She had done it again. She will have to pay for this. I promise, she will.

Seething with anger, he threw the paper down then grabbed it and tore it in pieces. He had wanted her to publish his *words*, instead, she wrote what she thought of him. It was her interpretation of him. *Not him.* How could she know how he felt about his people and their struggle? Reporters, he thought, always paraphrasing, always interpreting. One could not trust them. Even the best of them did not always get it right. How accurate were they anyway? Seventy-five percent? Maybe.

He grabbed his cellular phone and dialed the hotel where Kennedy Hunter stayed in Casablanca. It rang twice before he heard her voice.

"Hello," said Kennedy. There was complete silence on the other end. She repeated her greeting then heard him.

"Miss Hunter," he said.

She recognized his voice. "Yes," she replied, "I suppose you read the article and that's why you are calling me."

"Indeed," he said. "Miss Hunter, I'm a bit disappointed. I was expecting to see my own words in the paper. Instead, I read your analysis. *Your shallow interpretation.*"

Kennedy's hands shook. "I'm sorry you are not pleased with the article," she said, "but that's the way it is with reporters."

"Indeed," he repeated. His tone was so condescending Kennedy felt repulsed by it.

"Let me warn you, Miss Hunter, I do not like it when my orders are not followed diligently. I take it very personally, as you already know."

"Sir," she said, blood coursing to her head, "to be frank with you, your threats do not impress me. I have a duty to my readers. I did not become a journalist to please the likes of you. I'm here to tell stories and tell them truthfully."

"Which truth, Miss Hunter? Yours or mine? Isn't truth always something relative to the side you are on? To the position you are in? I beg to differ with you as to what is exactly truth." He paused. "Truth, Miss Hunter, is like beauty. It is always in the eye of the beholder."

"Sir," she said, "let me make a suggestion to you. Perhaps what you need to do is hire yourself some cracker-jack public relations firm. Because, if it is ink you are looking for, they will be able to get you plenty of that. Remember, we are in the business of uncovering the truth and they are in the business of manipulating it. Same coin, different sides. Good bye."

She was about to slam the phone down when she heard him say, "Not so soon, Miss Hunter." She brought the earpiece back to her ear.

"Miss Hunter," he said, "you are being particularly difficult."

"No, I'm not. I'm just telling you that the paper does not publish anything on orders."

"You may change your mind after you hear what I have to say. I suppose you got caught up on all your reading."

"Yes," she said, hesitating. She did not know where this conversation was leading.

"What do you know about Emily Carrington?" he said with glee.

"I know nothing other than what I read in the papers."

"What do you think happened to her?"

"I have no idea what happened to her," she replied firmly.

"You saw her in my compound."

Kennedy froze. Her mind was racing and her thoughts bounced with the force of a ball slammed against a wall.

"What are you trying to tell me?" she yelled.

"I'm trying to tell you that I want my manifesto published in every major newspaper. Put it on the wires. Let everybody read my own words. *My words*, Miss Hunter.

Not yours. And until you do, Emily Carrington will remain my prisoner."

"Sir, I happen to be a stickler for journalistic integrity," she said, "integrity is something you won't understand," she yelled back.

"And," he added, carefully. "Tell your chairman, tell him."

"You bastard!"

"Think of Emily Carrington, Miss Hunter." There was a slight pause. *Think of her.*

Kennedy heard a click. She could not believe the bastard was threatening her. She was hearing his last words. *Think of Emily Carrington. Think of her.*

Kennedy placed the phone down. Her hands shook so hard she felt she needed to do something to settle her nerves. She peered inside the hotel's refrigerator and found nothing but cokes and alcohol. She then looked into her medicine bag. Anti-inflammatory. Anti-diarrheal. Anti-bacterial. Anti. Anti. Anti. What she needed is an anti-anxiety. Finally, she found a kava-kava bottle. She filled the droplet and emptied it in her mouth. The stuff was so vile, it had to work.

Her mind speeding like a racing car, she shut her eyes and concentrated on her breathing. It always worked. Soon she began relaxing and her thinking process became clearer. She needed to take care of things in an orderly manner.

First, she needed to call the American College. Minutes later, Dr. Stevens came on.

"Dr. Stevens, I wanted to thank you for setting up the in-terview with The Torch. Although the way things went, I'm not sure it has been my most successful scoop."

"Miss Hunter, I'm not sure I have been very instrumen-tal on your behalf. I don't recall setting up anything." He seemed genuinely surprised. "However, I read your article and I must say you have captured the essence of the man."

She was wondering if he was being insincere about the

set up or that he had not truly arranged anything. "Well, thank you. It was not a pleasurable experience for me. I did not know if I was going to survive the Sahara."

"Oh," he said, "I see you have survived it nicely."

"There are some new developments today since my article has been published which may affect you."

She heard him take a deep breath. "And what are those?"

"Dr. Stevens, was Emily Carrington fair-skinned with blue eyes?"

There was a brief pause on the other end. "I'm not sure I understand," he answered hesitantly. "How does Emily Carrington fits in? Why are you asking?

"I have just gotten notice from him that he is holding Emily Carrington, your student."

The director felt as if a fist was slammed into his chest. "Why?"

"Blackmail. He wants his manifesto published and on the wires. And he is threatening."

"Manifesto?"

"Yes. A declaration of his principles and his philosophy, which I have in my possession."

"Is this some kind of bluff?"

"No. I don't think the man is bluffing. I saw such a woman in his compound."

"Miss Hunter, there are many blue-eyed women amongst Berbers. Was she veiled?"

"No, she was not veiled but most Berbers go unveiled. And my encounter with her was very brief."

"How do you know it was Emily Carrington?" Anger had seeped into his voice.

"I don't. But The Torch says so. And I did see a woman with blue eyes."

"You better notify the detective in charge of this investigation, Miss Hunter. This is taking an unexpected turn," he said.

"Dr. Stevens," she said, "I'll notify them but I'm afraid this is something the local police won't help us with. If I read the man correctly, this is going to be a quid pro quo situation. I don't believe the local police will interfere with him. They won't dare. It will create too much instability on the local political scene."

"Are you suggesting we do nothing, Miss Hunter?" His voice had risen.

"Certainly not. It's your call, Dr. Stevens. I will, however, notify you as soon as I hear anything from him."

Things were getting more complicated. She did not like the turn of events and felt impotent.

Kennedy grabbed the papers and scoured them reading everything that has been written about Emily. She scrutinized Emily's picture trying to recall whether it was the girl she had briefly met. Emily possessed blue-eyes, a pixie nose and shoulder-length chestnut hair. The kind of beauty Americans called "apple pie". There were millions like her in every city in America. Just like the girl in the tent.

Kennedy searched her memory bank for the face she saw in the tent and the face in the papers. Like instant replay, she recalled the girl's face repeatedly. And each time she reached the same conclusions. It must be her. It had to be her.

She recalled the girl's behavior. She had walked in quietly and walked out as surreptitiously as she had walked in. Could she have said anything to Kennedy if she had wanted to? Probably not. Did she have an opportunity to do so? No. Why did she not try?

Kennedy was puzzled. Her mind was churning the scenario over and over again. The girl walking in. The girl walking out. She could have slipped a note. She could have mouthed words. Instead, she stood frozen like a marble statue.

Was she there as a willing participant? Did she behave like a prisoner? Her eyes and body bore the language of fear. Kennedy recalled another time, another kidnapping. Images of Patricia Hearst, the newspaper heiress, abducted by the Symbionese Liberation Army. She was not a willing participant. She was kidnapped forcefully, then brutalized, then became a terrorist with a smile on her face and a machine gun in her hands.

She reached for the papers and read again. Maybe she missed something. Emily Carrington was born in Atlanta, Georgia. Her family was a direct beneficiary of the Coca-Cola fortune. The articles said she was missing, an unlucky prostitute found dead in the city's dump wearing her clothes.

Kennedy wanted and needed to know more. She was like a dog on a bone. She dialed the front desk.

"Do you have an internet connection?" she asked.

"Yes, we do," the clerk replied. "There is a plug in your room."

She looked at her watch. It was five o'clock in the evening. She quickly calculated. Ten a.m. East Coast time. The hell with the internet, she thought, then picked up the phone. She dialed Virginia Beach and at the third ring, a man's voice.

"Harry," she said, "it's me."

"Ken, am I glad to hear from you! Where have you been?"

"Traipsing in the Sahara."

"How bad was it?"

"Bad enough to never want to go hiking or spend a night on a sandy beach."

"I guess that did it for you."

"For sure."

"I read your article. Good writing," he said. "So, what's up?"

"Harry," she answered, "could you do a Net search for me? I need you to search the Carrington family in Atlanta.

Fax me or forward me everything you find. Also get me the phone numbers of the family in Atlanta."

Harry hesitated. "The Carrington family? You mean Emily Carrington? How are you involved with that thing?"

"I'm not. Yet." She paused. "Harry, please, check anything you find in old articles, particularly if it's related to the girl. Check the archives of *The Atlanta Journal-Constitution*. There should be plenty of stories on the family."

"What do you need all that stuff for?" Harry asked.

"Just a background check. Just curious," Kennedy answered.

"Curious? Well, we all know what happened to the curious cat."

"Harry, please spare me all your warnings right now, can you just do it?"

"Sure," he said, "but, listen, Kennedy. I've known you long enough to know that you won't go through all that trouble if you weren't sniffing something."

"Sniffing is all I'm doing right now."

"Come on, Kennedy! Tell me what's going on."

"O.K. Harry." She paused, then, "He's got the girl."

"Who's got the girl?"

"Him. The Torch."

"You're not serious."

"I'm bloody serious."

"Kennedy," he said, "keep your nose out of it. The family has got plenty of money to hire private detectives, fly them on a jet to Casablanca, and feed them lobster in the middle of the Sahara from now till eternity."

"You're right, Harry. Again. As always. Except."

"Except what?"

"Except that he wants his manifesto published in exchange for the girl. A quid pro quo. So whether I want it or not, I'm involved. Against my free will."

"Are you absolutely, positively sure he's got her?"

"Well, yeah. I saw a girl who would fit the description in his tent."

"What makes you think it's her?"

"Her eyes. The color of her eyes. And the fear that lived in those eyes."

"This is messy. I don't like any of it."

"Neither do I."

"All right," then reluctantly, "I'll get started on a Net search for you. What are you gonna do now?"

"Well, first I'm going to call the detective in charge of the investigation for a couple of quotes and then fire off something to Martini."

"By the way, on a lighter note, that finicky French poodle of yours really misses you. After a couple of days of snubbing hamburgers and French fries, he surrendered. Now, he'll eat anything. Even Pizza Hut. And he isn't doing too bad on the Colonel's glorified cuisine, either. What do you feed him, anyway? Filet mignon with buttered asparagus?"

Kennedy guffawed. It was the first time in days she had laughed. Or found any reason to.

"And how come you're eating so much junk?"

"Well, to be honest, I don't get too motivated to cook for myself. Eating alone should be a crime."

"Harry, his palate is going to be so bastardized by the time I return I will have to send him to you for dinner."

"It's a deal," Harry replied, "as long as you buy us an annual subscription to Burger King. I'll provide the cutlery and the Merlot."

Kennedy was still laughing when she hung up. It felt good to call home.

CHAPTER NINETEEN

"Detective Ahmed," said the detective as he answered his phone for the umpteenth time that day. He was worn down by the press, dogged to the point of harassment, and exhausted from the same questions.

"Detective Ahmed, this is Kennedy Hunter with *The Atlanta Dispatch*."

Ah, he thought, she is the one writing all those articles about The Torch. "Yes, what can I do for you, *Mademoiselle*?"

"I just spoke to The Torch and I believe he is holding Emily Carrington," she said directly.

"*Pardonnez-moi?*" The detective was trying to connect the points. Emily Carrington, The Torch?

"You have heard right. He is holding Emily Carrington."

"For what reason, *Mademoiselle*? Ransom? The Torch does not need any money."

"No, it isn't money he wants. It's his manifesto published."

"Ah, that." He paused as if he knew about the manifesto. "Miss Hunter, how do you know he's got her?"

"I was in his compound and I saw a girl who fits Emily's description."

"So you believe it's her?"

"Absolutely."

"I wouldn't be so sure, Miss Hunter" he said confidently.

"Well, right now, I'm sure until I find out otherwise."

"O.K.," he replied, "right now, I'm not sure until I find out otherwise." He had put great emphasis on the *not*.

"Detective, what are you doing to find Emily? Will you search for her in the Sahara if she's with The Torch?"

"Miss Hunter, the Sahara is a big place. Maybe you can tell us where he is since you've been to his compound."

"I have no clue where it's at. I was parachuted out of a plane to get to his compound."

"Well, we have no way of knowing where he's at. His communications are all via cellular phones."

"You mean to tell me your intelligence agency cannot find him?"

"I mean to tell you that *neither* your own C.I.A nor your N.S.A and all the sophistication of your American equipment can find him."

"I cannot believe you cannot intercept his communications."

"You better believe it. Your own intelligence agencies have not been able to find Ishmael Abdoulaziz, America's enemy number one. Neither will they be able to find The Torch."

"Why?"

"Because The Torch, just like Abdoulaziz, uses satellites, encrypted messages and scrambling devices made in America. Ironic, Miss Hunter, isn't it?"

"What you're telling me is that they're using our own technology against us."

"Exactly. This is the one time you have created a monster which you cannot control."

"Too good for our own good."

"*Oui, exactement.*"

CHAPTER TWENTY

John Martini opened his email and saw that there was a flagged message from Kennedy. In large block letters, the heading leaped out off the page.

ATTN: JOHN MARTINI. CONFIDENTIAL. FOR
YOUR EYES ONLY.

He glanced at the sender and the location. Kennedy Hunter, Casablanca. In capital letters, the headline read:

DISAPPEARANCE OF AMERICAN HEIRESS
LINKED TO BERBER REBEL.

He halted, blinked and read the headline again. This, certainly, was not the kind of development he expected. His fast eyes flew across the copy then he sat at his desk and read on.

Casablanca—In a stunning development, Emily Carrington, the American Coca-Cola heiress who disappeared over a week ago, has been spotted in the Sahara living in the compound of the rebel known as The Torch.

In a phone interview, The Torch admitted holding Emily Carrington. As a condition for her release, The Torch seeks the worldwide publication of a manifesto, a 5000-word personal mission statement he penned stating his personal philosophy, his dream for a Berber nation and the means he will employ to achieve his goals.

Local authorities, alerted of this new twist, are not considering a search in the three- million square miles desert. The Sahara is inhospitable and inhabited by dozens of warring tribes including The Torch's own Islamic Militia.

The Islamic Militia, considered the strongest in the region, is armed with state of the art weaponry and has been know to use it with impunity.

Little is known of the whereabouts of The Torch, a man notoriously famous for his sly and cunning disguises. Few people have ever seen him and fewer can describe him.

The Torch did not indicate what the consequences would be if his wish was not granted, but authorities believe his ruthlessness and past record of accomplishments suggest the man will stop at nothing to achieve his goals.

Local authorities, who until now were mostly concerned with Emily Carrington's disappearance, are surprised at The Torch's involvement and at the turn of events.

"We'll try to negotiate Miss Carrington's release," said Detective Ahmed in Casablanca, "The Torch," he added, "is highly unpredictable. Mostly, we are concerned with the well-being of Emily Carrington and her safe return."

Asked if local authorities will attempt to rescue Emily Carrington from The Torch, Detective Ahmed said that they would, if they only knew were The Torch was hiding.

The State Department, the branch of the United States government overseeing Americans living abroad, refused to comment on this particular abduction saying only that they do not rescue kidnapped Americans or those who get into trouble of their own volition.

Martini stood frozen. It took him several minutes before

he managed to grasp the full meaning of the situation.

He punched the number for his deputy managing editor, the woman in charge of the news division.

"Catherine," he said into his speakerphone, "could you come to my office? We have an emergency. I need to call our Chairman right away."

There was static and the answer came through the speakerphone. "Sure, John. I'll be there in few minutes."

He repeated his call to Malcolm Newberry, the newspaper's publisher then dialed the number for the paper's chairman, Aubrey Morrison.

Minutes later, Catherine Savich entered his office. Martini had just ended his conversation with the paper's chairman. Whenever he saw her, Martini was reminded of why she was nicknamed Catherine the Great. She possessed a physical presence many of her female colleagues envied. She was tall, with dark long hair and Mediterranean coloring. Modigliani in motion. She could have made it as a model but her keen intellect would have suffered. She wore a clingy black dress and the scarf around her neck hung casually, placed there almost as an afterthought. She was completely unaware of her beauty and her effect on the opposite gender.

She sat facing Martini as Newberry walked in. "John," said the publisher, "what's this about?" Newberry was a short, nervous individual with dark rimmed glasses and thinning hair. He wore a generic gray suit with a white shirt and Bostonian shoes. Although Newberry was the publisher, he had no interest in the daily operations at the paper and even less interest in small talk. Most of the time, he hid in his office crunching numbers and rarely interacting with reporters and editors.

"I have summoned both of you because of some decisions we need to make," said Martini. He placed his reading glasses on and glanced at a copy of an email on his desk.

"I have here an email from Kennedy in Casablanca. Here," he said, pushing two copies in front of them.

Catherine Savich scanned hers quickly. "Oh, no," she said. Newberry brought it closer to his face then read it. His face took on a somber look. "Not good for the girl," he said.

Martini held a copy of the manifesto in his hands. Fifteen typewritten pages. "And this is the famous document." He gave the stapled pages to Newberry who quickly scanned the pages.

Citizens of the World:

I, The Torch, descendant of the Great Prophet Mohamed, shall rid the world of the corruption that has befallen on us.

We have strayed from Allah, we have strayed from principles of virtue, and we have strayed from moral commitment.

We have embraced moral corruption, we have embraced greed, we have embraced self-aggrandizement.

Newberry slid the pages in front of Savich. "This looks like your typical radical Moslem propaganda," he said.

Catherine Savich read the first page, turned to the second page then halted. "I agree," she said, "pedantic stuff. It's full of references to other historical struggles." She stopped briefly and flipped over to the second page. "The man is an intellectual but his view of the world is distorted."

Martini's face took on an inquisitive look. "Any opinions as to how we proceed with this?"

Newberry spoke first. "Well, I think there's no debating this matter. We don't publish propaganda material on order."

Over his reading glasses, Martini glanced at Savich. "And you, Catherine?"

"Well," answered Savich, "the life of a young woman is at stake here, and we can't dismiss it so easily."

Newberry turned sideways eyeing her with intensity.

"Catherine," he said, "you're not suggesting we go along with this loony plan, are you?" His tone was one of incredulity.

"I'm not suggesting anything—*yet*. I'm saying we need to evaluate all of this and see how we can save this girl's life."

"Catherine," Newberry said in an exasperated tone, "we are not a charitable organization nor are we a commando organization. Dealing with terrorists is out of the question. We do not stoop to their level!"

Martini, who until now had maintained a controlled demeanor, interjected. "Undoubtedly, this is a tricky situation. Emily Carrington is not your average kid. She's an heir to a large fortune, a media sensation at that, and moreover, in the interest of full disclosure, she's the niece of our Chairman."

Catherine Savich leaped out of her seat. "I had no idea!"

"Well," replied Martini, "it isn't the kind of detail our Chairman wants publicized. It would make matters worse. Among the diversified assets the family possesses, they have many publishing interests, including this newspaper."

Newberry did not respond. He did not seem startled by the revelation, which made Savich think he must have known all along. He had a pen in his hand and he was whirling it around nervously.

"In trying to help Emily Carrington," said Martini, "we are opening the door to every terrorist organization with an agenda. We'll be setting a precedent."

"Forgive me, John," answered Savich, "but a precedent already exists." She paused and looked around her, her gaze traveling from Martini to Newberry. "Remember the Unabomber? It hasn't been that long. . . "

"I know," said Martini, "but, there lies the difference. The public interest outweighed the risk *The Washington Post* was taking. Their choice was clear. Somebody *did* recognize the writings of the Unabomber. It was a decision that proved to be wise. Ultimately."

Newberry interjected. "I was in total disagreement with them then as I am now. I fail to view capitulation as victory. The role of a newspaper isn't to serve as a propaganda tool for every loony under the sun."

Savich answered. "The Unabomber was not *every* loony under the sun. He was an intellectual, just like The Torch. These so-called loonies don't shrink when denied their wishes. They just up the ante."

"O.K.," said Newberry, his voice returning to its normal pitch "Assume we publish his manifesto. What happens if he *does not* release Emily Carrington? What if he's playing games? *The Post* did not have to worry about getting anything in return for their gambling. All they were hoping for was for somebody to recognize and identify the Unabomber's writings. Which is, in my opinion, a noble deed—however misguided that move was in deviating from journalistic principles."

"Setting aside any principles—what does Morrison know about our predicament and how does he propose to solve it?" said Savich.

Martini spoke. "He has been informed about this new development, the abduction of Emily by The Torch. He knew of the disappearance of Emily—of course. But The Torch's involvement is new to all of us. He read Kennedy's interview with The Torch and her latest article." He paused, ran his hand across his disheveled hair, and then continued. "Certainly, the only thing these two events have in common is they both happened in the same country."

"Very curious," said Savich.

"Indeed," replied Newberry.

Savich looked at Martini. "What does the chairman say?"

"I predict," interjected Newberry, "that he'll agree with

my position—notwithstanding the fact that his niece is held captive—that there's no negotiating with terrorists."

"What do you say, John?" said Savich.

John nervously adjusted his reading glasses and shifted in his seat. "Malcolm is right. Our chairman agrees with him. He's a tough old coot. And he'll stand firm on principle."

Savich was beginning to feel she was in a minority. Indeed, she was the only one who was willing to compromise. "Would he be willing to jeopardize his niece's life for a principle?"

"I'm afraid he doesn't see it that way," answered Martini. "He'll see it as capitulation to a renegade."

"I remember," said Savich, "sometime in the 70's, J. Paul Getty, the famous billionaire, was blackmailed by Italian kidnappers. They held his grandson in Rome and asked for a couple of millions in ransom money. He refused to pay up—the world was appalled that he would refuse."

"Yeah," interjected Martini, "the man was notoriously frugal."

"True," replied Savich, "anyway, the blackmailers did not capitulate and he received this grandson's ear in an envelope. The kid spent the rest of his life asymmetrical. I bet you he adored his granddaddy after that."

"Yeah, I bet. Anyway, I propose the following," Martini added. "We'll be running Kennedy's latest article as is. It will make the bastard cringe and we will get a response from him. We'll name him the abductor of Emily Carrington. Do we all agree on running Kennedy's piece?"

There was a unanimous "Yes" from Savich and Newberry. Martini stood up. "For all intents and purposes, I propose that we keep the family relationship between Emily Carrington and the chairman confidential."

Savich face showed her displeasure. "What about Emily? Who's going to save her from this?"

Martini replied. "For the moment at least, nobody. Certainly not this newspaper. Not the F.B.I, the C.I.A and certainly not the State Department. Remember the Beirut kidnappings? Well, the abducted rotted in prison for years. And that included one of ours—an A.P reporter named Terry Anderson."

CHAPTER TWENTY-ONE

Dr. David Stevens grabbed his phone and dialed a number. Then he remembered he should not use his regular phone and hung up. He moved to an adjacent room and picked up a cellular phone. He dialed a number and waited.

"*Allo!*" said a voice.

"Yes, get me The Torch. Immediately."

"Sure," replied the man.

He listened as the man made the connection and seconds later the familiar voice.

"Ibrahim, this is David Stevens, how are you?"

"I'm good, thank you. *Merci.*"

"You know why I'm calling you, don't you?" the director said crisply.

"I do."

"What are you doing with my girl? And why?" The director's voice trembled.

"David, listen to me. This has nothing to do with you or the girl."

"Excuse me? Then explain to me your logic because I'm dumbfounded as to the why of all this."

"It has to do with my vision, my manifesto."

The director laughed aloud. "And why this girl?"

"Because the girl is related to the largest media empire in the United States. And so is Kennedy."

"Let the girl go, Ibrahim!"

"The girl will go when my manifesto is published. *Nothing else!*"

The director paused. He could not believe what he was hearing. "Ibrahim, are you trying to get even with Kennedy for what she wrote ten years ago?"

"She came to my compound for an interview and she was as insolent and as disrespectful as she used to be. And it all came back to me. I remembered."

"Ibrahim, I thought you were over that. It's been long time ago. Let it go. Let go of it."

"The Torch never forgets," he replied bitterly.

The director was losing his patience.

"But then why Emily? Why not somebody else?"

"Because Emily is a rich American kid, not some poor Arab woman nobody gives a damn about. Do you think I'll get the attention of the international press if that was the case?"

"What are you saying, Ibrahim? That you are sacrificing Emily Carrington for your cause?"

The Torch's voice rose. "Yes, sometimes people need to sacrifice themselves or others to make a point! You understand that, David, don't you?"

The director felt the blood drain from his face. "No, I don't understand it!"

"That's what the Palestinians did! They died for their cause!"

"Let me tell you, Ibrahim," the director replied, "Arafat was a damn fool for turning children into human missiles, and the Palestinian people were bigger fools for listening to him! He always wanted more and more, never happy with what he got!"

"It was a noble cause!"

"No! It was the epitome of stupidity! They fought for their so-called cause for over fifty years and they never learned their lessons! Maybe what they needed is a good dose of reality accompanied with a healthy serving of sensibility and some new leadership!"

The director paused, his breathing had turned shallow, then, "Ibrahim, don't do that to your people! Don't turn them into martyrs! They don't deserve it!"

The director heard a click then a dial tone. He wiped the sweat that formed on his brow then immediately dialed another number. His hands quivered.

"Newsroom!"

"Can I speak to John Martini? Tell him it's David Stevens."

Seconds later Martini came on the line.

"David, it's been a long time. How is my old friend doing?"

"I would do better if I didn't have to deal with the Emily Carrington ordeal."

"Ah, we have to deal with it as well—"

The director got to the point. "John, are you going to publish his manifesto?"

"Well, we just had a meeting about it. If you want a yes or a no, then, bluntly put, it's a no."

"What does the chairman say?"

"From the very top—it's a no. You know we cannot bow to the whims of terrorists."

"What about Emily? Who's on her side?"

John Martini sighed. "Frankly, I don't know. We are just putting one foot in front of the other here. We don't know what will happen."

"Are we going to wait until he sacrifices her to react?"

"We hope not. All I can say is that we have a reporter on the site and maybe she can negotiate with him on something."

The director let out a nervous chuckle. "Are you kidding? Are you talking about Kennedy Hunter?"

"Yes, of course."

"Maybe none of this would have happened if Kennedy Hunter had stayed put in America where she belongs."

Martini shifted nervously in his chair. "What are you saying, David? What does Kennedy Hunter have to do with this maniac?""

"She has a lot to do with this, John. She *is* the reason behind all of this. She's the reason for everything."

"You care to explain?"

"Ask her. Ask her."

CHAPTER TWENTY-TWO

From the third floor of the Prefecture building, detective Ahmed eyed Place Mohammed V and its namesake boulevard. Lined with art deco buildings in a neo-Mauresque style, the boulevard was a remainder of French dominance, a past both rich and contentious.

A hazy veil fell on the city as dusk drew closer. Soon, shameful behavior will be tolerated and promoted and weaknesses will be catered to without scruples or accountability.

Down, at ground level, the streets overflowed with cars, bicycles and pedestrians in a never-ending bustle that crescendoed as darkness neared. The din of the city rose above ground level, its deafening sounds reaching the distraught detective whose obsession with the American girl and The Torch was the cause of recent insomniac bouts.

From above, the detective looked down the boulevard that lead straight to the old city, the medina. Down there, he thought, in the labyrinths of the old city is the answer I'm looking for. Down there, in the narrow alleys and hidden corners of the medina the truth hides.

The detective ran down the three floors of the building and walked straight into the sidewalk. The pleasant aroma of roasted chestnuts emanating from a nearby charcoal grill engulfed him as the vendor, a man with a complexion the color of smoked meat, brandished a roasted chestnut on a wooden pick.

"Des marrons chauds! Des marrons chauds!" Roasted chestnuts, he yelled.

Ahmed ignored the man's invitation and moved among the pedestrians crowding the sidewalks. He raised his jacket collar, stuck his hands into his pants' pockets and plunged into the crowd. The air was brisk and he wished he had worn a top coat. *Tant pis.* Never mind, he thought, a bit of cold won't kill me.

He traversed the boulevard ignoring cars honking at him and followed the sidewalks towards the old city. For a while, he walked along the dark streets and past merchants closing their shops. Outdoor cafes were already deserted, patrons deciding it was too cold to sit alfresco.

But the detective forged on, his mind winding through the details of his investigation, reaching dead ends and starting over like a rat finding his way in a maze. As he neared the edge of the medina, darkness had submerged the city and city lights, once ubiquitous, were now scarce and dim.

The wide boulevards gave way to narrow cobblestone streets flanked by houses and doors opening straight to the street. Behind the doors lay an intimate world of parents, children, and grandparents gathered around their dinner, a *tajine* or a *harrira*, served on low tables and on the floor. It was a world he was familiar with, a Moslem world where servitude to Allah was the most noble of all callings, but servitude to the material world was the calling most everyone followed. He passed whitewashed houses but now and then one would stand out, painted in bold strikes of blues, yellows, and reds as if Miro or Kandinsky had made an appearance while no one was looking.

Suddenly, the flat pavement turned steep, the climb

more laboring as the detective struggled to keep up with its incline. He was familiar with the medina, the narrow and unpaved streets that often ended with no warning. He often found himself in a cul-de-sac wondering how he would retrace his steps, and return to where he had started.

He saw a small plaza that he recognized. There was a tiny park fringed with palm trees and benches. The buildings surrounding it housed small businesses on the first floor and boarding houses on the second. The businesses were already closed and under the poorly lit porches stood girls in skimpy attire. There were two or three girls under each portal and they spoke in loud voices. Their carefree giggles traveled to the detective and he secretly envied their insouciant behavior.

He knew this world well. Sins of the flesh were so common they no longer counted as sins. Arab women, once chaste, pure, and veiled to the world were, at least in his city, no different from western women. Free to lower their veils and raise their skirts. For the freedom and power it gave them over males. For the love of money.

"*Salam, Monsieur* Detective!" a woman cried.

He recognized Samira's voice.

"*Salam!*" he answered. "*Ca vas*, Samira?"

"I'm fine, *Merci*," Detective. "What brings you to this part of town?" she said in a teasing tone.

She neared the detective, swaying on impossibly spiky heels, her narrow skirt riding high on her thighs, her breasts spilling out of her clinging top, seemingly unaware of the shivery weather. She brushed the detective slightly, her heavy perfume enveloping his space, her chest pushed against his, her face so near he felt her breath on his skin.

She grabbed the lapels of his jacket. "Are we cold, Detective? I know how to warm a man's body."

He stepped back, her false and simulated lust having little effect on him. "Samira, have you seen Mohamed?"

"Mohamed? *Pourquoi?* Why are you looking for Mohamed? What has he done lately?" She pivoted and looked away. She opened her purse, pulled out a cigarette, a lighter, and put the cigarette to her mouth. The flame of her lighter flickered and the Detective noticed that her hands trembled when she lit her cigarette. She expelled a cloud of white smoke and turned to face the detective. Under the dimly lit porch, the detective did not see the expression on her face but her body language told him plenty.

"Samira," he said in a paternal tone, "where's Mohamed?"

Her face took on an irritated look. "Detective, what am I? His mother? I don't know where he's. He's a big kid and he goes where he wants."

The detective retrieved a picture from his jacket pocket and placed it squarely in her face. "Look at this picture. Do you see who that is? Look at her face."

Samira turned away but he grabbed her arm, twisted it and forced her to look at the picture.

"Now, tell me who that is! Who is she?" he was yelling at her.

"Let me go!" she screamed as she tried to untangle herself from his clasp. "I don't know who she is!"

He stepped back. "Do you want to end up looking like her? Bloated in a dump! Then tell me who she is! Now! *Tout de suite!*"

The Detective reached into his pocket again and pulled out another picture. He held it in his hand. They were the ornate feet of the victim. The detailed tattoos were enlarged and their intricacies were clear.

"Who's she, Samira? Who's she?"

Samira did not reply. She grabbed the picture from his hand and stared at the geometric designs on the girl's feet. With her index finger, she touched the photograph and slowly ran her finger over it as if caressing it.

Finally, she spoke. Her speech turned grave, her tone altered from the teasing girl she was minutes earlier to a whisper. "We did this together," she said, "I applied the *harqus* on her feet." She stopped briefly, her eyes still fixed on the picture. "It was a rainy afternoon and there was no one on the streets, so we spent our day painting each other. It was the last time I saw her."

She averted her eyes from the detective and as she turned, the moonlight brushed her face. At that moment, he caught the expression in her shiny eyes and he knew then she would give him what he wanted.

"She's dead, isn't she?" she asked even though she already anticipated the answer.

"Yes," said the detective, "what was her name?"

"Her name was Hadouj. She was a friend. A very close friend. She arrived from a small village last month but we became close real fast." She uttered the last sentence in a composed voice but the silence that followed spoke volumes of the pain she felt.

"Detective," she finally said, "there were two men who came that evening. And they left with her. Two Arab men."

"Remember how they looked?" asked the detective.

"Like Arab men look, *Monsieur* Detective. Or like johns look. They're all alike," she replied sounding more resigned than angry.

"Anything you can remember about them?"

"Thin and tall with dark gray suits. Dark hair, dark eyes. One had a thick Marrakshi accent. Vulgar. Full of sexual overtones." She stopped and looked at her hands. "I remember the hands of the Marrakshi. His fingers were slim and long. And quick. I remember thinking he had the fingers of a thief. Or a magician. That he could do anything with those hands. They could get into your back pocket and lift your wallet, or shuffle a deck of cards."

"Or slide a cord around your neck," said the detective.

Samira raised her eyes and gazed at the detective. "Is it what happened?"

"Yes, among other things. Where did they all go that evening?"

"They went to a club. They said they wanted to have a good time. And they never came back."

"Did you notify the police, Samira?"

She chuckled bitterly. "You're not being serious? Since when do the police care about girls like us? *Vraiment*. Really."

The detective did not respond. He knew she was right. Girls like her were not a priority for the local police. He felt ashamed that human life was prioritized but he knew it to be the disturbing truth. In his precinct. And others. Even those in America. You are treated as if you are your profession.

"She wore the clothes of the American girl who disappeared. You have any idea why?"

Bewilderment fell on Samira's face. She looked confused. "I don't see the relationship between Hadouj and that girl. Do you, Detective?"

"No, I don't. Except that somebody wanted us to believe that Hadouj was the American girl. Temporarily, of course. Because once tests were performed, we knew that to be false."

He paused and scrutinized her fallen face. Her overstated mascara and lipstick gave her the appearance of a painted doll, an exaggerated caricature of herself.

The detective pressed. "Where is Mohamed, he might know something. He's the one who found the body."

"He's upstairs, on the last floor. The apartment to your right."

The detective entered the dark building into a large hallway where he found a black wrought-iron elevator. He pressed the call button and gazed at the marble walls before realizing that none was coming. Built sometimes in the thirties, the building carried the opulence of the era when

French architects had turned the city into an Art Deco center. Obvious deterioration had taken place and many buildings, although elegant, were inhabitable. Wide stairs flanked the elevator; he decided to walk up the steps. The middle part of each step was chipped as if someone had taken a bite out of it. He tiptoed all the way up as he held on to the metal rails. This building needs to be condemned, he thought.

When he reached the third floor, he stopped to catch his breath. He looked up between the rails and counted three more floors. Six floors, he thought. *Merde.* Shit. He wished Samira had warned him. He would have sent her up to fetch the little bastard.

Finally, he reached the last floor. Three apartments and an adjacent door leading to the roof. He knocked on the apartment to the right and heard nothing. He knocked again then pushed the unlocked door. The door creaked as he entered. "Mohamed," he yelled. Still no answer. He walked through a narrow hallway past the kitchen and a small dining room to the back bedrooms. One of the doors was open. He walked up and pushed it. There was a bed against a wall in a room devoid of flourishes. No wall hangings and no decor, just a bed and a naked bulb hanging from the ceiling. He neared the bed. Mohamed lay on the bed. The detective was not sure whether the boy was asleep but called his name again, then grabbed his arm and shook him.

"Mohamed!" said the detective. "Wake up, I need to talk to you!"

A faint sound came out of the boy's mouth. He flipped him over and bent down for a closer look. Mohamed's face was bruised, the eyes swollen. Taken back by his appearance, the detective sat on the edge of the bed. "Who did this to you, Mohamed?"

The boy recognized the detective's voice. "Don't know," he uttered his voice barely audible.

"Who was it?" repeated the detective, "Who would do this to you? *Pourquoi?* Why?"

The boy shifted in his bed. "I fell from my bicycle."

"You're lying to me, Mohamed! You did not fall from your bicycle. Somebody did this to you!"

The detective grabbed the boy's arm. "Who did this, Mohamed? And what did he want?"

"I don't know," replied the boy. "I don't know."

"He wanted something," said the detective "and you know what it is! Don't hold back, boy!" He pressed his face against the boy's face and whispered in his ear. *"Sh'koun hada?"* Who was it?

The boy did not reply. He just groaned. Seconds passed while the detective patiently waited. In the dimness of the room, the detective noticed the boy's pants on the floor. He picked them up and went through the pockets. He pulled a wad of dirhams and several American dollars.

"Where did you get this money, Mohamed?" he asked while brandishing the money.

"In the city dump," he said, "on the corpse I found . . . the girl…", he whispered.

"What else did you find, Mohamed?" asked the detective.

Silence, as thick as a wall. The detective pressed on. "Is that why you're beaten like this? Did you find something else there?"

Silent tears ran down the side of the boy's face. The detective waited. The boy sniffed.

"Is that all you found or there was more," asked the detective.

The boy hesitated. The detective felt that the boy needed to talk but was too frightened. "No, nothing."

Ahmed got up. "Anything else you want to tell me, Mohamed?"

"No," the boy whispered then turned his back and faced the wall.

The detective walked up to the door then pivoted. "Mohamed," he said, "the dead girl's name is Hadouj, Samira's friend. And yours, too. You could not have recognized her; she was already decomposed beyond recognition."

The detective heard faint sobs as he walked out of the room.

"Son, take good care of yourself, *Ya'bni'*."

CHAPTER TWENTY-THREE

It had rained all day and gray skies cast a dark and gloomy aura on the city. Unaccustomed to downpours and bad weather, Casablanca drivers turned a chaotic traffic situation into a state of complete anarchy.

Kennedy Hunter watched the chaos surrounding her with utter detachment as Sami navigated the Renault in and out of tangles. Her mind was elsewhere. She was accustomed to boxing things in little compartments, sorting and separating, following a thread until she found its genesis. Little could distract her from her thoughts when she was engaged in a pursuit. Her mind, keen, alert and focused, was laser-like. Probing, seeking, digging.

How, she wondered, did Emily, whose existence she knew nothing about until recently, become a pawn in The Torch's game?

She was about to find out. At least she hoped so.

"We're here," Sami said interrupting her musings. He had parked parallel on the street near a large building.

"It's the third floor, door to the left, *Mademoiselle*." He eyed her with a knowing smile and she did not bother to ask how he knew where the apartment was. He just knew. "Be careful," he said.

People moved in and out of the sidewalk as Kennedy exited

the car and ducked under the awnings of the storefronts. She quickly entered the building into a cold and dim lobby. There was a small desk for a concierge but no concierge. Good, she thought, I wouldn't have to rely on my wits. She hurried up the stairs bypassing the elevator. No need to alert the concierge. The building was strangely quiet and her steps echoed on the tiled floors. Each floor consisted of a large foyer and three apartments. No names or numbers. Just doors with peeping holes.

She reached the third floor and rang the doorbell of the apartment on the left. She listened closely. No answer. She rang it again. This time she heard a noise. Little paws on the tiled floor. Then the yapping of a little creature. Unnerving. She realized the dog lived in the adjacent apartment. She rang the doorbell for the third time. Still no answer.

She turned her back to the apartment where the noise box lived and lifted the pick she always carried in her bag. Thank you, Harry, for thinking about everything.

She manipulated the pick a couple of times then the door came ajar. She stepped into the foyer of a darkened apartment and stood still in the dark. She listened for noises. Maybe they were taking a shower. Maybe they were asleep. Seconds passed. Slowly she stepped in, her eyes now adjusted to the semi-darkness. Living room, dining room, kitchen and farther down the hallway, two bedrooms.

She stepped into the living room and eyed her surroundings. It was a typical students' apartment with a hodge-podge of furniture and leather hassocks on the floor. There was a television and a video. A stereo system, books and newspapers everywhere. Posters nailed on the walls with tacks. A Toulouse-Lautrec poster of the Follies Bergeres in Paris. A Casablanca poster of Humphrey Bogart with Ingrid Bergman. And a wall of photos of Moroccans that could have been shot by a National Geographic photographer. Berbers in traditional clothes. Berbers on horses. Berbers in the desert.

Kennedy turned on a light and studied the photos. They were originals that had been mounted and framed. She removed one from the wall and turned it over. To her surprise, Emily Carrington had signed it. Emily was an amateur photographer and her subjects were all Berbers.

From the living room, Kennedy stepped out into an unlit hallway and to the bedrooms. The first bedroom she came across belonged to Morgan Taylor. She found an unmade bed and books on her bedside bearing Morgan's name on the inside jacket. Kennedy left Morgan's room and stepped into Emily's. The bed was neatly made and covered with a chenille bedspread in a cranberry color. A small bookshelf sat by her bed with a dozen books. Kennedy glanced at the titles. *Peoples of the Desert. Travels in the Great Desert of the Sahara. Living Races of the Sahara. Sahara Unveiled.*

On the shelf, there was a framed photo of a smiling Emily and a young man. He was golden, a California surf boy. Kennedy turned over the frame. A handwritten note. *To my Emily, Love you forever, Brent.* The photo was dated May of that year. Kennedy made a mental note of it.

She opened Emily's closet and combed through her wardrobe. It mostly consisted of khakis and T-shirts. Hiking boots. A backpack. And one single item that did not fit with the rest of her wardrobe. A long *hendira,* the traditional garment Berber women wore over their garment just like the one Kennedy had worn during her trek in the desert. She also found tribal beads and coins to wear with the garment.

So there it is, she thought. Was Emily with The Torch of her own will? Or was she a prisoner?

Quickly, Kennedy opened desk drawers. She found school schedules and empty files. Nothing to warrant any further searching.

Kennedy glanced at her watch. She had been in the apartment more than five minutes. She felt like a thief and knew that most thieves spend less than three minutes in a place. Now she knew why. The pressure was too great. She needed to hurry out of there, return everything in its proper place and walk out of the apartment. She made another quick turn, turning over pillows, blankets and reopening drawers then finally decided she had seen whatever there was to see. She stepped out of the apartment, slowly shut the door behind her and called the elevator. Again, the yapping of the little creature next door startled her. She heard the muffled noise of feet running and felt the presence of someone behind the closed door eyeing her through the peeping hole. She turned her back to them and slipped inside the elevator when it arrived.

Once in the foyer, she found the concierge at his desk and a tall Arab standing by his side. They talked in an animated tone and immediately halted when she walked in. The concierge eyed her, a surprised look on his face. She walked out of the building with assurance but not before she made eye contact with the tall thin man. She recognized his face having seen it in local papers. He nodded gravely when he saw her and she nodded back. Their eyes locked and for a moment he scrutinized her face, his professional instinct telling him something propitious had just happened. Earlier that day, she had spoken to him but they had never met.

The Arab's eyes felt like a drill in her back when she walked out the front door and onto the street. Sami was still parked upfront and she quickly slid into the back seat. Looking out her window, she noticed that Detective Ahmed's piercing eyes had not left her.

CHAPTER TWENTY-FOUR

The Rif Mountains, rugged and remote, stood etched against dark hovering clouds as Brent Seymour traveled the road to Chechaouen. Soaring cedar and oak trees flanked the road and formed giant shadows with every turn he took. As he drove further and farther out towards Ketama and away from populated centers, Brent Seymour dove deeper into unknown territory.

He had been driving for more than five hours north of Casablanca and through the Mamora Forest when he finally began noticing a conspicuous change in the landscape. Cannabis plantations of tall, dense weed propagated the bordering fields where the cultivation and sale of hashish or kif went unabated despite its illegality. The knee-high weed was, for the farmers of this area, a boon that brought much needed prosperity and, alas, its uninvited kin—crime. The plant, once harvested, underwent many transformations. Dried, the leaf was named *kif*. Processed into resin-like bars, it became *hashish*. *Gaouza* was designer *hashish* served during tea ceremonies, and *ma'joun* when laced into homemade jam.

As Brent Seymour neared his final destination, he felt his chest fill with apprehension. It was the first time he had strayed this far from the city. It was all so alien, so remote.

The terrain, its people. He felt like a trespasser on their turf. They spoke Riffian, a dialect spoken only around the Rif Mountains, which no one understood. Their women wore large pom-pom sombreros, and red and white cloth called *f'touh* over their long white garments. Their faces went partially veiled, a white cloth covering their mouths leaving their slanted dark eyes exposed. The men possessed hard faces, sharp as a knife's edge and hair-trigger tempers.

Chechaouen stood high on the hills, its quaint little houses perched on steep and winding cobblestone streets. The town's main square, Plaza Uta el Hammam, was lined with whitewashed buildings and blue portals. Brent slowed down and parked his vehicle in front of a small grocery store. He stepped out of his car, looked right and left, scanning the street then neared the storefront.

A crisp chilly air hung over the town and the Riffian sun, as pale as straw, hovered over the plaza. Children played on dirt sidewalks as Riffian women hurried around the plaza. No one paid attention to Brent Seymour. An Arab dressed in a djellaba waved him inside the store. The man did not have to be told why the stranger stood there. He was accustomed to seeing outsiders in his town. Young, golden boys from California or Europe. Just like Brent Seymour.

Brent entered the little shop. Chewing gum, bottles of Coke and candy lined the shelves behind the counter. He walked to the back of the shop and up a flight of narrow stairs into a darkened room filled with men and smoke. He squinted in the dark, the pungent smell of *hashish* filling his nostrils. The sun never shines on this place, he thought. Men huddled around small round tables, some smoked *sebsis*, water pipes, while others played games of dominos. There were few men dressed in expensive European clothing—foreigners—just like Brent, there for business purposes only.

Brent walked to the back of the room. He saw his contact seated in the far corner, smoking *hashish*.

"*Salem,*" said the man. He extended a thin, dark hand to Seymour while adjusting his jacket with his free hand. He wore a dull gray jacket over a wrinkled, discolored white shirt on his wiry frame.

Brent shook the man's hand and sat down.

"Try this," said the man. "The best." He handed the hand-rolled joint to Brent.

Brent grabbed it and brought to his lips. He inhaled deeply, held it for a while then exhaled a white cloud from his mouth. "Yeah, it's good, real good."

The man looked on. A deep smile shaped his face revealing stained crooked teeth. His beady eyes glimmered with satisfaction. "The best *hashish* in the world."

"What did you bring me?" asked Brent.

"I have everything. *Tout.* Everything. *Kif, hashish, gaouza, ma'joun.* You name it."

Brent Seymour grinned broadly. He was feeling better already. This ought to satisfy all of my clients, he thought.

"You're overdue on your debts," said the man. The smile from his face disappeared replaced by a sinister look.

"Sorry, man. I have had trouble collecting. I'll catch up . . . soon. I promise," replied Brent, shifting uneasily in his chair.

The Arab canvassed Brent's face, his bony fingers still holding the joint.

"*Monsieur* Brent," said the man, "no promises. Just dirhams or dollars." His tone matched his face. Hard, unyielding.

Brent's gaze dropped to the floor, he was looking down between his legs. "I know . . . I'm sorry . . . like I said . . . ."

"How much money did you bring with you?" asked the man.

Brent did not respond at once. He was weighing his answer, something the Arab noticed immediately.

"None with me. I was hoping to extend my credit with you."

The Arab nodded, his eyes boring into Brent's face. He probed the American's face but all he met was the nervous facade of an unsecure young man. The Arab, however, was not convinced.

"O.K," the man said, "I expect payment a week from today. No more credit after this. And no more *hashish* if you don't pay."

Abruptly, the Arab stood up. His chair creaked and few heads wheeled around. Brent rose and followed the man out of the room and down the stairs, through the shop and to the street. Silently, he followed him to his car. The man opened his trunk. Inside there was a black bag. He grabbed it and handled it to Brent.

"*Bon voyage,*" he said and waved with his hand.

Brent walked to his car, opened the trunk and threw the bag in. The man remained on the sidewalk then turned around and entered the shop. Soon as he was inside, he pulled out his cellular phone.

"Police!" answered the voice.

"*Ishmah*, listen," said the man, "there's a young man, an American, in a white Peugeot. He's leaving the city on highway P38. Frisk him and clean him of any cash he has. The kid needs to learn a lesson."

"How bad do you want me to hurt him?" said the voice.

"Bad enough so that he won't lie to me again. Bruise him and scare him. Take back my black bag and bring it back to me. Of the cash you find on him, take your cut."

"Do you want him to spend few days in jail?" said the voice.

"Not necessary. Just work him over a bit and send him home," answered the man.

"*Mi'jiane*, good. It'll be taken care of."

The man snickered. "Wait till he founds out he still owes me the money on the merchandise!"

When the man turned off his cellular phone, he could still hear the brassy chuckle of his accomplice.

CHAPTER TWENTY-FIVE

For the fifth straight day, Atlanta woke up to an unnerving drizzle that poured on this southeastern city like fine sand though a sieve. Marietta Street had turned into a welling river flooding adjacent streets and spilling into the heart of the city. No one found relief from the downpour that was heaped on the city, engulfing it in the wet, liquid hell that nearly paralyzed everyone.

For Harry Bernstein, rain was nothing but a minor inconvenience barely affecting his movements. Truly, the messier it got, the more he liked it. Life, for Harry Bernstein, was a gratifying challenge. He was not interested in easy. Easy, Harry thought, rhymed with lazy.

He parked his SUV in *The Atlanta Dispatch* parking lot and walked to a small cafe across the street. He glanced at his watch noticing that he was right on time. One p.m. The cafe, a cozy room with wooden floors and handpainted walls, was already teeming with staff from the newspaper. Red and white checkered tablecloths adorned small tables and recycled olive oil bottles served as vases for red roses. The odor of olive oil, garlic and sweet Italian sausage saturated the air and made Harry hungry. A plump hostess, surely a distant cousin to Sophia Loren, escorted him to a table obviously reserved for those who were not on her A-list.

He settled on a small wooden chair and studied the menu. Pizza. Pasta. Spaghetti a la carbonera, Penne a la—

"Harry?"

"Ty!" Harry got up. The two men shook hands, then embraced. Harry had not seen Ty for two years since he had joined Kennedy at a New Year's Eve party organized by a colleague. Ty Johnson removed his raincoat, folded it neatly on the back of his chair and sat down. He wore a black suit with a crisp white shirt and a deep purple tie. His hair was cropped tight and the thin-rimmed glasses endowed him with a serious, intellectual appearance.

"Looking good, man," Harry said as he gave him the look-over. "Must be the best dressed man at that paper!" He chuckled.

"Yeah," replied Ty, "that's what I hear. You know, newsies aren't exactly clothes horses."

"You're right about the horses thing," replied Harry.

They laughed in harmony. Ty held up his menu but barely glanced at it. "How long has it been?"

"Ah, too long my friend. Too long." Harry's eyes shone as he eyed his old friend. He silently nodded.

Harry spoke first. "What are you hearing, Ty?"

"Many things, Harry. Many things." Ty turned around and looked over his shoulders. He was checking to see if other reporters were present. "How is Kennedy?" he asked.

"Well," Harry said, "she's doing O.K. But this thing has gone from an interview to an investigation."

"I know," said Ty. "The paper isn't going to publish the manifesto, you know that. I hear that there was a unanimous decision from Martini and from that asinine Newberry. Savich did not go along. She did not want to chance it." Ty paused as the server placed bread and drinks on the table. He waited for her to leave before he continued. He leaned across the table and whispered. "Now get this, Harry. The Chairman is Emily Carrington's great uncle or something like that." He paused for maximum effect. "If that ain't a story."

Harry was tackling the bread when he heard Ty's statement. He halted, a piece of Italian bread in mid-air. "Who knows about this, Ty?"

"Not many people, Harry. Not many. Well, you know how we are about our own news. We are more than happy to expose everybody, but reserve the right to be as secretive as we want when it comes to revealing our own dirty secrets."

"Full disclosure only applies to others." Harry's instincts told him this story had legs. "Is the chairman willing to bargain on his niece's life? Sounds to me like the man is taking some real chances."

"Yeah, he is. I'm assuming The Torch doesn't know she's the niece of the chairman. Or maybe he does know. And that's why he's pulling such a stunt."

"What do we know about Emily's family?" asked Harry. "I've been pulling things from the Internet and *The Atlanta Journal Constitution*."

Ty raised an eyebrow. "What are you finding out?"

"Well, the usual stuff about the Coke riches. I checked up their website and all I could find is a mega advertising campaign. With some history, you know, started in 1886, etcetera, etcetera . . . ." Harry paused, bit into a chunk of bread, then proceeded. "Atlanta is Coke's hometown, as you probably know. But all I found was stuff on international marketing, change of leadership and so on. Nothing on the family."

Ty leaned forward. "And here's something you won't find on the Internet."

"Oh," said Harry. "And what's that?"

"I hear stuff. All kinds of stuff. The rumor mill is alive and well at *The Dispatch*. Emily Carrington lives on a trust fund. Her deceased father has established it for her. You know, the Coke fortune. In addition, she has a married sister and a mother. The mother has multiple sclerosis, is in a wheelchair and is deteriorating quite rapidly. When she dies, Emily stands to inherit a large sum of money."

The server arrived pen in hand. "Made a decision?" she said. To the point, Harry thought. Harry was happy she was sparing him the cheerful introductions and endless recitations of late.

"Yeah. Pasta for me. A la carbonera. Ty?"

"The usual for me," not looking at her. Without as much as a nod, she took off to the kitchen leaving them to their conversation.

"Must be the most discreet waitress I have ever seen," Harry said.

"Makes you wish they were all like that."

Harry returned to his bread. "This changes the picture altogether." He took a sip of water. "What else are you hearing, Ty?"

"The sister, her name is Janet Carrington Fairfax. Married to Porter Fairfax."

"Humm . . . "

"I checked the social calendar at the A.J.C. too, Harry. You know Atlanta is an oversized hick town. With old money and new money," he chuckled. "By American standards, Coke money is old money. Everything else is *nouveau riche*."

Harry laughed wholeheartedly. "That so?"

"Well, yeah. Now, my sources at the paper tell me that Janet and Porter Fairfax have quite a social life. Porter, by the way, is *nouveau riche* to the core. She is a purebred. Pedigreed, and all."

"How did you get such information, Ty?"

"Easy, Harry. Easy. The reporter covering the fluff beat, you know, fashion and social events, is an old chum from the days we worked together at a Virginia paper."

"What is she saying about Porter Fairfax?"

"A lot. He's some sort of a rich slacker. Big house, fast cars, and a rich wife."

A smile came over Harry's face. "Nice. If you can afford it."

"Anyway, Porter Fairfax lives the good life. They live in a Northern Atlanta suburb in an equestrian estate. Horses and the whole bit."

"Does *he* horse around?"

"They both do," Ty said. "She owns several thorough-breds and teaches dressage. His horsing around is of a different breed."

Harry looked puzzled. "What the heck is dressage?"

"Not a Jewish thing, Harry. You know, they teach the horses to do some sort of *pas de deux*."

"You're right about not being a Jewish thing. Come to think of it, I don't remember ever seeing an African brother doing the *pas de deux* on a horse."

"I guess you never saw Blazing Saddles, buddy."

Harry made a thumbs-up sign then asked, "what does Porter Fairfax do for a living—other than spend his old lady's money?"

"I believe that's his full-time occupation. Plus pleasing his Georgia peach."

Harry snickered. "Man, some guys've got it made." They were both shaking their heads at the same time. "Ever seen any of the Carrington' at the paper?"

"Nope. If I've seen one, I wouldn't know it. Let me tell you something else though. The suits at the paper have been having editorial meetings that go on ad nauseaum and ad infinitum. Mind you, none of us is allowed to touch this story. This is Kennedy's baby. All the way through." Ty was shaking his head.

The server came back with the food. They waited for her to leave before they resumed. Harry pushed his dish aside and leaned across the table. "Are they on the up-and-up with Kennedy?"

"I don't know," replied Ty, "I sometimes wonder if she has all the facts she needs to do her job."

"Something to worry about," replied Harry. "In this case, ignorance is not bliss."

"In this case and just about any case." Ty's tone turned skeptical.

"What will happen if it was known that Emily Carrington was related to the chairman?" said Harry.

"Well, that's an easy one to answer. See, right now The Torch just wants his manifesto published. Or at least that's what everybody thinks. If he finds out there's big money involved, he might start having some serious demands— like a real ransom."

"That sure would complicate matters," Harry said.

Ty grabbed a piece of bread, buttered it and bit into it. "Of course, we don't know for sure that The Torch abducted her because she's related to the chairman." He shook his head. "Man, this case more and more resembles the case of Patricia Hearst, many years ago."

Harry nodded. "I remember that one very well. She was related to the Hearst publishing empire, if I recall correctly."

"Some of the same elements in this story. Publishing heiress. Social ideology. Renegades."

"You know what the French say?"

Ty nodded. "Yeah?"

"The more things change, the more they remain the same."

"No kidding."

Ty looked at his watch. "Time's up. Need to get back to the paper mill." He rose and slid his raincoat on.

"Harry, my friend," he extended his hand, "always a pleasure."

"Thanks, man."

"What next?"

"I think I'm gonna pay a visit to the Coca-Cola heirs. I have a hankering for the real thing."

CHAPTER TWENTY-SIX

In the northern section of Buckhead—a posh Atlanta address with soaring glass skyscrapers, manicured front lawns and sparkling lobbies—the offices of MyTrade.com differed little from those of insurance companies, public relations firms and advertising agencies.

Located on the 14th floor of a glass and marble behemoth, the front door of MyTrade.com—simple and plain dark wood with gold lettering—was surprisingly understated, as if the owners had preferred to maintain a lower than usual profile. Below the name, in smaller font, the subheading 24-hour Electronic Trading was the only sign indicating the nature of the business. Understandably. Earlier that year, a day trader in a nearby office had gone mad, shot his wife and children to death, then, to top it off, went on a rampage gunning down several of his fellow traders.

Inside the trading office, the mood was, on the surface at least, subdued. The news ticker on the wall flashed up-to-the-minute reports and in a corner, high on a wall, a muted TV was set on CNBC. Traders sat in pods large enough for a small desk and a computer, their eyes glued to monitors, their hearts fluttering at every turn the stock market took. The traders were in their twenties, forties and sixties, some even past retirement age, all commonly linked by their desire to strike it big. Some even participated in S&P futures trading—a leveraged gamble where complete losses could happen in the blink of an eye. They had bypassed their brokers and investment counselors for the thrill of the chase and the lure of a fast win. No gambling tables and no croupiers here, but a no-less-dangerous roll of the dice. Large sums of money were made or lost with the click of a mouse.

Occasionally, moans or winning cries were heard, depending on whether it was a loss or a win. More often than not, the losses were suffered in silence, a double ripping of the heart and the pocket.

In the far right corner of the room sat Porter Fairfax, his eyes fixed on a monitor that displaying color-coded charts of markets indicators. Dressed in the latest fashion attire, he was—undoubtedly—the best dressed man in the place. He wore a black turtleneck on a lean and well-defined torso, taupe velvet pants, a brown jacket made of buttery-soft leather and matching Cole Haan boots.

He stood out among the casually dressed traders with his style and polished manner. No one at MyTrade.com knew if Porter Fairfax was making any money but he smelled of money in the surreptitious way rich people do. Older women dotted over him like an incorrigible child, young ones swooned. No one hated Porter Fairfax, not even the men who saw him as the luckiest S.O.B. they had ever run across. They could only envy him. He was handsome, with large brown eyes, a smile that revealed near perfect teeth and hair that should have belonged to a younger man, a flock of which fell permanently on his forehead. He had a way of casually pushing it out of his face unaware of how packed with sensuality that gesture was.

At forty, Porter Fairfax was living the good life and the fast life, which is what he loved. Living on the edge gave him the adrenaline spike he craved. Porter Fairfax was a glutton for life and he feasted on it.

Daytime trading had given Porter Fairfax the daily fix he needed. It had taken him away from the Trump Casinos tables in Atlantic City and brought him closer to home where he indulged in his favorite pastime—gambling. Except that now he was gambling on the stock market, trading on commodities or on stocks, holding on to them for a few hours or a few days and moving fast, never stopping too long, win or lose.

Porter Fairfax had a rule. He called it the five-percent rule. A five-percent win or loss, he got out. He never lingered. Lingering could cost him big.

Now and then, he broke his own rules. Like today. He had bet on a new internet stock. Bought the stock at $28 a share, saw it rise to $32 when he should have gotten out but he held on to it for too long and before long the darn thing plunged to $18—a ten dollar loss on each share. Now he was biting his fingernails and kicking his butt.

"Stupid! Stupid! Stupid!" he cried in his pod. He quickly calculated his losses. Five thousand shares at $140,000. Now they were worth $90,000. A fifty-thousand dollar loss. Damn!

He yanked his cell phone out of his jacket pocket and quickly dialed a number.

An operator answered.

"Get me my accountant," he ordered. Then, "Jack, it's me."

"Yeah, Porter. What can I do for you today?"

"Jack, I'm gonna need more money for the remainder of the week," he said. "I just had a big loss, Jack."

"Porter," Jack said, "you always have losses. How big is this one?"

Porter did not answer immediately. "Pretty big. But I'll regain it soon. I know that." There was panic in his voice.

Jack pressed. "How big is your loss, Porter?"

"Fifty K." he said.

"Fifty K.? How are you going to regain it back?" Jack's tone was contemptuous.

"What do you mean, Jack?"

"I mean that there is no way I can keep covering up for you losses, Porter. Your wife is your banker. She's gonna find out—soon or later."

"Jack," said Porter, "are you my friend or not?" he yelled. "Are you?"

"Porter! Porter! Listen to me. I can go to jail for what I'm doing! I'm hiding expenses from my client. I'm doling out her assets like candy on Halloween."

Porter lowered his voice and whispered in the mouthpiece. "Jack, you listen to me. My wife is so loaded you never have to worry about her running out of money. You know that. Her mother, you know, that old woman is gonna kick the bucket soon and she'll be even more loaded."

There was no response from the accountant, just a deep and an uneasy sigh. Porter insisted. "Jack, listen. Just this time." He was begging. "Please, please. Just one more time. I promise this won't happen again."

"Porter, what I should do is call your wife and let her handle you. I'm not your keeper!"

"Jack, please. She doesn't need to know about this. C'mon man, for old times sake," he paused. "C'mon, my friend."

"I'll think about it, Porter. I promise that I'll sleep on it. And that's all I'll do for now."

"Damn!" said Porter as he slammed his cellular shut. "Damn accountants! Always ruling your life!"

Porter scanned the room. Traders were fixated on their screens, each living in his cocoon. He eyed the man in the next booth and raised his hand.

"Hey, I'm taking a break," he said, "I need a drink."

The man looked up from his screen. "I could use one myself. Care if I join you?"

"Sure. Why not," said Porter. "I could use some company." Porter stepped out of his cubicle. "I haven't seen you here before, must be new."

"Yeah, just started. This week, as a matter of fact."

Porter extended his hand. "Welcome aboard. My name is Porter Fairfax. What's yours?"

"Harry. Harry B. Smith."

"So, Harry, what brings you to Atlanta, all the way from Virginia Beach?" Porter Fairfax asked soon after he saddled his stool. He was scrutinizing Harry's face in the darkness of the bar.

A bartender approached the pair. She wore a flouncy skimpy outfit that barely covered her buttocks, her tiny breasts pushed up high—not much she could do with the little she possessed. Porter Fairfax eyes traveled up and down her body and they stopped right at her tiny cleavage. An incredulous smile covered his face, a why-bother smile that did not go unnoticed by her. Embarrassed, she took their orders and left with a little less bounce in her step.

"Are you familiar with Virginia Beach?" Harry asked.

"Somewhat. I remember spending some summers down the beach when I was a kid." He looked off in the dark trying to recall those days. "I remember a long boardwalk by the waters."

"It's still there. Our claim to fame, I suppose," Harry replied. "I live south of the city near Chesapeake in an area called Pungo where I raise horses."

Porter straightened up in his seat. "Horses, huh?"

"Yeah. Horses. I'm here to visit a farm out of the city where they raise and train horses. Up in Dahlonega." Harry took a sip from his drink. "Actually, it's my former wife's interest, more than mine."

Porter chuckled. "What's with women and horses?"

"I guess they prefer their company over ours," Harry replied. "My wife used to get up at 4:30 in the morning to shovel dung."

"So does mine," Porter said, chortling.

"Yours too into horses?"

"Yeah. You ought to see how many hours she spends brushing their coats. You know, pampering them." Porter was shaking his head. "I wish I could get as much fondling as they do."

Harry emitted a hearty guffaw. "Maybe because they don't answer them back."

"Maybe. What kind of horses do you raise, Harry?"

"Dutch warmbloods. They're good for dressage," Harry replied with assurance.

"Dressage," replied Porter. "Complicated little maneuvers. Horse ballet. What do you look for in a dressage horse, Harry?"

Harry did not reply immediately. He flagged down the bartender biding for time. He turned to face Porter. "Another round?"

"Sure," Porter answered, "I have already spent as much money as I'm going to today anyway. No going back up for me."

"Me, too."

"So, what were you saying about the kind of horses you like having for dressage?"

"What I look for in a horse is personality. Especially a dressage horse. I look for poise, balance and mostly pride. Whether it's a Shetland or a Shire, it doesn't matter. As long as he's got presence."

"You're right about that, Harry. For my wife, it's got to be more than that. She has to have the whole package. You know," with his hands Porter formed the outline of a horse, "his withers higher than his croup. Long neck. She even measures the angle of his shoulder and pastern. It's gotta be 45-degree angle for her."

"Not easy to please, your wife."

"Tell me about it!" Porter got up. He took a last gulp from his drink. "Harry, my friend, I need to introduce you to my wife. She would love to talk shop with you. You know, you people are a gray horse of a different color," Porter patted Harry on his back.

Harry laughed. "I know what you mean."

"You gonna be in town this weekend? Maybe you can come by and see us? We live just north of here, as a matter of fact not too far from Dahlonega, your stomping grounds."

"Be happy to oblige, Porter."

CHAPTER TWENTY-SEVEN

The cryptic message that Kennedy found under her door left her perplexed. The sender was anonymous but the message was clear. *Be downstairs at hotel bar at 8:30p.m.*

At first, she had been reluctant to play the game but after some consideration, her reporter's curiosity got the best of her. She calculated the risks involved and decided there was little she could lose by not showing up. After all, the bar in the hotel was a public place.

At 8:30p.m she descended to the bar. A hostess dressed in a flowing red caftan and gold velvet slippers led her to a corner table. At the counter, there were several men perched on high stools and a barman clad in a festive *djellabah* and a red *fez*. French pop music played over the speakers and a group of Germans at the counter spoke loudly. The lounge was sparsely furnished with carpets, mats and cushions. The walls were adorned with arabesques tiles and marble pillars separated the space into cozy corners for those who eschewed crowds.

She waited patiently until 9p.m., no one had yet shown up. Across the room, in the opposite corner, a single man dressed in a suit sat at a small table. From her position, she could clearly see his back but nothing else. He held a cigarette in the way hard-core smokers sometimes do, between his thumb and his index, and inhaled hard sending white clouds of smoke in the air. The clouds formed a halo around his head, which he chased with a quick gesture of the hand.

Unexpectedly, a waiter approached Kennedy with a cell phone in his hand.

"*Mademoiselle*, there is a call for you," he said in an accented English.

"Yes", she answered, uncertainty in her voice.

"Ah, Miss Hunter," the man said, "how are you doing tonight?"

She instantly recognized the sharp voice. He did not need to identify himself. Her heart fluttered as she tried to recover from the surprise. He followed his question with another question.

"How are you being treated in my country, Miss Hunter?"

"Doing fine, thank you." She paused and waited for him to go on. He did not.

"May I ask what this is about?"

"Of course, you may," he cackled. "I've read your last article and I'm not pleased with the doings of your paper."

"I'm afraid that it is something I have little control over," she replied, matter-of-factly.

He snickered. "Oh, really? An international reporter of your caliber having no editorial control?" A silence followed as she waited for him to resume. "What's the purpose of being a queen bee if you cannot control your subjects, Miss Hunter?"

"Control, *Sir*, isn't an issue I'm concerned with. I'm afraid that the control you like exercising over everything is your problem, not mine. I like controlling only what I write, not what is published. Nothing else."

"The world is made of leaders and followers, Miss Hunter. What are you? A leader or a follower? Or perhaps," he articulated slowly, "you fall in that area reserved for those who are neither. A scribbler of little relevance. A hack."

"Your insults have little effect on me. I'm accustomed to seeing and hearing the worst of what the human race has to offer," she paused momentarily, "you are no exception."

"What would it take to convince you that I'm the exception rather than the rule, Miss Hunter?"

She came back forcefully. "Release Emily and stop playing these mind games."

"These are not mind games, Miss Hunter. I'm serious in my purpose. *Deadly serious.* Emily will be released when my manifesto is published."

"How do I know you have Emily to begin with? I have no proof of that. Only you say so."

"Proof? If proof is what you want, then proof is what you'll get."

Suddenly the line went dead. She was left with the phone in her hand, startled by the sudden disconnection. She raised her eyes and that's when she noticed that the man across the room had slid his cellular phone inside his jacket pocket.

She watched the man's back, her eyes probing the dark room. She was not sure of his identity but she was certain of the way she felt. His presence had ignited in her a visceral response she could not ignore. Minutes earlier, she had been completely decaffeinated, calm and collected. Now, she felt like an animal whose senses were aroused. She tried to dismiss her response to him as an overreaction or even professionally induced paranoia but she knew to trust her instincts. They were, more often than not, undeniable. They did not fail her. Frequently, rationalization was an obstacle, like speed bumps on her reasoning course. Her eyes boring his back, she ached to walk across the room but her legs shook and she feared a confrontation with him. He picked up his glass and brandished it in a toasting gesture. She felt a cold wetness travel down her flanks as he lowered his drink.

Seconds later, he got up and walked down the aisle away from her. He slowed down and spun around. He was tall, thin with a dark complexion and thick black hair. Just like The Torch. An icy frisson traveled the length of her body and that moment she knew with confidence it was The Torch. As she watched him, he walked out of the room with the self-assurance of a man who knew his position in life.

CHAPTER TWENTY-EIGHT

That night, Kennedy Hunter sat by her window over-looking the city, listening to the gentle rustling of palm trees and the dimming city noises.

Beyond, she heard the distant barking of a dog followed by a chorus of dogs and then, the screeching sound of brakes that were slammed too fast.

She wondered if Emily Carrington could hear barking dogs or screeching cars or if desert noises were the only noises she heard. Or perhaps Emily Carrington was not hearing any noises at all, the noises silenced forever. Eternally.

Instinctively, she reached inside her bag and retrieved a photo of Emily. Again, she studied the face superimposing the image in her hands with the one in her memory files. And again, Kennedy found that her memory stored a blurred vision that could not be reconciled with the photo in her hands. In her mind's eye, she saw Emily with kohl lining her sapphire eyes. Russet palms. Bronze naked feet. *Harqus* lines following the contour of her toes. Clad in a white gossamer garment, her young breasts peeking like tender rosebuds under the sun. Emily as the desert girl. On a camel. In a tent. Forming balls of couscous with her gleaming white hands. Emily and The Torch. Without veils or clothes. Her nimble white fingers over his tanned and taut body. Naked bodies in the barren desert. Rolling on golden dunes. Rolling, rolling, rolling.

Kennedy ignored all sensory distractions as Emily stared in the celluloid of her mind.

Then she heard a noise. A faint and timid knock. Once. Twice. Followed by two consecutive knocks.

She walked to the door, cracked it open finding no one at her door. She lowered her eyes to the floor and saw a white envelope. Hesitating, she retrieved it and shut the door.

The envelope was bulky as if it held an object. She tore it open and a ring spilled out followed by a medallion attached to a chain.

She heard his voice. *Proof?* If proof is what you want, proof is what you'll get.

The gold ring was simple in design, adorned with small diamonds placed diagonally on the face. Kennedy held the ring in her hand and slid it on her own fingers. Too small. Emily was a slim person with thin fingers. Size five ring. The medallion was the locket genre and she opened it. Inside she found Brent's picture.

She was still lost in her thoughts holding the rings in her hand when the ringing phone stirred her out of her concentration. She answered it like an automaton.

"Kennedy! It's me." Harry's voice was full of vigor.

"Harry, I'm so glad you're calling. Where are you?"

"Atlanta. Visiting Porter Fairfax. We have become such chums, you'd think we've been golfing buddies for years."

She chortled because she needed it and because she was genuinely pleased he was calling. "How did you approach him?"

"Easy, Ken. All I had to do was get a quick lesson in daytime trading and dressage."

"Dressage? Don't sound to me like something you'd be particularly interested in."

"I'm a quick study, Ken. Just learn enough of the stuff to make them believe the lie."

"Just like reporters. So what are you finding out? What's the story behind the story? You know there's always one."

He paused. She could visualize him gesturing in the air. "First, let me fill you in on what's going on at the paper. The behind the scenes maneuvering. Courtesy of Ty. Get this. Your chairman is Emily's uncle."

Kennedy gasped. "No way!" Then, "I wonder if The Torch knows that."

"Did he say anything about it?"

"No, not yet. He only said he wants his paper published."

"I see."

"Wait a minute, Harry. He did ask to tell the chairman but I did not think much of it because it's obvious that the chairman already knows."

"Anyway—and as you already know there wouldn't be any negotiating with The Torch. Savich wanted to play the game, Newberry did not. Martini just wanted peace in the house. Newberry wins, of course."

"That figures."

"Porter Fairfax, from all appearances, lives off Janet Carrington's dough."

"So? What are you trying to tell me?"

"Well, I don't know—yet—if any of it is relevant to Emily's disappearance or not, but I'm on his trail. What's on your side?"

"I just received Emily's ring and a locket she wore. From The Torch. As a proof that she's with him. Now, my question is this: Is she with him of her own volition or is he holding her as he says?"

Harry snorted. "What supports your theory of her being there of her own will?"

"Harry, I found Berber clothing in her closet, books on the subject and plenty of photos. Coincidence? Perhaps."

"Humm . . . "

"Harry, get this. I think I saw The Torch tonight. Down-stairs at the bar." Her tone went down a notch.

"And?"

"Nothing happened. I just sensed that it was him. Call it feminine intuition. I think he gets a kick out of hurling flames."

"Bastard."

"Sometimes those who throw flames get burned by their own fire, Harry."

"In common parlance, it means that it'll come back to bite him in the ass."

"Very poetically put."

"Something else, Harry. I think him or some of his goons were in my room when I was downstairs. I actually smelled them."

"They take anything?"

"No, I have my discs in the safe and my laptop too."

"Good. So—what's your strategy with him, Kennedy? Do you have one or is it just action-reaction."

She scoffed. "Harry, you are a former soldier. And he is a freedom fighter or terrorist or whatever you want to call him. I'm just a lowly reporter trying to outsmart a big fat cat in a cat-and-mouse game."

"Kennedy, listen to me," he said with quiet authority, "think of him as the mouse. If you're gonna play with him, in your mind at least, he has to be the mouse."

"Well, he's a mighty fat mouse. Right now, he wants me to get him some ink. And if I don't, I'm afraid we'll lose Emily."

Harry lowered his voice. "Ken," he always called her Ken when he was mellow, "can I ask you to be careful? I'm worried about you. This is like a David and Goliath thing."

"Well, we know who won that one. Harry, I promise you I won't do anything foolish. I won't play by the rules but I'll be as careful as I can be."

"Promise me that you'll come home soon and relieve me from the prolonged agony I have been in."

"Agony? What agony?"

"Taking care of Francois, your mutt."

She exploded in laughter. "So, that's what this is about!"

"Yes and no. Beside," his voice trailed, "I miss you."

"I miss you, too Harry." There was a momentary pause between them, neither uttering a word, like the suspended silence in a play just before the curtain rises.

"Good night."

"Good night, Harry."

CHAPTER TWENTY-NINE

He had been driving for more than four hours south of Casablanca when, out of the stony and plain landscape, he saw the silhouette of the pink city. The sun had dipped low behind the ancient ramparts and the surrounding countryside took on a fiery glow as detective Ahmed neared Marrakesh.

He was apprehensive about this trip but felt it was imperative to follow his hunches. The pace of his investigation did not please him, having little to go on other than two girls enmeshed in a fatal dance. Detective work, as he knew so well, consisted of gathered evidence, instincts, and the ability to weave the two together. Deduction—the deriving of a conclusion by reasoning—was, for now at least, the only tool he possessed in his meager arsenal.

Right now, he concluded, he had an heiress who disappeared then resurfaced with the country's most sought after criminal. And he had a dead prostitute who had been substituted for the heiress.

Then there were two men who went with Hadouj, the prostitute, and who, he was certain, created the whole scenario.

If I could find the men, he thought, *they would lead me to the girl.* To The Torch. To somewhere.

His reasoning, rational and lucid under normal circumstances, was muddied by the incongruities of this case. Why, he wondered, did The Torch kill the Arab girl if his only goal was to abduct the American? What could be gained from it? What was the motive? He mused for several moments then gave it up. He was unable to connect the many elements because none of it made any sense.

What he needed, he felt, was to find that loose thread, the unraveled one, and follow it all the way to the end. All the way to The Torch. All the way to the girl.

Finding Emily Carrington had become his obsession. For no other reason than to appease the Americans. Her disappearance had been an unrelenting source of exasperation. The media circus that followed her disappearance was, at least in Casablanca, unparalleled. Media outlets had descended on the city like carnivores craving flesh for their literary diet. He knew she was the reason the throbbing headaches he occasionally suffered from had come back, en masse.

To detective Ahmed, Emily Carrington was not the real victim of this story. Not yet, at least. The death of the Arab girl gnawed at him and he felt a tightening in his chest when he thought of her. His own daughter came to mind. She, too, could have been a victim had the circumstances of her birth been different. Hadouj was not the privileged child of wealthy parents—a girl from the Atlas Mountains gone to the city to find work to support parents and a passel of brothers and sisters. Leaving the wretchedness of the mountains for the wretchedness of the city. Trading mud houses for shantytowns. Trading hunger for immorality.

She had died without identity and no one had claimed her dead body. Some dogs, he thought, died with a tag around their necks. Engraved pedigrees. It was as if her life had no other purpose but to serve as a substitute horse for a thoroughbred.

And so, as he entered the city, he hoped that his search for her killers was not in vain.

Dusk hung over the city and palms stood etched in the waning light as the city's main square, Djemaa El F'na, came to life with jugglers, fire-eaters and snake-charmers performing their daily feat in front of awed tourists. The detective, however, was not interested in the false front and artifice the city offered as he drove past it all and went straight to the old city, the medina.

He neared the narrow cobbled streets, parked his car, and continued on foot. He entered dark alleys flanked by houses and small shops, a universe rarely seen by the city's visitors. Behind closed doors, he heard nameless voices, laughter from men and women, and children giggle as he forged through the dim labyrinths of the medina.

He reached a dark cul-de-sac and for a flickering moment, his pulse quickened thinking he had lost his way. But then he recognized the old, rusty sign above a commercial building and he let out a deep audible breath. *Le Cafe du Sultan* was poorly illuminated but he recognized the carved wooden door and the lion paw that served as a knocker. He pushed the door and entered a room filled with men and smoke. The smoke, emanating from cigarettes and water pipes, formed a thick cloud that hung like a layer of smog above everybody's head. Mournful music played in the background amalgamating with the voices of the men who played cards, chess, or domino. There was alcohol on tables even though Islam strictly prohibits its consumption.

No one paid attention to the Arab detective who entered the room. He felt secure that no one knew him. Here, he was an Arab among Arabs, and he did not present any threat to the locals.

He found a small table away from the center of the room and settled in. Soon, a waiter came, small plates of cured olives and salted almonds in his hands. He placed them in front of the detective and went on to take his order. He was a rotund man, a fireplug of sort, moving swiftly in spite of his size.

"*Salem ya habibi,*" said the detective.

The man quickly spun around and eyed the detective. There was a flicker of recognition in his eyes and his face broke into a wide, friendly grin. "Ah, Ahmed, it's been a while since we saw you in Marrakesh!"

The detective smiled and nodded. "We've been busy in Dar-El Beida," he answered, referring to Casablanca by its Arabic name, The White House.

"We hear, we hear," the man looked around then bent down and whispered into the detective's ear. "Do you want your aperitif here or in the back room?"

"I'll go to the back room." The detective rose and followed the man out of the room through a small corridor and into another room.

The room was set with sofas covered in red damask fabric and adorned with gold lame pillows. Thick carpets covered the floors and the detective slipped his shoes off before he stepped on the carpet. He settled down and Salim joined him.

"My friend," said Salim as he embraced the detective, "how is your family? Your daughter, your wife."

Salim was an old friend. The detective had known him from the days he was a rookie cop, a time when he needed to create contacts and generate sources. Salim had always been his eyes and ears south of Casablanca, in Marrakesh and beyond where he had his fingers on the pulse of the city. In his cafe, news—fact and fiction—had a way of taking flight. Salim always lent an attentive ear to all, taking in information, absorbing it, and holding on to it until the opportune moment presented itself. The detective often thought that Salim would have made a good cop; his keen sense of observation did not allow any minor detail to escape him.

"Thank you, Salim. Thank you. Everyone is fine."

"What brings you to Marrakesh, my friend?"

The detective released a sigh. "Much is worrying me these days," he paused. "You heard the story about that American girl, right?"

"Right," answered Salim. His face took on an inquisitive look. "And?"

"I have an Arab girl that's dead and an American girl missing. The Torch says he has the American one. What are you hearing, my friend? Your place is well frequented by Berbers."

Salim pursed his lips. "Many stories. Some say he has the girl, others say he doesn't have the girl. Some say he killed the Arab girl, others say he would never kill an Arab girl."

"What do you believe, Salim?"

"I believe he would never kill an Arab girl."

"I have two guys who went out with the Arab girl. One is from here, Marrakesh. He is tall, lanky with a vulgar accent and thin, long fingers. Hands of a magician, I'm told."

Salim turned pensive. "Tall, you say, with thin, long fingers." He paused. "I think you're talking about *Seba'h Del Da'hab. Gold Fingers.*"

"*Gold Fingers?*"

"Yeah, we call him *Gold Fingers* for his reputation as a pick-pocket. A rotten little bastard. He grew up on the streets here and made his living pick-pocketing tourists in town."

The detective raised an eyebrow. "And who does *Gold Fingers* work for?"

"*Gold Fingers* always works for whoever pays him. An independent agent. He has no allegiance."

"Does *Gold Fingers* work for The Torch?"

"Not usually. The Torch has his own people and Gold Fingers isn't part of them." Salim grabbed an olive with a toothpick and dropped it in his mouth.

"Salim, my friend, are you sure that Gold Fingers is not a Berber?"

Salim nodded. "Sure. Very sure. He's a Marrakshi without a drop of Berber blood in his veins."

The detective patted Salim on the arm. "Thank you, my friend." He rose to leave. "I need to get back to Casablanca. It's a long drive back home."

"Ahmed, please stay for dinner. I'll have the cook prepare something for you. Maybe some grill, kebabs." He grabbed his friend's arm. "Please."

Ahmed sat back down. "Sure, my friend. I guess I better eat before I hit the road."

Salim disappeared behind curtains leading to the kitchen. Within minutes, Salim was back with a plate charged with kabbabs on skewers, smoke still emanating from them. He placed plates of salads and crudités on the table and left to attend to his customers.

The detective ate in silence, his mind straying, putting pieces together, weaving a web that seemed to have no weaver. He looked for a motive and each time he came up empty handed. The words kept coming back at him, bouncing in his head like a ball against a wall.

The Torch would never kill an Arab girl.

He was thinking of that thread again. Suddenly, the fog in his head dissipated. He had something, not much, but enough to point the way. Enough to get him going in some direction. Perhaps, he thought, he could now focus on the road ahead instead of wasting his vigor on the small venues going in many directions. In many ways, this was the genesis of his investigation, the spark he needed to get his fire going, the birth of that first cell from which it would grow.

The Torch would never kill an Arab girl.

He singled out that one sentence like a reporter who instinctively knows a great quote when he hears one. It stands out above the rest of the verbal din like a giant among Lilliputians.

He got up feeling satiated and suddenly envigored. He walked out to the main room and found the place nearly deserted. The patrons had gone home for dinner.

Salim saw him out the door. "Careful, my friend. Your picture has been splashed over all of the papers. Everybody knows what you look like." He raised a cautionary hand, "don't forget, this is The Torch's turf."

The detective shook his head. "I know, I know."

They embraced and the detective walked back through the dark alley where he had left his car. He descended the silent streets listening to the sound of his own footsteps as they reverberated through the night.

He stopped for a moment to catch his breath and heard the distant sound of other footsteps, the click-click of heels that played against his own like dueling banjos.

Finally, he saw the arched entrance leading outside the medina. From where he was, he could see out into a wider street and the small deserted plaza.

At once, he heard voices. There were many and they sounded as if a group of revelers were out for the night. They neared him and he smiled when he heard the booming laughter of his fellow citizens. He was briefly transported to the South of Spain where he had, years earlier, vacationed on his honeymoon. He remembered the Spaniards as being a nocturnal bunch who sang and danced in the streets way into the night just like this bunch.

Spinning around he noticed that they stood behind him. One had broken out in a song and the rest accompanied with hand clapping. To move out of their way, he pressed himself against the wall behind him. Soon as he did, they slammed his body hard against the wall with a force that surprised him. His throat was jammed so hard he was gasping for air. With one major blow to the head, they knocked him unconscious and he went down, melting into the ground like butter under the sun.

CHAPTER THIRTY

He opened his eyes to darkness, his temples hammered, his vision blurred by the blow sustained. His hands and feet were tied with rawhide ropes and he felt completely powerless. Numbness had settled in his limbs and his body shook like a dog waking up from a nap. The rough and cold cement floor felt like an ice sheet under his skin. He did not know where he was or how he had gotten there. The last thing he remembered was walking down an alley in Marrakesh.

Struggling, he opened his swollen eyes in a warehouse that smelled of seawater and fish. His tongue traveled the length of his upper lip and he tasted the salt of his own blood. It was then he realized he had been brutally beaten.

Suddenly, he heard voices. They had sounded like whispers but now he realized he just had not been able to hear them. The two men sat on wooden storage containers and smoked cigarettes, releasing smoke from their mouths like well-stacked chimneys on a cold winter day.

He stirred in his spot and coughed, spitting blood that was lodged down his throat. The men rose almost instantaneously and brought him up to his feet. They sat him up on a small wooden chair, interrogation style.

"Tell us your name," a man said. "And what you do," added the other.

The detective lifted his eyes to the dim light.

"Screw you," he said, his voice as rough as sandpaper. "You're messing around with a detective from Casablanca. You won't survive this."

He heard screeching laughter from one of them.

"Oh, yeah, *ya habibi*. What makes you think *you'll* survive this to tell your story?" They laughed in tandem and their laughter echoed in the hollow warehouse.

He did not respond. They eyed each other, goofy smirks on their faces. More chuckles. The detective saw bottles of wine on a table and small glasses.

"So, you are the famous detective Ahmed," the man said his thick voice drooling with venom. His accent did not go unnoticed. The man neared the detective. He raised his chin challenging him to a direct gaze then slapped him hard across the face. The detective caught a whiff of stale nicotine and liquor.

"Bastard!" cried the detective.

The man slapped the detective on the other cheek sending his face flying. "You should never call an Arab man a bastard, you bastard!"

The second man giggled nervously, then approached the detective. He touched the detective's face. His slender fingers caressed the face in a mocking manner, traveling up and down its sides, lingering like the fingers of a blind man. "Does it hurt, *Monsieur*, the famous detective? This pretty face of yours won't be so photogenic after we get through with you. You won't look so good in all those papers, brother."

"Go ahead, mess him up," said the man with the accent.

Gold Fingers slapped the detective, his hand slashing the detective's face like a leather whip.

"You're meddling too much with our work, *Monsieur le Detective*," said the man with the accent.

The detective licked his cracked lips. "You call killing innocent Arab girls and beating up on young boys *work*, you vermin!"

The detective caught a surprised glance exchanged between them.

"Necessary, sometimes. *Monsieur* Ahmed. *Honorable* Ahmed," *Gold Fingers* replied. "Besides, she was just a poor girl from a bled. What other crimes are you accusing us of committing? A boy? What boy are you talking about?"

Gold Fingers turned to his accomplice. "Rashid, did you hear? He's more interested in the prostitute than in the American girl." He neared the detective and pocked a finger in his chest. "Well, well, well. When did you guys turn into saints? Eh, tell me."

The detective did not respond. His face was burning like fire and his tied hands felt numb.

"Are you gonna tell us about the American girl? Where is she? Where is she?" *Gold Fingers* cried in his face.

The detective stayed silent, which increased their ire even more.

At that point, the man named Rashid got up, slid one hand in his pants' pocket and fished out a pocketknife. He rolled it between his fingers playfully then snapped it open revealing a thin sharp blade that glimmered in the dim warehouse. He then took the slow and unsteady steps of an inebriated man and placed the knife under the detective's chin.

"Where is the American?"

The detective felt the icy metal on his skin. Rashid moved the knife up and down his throat in a shaving motion.

"You read the papers, don't you? She's with The Torch."

Rashid pushed the sharp point of the knife right under the jugular. The detective flinched. He did not respond or move doubting he could entrust his life in the unsteady hands of a sot.

"The Torch?" He snickered. "You think so?"

Rashid's face flushed, his dark eyes filled with the rage of a man out of control. He grabbed the detective's hair and pulled his head back to where he could look down on him. "You stupid cop, you're dumber than a Berber. Tell you what. We'll find the girl and when we do, you'll have another corpse on your hand—except, of course, you won't be around to know the difference, you'll be in the hands of Allah."

Gold Fingers intervened. "Let's get rid of him. He doesn't know anything. Stupid cop."

Rashid still held the knife under the detective's throat seemingly enjoying the effect it had on him. He then moved the knife behind the detective's ear and held it there for what felt like an eternity. He slid the knife down in a straight line. The detective felt the burn of a raw cut followed by an icy trickle down his neck.

Suddenly, Rashid blew a fist into the detective's gut and followed it with a blow over his head. The detective collapsed in his chair, his body a mangled mess, his pride shattered.

———•◆•———

He awoke in a place he did not recognize trembling like a wet cat on a cold day. He felt himself rocking. Back and forth. Back and forth. Where am I?

Frozen in place, he listened to the curl and roll of the waves and the putt-putt of the motor boat as it moved across the waters. The cut on his neck burned like a flame under his skin. He opened his eyes and looked at the expanse above him. He gazed at the Big Dipper and found himself awed by the beauty of the stars that lit the night.

His senses nearly normal, his mind focused on the rocking motion. He had always suffered from motion sickness and he knew its symptoms. The air smelled of salt, wetness, and fish. He knew he was on a fishing boat.

Beyond, he heard the splashing of waves against the boat, a small and barely audible sound that went undisturbed in the night.

He began to wonder how he had ended up in a boat—

Marrakesh was right smack in the middle of the desert and nowhere near any body of water. The nearest coast was the Atlantic to the west and, farther, the Mediterranean to the north. He guessed he had been hauled to Essaouira, a resort area southwest of Marrakesh on the Atlantic side a few hours drive from where he had been. There were plenty of fishing villages on that coastal stretch and plenty of places where a body could be quickly disposed of.

He realized then he had become a disposable commodity and his heart fluttered when he thought of the certainty of his fate.

The boat was quiet but that did not mean he was alone. He was at the stern of the boat and from his position, he could see no one. But he knew they were there. Someone was there to do the job. He guessed there would be at least two men at the helm with the duty of tossing him overboard. He listened intently to voices and then heard the sounds of men moving about the boat. Footsteps. Ropes and nets dragged around. Noises in the dark. The bogeyman of his childhood was back and he was gripped with fear.

He moved his hands behind his back manipulating the rawhide ties. He was laying in a large puddle of water and the soaked leather ties were loose. They cut deeply into his skin and the manipulations left him with a raw burning sting. He loosened the ties behind his back until he felt them give in. Suddenly, he was free. He brought his hands in front of him and rubbed them together. He stayed in this position for fear of alerting the men. Hunched over, he loosened the ties on his feet. For several minutes, he wondered about his next move. Should I attack or escape? Or both. He brought his hands to his face fingering his skin, touching the cut, the swollen eyes. His tongue traveled his lips, a coarse crust had formed on the surface, and he felt repulsed by his own body fluids. He felt weakened by the blows and the exposure to weather and decided that his best move should come as a surprise.

He guessed the men would be armed and quickly gave up on the attack angle. He raised his head above the boat's rim and looked out. At a distance, he saw the sparse lighting of a village and the houses dotting the shoreline. Good, he thought, I'm not too far from shore. He was a good swimmer and tackling the waters did not intimidate him. Below, water black as ink glistened and the moon spilled silver on its surface.

Surreptitiously, he eyed the two men at the helm. They watched the night and talked. He was hoping they had forgotten about their cargo.

He stalled but he knew he needed to act quickly. He slid across the floor to the edge of the boat and in one quick move hurled himself above the boat. He let himself fall in the water and immediately went under.

The splashing noise made the men run to the stern. There was mayhem. He heard their shrill voices reverberate in the night and quickly dove deep under the boat. Their eyes searched the waters, roving here and there, but darkness gripped the night leaving them angry and helpless. He went under, holding his breath and surfacing just long enough to refill his lungs. He swam under the waters putting a great distance between him and the boat, and when he felt safe, he cut across towards the shore. He swam furiously as if mad dogs were gnawing at his heel

CHAPTER THIRTY-ONE

She remembered it as a spring day. The sky had been blue and deep and when she had raised her eyes, she had felt lost in its vastness. The wind was blowing, but it was not a fresh, spring wind. It was a hot and heavy wind, fraught with peril and it hung in the air like an omen of things to come. The *Shergui*, locals called it. A North African wind that came from the Sahara, swept across the plains and left people jittery and weary. It whistled and hissed, and on the days it blew, everyone knew that anything could happen. She knew that such wind could only be a foreshadow of events in her life and that, somehow, things will be altered after that day.

She had never been particularly superstitious but always paid attention to her inner barometer, which, on that day, told her that the events of the day would mark her in a way she had not anticipated. They would change her viewpoint, mold it, shape it, and alter it in an unrecognizable manner. She would become a better being, one less indulgent and more benevolent not unlike the detached doctor who feels compassion only after he, himself, becomes a patient, walks to the brink of death, and survives it.

She had been a young reporter, an observer, had kept herself at bay and out of the fray until the day when she became the subject of her own reporting. Her goal had always been to remain a chronicler of events and to maintain an emotional distance. She was like the photojournalist who keeps clicking his shutter long after the bullets are fired, but waits for the bodies to fall to snap his last shot.

But the events of that day, etched in her mind and her psyche, remain as clear and real as they had been some fifteen years earlier, when, she had been in Africa, fighting the same war, fighting the same man.

The Torch, she thought, *you and I go back a long way.*

He had trapped her, wanting to set an example out of her, just so that other reporters would know what their limits should be. He had abducted her, held her in absolute isolation until she thought she'd surely go mad.

Then he let her out on the day the *Shergui* blew.

At the time, she had interpreted it as a moment of fleeting generosity from his part. She had underestimated his reptilian soul and allowed herself to be transported by the moment.

He let her out of her dingy room on a rooftop where she had been held for over thirty days. She had walked out on to the flat roof amid the laundry that hung to dry and peered out and over its walls. The building was some five stories tall and she had remained all afternoon there. The *Shergui* hovered and danced over the rooftop and she had not sensed the ominous threat it presented. She did not want to. She did not care. She was out on the rooftop and if she could fly, she would have tried.

Suddenly the skies turned dark and dense and cries filled the air above her. She was standing still taking in the fresh air and rejoicing her first day out in the open when she was pummeled by herds of locusts. That year, the locust had invaded the North African skies and plains, eating their way through everything they met. Like the biblical curse of the ancient pharaohs, they blanketed the skies and formed a tight lid on the city. She lay on the naked roof as hundreds of critters entered every cavity of her body terrifying her so much she was certain she would not survive the onslaught. Buzzing like bees, they gnawed at her, through her clothing until they reached the tender flesh and began their predatory feast. They blanketed her body wrapping it like a mummy when suddenly—as if a telepathic message had traveled through them—they gave up on their meaty repast and took off like a flying carpet, away from her and in search of a more befitting vegetarian meal.

For hours thereafter, she had lain on the rooftop amid the countless locusts that had perished. Finally, she crawled back to her room, closed her door, and fell into a large, dark abyss. That night, the abyss felt like a womb, it drew her deep inside, then enveloped her and in it, she felt nurtured and safe.

The following day The Torch came in and brought with him a clay pot filled with smoldering embers. He placed the locust he had gathered from the rooftop on the burning coals and roasted them. The green insects sizzled and turned red. He snapped and tore their heads and legs then bit into their flesh as she listened to the crisp and crunchy sounds he made. Then, he served her a plate of locusts, red as blood, which she turned down.

After several days of just water and no food, he came back and once again offered her another plate of locusts. This time she relented and ate the locusts that ate her.

And when The Torch felt satisfied that she had learned her lesson, he set her free.

She had been freed, but not freed from the memories of that day. After that time, she could no longer remain the uninvolved eyewitness she had been. The observer. Often, she became a willing participant turning the rules of journalism upside down and making her own rules along the way.

Now as she sat in her darkened room holding Emily's ring and pendant in the palm of her hands, she wondered if she was—still—a subject of his manipulations. Rage filled her throat, but she knew that she could not allow it to take hold of her heart and head. Her head was to remain clear and lucid and she was to test whether self-restraint was one of her attributes. She was to become calculated, learn to anticipate and predict his moves, and then give it back to him in spades. Was she capable of such devious behavior, of outwitting him at his own game, of outmaneuvering him at what he was a master at? She did not know. And she was not sure.

She was sure of only one thing. She was sure that Emily's life mattered and that someone had to care.

She reached for the phone. She dialed Sami's number. He answered after the second ring.

"Sami," she said, "tell him that the rings won't do. Tell him that I think he's bluffing."

Sami sensed the gravity in her voice and bypassed the customary niceties. "Miss Hunter," his voice stalled, "I don't know where…"

She interrupted him. "Sami, I don't care how you get the message to him. I don't want to know. Just let him know that I want more proof. For all I know he could have stolen this stuff. You know how to relay a message to him, don't you?"

She hung up.

She lay on her bed watching the sky outside her window. For a while, she viewed the top of palms sway in the soft wind letting their gentle rustling lull her into a state of semi-consciousness.

She fell asleep. Deep, hard. And she dreamed.

In her dream, she was Emily. And she was herself. They were together and the same. Emily's face was juxtaposed with hers and she sensed a dark and heavy oppression pressing inside her chest. They were both behind the walls of their prison, both on the same rooftop.

And the locust was there too.

The locust was thick and dense, and black. And the locust wore a veil. Behind the veil, the locust had eyes, and those eyes shone like brilliant agates. They pierced her soul, and the eyes knew that the walls she was behind were the walls of her own inner prison.

———— • ◆ • ————

In the morning she awoke feeling as if she had been inebriated, her head feeling heavy, her limbs as if they belonged to someone else. She went to the bathroom and turned the lights on. She glanced in the mirror and was appalled at the sight of herself. Her face was drawn and her eyes hollow. There were deep dark circles under her eyes and the sparkle had vanished from them. Stress, she told herself, will kill you. She remembered once seeing a chart of the most stressful careers and being a journalist was right up there, among the top twenty. The writer of the article had pointed out that the amount of stress was not always commensurate with the amount of money one made. So, there you have it, she thought, plenty of stress and little money.

She washed her face, dabbed on some foundation laying it thick under the eyes, and completed her morning meta-morphosis. Once done, she marveled at her transformation and thanked the gods who invented war paint.

She called in for room service, turned on the television, and watched an Arab soap opera. She watched for a couple of minutes, found the acting too melodramatic, and switched the station to CNN International.

Emily was everywhere. There was the interview with the detective. Shots of Emily's sister and brother-in-law. The camera panning the estate in Atlanta.

She watched feeling both alienated and compromised. She viewed the happenings in America with a cool detachment feeling the distance between the story here and the one there. Here in North Africa, on The Torch's territory, the world evolved on a different axis, in a pace that did not include the frenzy of American life or its values. For America, Emily's story was a tabloid event. One more story to add to the countless others the grinding monster swallowed, chewed, and spat out. Emily was the story of the moment. Of this moment. Because in the next moment, there'll be another story that'll take its place, a story that'll bump off this one from the headlines, push it to second or third place and eventually turn it into an insignificant blurb buried deep inside the back pages of every paper. Soon enough, Emily's story will disappear from the headlines.

Just like she did.

Until an answer is found. Until she is found. Alive. Or dead. And then she will become news again.

There was a knock at her door. Breakfast was being delivered.

"*Bonjour*," said the young Arab. He held a tray with juice, croissants and coffee. She let him in feeling conscious about the way she was dressed, in her bathrobe. He placed the tray on a table and handed her a large envelope he held under his arm. When he left, she decided that getting coffee and food was more imperative than opening the envelope. She poured herself coffee and munched on her croissant as she watched CNN. She noted the flakiness of the local croissants, and remarked to herself how much better they tasted in that part of the world. Maybe one day, she thought, Americans will create a croissant that will rival its European counterpart.

When she was done, she opened the envelope. Inside she found another envelope, which she opened. The content spilled out in her hand and when she saw it, she let out a blood-curdling cry. Like acid burning a hole in her hand, she dropped it on the table. Nausea gripped her stomach and the bitter taste of bile filled her throat. Sweat poured profusely from her face and she held on to a chair lest she was going to faint.

The memento she had requested from The Torch was there. Alive and well. More alive than she had ever wanted. It was an earring. A dangling earring. And it dangled from an ear. A very live ear, small and dainty, as delicate as the earring hanging from it. But the ear was not attached to anybody's head. It came frayed and bloodied at the edges, solo, unpaired. Like fish bait on a hook.

She dashed to the bathroom and slammed the door open. She stood bent over the sink and emptied the contents of her stomach, croissant and all. When there was no more, she poured cold water over her face and stood there convulsed, almost too shaken to return to her room. Then she cleaned herself up, drank some water, and slicked her disheveled hair. She glanced at herself in the mirror and the reflection of herself staring back at her scared her. She had turned a jaundiced yellow and the makeup she had applied earlier had run down her cheeks. Now it really looks like war paint, she thought.

She returned to her room and saw the bloody note. She could not have missed it, it was a yellow sticky notes, the kind everyone uses. Two words scribbled in block letters and a question mark. More proof?

No, I don't need anymore proof. You've made your point, Torch.

Chapter Thirty-Two

Kennedy returned to the apartment she had visited earlier but this time she knocked at the door and waited for Morgan Taylor to answer it. Morgan's face broke into a strained smile when she saw Kennedy.

"Please come in, I'm glad you're here," Morgan said sounding relieved.

"Thank you for meeting with me," Kennedy replied. "I'm gonna need your help on this."

In the living room, Kennedy found Brent Seymour flipping through a magazine. His face was bruised, a black circle under his left eye. Reluctantly, he rose from his seat and shook Kennedy's hand.

"Glad you're here," Kennedy said as she faced Brent. Morgan had joined them and sat on the sofa near Brent.

"Tell me about Emily," Kennedy began. She wanted to ease into it, sort of feel her way first before she'd spring into full mode.

Morgan glanced at Brent before she replied.

"What would you like to know?"

"Well, everything. More specifically, what kind of relationship she had with Berbers?"

"Relationship?" replied Morgan, "I wouldn't call it a relationship. Maybe an interest, but not a relationship."

"O.K," Kennedy replied. Then, "where did her interest take her?"

Again, Morgan replied. "She went out a few times to Marrakesh. She was putting together a photographic collection that she was going to try to get published in the U.S."

Kennedy eyed Brent. "Did she have any relationship with The Torch? Was she, ever, in contact with him?"

"Not that I know of," he replied. There was certainty in his tone. "But of course, we haven't been dating for a long time and I'm not sure I know everything she was doing."

He offered this tidbit of information as if in a hurry to distance himself from Emily and Kennedy wondered why.

"Oh," Kennedy said, "how long has it been since you two dated?"

"More than a year," Brent said as he leaned back into the sofa and crossed his legs.

Morgan eyed Brent, a puzzled look on her face.

"Oh," Kennedy said. The dated photo in Emily's room came to mind and she connected the dots.

Brent shifted nervously in his seat.

"I have some things that belong to Emily. I want you two to confirm that they belong to her," Kennedy said. She reached in her pocket and opened an envelope from which she pulled the ring and the pendant.

At their sight, Morgan's face took on a confused look. "Oh, my God!" she said. She reached for the jewelry. "Can I?" she said. She held the jewelry between her fingers, a pained expression on her face.

"Yeah. They are hers. Both of them." Morgan opened the locket, glanced at the picture inside, and then showed it to Brent. He forced an awkward smile and looked away.

Kennedy eyes traveled from Morgan to Brent. "There's another thing here I'd like to show you," she said, then reached inside her bag and pulled a small plastic envelope. "This, here, is also something from Emily."

She handed the envelope to them and Morgan reached out and grabbed it. She opened it while Kennedy analyzed their faces. Morgan let out a loud scream, dropped the envelope in Brent's lap, and ran out of the room. Kennedy heard the loud slam of the bathroom door followed by a coughing fit and running water.

Brent picked up the envelope and opened it. He peered inside, his face vacant.

"Pretty gruesome," he said, closed it and placed it on the table.

Kennedy thought, This kid is hiding something and if that is the case, then he's doing a lousy job of it.

"Brent, how did you get those bruises?" she asked.

He shifted in his seat. His hand instinctively went up to his face and he fingered his black eye.

"Oh, this. I fell from my motorcycle. A small accident."

"You fell on your face?"

"Oh, yeah."

"O.K. You ride a motorcycle in Casablanca?"

He scratched his head. "Well, yeah, one of those scooters, you know, a Vespa."

His lack of cooperation and monosyllabic answers riled her. She canvassed his face and watched his body. He was taping one foot, a smirk firmly planted on his face that she was aching to wipe off.

She stared quietly at him while Morgan was still in the bathroom.

"What do you think happened to Emily?"

He twisted his fingers nervously and looked sideways. Then he answered her question with a question. "How would I know?"

"I'm asking you to speculate. You think you can do that?"

"That's what everybody else is doing, if you ask me."

"I'm not asking everybody else," she said forcefully, "I'm asking you."

His answer dribbled like a leaky faucet. "I can't speculate and I don't know."

She pressed. "Do you believe the Berber story? Or do you think something else is going on?"

"You are asking me if I believe the press. I don't know if I should. *You* tell me if I should believe them. You're the reporter." He said with contempt, as if challenging her.

"Yes, I'm the reporter, but what I'm asking you is to tell me what you think, not what the press says. I know what the press is saying. I'm the press."

"Tell you what, leave Emily alone," he answered.

His unintentional slip startled her. "You know something, don't you?"

"I know what you know. Which is nothing. Or something. Depending on your point of view."

"Tell you what, Brent. If you are hiding information from the authorities, you'll pay for it with blood in this part of the world."

"I'm not hiding anything. If I'm, prove it."

Kennedy got up. His contempt and arrogance were infuriating her and she felt like slapping the snotty-ass kid across the face. "I'll do just that. Promise you."

Morgan had returned to the living room. Her face was pale and her sweater was drenched from the water she had splashed on her face. She looked at both of them, trying to comprehend the situation.

Kennedy extended her hand to her. "Thank you, Morgan. I'll be in touch."

"Sorry about this," she was pointing to her clothes, "if there is anything I can do for Emily, I will. Just let me know."

"Let's stay in touch," said Kennedy. "Thank you."

Kennedy walked to the door then said, "By the way, Brent, whose ear is it?"

"Van Gogh," he replied.

CHAPTER THIRTY-THREE

The hotel's conference room had been turned into a pressroom but the space, large and filled with tables and hook-ups for computers, was, more often than not, vacant. The atmosphere was not conducive to mingling or socializing lacking the necessary ingredients that turn a room from cold to cozy. And so, the bar, noisy, filled with smoke and body heat became the nerve center of the story. And in spite of the competitive spirit of the profession— reporters, producers and television crews—love to commiserate. Some out of boredom, others out of solidarity, and the rest do it because misery, indeed, loves company. Rumors, gossip and, now and then a genuine fact, circulated as reporters scrambled to separate fact from fiction.

Until now, Kennedy had kept away from it all, knowing all along that eventually she would need to join the fray. When she entered the bar, she recognized several reporters from other news organizations huddled around the counter. Kennedy straddled a stool. She overheard two reporters talk about renewed skirmishes outside of Marrakesh and about The Torch. No one had seen him or interviewed him and Kennedy's arrival stirred the group. They knew she was the only one with the scoop and they— surreptitiously—envied her.

They had been waiting for something to happen and boredom had sunk in. Soon as she sat down and ordered a glass of wine a reporter accosted her.

"Kennedy? Hi, my name is Stone Richards, I'm with *The Trib.*" Everyone in the business referred to *The International Herald Tribune* as *The Trib*. He offered his hand and shook Kennedy's. Clad in khakis and a photographer's jacket, he possessed the taut and lean look of the seasoned reporter.

"Hello, Stone, how you doing?" She was familiar with his byline and frequently read his articles while on the road.

"Not too well. Care if I join you?" Without waiting for a reply, he pulled the stool near her and straddled it.

"That was quite a thing you pulled, The Torch interview, and the girl missing," he nodded his head.

She took a sip from her glass. "Call it luck. Or maybe luck and hard work."

"False modesty? Not many reporters with those qualities around. I'd say it's more than just luck. Excellent reporting job you did."

She smiled at his remark. "Thank you, I guess hard work always shows. That's what they taught us in school."

He scanned her face. "Ah, journalism school. That was a long time ago." He turned pensive as he said that.

"So, what do you guys do with all your time?" Soon as she said it, she wondered why she asked because she knew the answer.

"You know the drill. Hang around bars and try to get an interview with the man." He paused. "Then of course, we drink too much, smoke too much, eat too much, and sleep too little. And in between, listen to everybody's war stories."

She chuckled. "Yeah, they are always there, those skeletons."

"Sharing those helps," he answered, "they take less space in your head."

He avoided her eyes and a momentary silence fell between them. When he looked at her, she discerned a flutter of discomfort and looked away feeling as if she had trespassed on a private reflection.

Then he changed the subject rapidly. "Listen, where does the story of the girl stands?"

She raised an eyebrow as if saying you-don't-really-expect-me-to-tell-you, do-you?

"It stands still. There are no new developments at this time."

"I see," he replied without pressing, a hint of a smile on his lips as if saying you-don't-expect-me-to-believe-you, do-you?

She returned a faint smile thinking how reporters trust no one and never believe what anyone tells them. The mantra is—if your mother tells you something, check it anyway. You have to be born a skeptic to be a good one, spend any time at it and the profession turns you into a cynic. Poisonous combination.

"So what are you working on right now?" he asked.

"Doing the same stuff you're doing. Hanging around for my next interview. If there is one."

"Oh, there'll be one," he said with certainty.

"What makes you say that?"

"Instinct, Kennedy. I've been at this game for a long time and the guy isn't going to give up right now. He won't."

"A testosterone test from the alpha male?"

He lifted his glass and began swirling the ice cubes. "You bet it is. It always is with guys like him."

"You seem to have some insight into the male psyche," she said. "What do you think he'll do next?"

He paused before he replied. He was weighing his answer.

"I think he'll push you to the edge," he said, holding his hands up and making a pushing motion with them. "He wants his manuscript published—come hell or high water. And he'll go to the highest bidder."

"Are there other bidders out there?"

"You never know. There are always papers and mags ready to make a name for themselves. Some intrepid reporter out there who would kill to get this scoop. Some tabs might even be willing to put out some hard cash for this."

Like hell, I'm going to let some hungry reporter move in on my turf, she thought.

"You know the game," he added.

"I sure do. Dog eat dog," she said thinking how cutthroat the profession was.

"And vice versa," he said. They laughed in unison finding release in laughter.

"Except," she said, "he isn't interested in having somebody else do the bidding for him. It's me he's after. We two go back a long way. As a matter of fact, more than ten years."

"Oh, I had no clue."

"Oh, yeah. It's a personal thing with him. I'm the chosen."

"The chosen?"

"Yeah. His personal pet. I was here before covering his war in the Sahara and," she paused wondering if she should say more, then, "oh well, it's a long story." She took a sip from her drink.

"Come on," he said, "tell the rest of it."

She hesitated. "I was green then and maybe he decided he was going to toughen me up. It's too difficult to explain or analyze."

He pressed. "What happened then?"

"Oh, I made all the mistakes rookie reporters make." She stopped momentarily transporting herself back to that time. "I first built up the mystique then decimated him with words. You know, construction-slash-deconstruction. We do a lot of that. And he took it very personally. Call it the arrogance of youth or whatever but he sure did not like the deconstruction process."

"Humbling experience, I'm sure."

"Oh yeah, it teaches you not to mess around with people's lives and to respect that. Not to play executioner only because you can." She was vague because she could not bear going there. She did not want to talk about the rooftop, the locust, the captivity. Or the desert. Telling it and reliving it. Being right here on The Torch's turf was enough to open that gate and bring forth a flood of painful memories.

Stone tossed a peanut in his mouth. "I'm sure you've learned some lessons from this."

"Oh, yeah," she said, "I learned that words are like weapons, once you fire them they can kill. Verbal combat."

"It's an interesting story. Maybe you need to write it. Cathartic. A good way of exorcising your demons."

"In due time," she answered. She turned reflective. "There is a place and time for each story. This one will be told when the final chapter is written. Thus far, it is not near its end. There are few more chapters in the making."

He nodded and his eyes probed her face. "Interesting how we develop relationships with our subjects. Although theoretically, we are supposed to remain neutral and unbiased. And certainly unmoved and unattached."

"There's no such thing as unmoved and unattached— and there's no such thing as unbiased reporting. All reporting is tainted by our experiences and our beliefs. And all our experiences are personal and subjective."

"Amen," he said and raised his glass in a toast. She returned the toast.

"Don't you wish that sometimes you could just go someplace where the dogs don't eat the dogs?"

He took a swig from his drink. "Yeah. You gonna need to get someplace away from the American media to do that."

She shrugged hinting at the impossibility of his suggestion and looked across the room. The place had filled up and the noise level made it nearly impossible to maintain a conversation without resulting to screaming.

As if reading her mind, he said, "Let's get out of here, it's really getting loud. How about dinner across the street?"

They exited the hotel, walked out, and crossed the street on to a wide ocean promenade with few pedestrians. The night was clear and the biting wind kept locals away. The soft moon hung above the waters like a drifting balloon and curling waves rolled at Kennedy's feet in a fizzle of white foam.

Instinctively, they huddled and he placed his arm around her waist in a protective manner as they walked towards the row of restaurants that peppered the coast.

They entered a dim restaurant where diners talked in hushed tones and waiters moved about the place with the reverence reserved to a holy place. In a corner, a piano man dressed with a tuxedo played soft music.

They sat at a corner table, placed their orders.

"So how many wars have you witnessed?" she asked.

"Most of them. Catholics and Protestants. Jews and Arabs. And many more. The list is endless, the human corruption unending and as long as the list." She listened without interrupting, hearing the cadence of his words, the choice of his words and the pauses between the words.

"Tell me about yourself," she said.

He told her he was born in the South but he did not have to, she knew that. There was a lilt in his voice, a musical note she noticed when he first accosted her.

"How long have you been a stringer?" he asked.

"Over ten years," she said, "ten long drawn out miserable years."

He laughed hard, wiped a tear from the corner of one eye.

"Bet you have some scars to show," he said.

"None I can show you right now, at least not in public," she said then winked.

"Well, I have some I can show you right now."

"Oh. And they are where?"

"Here and here," he said, pointing to a knee and an elbow, "I'm not joking."

"Beautiful mementos," she said.

"They are service stripes," he replied. "Each one marks an event in my life, a moment when my life hung in the balance."

"The main thing is to learn something from those moments, let them be a lesson," she paused then, "what have you learned from them?"

"I have learned that when I have a bottle of good wine in front of me, I should finish it before I go home."

They laughed in harmony. He had a way of throwing back his head with total abandon, his laughter reverberating in the hushed room like sparkling water from a spring.

Once he found out she liked risqué jokes, he spilled out his entire repertoire, and she laughed until tears ran down her cheeks.

Suddenly the piano man played "As time goes by" from the movie Casablanca, they looked at each other and burst in laughter. She hummed along *You must remember this, a kiss is just a kiss* . . . he joined her adding his voice to hers.

"I can't believe this," she said, "the piano man is playing Casablanca, right here in Casablanca."

"He's well trained," he replied, "somebody must have told him that Americans like it. How many times have you seen the movie?"

"Every year, when they show it on American Movie Classics," she said. "I always wondered about her, Ilsa." Her face took on a wistful look. "She loved Rick desperately, passionately. Yet, she also loved her husband. In a different way, perhaps. I sometimes question if a woman can have a heart big enough to accommodate two men."

She instantly thought of Harry. How, over time, he had taken a corner in her heart and made himself nearly indispensable. Harry was as comfortable as the proverbial old shoe, one that's broken in, feels good and is hard to discard. He was the mature man in her life and he balanced her with a mix of poise and calmness, steadying her footing and slowing her down when needed. The brakes on her engine.

"Sometimes I wonder if there's space for even one person." His voice trailed. "Some of us cannot even accommodate one singular being."

She nodded, then, "in the end, Ilsa left with her husband. She left smoldering fire for the ease and comfort of the known. The comfortable shoe."

She eyed him imperceptibly. He had leaned back in his chair and was listening carefully to her words.

"She made the right choice, not the easy choice, but the morally right one. She had a commitment to her husband and she chose that over passion," she said.

He said shrugging, "life is sometimes about choices. Making the difficult choices as opposed to the expedient ones." He paused studying her face. Their eyes met. "Indeed. Is Emily the morally correct choice for you?"

"I think so." She paused then added, "let me correct that. I know so, not just think so. Emily is me twelve years ago. I was where she is now. He possessed me. He owned me. I was his."

"Does he still?"

"In a very marginal way, yes. Except that this time I call the shots. It's my web and he's caught in it."

"Kennedy Hunter, the black widow!"

"You see, he sees himself as the puppet master. He pulls the strings and I dance to his tune."

"Do you?"

"No. But I lead him to believe so—not by being submissive but by opposing him. He likes the challenge, the give and take. As long as he thinks he's in control."

"The games people play." He was nodding his head in

disbelief. "It shouldn't be that difficult to get an interview, should it? You'd think it's a cut-and-dried thing."

"With him nothing is that simple. He almost has delusions of grandeur. He believes his mission is to lead his people and to believe it you'd have to have a rather lofty opinion of yourself. Think of Franco. Or Castro. These are people who had a disproportionate image of themselves. He thinks Allah choose him. Don't forget, his nickname is The Torch. He literally believes he carries the torch for his people."

"Torches can burn, Kennedy. They can be carried and passed on, but they can also crash and burn." He hesitated. "The world is full of egomaniacs. Megalomaniacs, you name it."

"The world is full of control freaks."

"And I'm one of them," he guffawed. "Allow me to control this situation. Another drink?"

"Yes, wine meister. As long as we are talking about you controlling the fluid situation—have at it."

They drank until the bottle of wine and the restaurant were nearly empty. They reluctantly rose, postponing the inevitable, not wanting to break the spell of the moment, and walked back to the hotel. He walked her up to her room, lingered at the door, kissed her on the cheek and walked away.

As she lay in bed, she thought this was the first enjoyable night she has had since arriving to Casablanca. The first time she had laughed. The first time she—temporarily at least—put Emily and The Torch out in the open and out of her head. She closed her eyes, thought of Stone, then drifted feeling warm all over.

CHAPTER THIRTY-FOUR

In a northern suburb of Atlanta, horse ranches sat amid magnolia and willow trees in a serene setting reminiscent of an older South. Stately and imposing, the homes were fringed with porches and picket fences behind which lived a privileged world of old southern fortunes made in tobacco or textiles, or nouveau riche money made in hi-tech speculations by, mostly, northerners. A co-existence born of necessity, an uncomfortable alliance, neither side liking the other. Old money was too stuffy. New money was too crass. But for the unacquainted and unfamiliar eye, this genteel image hinted of charmed lives, of polite conversations, of hot lazy summers and tall glistening glasses of ice tea sipped under shaded porches.

At Winthrope Estates, the mood was anything but tranquil. Janet Carrington Fairfax, heiress to the Coca-Cola fortune, sister of Emily Carrington, wife of Porter Fairfax, felt a growing sense of helplessness. She found no pleasure in her daily activities feeling mostly like an automaton. Automatic pilot, she called it. Nervousness and a deep anxiety had settled inside her very core leaving her in a state of permanent tumult. She was jolted each time the phone rang and patience—once an attribute she was proud to possess—was as scarce as the proverbial rain in the desert. Somehow, she had managed to keep in line her cool and collected temper but now her tightly snug lid was about to explode.

It has been several days since Emily, her baby sister, had vanished without a trace and no one had cracked the case. Or even made a dent in it. Not the embassy, nor the local authorities who seemed, in her opinion at least, as phlegmatic as an escargot. Moreover, Porter, the one in charge of maintaining contact with the authorities, had spent more time at his dot-com than ever, seeming aloof and acting as if this was nothing but an inconsequential and minor inconvenience in his life.

He had done what people in his financial standing do. He hired himself a P.R. firm, spinners adept at issuing denials, at keeping at bay the media beast and at feeding its giant appetite with canned morsels of recycled food. Most intrusive of all, she felt, were the trash tabloids, debasing and dehumanizing, who went as far as—practically—to dig into people's trash.

So much was said, so many untruths, so much fabrication, so much deception. When she read the tabs she felt she was reading someone else's life. She knew it was done in the name of profits; it filled pages on slow news days and sold papers to those who lived life vicariously. Emily. Poor little rich girl.

Emily was today's news. There were many others before her and there will be others after her. Far back in the seventies there was Patty Hearst and then there was O.J., Buttafueco, JonBenet, Monica, Chandra and countless others that will follow in their footsteps. Footnotes in the annals of celebritydom. And when everything had been said ad nauseaum, they will eventually become a Trivial Pursuit brainteaser.

Who would have thought that by going to Casablanca Emily had put herself at risk, endangered her life and became an international *cause célèbre*? Emily, certainly, would not have brought that kind of attention on herself. Good, sweet Emily was anything but conspicuous. The salt of the earth. A little girl who nurtured and healed wounded rabbits and birds. A girl whose love for nature was almost mystical. A girl who felt shame for having too much and who, reluctantly, carried the burden of her family's name and wealth.

Her eyes filled with tears when she thought of Emily. She pushed them back because she needed to stay strong for Emily, because Emily would have wanted her to, and because the alternative was just unbearable. For now, however, she needed to keep on marching—in spite of herself.

And today—of all days—Porter was about to bring along a friend, a horseman, he said. Someone he had met at his dot-com or in a bar, she was not sure, but she was in no mood to entertain, feeling exasperated and tired from all the sleepless nights.

———————•◆•———————

Soon, Porter showed up, Harry in tow. A housekeeper in a black and white uniform let them in. Harry found himself inside a large foyer with rich, dark wood floors the size of his den. He was led to a living room decorated with plush leather sofas and walls adorned with equine motif accessories. Browns, rusts, and earthy tones dominated the room and a rustic fireplace burned silently adding an element of coziness to the large room. Harry estimated it was her house; the caring displayed in the decorating had to come from her. Glass doors opened to a deck and to a manicured lawn and pasture. Beyond, there was an enclosed dressage ring and he saw Janet on a horse. She wore riding boots, pants, and a hat and to him, she looked stunning, elegant, and nearly regal in her posture. She sat erect on her horse while guiding him backward and forward until a series of steps was completed. Harry knew the steps had a specific meaning but was clueless as to their origin and interpretation.

He settled on the deck with Porter while she completed her routine. He watched her get off the horse and stride towards them. She arrived followed by two lapping dogs.

"Mr. Smith," she said, "welcome to our home."

Harry got up and raised his hat. He shook Janet's hand with a firm grip. She took it and eyed him. He was decidedly masculine and his mien was that of a man comfortable in his skin. Harry possessed the rugged look of the outdoorsman—cowboy hat and boots—but moved with a fluid grace few tall men bore. He was relaxed, at ease at the ranch, even more so than Porter was.

Harry considered himself—tongue firmly planted in cheek—a Jewish cowboy. An oxymoron, if there ever was one. Yet, he seemed willing to accept his new role, not feeling at all displeased by his new physical appearance and by the assumed role he was playing. A gentleman. A cowboy. A rancher. Why not, he thought, I'm the sum of all my parts. Real or made up.

"Ma'am, a pleasure meeting you. Please call me Harry. That's what my friends call me." He assumed his best Virginian accent, lingering on his drawl and words.

"Harry Smith," she repeated, "like the T.V reporter, you two have the same name."

"Yes, Ma'am, except that mine is Harry B. Smith and I'm no famous reporter."

"What does the *B* stands for?"

"Oh, it's my mother's maiden name. Not of any significance."

"Porter tells me you're a fellow horseman from Virginia."

"Yes, Ma'am—on both counts. I'm here to visit a ranch up in Dahlonega. And I'm from Virginia Beach. The Tidewater area as they use to call it. Although the Chamber of Commerce changed it to Hampton Roads lately. Are you familiar with the area?"

"Certainly. I, myself, have been several times to Virginia.

I attend the Upperville Horse and Colt Show every year. Wouldn't miss that for anything in the world. Do you attend it?"

"Yes, Ma'am. Best show in the nation. Nothing like it." He looked over to the dressage ring. "As I was saying, Ma'am, about the Tidewater area. Now that it's called Hampton Roads, nobody knows where it's at. A while back, I invited an out of town buddy to visit when the stewardess—I mean flight attendant, as they like to be called today—announced they had arrived to Hampton Roads. The poor fellow nearly had a coronary thinking he had boarded the wrong plane! Imagine that."

She laughed and her eyes sparkled. The dogs were nudging themselves against her, their tails waging furiously. She reached out and scratched them behind the ears as they competed for her attention.

"Now," he went on, "I tell my visitors ahead of time that they're not coming to Virginia Beach, Norfolk, or Chesapeake—they're coming to Hampton Roads."

Porter was semi-attentive to the story, his mind seemingly elsewhere. He cast a glance at them then forced a smile.

The conversation moved from horses to the weather in Georgia and the similarities between the two states.

Harry eyed the horses in the dressage ring. "You have some beautiful horses there."

Janet had already decided that this tall, mannerly and completely charming cowboy from Virginia was worthy of her attention. He had an old world charm especially when he peppered his language with the obligatory "yes and no, ma'am" which he added after each sentence. Although she had counted on only displaying a modicum of civility towards him, she was now ready to show him the horses in the dressage ring. She was assured that Porter will not bother to accompany them. He never did. Horses were, in his view, as inconsequential as their manure.

"You two go ahead," Porter said, "I'll be inside watching CNBC and the stock market." He left them and entered the big house.

Together, they walked to the dressage area. Harry followed her with his eyes. Wide shoulders, narrow hips, etched leg muscles under faded jodhpurs. Her pants and boots were soiled with mud but she displayed no self-consciousness about it. Harry knew he was in the presence of a woman who was not afraid of getting dirty and who possessed little, if any, vanity. Once out in the sun, he noticed her pallid face and the dark circles that formed under her eyes. He knew it to be the result of the stress she had endured recently.

The horses stood behind a fence, their faces to the sun. Janet reached to a majestic dark horse and petted him. He rubbed himself against her in a tender gesture and she responded to him by rubbing his nose and neck.

"This is Tennessee Williams, my favorite pet. He's more like a puppy than a horse." Her face took on a tender expression.

"I'm not going to ask who he was named after. And I take it he's a Tennessee Walking horse." Harry neared the horse and ran his hand over his shiny coat. The horse responded by sniffing Harry's hand.

She moved to a tan horse standing nearby and petted his striking silver mane and tail. "And this is Maroc, he's my sister Emily's favorite horse," she said. "He's a Palomino. Of Spanish descend, as you know. He's rather sad these days; she isn't here to love him." She paused. "She named it Maroc. It means Morocco in French. God, she loves that country," she whispered tenderly. A faint smile covered her face. "You know about Emily, don't you?"

Harry was waiting for this opening. "Difficult to get away from it. The media has been covering it like a blanket."

They lapsed into an uncomfortable silence. There was visible pain on her face.

"Yes, indeed. An understatement, if there ever was one." She turned away and continued to pet the horse.

"The wrath of the first amendment," he said, "the other side of the free speech stuff. The ugly side of it. You could almost call it harassment."

"I wish for it to end. Or that something could be done." Her voice lagged. "Instead of all the speculations, innuendoes, and falsehoods."

He wanted to allay her fears and came close to telling her that something was being done but he held back knowing that he could not. Should not.

Instead, he busied himself with the horses, running his hands over them and for a moment he forgot the deception he was engaged in. His knowledge of horses and dressage, such as it was, could only fill a few paragraphs. What he knew for sure was that horse people, as they call themselves, were distinct, a breed of their own who felt more at ease in the presence of the four-legged beauties than they did among the two-legged kind.

And now that he was in her presence, he knew he did not want to cause her anymore pain nor add his imposture to the rest of the herd. He was hoping to steer the dialogue between them to topics other than dressage and horses for he feared his mask would be unveiled and she'd see right through his masquerade.

"Have you been to North Africa?" he asked.

"Yes. Long ago. Before Emily went there. Porter has been there recently, alone."

How strange, he thought that Porter would go there to visit Emily without her.

"Business?" he asked, trying to be as inconspicuous as he could.

"Yes, to the south of Spain. Marbella, to be exact. He was so close to Casablanca he decided to visit her." She paused. "Have you, Harry?"

"Have I what?"

"Been to North Africa."

"Oh, yes, Ma'am. A while back. Years ago. He quickly changed the subject.

Why did Emily choose Casablanca for her schooling? Not exactly your regular Ivy League school location."

"Emily is unique in every way. Ivy League was not for her. She wanted an exotic place where she could learn more. She had a vast interest in cultural anthropology and a love of photography." She ran her hand through her long hair, "beside its French influence and its vicinity to Europe, Casablanca offered her both."

"What kind of cultures was she interested in?"

"Ancient cultures like the Berbers," she answered without hesitation. "There are many cultures that have been studied intensely. Like the Incas and the Mayans. She found the Berbers fascinating. A race with a rich past and a future of integration that leads to disappearance. They have been swallowed by the Arab culture. Both cultures are merging and the Berbers will eventually fade away. Like so many other cultures."

Immediately, he thought that it was The Torch's argument too. Ironically, they both thought alike.

"Emily knew that." She paused realizing what she had just said, "I mean Emily knows that," she said correcting herself. She put her hand to her head. "Oh, my God, I was talking about her in the past tense. It scares me that I'm starting to think of her in the past tense."

"Understandably. You're forgiven." he said, offering her a knowing smile.

"Yeah, but I have to be careful how I speak about Emily to Mother."

"Your mother?"

"Yes, our mother. She's bedridden. Quite ill, as a matter of fact. I'm afraid that I'd lose her if I start talking about Emily in the past tense."

He did not want to press so he let that one slide by, but she continued.

"I have kept most of the details from her. Not letting her know more than she has to. This may prove to be too much for her."

"Has she been ill for long?"

"Oh, yes. I don't know how much longer she has. She has surprised us all, a few times already. Every time we think she's going to leave us, she surprises us by hanging on. She's more tenacious than I thought she'd be. Emily has some of that. An underlying tenacity that isn't obvious to the naked eye."

"She'll need that if she's somewhere fighting for her life."

"I'm counting on that. I'm hoping that it will sustain her, wherever she is."

"Where do you think she is?"

"I don't know. I don't know what to believe anymore. Maybe with The Torch, like he says, maybe not. In a way, I'm almost hoping that she's with him. At least it tells me she's alive."

"I understand," he said, "who's taking care of talking to the authorities and staying on top of it all?"

"Porter, of course. He knows the people in charge of the investigation, if you can call it that. And I have been following the articles of that American reporter in Casablanca, Kennedy Hunter."

Harry froze. Damn, he thought. She might make the connection between Kennedy and me. The articles picked up from the wires had all originated from *The Virginian-Dispatch* in Norfolk.

"I, myself, don't read much of the papers these days," he moved behind a horse so that she could not see the deception in his eyes, "only the sports pages, and the business pages. Wall Street is better than Vegas these days, if you ask me."

"Indeed," she replied, "Porter can tell you quite a lot about Wall Street. Nothing about horse trading, but a lot about stock trading—I.P.O's, internet stocks, commodities, name it . . . he's done it."

He was relieved she moved beyond the subject of newspapers. He was hoping she had not made the geographical connection between Kennedy's paper and him.

"Yes, he is a connoisseur of the medium—excuse my pronunciation of the word—French words get me every time."

"It's quite charming the way you say it," she replied. "Like southern French."

He chuckled at the definition. "I take it Porter does little else other than play the market."

"Nothing else. Porter is a big dreamer. He is always striking it big. Always."

"Maybe he will one day. Dreaming is a good thing. Sometimes it keeps one alive."

"Yes, I see what you mean," she said. "As long as the dream doesn't become an obsession. Dreams can sometimes turn into an irrational occupation. A mania, almost."

He thought of his own passions. Passions that turned into obsessions. He remembered a time when everything he did was enacted with passion. When life was a big cornucopia of abundant, savory bites which he devoured with reckless abandon. Without worry of consequences or repercussions. And he wondered if ever, there'd be a time when he'd feel that kind of audacity again.

Perhaps, he thought, youth was just a temporary malaise from which one eventually recovers. Way too soon. His days of courting danger were over and his bravura was now tempered with moderation. He was reduced to taking calculated risks and despised how it made him feel. Aging, he thought, is a chronic disease from which one never recovers.

And as he eyed Janet, he wondered if under the semblance of civility and nobility there was an underlying recklessness running below the surface, seething and fermenting. And he secretly wished there was. For a life without passion was a life without purpose, he felt.

But as he looked beyond, on the front lawn, he realized what her passion was. It was right there, under his nose. Her horses. Her connection to the species was apparent and clear and he knew that her lifelong passion had been found and that no one could interfere or compete with it. No human. And certainly not Porter.

"And what is Porter's mania?"

"Money. The pursuit of money. It's the chase he likes, more than anything else. It's all consuming and it's as addictive as any Vegas table. An adrenaline high he can no longer live without, I'm afraid. Sometimes it worries me, to be honest."

He nodded. He knew right there and then he had found Porter's Achilles' heel, the flaw that would break him. Everybody had one. It was just a matter of finding it, defining it and in some cases, exploiting it. He had guessed it, but now he was sure of it. Greed, he thought, was the blinding force behind Porter's behavior.

They walked back towards the house, dogs at their heels yelping and entered the living room where they found Porter in front of a television. He was on the phone speaking French to somebody. When he saw them, he nodded in acknowledgment and carried on with his conversation.

Harry removed his hat and sat on a couch. "Porter speaks French?"

"Yes, he does. He loves the language and the culture."

"Do you?"

"No, not a word. Or maybe I should say that only the words I speak to my horse for dressage—they are in French. My second language was high school Spanish. Emily speaks beautiful French."

"So was mine, but somehow I manage to make myself clear when need be," he replied.

She lifted a small bell from the table and rung it. A uniformed maid showed up immediately.

"Would you like some ice tea? It's freshly made."

"Sure, Ma'am. Would love to have a glass."

"Sweetened, unsweetened?"

"Sweetened, please."

She turned to the housekeeper. "Maria, *por favor, dos* ice teas. *Con azucar*. Sweet for the *senor* and for me *sin azucar*."

The maid nodded and immediately left.

Janet turned to face Harry. "Yes, as I was saying, Emily speaks the local dialect in Morocco."

"She does? Quite amazing. What is it, this dialect?"

"They refer to it as Arabic but it isn't the real thing from what I understand. It doesn't resemble any Arabic spoken in other countries. Emily tells me that Moroccan Arabic is different, a dialect of some sort."

"And how did Emily learn such a complicated thing?"

The maid came back and placed a tray with two tall glasses on the cocktail table.

"Thank you, Maria." The maid nodded, "*mas*?"

"No, nothing. *Nada*."

Janet resumed the conversation. "Emily learned it from the natives. I think she was trying to learn some of the Berber languages, just so that she could communicate with them."

Harry nodded. "Berber. There is an obscure language. Has she ever met The Torch?".

At the mention of The Torch, Porter, while still on the phone, wheeled around and eyed Harry. Their eyes locked.

"She may have," Janet responded, not paying any attention to Porter.

Porter abruptly shut his cell phone and joined the two. Harry decided that this was the time to make a graceful exit. He picked up his hat and rose to leave.

"Ma'am, it was a pleasure meeting you," he placed his hat on his chest and bowed.

"Would you stay with us for dinner?" she asked.

"Thank you, Ma'am." He turned to Porter who had already gotten up. "Porter buddy, I reckon it's time for me to leave and return to my hotel." He extended his hand.

Porter did not insist on him staying. He rose and shook Harry's hand. "Take 400 south to Buckhead. Get off at the first Buckhead exit and make a left. The Ritz Carlton is right there on the right."

Harry turned to Janet. "Thank you, Ma'am, for the delicious ice tea and the guided tour. Most appreciative."

"Perhaps you could visit some other time. Maybe I could show you the barn and the rest of the horses, Harry."

"Thank you, Ma'am. My pleasure." He eyed Porter as if asking his permission. "Surely." He opened his jacket pocket, took out a business card, and scribbled the number of the hotel room on the back of it.

Janet extended her hand to Harry. She was holding the card in her hand when he spun around and exited the house.

———•◆•———

He drove out of the estate traveling through horse trails and country roads and somehow ended in the heart of a small town. Quaint shops flanked both sides of Main Street where old homes had been turned into antiques shops, coffee houses, and galleries. He found the City Hall building, an American flag proudly flying above it. Ensconced from view by old Bradford pear trees, the brick building faced a small park with few benches for city workers. The town, an old trading post from the late 1800's, maintained its old charm by conserving and renovating its quaint downtown and bucking the trend of sprawling malls and strip centers that had become the norm in Atlanta's suburbs. Harry drove his car behind the building and parked in the spot reserved for visitors only. At the entrance, he tripped on the brick steps and cursed the cowboy boots he was wearing. His toes were squashed inside the lizard boots and a sharp pain shot up his legs. The man that sold him the boots had told him the leather will soften up but never said when. Probably between now and eternity. They could survive a nuclear disaster, he thought.

He negotiated his way to the entrance and entered large double doors leading to the reception area.

"Howdy, what can I do for you?" said the woman behind the desk. Harry removed his hat.

"Yes, Ma'am. I'm here to check probate records."

She raised an eyebrow and gave him a quizzical look all the while chomping on gum.

"May I ask, Sir, whose probate records do you want to check?" She brushed her wavy blond hair with one hand and placed the other on her waist.

He leaned on the counter, elbows down.

"I'd like to see the records for Emily Carrington."

She smiled, showing a gap between the two front teeth. "Well, cowboy, you're not the first one asking for them. I don't even bother to file them anymore—they're right here on my desk. Are you one of them nosy reporters?"

"No, Ma'am, I'm no reporter—as you can tell by my costume."

She cracked a smile and leaned forwards revealing a cleavage that had seen better days. "Well, mister cowboy—what did you say your name was—the Carringtons have mucho money. You want her daddy's records or Grandpa's?"

"My name is Harry B. Smith and her daddy's will do."

"You're not that Harry Smith from T.V?" She eyed him suspiciously. Her eyes traveled to his head and stopped.

"No," she said answering her own question, "you're not that Harry. His head is as smooth as a baby's butt."

"And I'm a lot prettier than he is."

Her smile dissolved into laughter.

"Has anybody else filed anything recently?"

"No, cowboy. Not until her mama kicks the ole bucket— then I'm sure there will be more for the little princess."

He made a mental note. "Makes sense."

"Now, mister Harry—if you're no reporter, why would you be snooping around? The Carringtons have many secrets," she winked and lowered her voice to a whisper, "in this town we all know each other."

"Ma'am, with all due respect—"

"I could tell you some of them little secrets over at Rio Bravo where they serve some of the meanest margaritas this town has to offer."

"Ma'am—"

"I just have a weakness for cowboys. They just melt my heart." She closed her eyes and placed a hand on her chest.

"Ma'am, what did you say your name was?"

"My name is Darlene. But you can call me Darling. And after the margaritas, there's this place right up the highway," she gestured towards the door, "where some of the finest country music is played. You know, Garth, Wynnona, Reba."

"Sure. Why not? I'll leave you my phone number and we can connect. For drinks. I'm not much of a line dancer though."

He took out a card and scribbled his room number in the back. Silently, he thanked the genius who invented software to create instant business cards. Thirty bucks at Office Max and pronto, in ten minutes on your laptop, you have created a business card for your multiple personalities. The ideal software for schizos.

She grabbed the business card. "You don't have to be no Fred Astaire for line dancing. Just follow the herd."

"Sure. I can do that." He glanced at her and thought she needed an urgent makeover. The woman was stuck in the eighties. She hadn't had a change of hairstyle since Farrah Fawcett was a poster girl. Frozen in time.

"Where are you staying, cowboy?"

"In Buckhead. At the Ritz-Carlton."

"No way," she replied, "a cowboy at the Carlton? Why, that place is at least fifteen miles from here. You need to be staying up here with us." She paused, "the Carlton. That's no place for a cowboy. We have some fine motels right down this here road."

"Thank you, Ma'am—Darlene—but I'm fine where I'm. I promise to consider your suggestion next time I come around this place."

"Good. We can go river rafting on the Hooch—that's the Chattahoochee river—if you've got a hankering for the wild," she paused and gave him a conspiring look. "Now if you prefer more tame activity, I'll take you to a horse show right here, in Wilson Park. The Carringtons have horses that look better than many of the people living here."

He chuckled and silently agreed with her. He was starting to enjoy the banter with Darlene and almost forgot the boots. "No kidding. Either the people are very ugly or the horses very beautiful."

"Your pick, Harry B." She began leafing through a file. "Does the B. stand for *baby*?" She looked up. "Here it is, the distribution of the will of daddy Carrington."

She placed in front of him a stack of papers. Then she leaned and whispered in his ear. "Tell you what, I'll do something for you I'm not supposed to do. I'll make copies of this stuff for your perusal at your leisure in your Carlton suite. O.K.?"

"Much appreciative, Darling."

She liked that. She gave him a broad toothy smile and left for the back room. While she made the copies, he grabbed a copy of the local free rag, *Our Town*, and leafed through it. Front page, above the fold, photo of Emily Carrington. Front page, under the fold, photo of Janet Carrington Fairfax and Porter Fairfax. The stories were from the wires with no new developments with one exception—the local reporter had added his own personal touch and embellished the story by adding the requisite local spin.

Darlene returned with copies in hand. "Here we go, cowboy, all set."

He grabbed the stack from her. "I'll make it my bedtime reading. Thank you, Ma'am. If you remember anything else, please call me."

"You're starting to sound like a cop!" she cried.

"No, Ma'am, I'm no cop. Now, I promise a round of margaritas and that wild trip down the Hooch on my next trip, Darling. No time for fun on this one, but next time, next time . . ."

Her eyes conveyed disappointment.

"Can I call you sometime? I mean when I get back home to Virginia."

"Sure, Harry." Her pitch had come down by at least two octaves and he almost felt sorry for her. She shrugged. "Why not, Harry."

He placed his hat back on, nodded, and walked out the door. He could feel Darlene's eyes on his back. He entered his car,

tossed the hat in the backseat, and tried to remove his boots.

After tugging on them for several minutes, they came off abruptly nearly maiming him in the process. He placed his bare feet on the pedal feeling an odd and uncommon physical pleasure.

CHAPTER THIRTY-FIVE

Kennedy found three messages in her voice mail, all from John Martini. The messages were identical, except for the urgency in Martini's tone, which increased after each message. *Call me A.S.A.P.* His voice was firm—enough to make Kennedy squirm. At once, she sensed a tightening in her viscera. She dreaded this moment for the past few days. A confrontation with Martini was anything but a joyful experience.

She conceded to herself—albeit reluctantly—that the postponing of the inevitable was a stalling device from her part, and that, eventually Martini was going to ask for a summary of her activities. There was always accountability in journalism. To the profession. To the people she wrote about. To the people she wrote for.

She needed to brace herself against his railing. In spite of his friendly demeanor, Martini's rage could make any reporter tremble. Under his hide lived the ambitious spirit of a man who got there by fighting and winning his battles. He had a keen and discriminating mind and by the time he got through with a reporter—or editor, for that matter—they'd wish they had chosen sweeping parking lots instead of journalism. In his opinion, there were only two kinds of journalists. Good ones or mediocre ones. And if you belonged to the latter category, well, good luck. Because no one could loathe mediocrity with as much passion as Martini did.

Reluctantly, she called his number in Norfolk. Maybe I'll get lucky and all I'll get is his voice mail, she thought. Maybe he is in one of those endless meetings editors love. Maybe—

"Kennedy! Well—finally!"

"Yes, John, how are you?"

He plunged in. Both feet. "Maybe I should be the one asking that question. What's going on over there?"

He interjected. "Why is it that I'm not getting a follow-up? And what are you up to?"

Calmly, she let it out. "I'm trying to find the girl, John."

"Kennedy—are you out of your damn mind? It isn't your job to try to find the girl. That's the police's job, not yours."

She took a long deep breath before answering. "Yes, I know. Except that the cops aren't doing anything and I'm the only one in any position to try to help her."

"Kennedy, let me remind you that you are a reporter and your job is to report."

She was beginning to feel her face flush with anger. "John, I'm an investigative reporter and my job is to investigate. I don't suppose you want me to walk away from this story, do you?"

"Don't give me your job definition, Kennedy! I know damn well what and who you are!" His cries slit her eardrums like razors.

Damn, she wished she didn't have this stupid confrontation with him. "John, please, listen to me."

"No! *You* listen to me. If you are the subject of your reporting then you can no longer report on it. I will have to pull you off. Get that? You know the rules. You cannot have it both ways. You are either reporting it or getting involved to the point that you're no longer objective about it. So what's it gonna be?"

"John, please hear me out. This is what's going on. The

Torch insists on having his manifesto published. And I'm trying to keep the girl alive. If she is with him—and I have good reasons to believe she is—then maybe we can rescue her. After all, she's the niece of our chairman, isn't she?"

"Where in the hell did you get that information from? No one is supposed to know that. Who told you that?"

"I hear things."

"You have some mighty acute hearing. You are in Casablanca and you know about the private conversations we have in here."

"John, what I want to say is that no one is doing a thing about this girl. Not the cops. Not the embassy. And certainly not the FBI. I'm here and I can do some checking. Why not?"

"Why not? How about because you're endangering your life going against a maniac like The Torch. He's no amateur act and I don't want you to come back in a body bag."

"What if I say that I'll be cautious and I promise to be doubly cautious."

"It has little to do with you. It has more to do with you going against that country's enemy number one. When he finds out we have no intention of publishing his manifesto and, that you're stringing him along? What do you think will happen to you?"

She remained silent while trying to formulate an answer for him.

"Kennedy—?"

"Yes, John. I know there is danger here but, without some sort of risk taking, I doubt very seriously that I'll have *anything* for you."

She knew she had to find another way of convincing him. She was getting nowhere with him.

"I'm telling you, Kennedy, that the chairman—who is as you so knowingly said—the uncle of the girl, wants you out of there if you're not reporting on the area. He won't publish the manifesto and won't deal with the bastard. There just isn't any dealing with the man. Under any circumstances. You get that?"

"I get it. I understand, John. Look John, let me put in a word or two."

She heard him sigh. "O.K., go ahead."

"John, I'm a stringer and as a stringer I can get out of this story anytime I want to."

He cut in. "Kennedy! Don't threaten me! It won't work."

"I'm not threatening John. I'm damn serious."

"O.K., go on, say your piece."

"So, what I'm saying is that if you want to pull me off of it, it's fine with me. But I feel a moral responsibility and I have to do something. For Emily. For myself."

"You have no responsibility. Only an obligation to report the facts, as far as I'm concerned."

She swallowed hard. "No, John, I have an obligation to do something. It's between The Torch and me. This is a dog fight."

"A dog fight? You are really crossing your boundaries now, Kennedy. What the hell are you talking about? What do you mean by a dog fight? It's getting personal."

"It is personal. All of it is personal. You don't really know the story John, but The Torch and I go back a long way."

"And?"

"And he was a son of a bitch then and now he's doing it again. He's repeating the same thing."

"Repeating what? You care to elaborate?"

She wondered how to tell him or how much to tell him. "I don't know if I can, John."

"Try. You have my full attention. I'm all ears."

"I'll give you *The Reader's Digest* condensed version. Years ago, when I was here during the Polisario and Mauritania mess, I covered him. He was around then too. I wrote some articles he did not like and, as a result, he held me captive for thirty days." She halted while he absorbed the information. "And that's all I'll say about it. Please don't press for any details."

"Is that what David Stevens meant? Now that you're telling me all of this, I want you out of there yesterday!"

She heard his labored breathing. "Sorry, I won't leave."

"So you tell me what *you* want to do!" He put a strong emphasis on the *you*.

"If you and the chairman won't let me do my work, I'll stay anyway and do what I have to do. I don't give a damn about the reporting. This is about settling scores, and about Emily."

"Damn, Kennedy. You are complicating matters for me. Had I known of your previous relationship with the man, I would not have sent you there. Damn it!"

"Sorry about that, John. I did not know the bastard was going to repeat his previous performance with me. And I certainly did not anticipate this Emily mess. I'm truly sorry."

"What will you do when it's over? Sell your story to the highest bidder?"

"When it's over, I will. I'm a reporter and I have to tell my story. But it will have to be on my terms. There'll be plenty of takers on an exclusive story, I promise you."

"Kennedy, you have painted me in a corner and I don't like the feeling. This could be the end of our relationship; you know that, don't you?"

"Sorry about that. I'll take my chances. I have too."

"What will you do if I say no?"

"I'll say good bye, John. And I'll mean it."

"Allow me to be lyrical. You've got me by the balls and I don't like your squeezing."

She chuckled unable to contain herself.

"Your position is pretty firm, Kennedy."

"Firm and definitive, John."

"O.K." There was an empty silence as he pondered how to continue. She sensed he was rethinking his position and she gave him the space and time he needed.

Finally, he said, "Since you have made your decision, I'll tell you mine. I'll acquiesce on the furthering of your investigation with the clear understanding that you'll keep me posted on all your moves and discussions with The Torch. As needed, you'll provide me with follows and the final story will be ours. Exclusive. No sharing with anyone else. It will go on the wires and everybody will know the source. It may even win you an award or two."

She could already sense he was thinking Pulitzer and it bothered her that his prerogative had more to do with furthering himself and the paper than saving Emily. Get the story. Get the scoop. Don't let anyone scoop you. But then she thought, he was, after all, a newsman and he was acting accordingly. "O.K. It's a deal. Except that we'll have to play it safe, as far as Emily is concerned. We cannot endanger her life for the sake of selling copy."

"I can't deceive my readers, Kennedy. No deception." He turned adamant.

"I'm not talking about intentional deception. No outright lying. I'm talking about deception by omission."

"You mean to say that we won't say anything when we have something?"

"I mean to say that if we have something, we won't say it if it imperils Emily."

"Holding back?"

"Yes, holding back. For the sake of Emily."

"What if he decides to give the story to somebody else?"

"Then we'll go public with the full story. No holds barred."

"Then we won't be the first ones with it."

Damn it, she thought, it's always about the story. It always boils down to that. Being the first one, getting the credit first. Beating the competition. Even if this is the niece of the chairman, the story came first. She could never get used to this one thing about journalism.

"It's a chance we take, John. But I don't think he'll do that. He is not interested in anybody else. I'm the chosen. Remember that."

"The chosen," His voice lagged. "You better be right Kennedy."

"My instincts are right about this one. And about him."

"All right."

She could visualize him in his office running his fingers through his thick salt-and-pepper hair and pulling at his tie. "By the way, you'll have the first North American rights. Beyond that, I'm a free agent. I can also sell a variation of the story to any paper or mag."

"You're tough, Kennedy. I'll remember that next time I'm assigning you a story."

She ignored his remark. "I have bills to pay, John, and unlike some of your salaried reporters who take three months to tell a story, I actually have to write to make a living."

"All right, all right, all right. Send me a follow-up immediately."

"O.K. I will."

"What do you have?"

"I have quite a lot."

"You haven't been holding back, have you?"

"No, I haven't been holding back. Just trying to figure out where I go from here with him and with the story."

"So, what do you have?"

"I'll file it right now. Read it."

"O.K." He paused. "Kennedy? One more thing worth repeating. If you become a participant in the story then all bets are off. You'll be pulled off immediately."

She heard the click of the disconnection then silence. She stood in her room dazed from it all. She had won this battle with Martini but she knew he was going to make it very difficult for her, fighting her all the way through. The climax was yet to come. But she was ready. For him. For The Torch.

Kennedy called the paper's number and connected to its main computer. She heard the sound of the connection being made and pressed the Send button. Instantly, the transmission was made. Now all she had to do was wait for Martini to receive the information.

* ◆ *

Casablanca—In a startling new development, The Torch, the Berber rebel responsible for the abduction of Coca-Cola heiress Emily Carrington, has sent evidence of her existence to representatives of this newspaper. A gruesome package containing a cut off ear adorned with a dangling earring was delivered to reporter Kennedy Hunter at her hotel room in Casablanca as proof of Emily's existence. There is no evidence that the ear belongs to Emily Carrington until DNA testing is performed in the U.S.A.

Additionally, rings and a pendant belonging to Carrington, were also sent to Hunter who is reporting from North Africa.

The Torch continues to insist on the publication of his manifesto by The Atlanta Dispatch as a condition for the release of Emily Carrington.

Moroccan and American authorities have been notified of the latest developments and are evaluating the current situation. The Carrington family has been contacted but refused to comment on the latest happenings citing that any comment they make might jeopardize Emily's chances of survival.

Minutes later, her phone rang.

"Kennedy! You were holding this back?" He was angry and did not try to disguise it. She felt every bit of his ire across the lines.

"I was trying to figure out how to proceed with this. I'm not sure it's Emily's ear like he says. I had to check things out before I attributed this to him."

He was trying to control his anger. "And how did you determine that it was *her* ear?"

"I don't know that it is. I showed it to Emily's roommates and of course, they could not identify it either. How can one identify an ear? Unless there's something peculiar about it or one knows somebody intimately, an ear is an ear is an ear."

"I see. So enlighten me about your thinking process. Tell me your plan—if you have one, that is."

"I do. I want to bring him out in the open. He needs big bright spotlights on him. I want to expose him for what he is." There was urgency in her tone. "Truth is the biggest antiseptic, John, you know that."

"O.K. Then, what's next, Kennedy?"

"Well, I'm working on something else. I'll file it in soon as I have it. Can I ask you to trust me?"

"Mighty big request but I guess I can do that," he said reluctantly.

She knew that in spite of his promise to trust her, he would intervene and question her all the way through. Martini could not help being Martini. But it was a reprieve of sort—albeit temporary—and she was going to take advantage of it while it lasted.

"Thanks, John. I'm going to need your support to pull this one off. Can't do it alone."

"Alright, Kennedy. By the way, what did you do with it? The ear, I mean."

"It's in the frig, in my room, here."

"Nice. Cute memento, Kennedy. Hope you don't believe in ghosts."

"I don't think about it. It's out of my mind."

He hung up and she did too. Without wasting any time, she dialed back the fourteen-digit number to *The Dispatch*.

"Ty Johnson."

She was glad to hear his voice. "Ty, this is Kennedy in Casablanca."

"Kennedy, my African sister! What's up?"

"I need your help, Ty. I need you to use some of your muscle to gather information for me. I can do some of it from here, but the rest needs to be done stateside."

"What do you need?"

"I need anything you can find on The Torch. What I have of his past in the U.S. is skimpy but I know there's more. There always is. Here is what I have. You're taking notes?"

"'Course. Diligently."

"O.K. He went to UCLA over ten years ago. He lived, I bet you, in Westwood or in Bel Air, so that constitutes Los Angeles County. Now start with any traffic ticket violations, which should give you former addresses. He did not vote because he isn't a U.S. citizen but check the civil court system and see if there was any lawsuit, either as a plaintiff or a defendant. Check everything, family court, civil court. Also check the county's Recorder's Office for marriage and birth records."

"What are you hoping to find there?"

"Anything. Maybe he had an alliance, who knows? He was several years in the U.S. I'm certain he had relationships with women. You know what the French say? *Cherchez la femme*. Find the woman. If you want to get a man, find his woman, and follow the trail, she'll lead you to him."

"Good thinking, Kennedy. The French aren't stupid."

"No, they aren't. Depending on where your research leads you, you might want to check the Passport Office and Immigration records. Now, I doubt if there is anything in criminal court, but if there is, use your FOIA power, and get it for me." The Freedom of Information Act was always something a reporter had on his side.

"I may have to use the paper's attorneys for that. Martini knows about this?"

"Yeah, he does. He doesn't know what I'm doing but he knows I'm on The Torch's trail."

"Got it. What do you want me to do with all this once I get it?"

"Put it in my basket at the paper and I'll retrieve it later or better yet, e-mail me the results on my computer. I would like to see everything for myself."

"O.K. Anything else?"

"Yeah, Ty, what's the rumor mill up to? Unofficial, that is. I'd like to know who's with me on this."

"Savich's delighted you're investigating. Newberry's pissed. He wants you out. Martini's the ham between the sandwich."

"Thank God he isn't Jewish. Not a kosher position to be in."

He chuckled. "Glad to notice you haven't lost your sense of humor. Anyway, let me get started on this. Keep your lines open, I'll e-mail everything I find."

"Thanks Ty, I owe you one. Keep your findings confidential—for my eyes only."

"You know that's my M.O."

"Lunch on me at your fav place when I get back. Tata, *mon ami*."

She hung up, dropped on her bed exhausted from the adrenaline.

There always is a thread. Unravel it and follow it to the end.

———•◆•———

She could not relax or get her mind off The Torch. She sent Sami away and had her meals delivered to her room. She

told him she was not going to need him for the day—she
had some writing to do. She paced her hotel room for what
seemed like hours while watching terrible Arab TV. Now
and then, she checked her e-mail wondering if Ty had
found anything. Patience, she thought, is not one of my attributes.

Then she went down to the hotel's coffee shop and sat
down at a small table. She ordered coffee and pastries and
nibbled on them while biding her time. She scoured the
newspapers for stories about Emily and found none. The
local *Petit Matin* ran a small blurb rehashing old news together with the now-famous photo of the Arab detective in
charge of the investigation. Maybe, she thought, local cops
investigate in the same manner they do back home. When
they run into walls, they just wait for somebody or an in-
formant to come forward.

Finally, she went back up to her room. She sat down and
began writing her next article. She began forming the lead
in her mind but her thoughts were too disordered and she
couldn't concentrate on what exactly she wanted to say.
Her eyes were fixed on the screen when she, finally, heard
it. A new email. Her heart skipped a beat. Ty had something. She sat transfixed. First, she opened the e-mail from
Ty. I read, Ken! I found the woman! He underlined the
word woman twice. She screamed and sent her fist into the
air. My God, she thought, incredible. A woman had been
his lover once.

Document after document, it came. Then there was another e-mail from Ty summarizing everything he found.

She read that first.

Kennedy, by golly, you're right! Except that I had to play detec-
tive to find anything on your man. The search with L.A County
did not pan out. I remembered a friend of mine (a cop now) who
went to U.C.L.A about the same time your man did. He told me

that Al Maghrebi (before his incarnation as The Torch) was quite a ladies' man. Girls loved his mysterious personality, his dark looks, and his intellect. Get this—he used to be driven to the campus in a chauffeured Mercedes and lived in a fancy house in Westwood Village. I asked my friend about any liaisons and he said that there was a girl who hung around more than the rest. Then he made a suggestion that turned out to be brilliant. He said that the guy was so secretive that if there ever was a marriage nobody would know about it AND he certainly wouldn't get married in L.A. He suggested to check Las Vegas records. I did. And bingo! The woman is American, her name is Christine Carter. She lives on Barrington Avenue, on the Westside. Her phone number is (310) 555-0301. So I went back to L.A and checked family court and there too I hit pay dirt. The plaintiff was Christine Carter. There's a kid whom your man supports. She had gone to court to enforce and increase child payments. Also, there's an outstanding ticket for him with interest and penalties accruing for years. It's in the books. It's a jay-walking ticket in Westwood. Your guy crossed a street without going to an intersection. (Don't the West L.A cops have anything better to do than to issue jay walking tickets (!?!) Here the documents you have asked for.

Kennedy paused, her hands trembling from excitement. Christine Carter. She was the woman in The Torch's life. *Femme trouvee.* Woman found.

That was all she needed. She looked at her watch. It was 6p.m. her time. L.A time was 8a.m. She called L.A. She heard the phone ring and finally the sleepy voice of a man answer.

"Hello," he said.

"Vince, sorry to be waking you up at this hour."

He recognized her voice. "Kennedy?"

"Yeah, it's me. How you doing, Vince?"

He yawned. "Hey, Kennedy, where are you calling from? You sound far."

"I'm calling from Casablanca."

"Casablanca?"

"Exactly."

"You mean there is a Casablanca? It's not just a movie?"

She chortled. It was a question Americans often asked. "Yeah, there is. And there even is a *Rick's Cafe.*"

"No way. Kennedy, hold on, let me get a cig, can't get going without one."

"Alright, take your time. I'll hold."

She heard him put the phone down. Then she heard the click of a lighter being lit and his voice again.

"So, I don't suppose this is just a social call, is it?"

"No, it isn't. I need you to do something for me, Vince. Still freelancing?"

"Oh, yeah. What do you need?"

"I need you to go to an address on the Westside and get me a couple of shots of somebody. Her name is Christine Carter. Here's the address." She gave him the address and phone number. "And Vince, be discreet. Use your telephoto lenses and get the kid too."

"There's a kid?"

"Yeah. I need long shots and close ups."

"And who are these folks, if I may ask."

"I need it for some background investigative thing I'm doing. No, they're not celebrities or anything like it. Just common folks."

"And who do I send the bill to, Kennedy?"

"Send it to me; I'll make sure you get paid on time."

"O.K. Will do. Thanks, Kennedy. I appreciate the work."

"You're welcome. I may have to use you again. At a later date."

"Sure, no problem."

"Thanks, Vince. Ah yes, when you get them, scan the things and e-mail them to me. I'll retrieve them right here in my hotel room." She gave him her e-mail address.

"Will do. The power of technology. The road to Casablanca. Hey, that sounds like a good name for a flick!"

"Too late, Vince. There already was one, it's called, *The road to Morocco.*

She heard his loud laughter followed by the asthmatic wheeze of a smoker.

"When can you get to it, Vince?"

"How fast do you need it?"

"Yesterday."

"I'll push you upfront. I'll get it done today. You'll get your photos within hours."

"Thanks, Vince."

"Kennedy? One more thing. Is Casablanca in Morocco?

"Well, yeah, of course."

"Can you get me some of that weed they have there? I hear it's pretty good."

"Vince, I don't look good in black and white stripes. Especially the horizontal ones—they make me look fat."

"That bad, eh? Forget it. It's just a joke."

"All right. I'll hear from you soon then."

She felt the rush of blood coursing through her veins. A good day's work, she thought. Torch, the ball was in your court, now it's in mine, and it's rolling.

CHAPTER THIRTY-SIX

He heard the sounds of a rooster crowing followed by a chorus of other ones near and far and opened his eyes to the rays of light that filtered through the shutters of his small apartment.

Momentarily, Detective Ahmed sat on the edge of his bed then turned and gazed at his wife who lay curled like a child, her hair fanned on the pillow, a breast spilled out of her disheveled gown. He listened to the cadence of her soft breathing and wondered what dreams her mind was unraveling and what mysteries lain in her heart. He wondered if her dreams included him and if, any woman, had any dreams in her heart that she could call her own. How, he pondered, can she do it? She gave and gave until her spring grew dry and demanded so little in return. Of course, he thought, I was there, but never enough. Never wholly. Always torn between the job and the obligations that came with raising a family. But she was there. Always. Never torn. Always knowing that her most important duty was to be present, as a mother, as a wife, as a companion, as a friend.

But guilt, ah, guilt, was forever present, never leaving, cutting deep into his heart and soul, leaving chasmal wounds that grew deeper as years went by, as the children grew into adults, as she grew into maturity settling into a life of banal routines, giving up her dreams for the good of all.

Could I do that? Could I give up my self-ness for others? I don't think so, he thought. Not in this way. Not like she does.

Yet, he had given up his self for others. Ironically, these others weren't his own. They came in and out of his life, took in small bites, bit by bit, nibbling at his self until there was nothing but erosion.

As he listened to early morning city noises rising from the streets below, he wished for his daughter a better life, a richer life, one filled with laughter and beauty and awe and wonder.

He rose from his bed and tiptoed to the bathroom. He passed his daughter's room and heard her faint breathing through the door. He peeked in and saw the dark mass lying there in all its youthful abandon and smiled. He closed her door and went into the adjacent bathroom, turned the lights on and closed the door behind him. Gingerly, he turned the faucet on and waited for the water to warm up. He put his shaving kit by his side then laid a thick layer of foam on his face. He cut through the thick facial hair and shaved the mustache he had worn for years. It's just hair, he told himself not so convincingly, it will grow back. Nobody will recognize me without it, he thought. And, of course, that was the point.

Once done, he felt his bare skin above his lips and thought that he looked younger and softer without it. Oddly, he felt naked. As if shaving it off made him more accessible to other.

Then, he proceeded to get dressed. He opened a narrow and crowded closet in the hallway and peered inside. He saw his cop uniform hanging there but opted for the long white djellabah beside it. In the semi darkness, he slid into a pair of pants and a shirt then slipped his djellabah over it. He placed the hood of the djellabah on his head, eyed himself, then opted against it and took it down. He stepped back and looked at himself again. He looked like many of his fellow citizens who wore the loose garment, certainly not modern, but humble. Somehow, the garment had a way of taking the edge off a man, of making him less threatening and more spiritual. He liked the transformation, both for the way he looked and for the way he felt. It was as if he was taking a day off from being a cop. Something he was not sure he could still do. For being a cop was an inherent part of his persona, not just a vocation, but also an avocation.

He left his apartment as dawn was pushing the night away and morning entered the city with a cacophony of sounds. He found his Renault not at the curbside where he had parked it the previous night but on the sidewalk, a distance away. Probably, some guys looking for parking had lifted it and placed it there. There are too many damn cars in this city, he thought, and not enough parking space. One day, parking will be as expensive as renting an apartment.

He drove off joining the increasing traffic and listening to the blaring horns his compatriots seem to enjoy so much. Horns in his country served as a warning device—someone had told him that in America blowing your horn was tantamount to a verbal insult. To each his own, he thought, as he dove into traffic.

He extricated himself from the morning mayhem and took the road to Marrakesh. There were fewer cars but many more trucks with hazardous cargoes. Mattresses, refrigerators and animals, none tied down, rode in the back of trucks as they bounced up and down the highway. He slid a disc from the Berlitz School of Languages into his CD player and began his English lesson. Four hours, he thought, I ought to learn a few more words in English by the time I get to Marrakesh.

Good morning, said the voice. *Good morning*, he repeated as he shut his window to the outside world.

He arrived to the medina around noon. He covered his head with his hood and placed dark glasses over his eyes. He took his revolver out of the glove compartment and placed it under his djellabah. He had a natural dislike for guns—he knew of no positive outcome from either their possession or use—but realized that sometimes drastic problems demanded drastic solutions. Like he had done many times before, he left his car at the entrance of the medina and proceeded by foot. He walked down the cobblestone streets adopting the mien of his fellow citizens, calm and unhurried.

It was lunch hour at *Salim's cafe*. The place had already filled up with customers. He entered the smoke-filled room and went straight back to the kitchen where he found his friend. He grabbed him by the arm and whispered in his ear.

"Salim, my friend,"

Salim stepped back and eyed him surprisingly. "Ah, Ahmed, I did not recognize you!"

"Undercover, Salim. Just did not want to look like my old self."

"What's happening, Ahmed? Why the disguise? You're going to the mosque or something?"

"No mosque, Salim. I don't want to look like a cop today. Too easy for my foes to recognize me." He paused and then added, "I need to know where *Gold Fingers* and his buddy live."

"They're here often, but I can't say when. It varies. I understand they spend their days asleep and prowl around at night."

"Where can I find them?"

They walked to a table and sat down. "Can I get you something to drink?"

Ahmed raised his hand. "No, thank you. I need to get going. Where did you say I could find them?"

"I don't know for sure, but I hear they live someplace around the tanneries across town. Know how to get there?"

"Yeah, somewhat."

"Well, get out of the medina and go west towards the city's ramparts. Take Rue de Bab Debbarh and it'll take you there."

"Thanks, my old friend. I guess I'll pay them a visit."

Ahmed rose. Salim followed suit. Salim said, "Careful my friend." They embraced and Ahmed left from the back door.

He walked out of the medina, retrieved his car, and drove towards the tanneries. He drove for several minutes through narrow streets before he began noticing the peculiar odor. Now all he had to do was follow his nostrils. The overwhelming and pungent odor of dye mixed with cow urine and human sweat saturated the air and filled his lungs. It nauseated him and he wished he had brought with him a gas mask even though he was certain it would not be of any great help.

Large stone vats flowed with dye as young boys jumped from one vat to another dipping hides into the colored pools. They were skimpily dressed, their shorts riding high on their bare legs and sleeveless shirts, their hands and feet stained in indigo, saffron and poppy dyes. They paid no attention to the people around them, not even the tourists who were determined to photograph this primitive and archaic way of treating leather.

The vats were surrounded by dilapidated houses and stone buildings several centuries old in deplorable conditions. Families lived and died here, raised children, and judging by the amount of antennas jutting out of roofs, watched plenty of television. Dirt alleys lead to more alleys and into plazas and souks where people do not fret about the sweat or urine odors that impregnate their own hides. They have grown accustomed to the foul smells, many never knowing of anything else. Only those who do not belong strut around with mint leaves held under their noses and unblemished complexions. On nearby rooftops, hides hanging to dry formed a stitched quilt, a bovine tapestry of multiple hues.

Ahmed parked his Renault in front of a coffee shop. Many tables were occupied and he guessed that this café was a popular one. He chose an empty table on the sidewalk and settled into it. Momentarily, he closed his eyes letting the sun, bright and clear in the center of a perfectly blue sky, brush his face nearly forgetting he was not there as a tourist. Immediately, a rotund waiter wearing a *seroual*—large billowing pants—and leather *babouches* on his feet placed tea glasses on the table.

"Tea?" he asked. Ahmed nodded. The waiter disappeared inside the coffee shop and came back with a tea pot. He poured the sugary concoction in a glass.

"Salem," he said.

"Salem," answered Ahmed. "*Ya habibi*, I'm looking for a friend called Rachid. Do you know where I can find him?"

The man cast a distrustful glance. "Rachid? Which Rachid?"

"He shares a place with *Gold Fingers*."

At the mention of *Gold Fingers*, the man stepped back. "I know no Rachid and no *Gold Fingers*," he said adamantly.

Ahmed pressed. "*Ya habibi*, it's important that I find him. There's a pressing family affair he needs to attend."

"Sorry, don't think I can help you."

Ahmed reached inside his pocket and pulled out a fifty-dirham bill. He held it in plain view of the waiter and placed it under the teapot.

The man immediately grabbed it and stuffed it in his pant pocket. He scanned the coffee shop, his narrow eyes roving right and left and back at Ahmed.

He said, "Look, we never met, O.K.? That clear?"

Ahmed nodded. "Clear, my friend. Don't worry."

"O.K. You go down the first street to your right. Then you count three alleys, at the end of the third alley, make a left. You'll see a house with a blue wrought iron gate. That's the one."

Ahmed could not bother with the tea. He rose to leave. "*Salem*, and thank you."

The man held up the teapot and shrugged, a resigned expression on his face.

Ahmed quickly left. Nonchalantly, he walked the three alleys dodging a dozen kids and immediately spotted the blue gate. Untamed bougainvillea and hibiscus climbed over the gate and the stucco fence surrounding it. The air smelled of orange blossoms and jasmine. The house was typically Mediterranean, red clay roof and white stucco. Ahmed peered inside beyond the gate. Gardening, certainly, was not their priority, he noted. Plants just withered on their vines. The blinds in the house were shut tight and he wondered if anybody was inside. Then he remembered what Salim had said about their nocturnal prowling.

He found the gate unlocked. He pushed it slightly. It creaked. Cautiously, he walked to the back of the house where he was sure to find a back door. He crouched low listening to internal noises. No music, no T.V. When he was sure that his presence was not felt, he removed his djellabah and tossed it on the ground. He did not need the cumbersome garment to constrict his movements.

There were two windows at the back. He guessed they were bedrooms. The blinds in one of the rooms were cracked and he rose on his toes to peer inside. The window was beyond his reach so he placed a large garden rock under his feet. He stuck his face to the glass and cupped his hand. He saw a mass in a disheveled bed and quickly pulled away. He tiptoed to the second window. The blinds were so tightly shut he could not tell whether there was anybody inside.

The back door was locked. He pulled the pick he carried with him and jiggled it until the door gave in. He held his gun in his hand and pushed the door ever slightly. It creaked and the noise echoed throughout the silent house. "Damn," he murmured.

He entered a cool and dark living room. A tattered old sofa in gold brocade sat against the wall and two old leather hassocks took center stage. Shoes, newspapers, and dishes were strewn around the place.

He walked across the floor his loafers making a squeaking sound on the ceramic tile. He halted and listened. He thought of taking off his shoes but decided against it. Walking with socks would make him slide across the room and lose control. Not a good idea. He tiptoed on the floor, reached the first bedroom door and found it ajar. He dashed in and quickly placed his hand on the man's mouth. Startled, the man responded by rising abruptly from his bed. Before he reached full awareness, Ahmed had already placed tape on his mouth, had him in manacles, and hooked to the bed railings. In a swift move, he hog-tied him with cut rope he always carried in his pockets. The man's eyes displayed utter shock. At once, their eyes locked. They had recognized each other simultaneously. Gold Fingers, still groggy, was too startled to fight back.

Ahmed put the gun to his temple and whispered in his ear. "One move and I'll waste your friend next door."

The man's eyes grew wider, a curtain of fear over them. He nodded vigorously as if saying, I get it.

Ahmed stepped out to a dim and narrow corridor closing the door behind him. There were two additional doors, one to his left and one to his right. Both were shut. He knew one to be a bedroom and the other probably a dining room, or a bathroom he was not sure if it was Rashid's room. He put his ear to the door. All quiet. Birds in the garden chirped in a joyous chorus and he was struck by all the paradoxes life presented at any moment. Here he was about to waste a man and birds were chirping.

He pushed the door open when a door across the hall flew open. Rashid walked out, half asleep, rubbing his eyes and obviously unaware of the happenings inside the house.

He eyed Ahmed, consternation on his face. His eyes traveled to the gun in Ahmed's hand and surprise registered on his face. With the butt of his gun, Ahmed hit him hard on the head and followed it with a knee in the groin. Rashid let out a loud grunt, doubled over holding his groin and quickly went down. Nothing like surprise to overpower your enemy, Ahmed thought. He dragged him inside the bedroom and tied him to the bed. Before he left, he placed tape on his mouth and hog-tied him.

"One move and I'll waste your buddy next door."

Rashid nodded, his dormant eyes filled with pain and horror.

Ahmed left through the front door and stepped quickly to the street. Outside the world appeared strangely normal, children still played on the dirt street. Across the street, a woman walked out of her house and eyed him, a frown on her face. He forced a smile and nodded. She hesitated then nodded back. She ran after a toddler and quickly yanked him inside the house.

Casually, he walked back to where he had left his car. He looked inside the cafe before he went to his car. The waiter who had given him the address was watching him. Ahmed waived. The man did not respond. Slowly, a frown covered his face then dissolved into surprise and suspicion upon recognizing Ahmed. Minutes earlier, Ahmed had been wearing a djellabah and a hood over his head. The man hurried back inside the cafe and disappeared.

Ahmed drove the three blocks back to the house. He

parked in front of the house and hurried inside. Everything appeared as quiet as he had left it. Nonetheless, he held his gun cocked and ready. He entered Gold Fingers' room. He found him in the same position he had left him. He unlocked the manacles from the bed and immediately snapped his wrists together. He untied his feet while holding the gun to his ribs and lifted him up. The man rose reluctantly. He thrusted him upfront.

"Move, you scum bag, move!" he said.

Gold Fingers shot him a glance, a cobra spitting venom. Reluctantly, he followed and together, they walked out to the bright sunshine. The children broke their game and pulled back. Ahmed shoved him in the backseat and closed the door behind him. The kids formed a ring around the car squealing with delight at the action. He chased them away and went back inside the house to retrieve Rashid.

As he walked back inside the house, he heard a muffled pop and the sound of a door closing.

Gun in hand, he rushed into Rashid's room. He found him slumped in his bed, a trickle of blood running down his right temple. A door slammed. He tore out of the house to a deserted backyard, but there too he found no one. Suddenly, he heard a second pop. He recognized the muffled sound of a gun with a silencer.

He dashed to his car. The kids had disappeared and the car sat alone on the deserted street. Gold Fingers was still in the backseat but when he neared his car, he found him slumped in his seat, a bullet firmly lodged in his forehead, blood running down his face.

"Damn!" he thought.

He crouched near the car, his gun drawn, using the car as a shield. His temples throbbed and his jugular pulsated like a strobe light. He wiped his brow but sweat, icy and hot, gushed under his shirt. His dilated pupils journeyed the length of the narrow alley and houses across the street.

Suddenly, he heard a door slam and a cry. He wheeled in the direction of the noise, hands fully extended in front of him when he noticed a toddler run across his yard squealing with excitement, his mother dashing behind him. Angered, Ahmed lowered his gun. The woman grabbed the kid and ran inside the house.

"Son of a bitch!" He cursed loudly. He was angry with himself for letting the intruder flee. Whoever killed the two had already escaped him, he knew that. Probably jumped the stucco fence and raced through the back street.

He hurried inside the house and ransacked the place. He emptied pockets, rummaged through drawers, turned over mattresses and took anything he thought might be of any usage to him. Gold Fingers' back pocket held a small address book. He opened it. On a torn page, he had written a ten-digit number. Ahmed carefully eyed it and placed the whole book in his shirt pocket. Intuition told him he better keep it.

He retrieved Gold Fingers' body from his car and dragged it back inside the house. He needed to call the local cops, but that would come later. Right now, he just wanted to get out of there and try to sort out this mess. Outside, the street had returned to its stillness. There was no one in sight. Not even a cat or a dog. Just the hard blue sky looming large above his head and the unforgiving southern sun.

CHAPTER THIRTY-SEVEN

She turned her hotel room into a combat zone. Her theater of operations was equipped with the necessary arsenal to conduct her war of nerves—a portable printer, a scanner, a state of the art laptop Martini had been less than happy to invest in, and a 35mm camera with lenses so powerful they could zoom into an eagle's eye in mid-flight.

She downloaded and studied all the materials Ty had sent her. Documents from Las Vegas and Santa Monica included The Torch's marriage certificate and a copy of the court settlement. It was all of the documentation she needed to make and support her case. *Always follow the paper trail and back up your case with hard copy.* Evidence.

She connected to the Internet and waited with much anticipation, her hands trembling with excitement. The little red flag on her mailbox rose up—which meant there was mail for her. There were several mail attachments from Vince—more than enough to serve her purpose. She opened her JPG files and soon the screen filled with the face of a woman and an adolescent. The picture was taken in front of an apartment building. The woman was in her mid- to late thirties and the adolescent was about twelve years old. She appeared tall, with straight hair cut below her ears in a classic bob and the scrubbed look of the girl-next-door.

She wore a tight tee and slim pants that revealed her curves nicely.

The adolescent was of mixed ethnicity. American and Berber. Honey colored with high cheekbones—definitely a Berber trait—and blue eyes. His hair was light golden brown and curly. He dressed like his peers—baggy jeans that rode below his waistline and a large cotton tee with a printed logo. In a close-up shot, she identified the initials A&F. Abercrombie & Fitch. A pricey and popular brand for hip kids.

The next shot was of Christine again. Face and neck. Around her neck, she wore a small cross. Interesting, Kennedy thought. Small detail The Torch's followers will not cherish.

She went back to the boy's close-up—the birth certificate had him listed as Ryan Al Maghrebi Carter. There, right above the A&F logo, hung a tiny cross too. So, she thought, the son of The Torch, descendant of a fierce Moslem purist was having his son raised as a Christian. Raised like the infidels and heathens he and his Islamic fanatics loathed. It may not have mattered to The Torch, but she knew this mattered greatly to his people.

She clicked on her Print icon and photos of Christine and Ryan Carter floated out of her printer like dead leaves in the wind. She gathered her scattered crop, laid it out on the bed, and studied it carefully. She found it peculiar to peer inside The Torch's life feeling like a voyeur, peeking into a life she was not authorized to know anything about. Except, that's what reporters do, she thought. If you wait around for information to come your way, you could wait until the earth stopped rotating around the sun. She was certain she had uncovered The Torch's Achilles' heel. And, she had to admit to herself that she felt a certain glee at finding him out. A gotcha feeling she could not shake. Although it felt like cause for celebration, she knew she needed to temper her elation with reasoning. Could not allow herself to be transported by small victories. Because confidence coupled with carelessness could be deadly. So she brought herself back to the task. Viewing the woman he had chosen as the carrier of his ancestral progeny, she was gleaning facts about him—as both a man and adversary—that had not been revealed publicly. Did his choice of companion reveal more about him? Did he seek a woman that mirrored him, one that complemented him or were they completely different from one another? And what did it say about him?

How strange, she thought, so often one deduces more about a person, not by what they impart us, but by the company they keep and the choices they make.

For a while, she held Christine's picture in her hand, going back and forth between the close-ups and the long shots. She felt an intense desire to know her but cracking the mystery that was The Torch would require more than gazing into Christine's picture, she concluded.

Beside, she thought, how much can be told by a picture? Are the choices we make in clothing telling of whom we are? She recalled that once she had undertaken an exercise for an upcoming article she was writing. A social experiment of sort and if, indeed, as the cliche goes, clothes made the man. Her goal had been to test whether people reacted to her differently because of what she wore. So she donned different clothes, taking on different appearances to make her point. She wore a skimpy dress, a push-up bra, spiked heels, lifted her hair in a soft, sexy do, and trotted to the first bar. Later, she returned to the same place dressed conservative with a stylish, but demure outfit and glasses. As she had predicted, the reaction from both men and women was based on her outward appearance. Albeit dissimilar—men were drawn to the skimpy attire like bees to a flower and women discounted her seriousness. She had been judged by what she wore—supporting her case—that perception was reality. You are what you wear. Our bodies are canvasses, clothes are the paint that goes on our canvas, and the way each one of us paints that canvas is a reflection of the artist we are. She had concluded that people, in most cases, wore their identity on their sleeves. Literally. There was such a thing as looking like a banker, or a lawyer, or a librarian, or an artist.

As she viewed Christine's attire, she noted that she was a woman accustomed to nice things. She guessed she was upper middle class or higher. With education. Probably liberal arts. She exercised and went to the theater. She probably lunched with friends at fancy Westwood cafes everyday, drove an SUV, held a Nordstrom credit card. She smiled when she realized what she was doing. Giving a life to strangers. She often engaged in this exercise. In coffee shops. In parks. Anywhere actually. She gave women husbands, men wives, and lovers to young adults. It had started once on an airplane when she was traveling overseas on one of those long, tiring trips. She had sat across from an intriguing man. Tired of reading and out of boredom, she began her guessing game. Who was he? What did he do for a living? By the time she arrived to her destination, she had assigned him a life, a wife, kids and he no longer seemed alien.

Finally, she selected two pictures of Christine and her son and placed them inside an envelope. Then she made copies of the marriage and birth certificates and added them to the photos. On a sticky note, in large capital letters, she wrote, *Emily—or I go public with this*. She sealed the envelope leaving the outside blank. She called Sami.

She felt uncertain when she hung up. Soon thereafter, a surge of anxiety coursed through her body upon realizing the possible outcome of her actions. She knew that this time the consequences of her actions could turn fatal. She remembered the case of a reporter in Colombia who knew with certainty that naming a drug dealer will result in his death. And it did. Heroes, she thought, rarely change the world. They just die young.

For a fleeting moment, she wanted to backpedal, get out of the deal, run fast, run out of this place, go somewhere safe. Harry had called it a case of David versus what's-his-name. And this David right now felt anything but heroic.

Minutes later, Sami showed up at the door. Her hands quivered when she handed him the envelope. "Submit this to The Torch."

He noticed her seriousness and the tremors in her hands and remained silent. He accepted the package from her and nodded. Instinctively, he understood that she was not in any mood to chat and that the gravity of the moment called for his silence. He left quickly.

She opened the small refrigerator in her room and found mini bottles of liquor. Whiskey. Rum. Gin. White wine. She opted for the least damaging option and settled for white wine. She poured herself a cold glass, opened her balcony door, and sat on a patio chair.

Immediately, her focus changed from The Torch to the city noises drifting from below. She closed her eyes letting the noises fill her while she listened to the life that existed outside of her. Somehow, she found the din comforting and life affirming.

———•◆•———

She was still on her balcony when darkness blanketed the night and the stars, sparse and dim in the January sky, burned dimly. The night air was crisp and smelled of wetness but she hadn't noticed the chill that had descended on the city. She had been lost in her thoughts, in her past, in a universe with The Torch, her life intricately intertwined with his. Like Siamese twins who have no choice but accept each other's existence, clasped together, simultaneously loving it and loathing it.

Theirs was a karmic connection she was trying to comprehend and unravel. She was certain this slow dance with The Torch, this deadly tango belonged to the past. Perhaps, she thought, this incident with him was a way of restoring spiritual justice. And she wondered if she could—this time—extricate herself from his tangle, from this intricate web he had built around her. She did not know. She was not sure. She was only certain that now, more than ever, she was David. David naked and vulnerable. David with nothing more than a little rock in his hand.

When the phone finally rang, she hoped that his verbal assault would not affect her. She wished that, somehow, she could be eased into it, eased into the lynching that was about to commence, allowed a prisoner's last meal with all the deserving respect.

"Miss Hunter?" His voice was firm and commanding.

"Yes."

"I received your last missive," he said. "Impressive detective work, Miss Hunter. Good research. It explains your reputation as a hard-nosed reporter."

She did not reply.

"I propose we meet," he said crisply.

"Alright."

"How about if we meet soon. Real soon."

"O.K.," she said tentatively.

"I'd like to meet you on neutral ground."

"And when and where would that be?"

"Your driver will be told."

"I'd like to know now where I'm going," she replied. "I don't want any surprises."

"There'll be no surprises. Only safety issues with me," he said. "Your driver will inform you on the when and where."

"Alright," she replied, reluctantly. "Sir, let me clarify something. We are meeting for an exchange, nothing else."

"Indeed, Miss Hunter," he said. "An exchange." He chuckled.

The chuckling annoyed her. She did not find it amusing. There was nothing amusing about this situation.

"How do you propose to conduct this exchange?"

"Simple, Miss Hunter. I get the documents, you get the girl."

"I mean, who gets what first?"

"Like I said I get the documents and negatives of photos, you get the girl."

"How about if I get the girl first, then you get the documents," she said. "You know you'll get the documents once I see the girl. You're aware of my professional integrity."

What she wanted to say was, I don't trust you. But she didn't.

"Are you implying that I'm not to be trusted?" he said with scorn.

"No. I'm not implying anything. Just playing it safe," she said. "Just like you do."

"Then, *Au revoir*, Miss Hunter," he said. "We shall meet again."

The line went dead. She plopped in her chair, her hands shaking from the exchange. She reached for her glass of wine and in one big gulp consumed the rest of it.

CHAPTER THIRTY-EIGHT

They left the coastal sand cliffs of the Atlantic and drove first south and then east towards the Great Atlas Mountains. As they dove deeper and farther inside the country's heart, the roads turned dangerously sinuous, the terrain stony and harsh and the altitude rose to nearly 10,000 feet.

Kennedy felt the diminished oxygen in her lungs as they climbed higher and Sami pushed his 4-cylinder car in second gear. The car emitted strangling wheezes as the ascending got harder and the air thinner.

At the foothills, flanked by jagged peaks and mountaintops eroded by wind and rain, the Ourika River flowed through a deep and luscious valley irrigating orchards and winter crops. Hugging the base of the mountains, villages made of mud and rubble stemmed from the alien landscape.

When they reached mid-altitude, the mountains were blanketed with thuja, pine, cedar, and oak trees. Farther, they found thorny xerophytes and junipers growing wild as Barbary sheep roamed the rocky landscape and soaring eagles haunted the mountain range.

At its highest, the vegetation became hardy and sporadic, springing, here and there, from limestone plateaus and alluvial plains.

Finally, they saw the peaks and ridges of the High Atlas capped with snow but as they looked down below, lava from the Jebel Siroua recent volcanic eruptions had blanketed the plateaus with ash.

Arak, a quiet and remote village, spiritual home of Berbers, lay deep in a valley surrounded by a desolate landscape of prickly argan trees and mountainous slopes. Tinted like the mud it spawned from, it melded with the mountains and formed one solid mass against an unblemished blue sky.

Here, during the 12th century, Ibrahim El Maghrebi, nicknamed The Torch, spiritual leader of the Berbers and ancestor of the current Torch, had founded the Almohad Dynasty and conducted his spiritual war against the reigning Sultan. He preached strict adherence to Islam and died for his cause. After his death, the mosque in Arak was built in his honor.

They neared the weather-beaten ramparts of the village. An army of donkeys, saddled with huge cargoes, eyes filled with resignation and sadness trotted by the ramparts. Donkeys in North Africa, Kennedy mused, were the most mistreated of all animals.

Somewhere behind these walls, The Torch and Emily are waiting, she thought.

She had kept quiet for most of the trip, looking inward and rehearsing the last conversation she had had with The Torch.

There were few Berber pilgrims at the entrance of the village. But her mind was crowded with only one Berber, the one who for the past fifteen years, had made her question her vocation and pushed her, more than she could bear, to the threshold of rage.

Now as she stood in the place where he sought spiritual inspiration, she hoped for a closure, a conclusion to the chapter he had written for her and for a complete and final breakup in their deadly alliance.

But she was not sure it would happen. She was not sure of anything relating to him. Certainly not of the bizarre and distorted relationship they had. His profound intellect and persevering character, traits she usually admired in others, terrified her. He was so driven and blinded by his mission, she was certain he would never live to fulfill his promise to his people.

Sami parked his car. He opened the trunk and retrieved a djellabah and a veil.

"Wear this," he said as he handed her the garment. "You're going inside the mosque. This is one of the few mosques where non-Moslems are allowed in."

"So why do I need it if I'm allowed in?"

"I think it's better for you. You'll blend in."

She nodded and thought better than argue with him. She was thinking how the garment would restrict her movements. She slipped it over her clothes and placed the hood over her head. Then she placed the gossamer veil over her face as Sami looked on.

He grinned broadly when he saw the transformation, then laughed aloud.

"What?" she said, "I look funny or something?"

He was laughing hard and shaking his head and that broke the tension she was feeling.

A sheer azure sky blanketed the town and a biting mountain wind hollered over the snow-capped Gourza Mountains.

She grabbed the brown envelope with the documents, placed it under her garment.

"Sami, tell me, it's awful quiet in here. Is it always like this?"

He scanned the place before he replied. "No. Usually there are more people around here."

"Is it some special Moslem holiday?"

"No," he said. "As a matter of fact during holidays there are more people, not less."

"I see. Where is the mosque?"

"Inside the ramparts. We are going to have to walk through the gates first. There are several naves inside."

He pulled a cigarette from his shirt pocket, lit it cupping his hand, and took a long drag. The wind blew the smoke around.

"Have you been here before?"

"*Oui*. Many times." He spun around, his dark eyes roaming across the landscape.

"What's missing?"

"The tourists," he said. "I don't see any."

"What else, Sami?"

"The camel herds in the background. The ones at the foot of the mountains. They're always there."

"So there are no tourists and no locals, right?"

"Right."

"What's going on, Sami?"

"I don't know but I don't like it, *Mademoiselle*."

"Who could orchestrate such a thing? The Torch?"

"Oh, no. These people are not afraid of The Torch. They are Berbers. Just like him."

"Then who else?"

"Others. Enemies of The Torch," he said. "They know something is happening."

"Oh, my God," she said. "Sami, do you have a gun?"

"Yes. Obtained illegally. We are not allowed to own guns in Morocco."

"What's your advice?"

"My advice is to go back, *Mademoiselle*."

"I can't do that, Sami. I told him I'd be here. He's expecting me to deliver something."

"I understand." He was leaning against the car and kicking dirt with one shoe.

She made a quick mental assessment. She'd have to get inside the mosque, get Emily, walk out of the mosque, run to the ramparts and out of the ramparts where Sami would wait. It seemed as if she and Emily would be out in the open for too long—long enough for anything to happen.

"Why is it that he wants to meet inside the mosque?"

"Because he knows it's a holy place and nobody would attempt anything there."

"Why couldn't we meet outside the ramparts instead of inside?"

"Because no one can drive a car inside the walls. There are only narrow dirt alleys. It keeps everybody out."

"Great. That's including me."

"That's the whole idea. You'd have to walk in and walk out. There is no other way of getting in and out."

"Sami, I'm going in anyway."

"I would advise against it," he said. "The eyes of a cop can see things others don't see."

She wheeled around and eyed him. "You're a cop?"

"Used to be. Before my injury."

"You never told me," she said.

"You never asked anything about me."

She let his comment slide. "I want Emily out. I don't care what dispute The Torch has with the authorities. All I want is Emily."

"Of course. And all they want is The Torch."

"Sami, walk with me to the mosque." She stared at him until he looked away.

"O.K. I cannot let you go in alone. I'll go with you."

"Thank you, Sami. Thank you."

He grabbed her hand and together, they crossed the street. They looked just like any other Arab couple—she, with her traditional wear and he, with casual western clothes.

They entered the ramparts and hurried towards the mosque. They strode out of step, his steps longer than hers. She detested the long garment she wore, it slowed her down, and she had broken up in a sweat under the veil. Damn, she thought, what a stupid costume this is.

Her pulse quickened as they neared the mosque. There were no shoes at the front door of the mosque where Moslems customarily leave them. She thought it strange.

"There is nobody in. The mosque is empty," he said. "I don't like this."

"I need to go in, Sami. He has to know I kept my promise."

"*Mademoiselle*, I can't use my gun inside a mosque. It's sacrilegious," he replied, adamantly. "If anything happens, I'd have to let it happen. For either one of us."

They entered a tall arched portico. The mosque had been recently renovated to accommodate the many visitors. Inside, there was a courtyard flanked by more arched entrances. In the center, there was a fountain used for ritual cleansing.

They went inside a vacant prayer hall, the *haram*. It was long and wide and it lead to many outside naves. The central aisle led to niches facing Mecca, the *mihrab*. Walls were decorated with geometric designs and palm motifs favored during the Almohad Dynasty. At the end of the prayer hall, there was the *minbar*, a pulpit used to call the faithful.

The mosque was dim and cool. And strangely quiet. Only the sound of the outside wind could be heard echoing though the walls. Their soft footsteps reverberated throughout the mosque as they tiptoed across the naked floor.

Sami halted and Kennedy did likewise. He pressed her against a column and slid off his shoes. With his eyes, he ordered her to do the same. She did not like the idea but followed suit.

She felt odd about this role reversal. Sami the driver had become Sami the protector. All along, she had known there was more to him. As a driver, he was the Rolls Royce of drivers. The intelligent eyes did not lie. The coy smile hid untold secrets. He had been private and she hadn't pried. All she knew was that he had been extremely efficient and he had means of uncovering anything she needed. He had been the perfect partner and she had come to rely on him for more than just driving. He was better than many of the so-called pros she had worked with. Knowledgeable, accessible, yet, non-intrusive in his demeanor.

Across the hall, rays of light filtered down from the cupolas and formed geometric patterns on the tiled floor.

Suddenly, from a far corner a man appeared dressed in Berber attire. Kennedy elbowed Sami. He put his index on his lips in a keep-quiet gesture.

The man was alone. He looked around as if seeking something or someone. Seconds later, a woman neared him and stood by his side. She too wore Berber attire.

Kennedy's heart leaped. She wanted to tear across the hall but Sami grabbed her arm. "Not yet," he whispered. "Wait!"

She hid behind the column. She yearned to remove the veil so she lifted it over her head. Sami shot her an angry glance.

"Not yet!" he whispered.

Reluctantly, she left it on. The veil was starting to feel like a muzzle.

Sami grabbed her hand and moved out from behind the column. They were now out in the open. They walked across the hall but halfway through, a shot rang out. Startled, she eyed Sami in disbelief. She remembered his comment about the holiness of the place.

They tore across the hall still holding hands. Then more shots rang out. The shots came from a distant nave.

Meanwhile the couple disappeared behind a column. Sudden voices echoed in the hall and the place broke in a tumultuous chaos. From behind columns and out of the many naves, several men appeared.

They did not speak Berber.

When they reached across the hall, she found herself face to face with a man she had seen before.

It wasn't The Torch.

Detective Ahmed grabbed her by the arm. He tore the veil from her face and pulled the hood down.

"Miss Hunter. Finally, we meet."

"Damn!" she replied. "You almost got us killed!"

She was so furiously mad she could have used his gun on him. "Not so, Miss Hunter. The bullets were not intended for you," he said. He led her by the arm. "I believe we need to talk."

Sami interjected. "Detective, I need to take my client back home."

"Not so soon," said Ahmed. "You go on, Sami. I'll make sure your client gets back to her hotel room."

"I will not leave without Miss Hunter," Sami said.

"*T'fadal*. As you wish, Sami. It's your decision to stay or leave, but your client is to remain with me."

"Alright," said Kennedy. She turned to Sami. "I'll stay to talk to detective Ahmed. Where are we going, Detective?"

"To the local police station. There is one around the corner. You need to follow me."

Kennedy eyed Sami. He was not happy about the situation. She touched his arm in reassurance and patted it.

Together they walked out of the mosque. Two additional cops, none in uniform, followed Ahmed.

They walked behind the mosque and into an unpaved alley. They passed few houses and reached a dilapidated commercial building with a grocery store as a front.

They followed Ahmed into the cop shop then entered a room furnished with metal furniture that had seen better days. The man at the desk rose immediately.

"*Salem ya habibi*," the man said to Ahmed. He pointed to the chair inviting him to sit.

The man left the room and Ahmed pulled two more chairs for Kennedy and Sami. The other cops remained outside.

Kennedy spoke first. "Detective, before we get started, would you object if I use your facilities?"

He eyed her suspiciously and then turned to Sami who just shrugged.

"I'm afraid they won't meet your standards, but you're welcome, of course."

She rose. "Where is it at?"

"Outside. The small room behind the building."

She stepped out and walked behind the building. Great, she thought, an outhouse.

She pushed the door open and found herself in total darkness. A swarm of buzzing flies launched at her attacking her face before she adjusted to the surroundings. She groped the walls while her eyes adapted to the dimness, then fumbled for a light switch realizing there was none. She stepped forward, lost her footing, and slid further down. She steadied herself just in time. Finally, she stabilized. The cubicle held a ceramic slab in the shape of two footprints separated by a hole in the ground. An old French squatting toilet, a remnant left from colonial days. Above it, there was a water tank with a pulldown metal chain.

She lifted the envelop from under her garment, tore it in pieces, pulled the chain and watched it all disappear.

When she returned, Sami and Ahmed were in the midst of an animated conversation but halted when she came in.

"Miss Hunter," Ahmed said, "what are you doing in Arak?"

"The same thing you're doing. I'm trying to meet The Torch. And you just blew it for me."

"The Torch, Miss Kennedy, is our problem, not yours."

She took a deep breath. She could feel the blood speeding to her head.

"Detective Ahmed, The Torch may be your problem but Emily Carrington is an American girl and you haven't done a thing to rescue her."

Ahmed's face turned red. He tightened his jaws and she noticed it.

"Miss Hunter, he said, "let me remind you that I have no obligation to inform you on the progress of my investigation." He paused. "But, you," he added, pointing a finger at her, "you're interfering with my investigation and you're neither qualified nor authorized to do so!"

"Perhaps," she replied. "But I have the right to do whatever I can to find a fellow citizen."

Ahmed held a hand upfront in a stopping motion.

"In America, perhaps. But not here. Not in my territory. You'll be wise to tell me what communications you've had with The Torch and what you know of this case."

Kennedy leaned back on her chair, arms folded.

"I'm afraid I'm under no obligation to tell you of anything I know. It's your job to find out."

"Miss Hunter. You're engaging in an illegal activity by refusing to answer my questions and by communicating with a criminal."

Sami interjected and uttered something in Arabic she did not understand. Ahmed replied, anger in his voice.

"Detective Ahmed, I'm a reporter and as such I have the right to investigate as long as I don't break the law."

"You don't have such a right in this country. You'll answer my questions as to what you know about this case."

"I'm afraid not."

"Then I'll have to hold you until you answer my questions."

"O.K.," she said. "As you wish."

Sami's eyes flashed. She could tell he was thinking she had gone mad. He turned to Ahmed spewing words like lava from a volcano.

Ahmed rose from his seat. Sami could hardly contain himself. He pushed back his chair and took Kennedy by the arm. He turned to Ahmed and said, "Can we walk out for a minute, I need to talk to *Mademoiselle*."

Ahmed nodded in approval.

Sami grabbed Kennedy by her elbow and led her out to the street. When they were at a safe distance, he stopped.

"Miss Kennedy, you need to compromise. *Vous avez besoin d'ecouter.*" He was agitated speaking a hybrid of French and English, mixing them both in one sentence.

"Listen, Sami. I will not tell him anything. I'm not going to do his work for him. Let him find out on his own what's going on."

"*Non, non, non.* You don't have to tell him everything. Just give him something to make him happy and we go home."

"How much do I give him?"

"A little. *Juste un petit peu.*"

"Sami, do you think he's stupid? He knows I know a lot and he'd want everything."

"Then give him everything. And let him conduct his investigation."

"Are you nuts? He's only interested in The Torch and the Arab girl. You think Emily is on his agenda?"

Sami turned sullen. "Then you'd have to suffer the consequences of your refusal. I may not be able to negotiate anything for you."

"I know. And I'm willing to see where this will take me."

"*Aye, aye, aye. . .*American women. Just like men." He was nodding in disbelief.

"Let's go in. What's he going to do? Throw me in jail?"

Sami eyed her as if saying, you're damn right.

They walked back in. Ahmed was on the phone, he, too, was agitated. He hung up soon as they walked in.

He repeated, "What brought you to Arak, Miss Kennedy?"

"I was going to meet The Torch, as I said before."

"What for?"

"To get Emily."

"And?"

"And you interfered."

"Why would he return Emily to you?"

"Because."

"Because what?"

"I'm afraid that's all I can say about it."

"Where is the ear?"

"What ear?

"Let us not play games. *The ear*."

"It disappeared from my room."

"The ear is evidence, and for withholding evidence I can throw you in jail, you know that."

"I said I don't have it. Somebody took it out of the refrigerator where I kept it."

"O.K.," he said. He surprised her by giving up easily and switching to another topic. "Then, what do you know about the Arab girl?"

"Nothing."

"Nothing?"

"Yes, nothing."

"Miss Hunter, I advise you to tell me what you know about The Torch's location and this investigation."

"Mr. Ahmed, I have nothing to tell you about The Torch or about Emily."

Ahmed turned around and said something in Arabic to Sami. Sami raised a hand in protest.

Ahmed rose from his seat and came around to Kennedy. He leaned over her chair, his lips so close to her ears she could feel his breath.

"Miss Hunter, I'm afraid I'll have to incarcerate you until you tell me what you know."

Before she responded, he went behind her back and

snapped a set of manacles around her wrists. "Few days in a Moroccan jail might convince you that I'm serious about this."

Sami went ballistic.

"Sami, call Stone," she said, "He's staying at my hotel. He'll know what to do."

"Your embassy won't do a thing for you, Miss Hunter. You're in Morocco and you must adhere to Moroccan laws."

"Detective Ahmed," she said, "I'm going to be such a headache to you, you'd be glad to get rid of me."

"We'll see."

———•◆•———

She convinced herself that it could not be any worse than the thirty days she had spent on a rooftop.

But she wasn't sure.

The cell was icy, dark, and windowless. It was about six feet long and just as wide, and it felt as cavernous as a subterranean dungeon. The uneven dirt floor was hard and bumpy and a stagnant urine and damp odor saturated the air. It hit her nostrils with such force she heaved involuntarily and immediately wondered if she had made a poor decision.

Perhaps, she thought, I should have heeded Sami's warning and compromised with Ahmed. But there was no turning back now, she was irretrievably compromised, uncertain about her immediate future and in no position to negotiate.

A thin mattress rested on the floor. It smelled of dead flowers and cat piss. She ran her hand on the lumpy texture and fell down on it, weary from the journey and the turmoil of the last few hours.

She leaned against the hard cement wall feeling the damp walls behind her, no longer questioning the scarcity of crime in Morocco. Spend sometime in here, she thought, and you'll never want to come back.

She was alone in the prison. She was certain there were men in other cells, but in this corner, she was the only female. She looked out her cell bars and saw a guard in the corridor. A ray of light filtering through a nearby window landed at his feet cutting the fetid air. The mournful sounds of Arabic music rose from his radio and drifted to her cell like smoke from a cigarette.

Distantly, she heard sounds she could not identify. She imagined them to be hollering winds, giggling children, moaning lovers.

Finally, she lay on her mattress. She was still wearing her djellabah, glad she had kept it on. She stuck her cold hands in her pant pockets rummaging through notes and found money. She always kept money in her pockets, which she used for tips—tipping was expected everywhere, even for parking your car on a public street.

She called out to the guard upfront.

"Monsieur! Hello!"

He came rushing. A jittery man with a thin and wiry body and the leathered face of a sheepherder.

"I need a phone!" She put her hand to her ear and formed a phone with her fingers.

"Sh'ouiya," he said, holding his hand up. Calm down. He was not accustomed to seeing foreigners or women in his jail.

"La, la, la!" He refused.

She repeated her demand.

He said something she did not understand but from his demeanor she understood all too well the language of denial.

She dug inside her pocket and retrieved a couple of bills. Through the bars, she handed them to him. He immediately grabbed them and walked back to his spot. He returned with a rotary phone in his hands attached to a very long cord. He handed her the phone and when she grabbed it, his hand touched hers and lingered longer than needed. Her eyes flashed when she looked at him.

She dialed the hotel number and requested Stone's room. He answered immediately.

"Stone, this is Kennedy."

"Hey!" He sensed the urgency in her voice. "Kennedy, what's up? You sound far away. Where are you?"

"In Arak—know where that is?"

"I'm not sure. Where is it?"

"South east. In the Atlas Mountains. Deep inside the country."

"Geez, what are you doing there?"

"I've been incarcerated. I can't explain right now but I need to get out of here."

"What do you need?" His tone turned authoritative.

"The man who threw me in jail is Detective Ahmed in Casablanca. He accuses me of interfering with his investigation. Can you make him believe that you're gonna write something about it . . . you know, he imprisoned a journalist for no apparent reason."

"I see." She could almost hear his thinking. "Well, there definitely is a story there."

"That's the point. I don't want to be the story. I cannot be the story. If I become the story, I'm out of the game. Do everything to keep me out of the paper."

"So you want me to bluff?"

"Exactly." There was a long pause at the other end. "Stone?"

"Yeah, Kennedy. I'll do that. What if he calls my bluff?"

"Then I'll worry about it later."

"O.K. Consider it done."

"Stone, another thing. Could you also alert other reporters at the hotel, you know, to call him for quotes. I don't think he's gonna like the P.R. nightmare this will cause him."

"Easy to do. We'll assault him. At least verbally."

"Thanks, Stone. I owe you one. And if it doesn't work, use any arm-twisting method you want to get me out of here. You have my permission."

"You want me to call your editor?"

"Hell, no! A jail sentence is better than having to deal with him."

"Kennedy?"

"Yeah?"

"How are they treating you?"

"What do you want to know? The jail conditions or the ambiance?"

He chuckled. "I mean, the menu."

Well, she thought, he has a sense of humor even under the most rotten circumstances. "It's probably a la carte. I'll let you know as soon as I'm served my first Cordon Bleu meal."

"Yeah, right. I can imagine."

She hung up feeling energized by the conversation with him.

She slid the phone under the door and leaned back on her mattress. The rays of sunshine that had filtered through the bars had died and an orange glow fell inside the jail.

She shut her eyes and found solace in the sounds that infused the place. Soon, the music from the guard's radio filled her head and body almost to the exclusion of everything else. Berber and Andalusian wails took her on a voyage deep inside herself and she remained there for a long time. How long she did not know but when she opened her eyes, the cell had turned completely dark and the guard was standing with a terra-cotta bowl of *harira* and flat bread in his hand.

"*Kol, kol,*" he said. Eat.

She accepted the bowl from him. Again, he held on to her hand and when she looked in his eyes, she saw unsolicited lust. The soup was thick with ground legumes and lamb. The scent of lamb overwhelmed her but she had been without food for a whole day and this was no time to be finicky. She chewed the bread quietly feeling soon satiated.

The temperature in the cell had dipped, her feet were numb, and the black that surrounded her was as thick as the walls of a fortress. She shivered quietly.

She eyed the guard outside her cell. He was firmly planted in his chair, a half-consumed bottle of wine on his table. His radio played a vivacious tune with tambourines and he was taping on the table.

She tore three buttons from her shirt and crammed them deep inside the keyhole of her cell door. She emptied the content of her *harira* bowl in a corner of the cell, held the bowl between layers of her *djellabah* and split it on her knee in several pieces. She hid the shards under her garment.

Later, the guard showed up with an untreated sheepskin smelling like stale urine, which she placed on her legs and feet. He returned to his spot and turned off his radio.

She listened to the barren silence of the night until sleep baited her, then shut her eyes and surrendered to the lure of darkness.

CHAPTER THIRTY-NINE

"Hello, cowboy!" The high-pitched voice, the flirtatious overtone, and the thick Georgia twang added all to one person only.

Harry smiled. "Well, hello beautiful!"

"Are we still on for that margarita, cowboy?"

"Sure. Why not? Where would you like to have it?"

"Right here in Atlanta, darling, right here."

"Happy to oblige, Ma'am."

"I'll even serve some juicy tidbits with it—"

"What kind of tidbits, Darlene?"

"The kind you can really sink your teeth in." The double-entendres were killing him.

"Aha. I'm dying to know. Are you going to keep me hanging in there till the margarita is served, or you think you can grant me a bite."

"I'll grant you a bite if you promise to show up here for the whole meal, cowboy." The innuendoes, the playfulness. Ah, he thought, Darlene, you are a piece of work.

"It's a deal, I'll fly out A.S.A.P."

"Sitting down, cowboy? Here we go." Her voice lowered to a whisper. "The ole woman kicked the bucket and a will has been filed in court."

"That so? Damn. You know any more than that?"

"Guess what?" She paused. "Well, the heirs are Janet Carrington Fairfax and Emily Carrington. And they inherited the whole kit-and-caboodle."

"How much?"

"Enough to buy the whole state of Georgia."

"Anything else?"

"Of course, cowboy," she said, "Now, hear this. In the event of the death of either one of the sisters, the other one inherits the dough."

"That means if Emily dies, then Janet ends up with the loot."

"Exactly."

"What happens if Janet dies after Emily dies?"

"Well, it just means the playboy will end up with it," she said. "That scoundrel will piss it away like there ain't no tomorrow."

"Wouldn't it be just great for him if they both die?"

"Sure will. He'll just hit the jackpot."

"By golly, some people just have it easy."

"No kidding, cowboy. The rest of us peons have to work for a living."

"Well, Ma'am . . . I mean, Darlene, I can't thank you enough. This is just wonderful information."

"Well, cowboy, don't thank me. Just take me out when you make it down here."

"I shall oblige, Ma'am. It'll be my pleasure. A gentleman's promise."

"Harry?"

"Yeah?'

"Don't y'all say that Virginia is for lovers?"

"Yeah, we sure do. Or at least that's what the state's tourism agency wants us to believe."

"Well, then, I'd love to meet one of them."

"It's a deal, lady," he said. "Georgia is on my mind."

She chuckled at the joke. Boy, he thought, Southerners love clichés. They talked in clichés.

He hung up and immediately dialed Casablanca. He could not wait to tell Kennedy. He let the phone in her room ring ten times. Finally, he left her a message.

He glanced at his watch. It was still very early in the day and he knew he could catch the next flight out of Norfolk to Atlanta. He could be there in one hour. Tempting. But no, he thought, maybe I ought to wait for Kennedy to call back. He quickly calculated. Casablanca was six hours ahead making it late there. Where was Kennedy at this hour, anyway? Where could she be this late at night that she was not in her hotel room?

He was puzzled. Of course, he thought, she could be downstairs at the hotel's pub hanging out with a bunch of reporters. Yeah, that's it. She is probably at the pub.

He picked up his phone and pressed the redial button. This time when he got the concierge, he requested the bar.

A man answered.

"Hello, Monsieur," Harry said, "*Mademoiselle Kennedy, s'il vous plait.*"

Harry heard bar noises in the background.

"*Attendez, s'il-vous-plait.*" Hold, the man said. The man yelled in French. Has anybody seen Kennedy Hunter? The man came back on the line. "*Non, Monsieur. Ca fait trois jours qu'on a pas vu Mademoiselle.*"

It's been three days since Kennedy Hunter had been seen.

Harry thanked the man and hung up. *Three days.* Three days that no one saw her. A lot can happen in three days. One can be dead and decomposed in a lot less time than that.

Suddenly panic gripped him. He was always able to remain calm when it concerned him, but when it came to those he cared about, he was not always in control of his emotions.

Where could she be for three whole days? Let's see. The Torch could have her. The rebels could have her. The police could have her. Damn, the list was unending. Anyone could take a shot at her.

Maybe I ought to call her editor. No. Not a good idea. She hates to be chewed out by Martini. She'll hate it even more if it turns out she is O.K.

Again, he eyed his watch. There was an afternoon flight to Atlanta in an hour. If he hurried, he could make it. He thought that since it was night in Casablanca then perhaps the best thing he could do was get to Atlanta. He was too agitated to remain still. Waiting for the phone to ring was pure agony.

He picked up an overnight bag and filled it with a change of clothing. He heaped Francois' bowl with food and water and headed out the door.

As soon as he got in his SUV, he remembered the cowboy guise. Damn, he thought, the hat. I need the stupid hat. Screw the shoes. I can't handle them sum'bitches.

He dashed back in and picked up the hat. The monstrosity will fit in the overhead compartment.

He drove to the Norfolk airport in less than twenty minutes. He liked that little airport. Never any hassles out of there. Unlike Atlanta's. The airport from hell. Or may be the airport in hell.

———•◆•———

Delta's flight was about to depart. Passengers had already embarked and he was the last one in. He crammed himself into his seat and crammed his new umbilical cord in the overhead compartment. The woman next to him could have used both seats and judging by her expression when she saw him approach, she was just as delighted to share the space with him as he was with her.

Good reciprocal dislike, he thought. From the get go. Now, lady, don't say a word. Just shut up. I'll do what men always do. Roll over and snore.

He arrived just in time for Atlanta's notorious traffic jams to kick off. Getting out of the airport was tantamount to prying the jaws of a dragon.

He reached the 75/85 junction and took it straight out to Highway 400 North. He had no idea why they called it a highway because right now, it was more like a parking lot. Cars piled on for miles on end, inching their way. Slow misery. And if misery loves company, he thought, then I have plenty of it.

Right now, he was cussing himself for not staying in town instead of the suburbs, farther from the action, but nearer to Janet and Darlene. Oh well, he thought, eventually I'll get there. Turn on the radio and chill out. He stumbled onto a radio station named Peach-something-or-other and wondered if there was anything left in Georgia not named after peaches. Atlanta alone had over fifty streets named after peaches. Peachtree this or Peachtree that. Enough to make you hate the damn things.

Finally, he reached the northern suburbs, exited, and sighed heavily. Geez, he thought, I feel sorry for the poor slobs who have to do this everyday.

As soon as he exited the highway, he located his hotel. It was one of those generic ninety-bucks-a-night and all-you-can-eat-breakfast hotels and it suited him just fine.

He pulled into the parking lot. It was past 6p.m. Too late to stop by City Hall and visit Darlene. He was still hoping he would see her—otherwise the evening promised to be as boring as television reruns. At least Darlene was entertaining.

He checked into his room and dialed Darlene's number. She answered the phone as if every caller was a candidate for an amorous relationship.

"Hello." She stretched the second syllable like gum between her lips.

"Hello, Darling," he said, "Where did you say they serve those margaritas?"

"My, my, my . . . you're here?"

"Sure am!"

"By golly! You gotta be the fastest cowboy in this part of the country!" She chuckled like a giddy teenager.

"How 'bout if I pick you up at 8p.m.?"

"Perfect. That'll give me enough time to freshen up."

"Ditto."

———•◆•———

Darlene wore the best get-up she could find in her closet. It was red, with overflowing cleavage, as tight as skin on sausage and rode six inches above her knees. When Harry saw her, he thought, My, my, the wonder of Wonder Bra.

In the dim light of the cantina amid bold, brash colors, salsa on the table and salsa from the loud speakers, Darlene beamed.

Harry could always tell when a woman was falling for him. The blushing, the averted glances, the giggles. The seduction game. It did not matter their age, inside, beat the heart of a little girl. He knew Darlene had a gargantuan crush on him. If he measured her pulse, he was certain he'll discover she suffered from a severe case of circumstantial tachycardia.

He eyed her across the table, a smile on his face. He was thinking, I'm going to break your heart, little girl. Not because I want to but because you are falling, falling, falling.

She grinned back, one eyebrow raised, quizzically.

"So, what's with the Carrington-Fairfax story?"

"What do you wanna know, cowboy?"

"Everything."

"Everything, humm . . . like what?"

"Tell me more about Porter."

"Porter, Porter, Porter. Well, he's slick—"

He interjected. "Oh, I already know that. I mean tell me something I don't know."

"Alright." She looked around the room then whispered. "There are rumors," she lowered her gaze, "you know."

"What kind of rumors?"

"The kind people love to spread. Like sex and money."

"So he's a ladies' man. Everyone knows that. Tell me about the money."

"Now, I heard he's always in debt. Always stranded for money and—get this—lately she's refusing to bail him out from his messes."

Harry nodded. "I see."

"I know this gal who used to work for them and she told me they have huge fights over money. You know, Janet and him."

"I could have guessed that one. He seems to me like he knows how to spend it."

"She spends it too. Did you see them horses? She even got a trainer right there on the premises."

"I didn't know that."

A waiter showed up with another round of margaritas. They waited until he left.

"Next time you go there, Harry," she said, "You need to check out that trainer." She snorted.

"What's with the trainer?"

There was complicity in her eyes. "I wonder who he's there for. Her or him?"

"What do you mean?"

"What I mean, cowboy is—"She picked up her drink and licked the salty rim off her glass. "He's from one of them countries, you know. Dark eyes, dark skin. Black hair. Like an eagle."

"What country is that?"

"You know, where we had that princess of ours." She turned pensive. "Princess Grace, that's it."

"Grace of Monaco?"

"Yeah, Monaco. That's it."

Harry thought for few seconds. Then, it hit him.

"You're sure it's Monaco? Not Morocco?"

"Ain't that the same?"

"No. One is in Europe, the other in North Africa across the continent from Spain."

"Same to me. Sure sound the same."

"So the trainer is from Morocco, huh?"

"Yeah." She raised an eyebrow. "Check him out next time you go there, Harry." She waved her hand in a dismissing manner. "Check him out."

Harry suddenly felt a tingle in his spine. A prehistoric, primitive response, the kind that told him of something amiss. His senses were on full alert now.

"I will," he said. "I will."

"What's said about the man?"

"Well. He goes out to this feed place. The owner tells me he hardly talks. He's strange. Dark. Quiet."

He nodded quietly, churning the tidbits in his head.

The music was so darn loud; it intruded on his thinking process. Finally, he said, "what do you think is going on over there?"

"Ain't Emily in Monaco—or whatever?"

"Sure is."

"Sure smells funny to me, cowboy."

Harry grinned broadly. She was figuring out the whole thing. His purpose in town. His questioning. The paper trail. She probably knew all along what he was doing. Knew it and went along with it. Clever girl. Not so ditzy after all.

"Well, cowboy, you've got your hands full. Money can buy lots of things."

"Including murder?"

"Especially murder."

"Why, Darlene?"

"Greed."

She poked a long nail in her glass and gyrated the ice cubes. "Some people will kill for the five bucks you've got in your pocket, Harry."

"I've got more than that right now in my pocket, so that's makes me a desirable target."

She giggled like a little girl, covering her mouth with her hand.

"Who you're working for, Harry?" The smile had vanished replaced by an uncharacteristic seriousness.

"I'm self-*unemployed*, Darlene."

She loved the joke and burst in laughter. "Now, now, now, cowboy." Her tone turned cajoling. "I can spot a liar miles away and I know I've got one right under my nose."

"Me, a liar? Never. I only lie about being a liar."

"So why would you need to know all of that? You know Emily or something?"

"It's the something, Darlene."

"You're not gonna tell me?"

He got up and she followed suit.

"I'll tell you later. When it's all quiet. A lot quieter."

A smile, coy and knowing, covered her face.

He held her by the arm and they exited into the night.

———— •◆• ————

He awakened in his hotel room with a slamming headache. The margaritas were followed with red wine and none of it went too well with him. Maybe what they say about mixing liquor is true, he thought. He went into the shower and stayed under the cool water for a long time. Then he downed a cup of coffee and got dressed.

It was ten-thirty a.m. Good time to call Janet, he thought, Porter should already be on his way to his trading post.

He called her number and the Hispanic housekeeper responded. Janet was out in the dressage ring and there was no way to reach her. Perhaps he could call back later. No, he thought, I'll just drive there.

He remembered to don his usual costume and drove to Beaumont Estates. He parked his vehicle in the sweeping driveway and walked straight back to the dressage area. Janet was on a chestnut horse guiding him through steps, her attention completely focused on the horse. She was so achingly beautiful, Harry watched her spellbound.

She turned around and noticed the man with the cowboy hat. Seemingly surprised, she waved at him then guided her horse to where Harry stood. She descended from her horse.

"Well, Harry! What a pleasant surprise!"

"Ma'am," he said raising his hat, "I apologize for showing up without notice but—"

"Oh no, it's fine. Don't worry about it. I'm glad you came."

He removed his hat. She took off her gloves then shook his hand.

"Thought maybe I'd say hello since I was in the area."

They walked up to the porch.

"Please sit down, Harry."

"Thank you, Ma'am." He placed his hat on the table in front of him.

"What are you doing in town, Harry?"

"I'm back in Dahlonega for some horse trading."

She beamed. "Well, good place for it, Harry."

"And how have you been, Ma'am?"

Her smile flickered. "Oh, Harry, you can call me Janet, you know that."

"Well, yeah, Ma'am."

"Actually, things have not been so good. My dear mother passed away. And, as you know—"

"I'm sorry to hear about Mrs. Carrington's passing. My condolences, Ma'am"

"Thank you, Harry. It's been expected for a while now. It was a matter of time."

"Yes, I know."

"And as you already know no word yet from Emily."

He just nodded then, "and how is Porter doing?"

"Oh," she said as if she had forgotten of his existence. "Yeah, Porter. Well, Porter is up to whatever Porter is always up to. Come to think of it, I don't really know."

She seemed eager to change the topic. "Harry, forgive me, I'm so distracted! Would you like something to drink? How about coffee or ice tea?"

"Sure, Ma'am."

"Let me call Maria."

She went inside the house. He heard her call the housekeeper then she returned to the patio.

"That's a beautiful horse you rode there."

"Yes, it is. It's—"

"I did not see him last time I was here."

"No, you didn't. Come to think of it, you hardly saw any of my horses."

"True."

"Well, then maybe we will now. As a matter of fact while Maria is getting us some coffee."

"Would love to."

They crossed over to the dressage ring and walked the distance to the barn. Inside there were several stalls and five horses. Maroc, Emily's horse and Tennessee Williams stood side by side.

"Ah!" he said, "I see Maroc and Tennessee Williams are here!"

"Oh, you remember their names."

From behind the barn, Harry saw the silhouette of a man.

"Ah," she said, "let me introduce you to my horse train-er. Here he is."

"Wahid," she called, "come and meet my friend Harry. He's also a horse lover." She turned to Harry. "Wahid is from Casablanca."

The man neared them. He was hawk-faced, bow-legged and with the lean body of a jockey. Dressed in a rider's hat, tall boots, and a polo shirt, he held a saddle in his hands that he dropped on the floor. His handshake was solid, his eyes hard.

"A fellow horseman!" Harry said.

The man only nodded. Then he picked up his saddle, ex-cused himself, and walked away. Harry watched him go inside a barn.

"How did you come to have a Moroccan horse trainer?"

"They have a great tradition of horse training and rid-ing," she said. "Porter was there to visit Emily and that's when he thought about hiring one from there."

"I see."

"Wahid does a wonderful job. A loyal and hard working employee."

"A quiet man."

"Yes, he is."

"Looks mysterious."

"Yes, indeed." She spun around. "Very perceptive of you, Harry. Arab men are not as ebullient as we are. But he's particularly quiet."

Together they walked out of the barn and he followed her into the dressage ring. A pale sun filled the morning sky and the air smelled of horse manure and freshly mowed grass.

"Does he live on the premises?"

"Oh, yes. Right there in the small guest house." She pointed in the direction of the barn and right behind it there was a small building.

"Harry, would you stay for lunch?"

He lifted his hat. "Thank you, Ma'am. I'm afraid I'll have to be on my way."

Her composure changed and her face registered a hint of disappointment. It made him want to stay but he knew it was time for him to leave.

"Sorry about that. I wish you could stay. Porter won't be home until late tonight. Where are you staying, Harry?"

"Oh, right here in town. That first hotel right off Georgia 400."

They shook hands and she walked him to his car.

He drove out of the estate, circled the road, and went straight to the backside of the estate behind the barn. Privets and various evergreens protruded behind a tall brick fence where he located the back of the barn and the guesthouse. He parked his car at the curbside and looked around. It was mid-day and the street was deserted. He saw no one.

He opened his trunk and took out a camera with a long lens and a pair of binoculars. He slid both around his neck. Then he held his binoculars on the barn.

As he scanned the landscape, the Arab came into the picture. He was standing behind the barn, cell phone in hand and talking into it.

The Arab looked straight ahead as if he was looking at Harry and for a moment, Harry thought the man had detected him. But then he turned his head and pursued his conversation on the phone.

Harry held his camera and adjusted his close up lens. The Arab's face came into sharp focus. F5.6, one-eight of a second. *Click. Click. Click.*

Satisfied, Harry walked away from the fence and got back into his car. A sense of urgency filled him as he drove off. Emily, he thought, hang in there. We may be closer to finding out what really happened to you.

When he opened his door, he was truly surprised to see her there, not expecting any visitor at his hotel room and certainly not her.

She appeared at Harry's doorstep in full equestrian regalia. Janet Carrington Fairfax was in jodhpurs, tall boots, and a Ralph Lauren shirt tucked inside her pants. Her face was grim as if she had cried and Harry noticed she was slightly inebriated.

She came in, awkward, full of self-consciousness.

"Please come on in," he said, not knowing exactly what to make of it.

"Oh, Harry," she said, "I hope you're not expecting anybody."

"No," he said, "come on in, I do not expect anybody."

"When are you leaving for Virginia Beach?" she said, scanning the room. She was filling the silence with words trying to erase the awkwardness of the moment.

"Tomorrow morning, first flight out of Atlanta."

She sat at the edge of his bed, looking down at her soiled boots, then suddenly, she exploded in tears.

"Oh, Harry, I'm so sorry! I'm behaving like a little girl. I'm so sorry." She sniffed and pulled out a Kleenex out of her pocket.

He neared her. "No, it's O.K.," he said, "don't worry about it. It's fine."

"I'm so miserable!" she said, "and there is no one to talk to. Just no one." She hid her face between her hands.

He grabbed her hands and raised her chin towards him. "You'll be fine."

"What do I do, Harry? What do I do?"

"Things will work out, you'll see." He was trying to comfort her, feeling awkward, not knowing what or where his boundaries were.

"Oh, I'm so alone. I miss Emily so much. Mother is gone. Porter is never there." She opened her eyes and looked at him.

She is so beautiful, he thought, as beautiful on the inside and she was on the outside and I could spend the rest of my life getting lost in the azure of her eyes. Like gazing into the bottom of the ocean. He gently wiped her tears. She held on to his hand, turning it over and filling the back of it with soft kisses. He did not resist. He responded by kissing her gently on the lips, kissing her face, her eyes, her forehead. She reacted by closing her eyes and letting him travel the contour of her face. His lips reached her ears and she shuddered when his tongue followed her neck down to that nameless little dip at the back of her neck where he lingered. And that moment, he knew that he could not stop. He could not let her go. He had to have her whole, in her entirety, without reservations. The floodgates opened and he let go of all constraints filling himself with her body, drinking her like a tall cool drink on a hot summer day.

CHAPTER FORTY

Sometime during the night, she heard noises that awakened her. She felt heavy and weary as she opened her eyes to the sound of metal chaffing against metal. At first, the noises were faint, then they escalated, as the intruder grew more impatient.

In the dark, she saw the silhouette of a man standing in front of her cell manipulating a key into the keyhole. He inserted his key repeatedly before he realized the keyhole was jammed.

He rattled the door with both hands. Back and forth, back and forth. *Clang! Clang! Clang!*

The din resonated in the night and reverberated throughout the place like church bells in a ghost town.

She pressed herself against the cell wall as he went on with his relentless thrusting.

"*Heil el bab!*" Open the door, he cried.

She ignored his cries, which raised his ire even more.

But he continued pushing and slamming and hitting, and crying and by now, she had her hands to her ears trying to mitigate the assault on her senses.

Finally, she rose from her mattress and walked the distance to the door.

"*O.K.! O.K.!*"

In the darkness of the cell and with just a glint of light crossing his face, she saw a glimmer of lust in his eyes coupled with rage. Instinctively, she knew this was not just carnal hunger. This, she thought, was the face of uncontrolled savagery.

She neared the metal bars and he reached out and grabbed her.

She let him.

His fingers were slim and bony and moved with quick dexterity, grabbing and tugging and pushing and shoving.

She let him.

Then his hands reached around her waist and he slammed her hard against the cold metal bars and against him. She smelled him, hot, heavy, booze and hashish.

His nervous fingers traveled the length of her garment, down around her hips feverishly seeking, fumbling as he reached between her legs.

She let him.

With his tongue drooling like a dog's, his mouth feverishly traveled her neck seeking hers. At that moment, with his face so close to hers, she raised her hand from under her garment and with one swift motion, slashed the side of his face with a razor-sharp shard. She felt the soft flesh tear under her fingers.

Wounded, he cried like a hunted prey, doubled over and left the cell cradling his face in his hands.

"Putaine! Putaine Americaine!" Whore, he called her.

He scurried to his post and she heard him moan and curse and wondered if she had, unwittingly, exacerbated her situation.

She huddled on her mattress and for a while, she trembled in the dark, alternating between chills and sweats. Cold and fear occupied her mind and she found herself unable to focus on anything else.

He stopped moaning and total silence filled the jail. For a

while, she welcomed the quiet then realized it was too quiet, too eerie. It was as if he had vanished from the place and that frightened her even more.

Her eyes pierced the blackness around and beyond her but all she saw was a curtain of blackness. Then she closed her eyes and let her mind focus on the smallest of noises but then too, she heard nothing.

Suddenly, she turned tense. She did not like the stillness and dread filled her. The lub-dub of her heart echoed in her chest cavity hammering at her throat and temples.

Dear God, come *to the rescue.*

She neared the cell door. Briefly, she held on to the bars and scanned the space.

Seconds later, she felt it.

Then she saw it.

Sonofabitch.

It had traveled up her shoe and was now making its way up her leg. Its shiny orange coat glistened in the dark, the scissor-like claws opened and closed as it moved up her garment, slow as phlegm on a cold winter day. A Languedoc scorpion, deadly creature of the desert, feared by the fiercest of desert people.

One sudden move and you're dead, she told herself.

She wondered if scorpions could smell fear. Because if they did, she might as well say her final prayer.

With a broken shard still in hand, she stooped down, ever slowly, her eyes never leaving the scorpion. She halted. Suddenly, in mid-air he stopped his upward march. Then she did something so daring it bordered on insanity. But she felt she had no choice. It was do or die. She held the shard in front of him touting him and hoping he would take the bait. And he did. He pursued it like a dangling carrot as she guided him away from her garment. He followed her hand like a domesticated pet down to the floor.

She exhaled hard.

Monique Williams

Then she threw the shard under the door a distance away from her hoping he would continue to pursue it. He did.

Slowly, she moved backward one step at the time until she was completely away from him. She slumped on her mattress, her eyes firmly fixed on the scorpion as he traveled in the opposite direction and away from her.

Depleted from any residual strength she had, she lifted her thin mattress and used it as a shield behind which she hid. Who knew how many more scorpions roamed in her cell.

She remained on the hard naked floor until the night veil rose and the delineation of objects around her became sharp and clear.

At last, she heard voices followed by the clanging of metal doors. She quickly rose up.

Ahmed walked in followed by Sami. No sign of the guard. They spoke in loud voices but halted when they reached her cell.

"Miss Hunter," Ahmed said, "you're free to leave the area." His face registered anger coupled with impatience.

Sami stood by, a winning smile on his face.

"You're free to leave. For the moment. But you're not free of me—yet," he added.

Kennedy didn't respond. She wasn't going to jeopardize her position.

Ahmed inserted his key into the door and turned it. The door did not yield.

"You can't open it," Kennedy said, "the keyhole is jammed."

"Who jammed it and why?"

"I did. And you know why."

He did not reply. He looked over at Sami.

"Sami, get me a pry bar from the outside."

Sami hurried out and immediately returned with a pry bar in hand.

The detective grabbed it, placed it behind the bars, and in one quick move snapped the lock open.

The door opened and Kennedy walked out. Sami grabbed her by the arm and together, they walked out into a clear crisp day.

The snappy mountain air swelled her garment and made her shiver. But Kennedy did not care. She was free. And for a moment, she recalled that day on the rooftop, when The Torch had freed her, when she had walked out into the fresh spring air, when he had thrown her into the sea of life.

They walked to their car parked outside the walls. Ahmed followed. Sami opened the door for Kennedy.

"Mr. Ahmed," she said, "if you want to find Emily, you need to go after Brent Seymour. I'm certain you'll find your answers right there."

He canvassed her face, a look of consternation on his, then nodded.

———— •◆• ————

They drove off leaving him standing by the sidewalk. When she looked back, he was still standing, his hair disheveled by the strong wind, a solitary figure in the early morning glow of the Atlas Mountains.

"Sami, who got me out?"

"Stone. And other reporters. He told me."

"I'm glad." She paused lost in her thoughts. "What happened there Sami, with The Torch."

"Somehow Ahmed knew of this meeting. And The Torch knew it was a trap."

"Who do you think tipped off The Torch?"

"First, who tipped off Ahmed, and second who tipped off The Torch that Ahmed was on to him?"

"Yeah. More than one question here. Like most of this story. Many questions."

Sami looked in his rearview mirror. "Tell me," he said, "Brent Seymour, what do you think he knows?"

"Something. I don't know what but if I sic the detective on him, I might get some answers from him."

He grinned. "I see. You want Ahmed to do your work for you."

"Yeah, kinda. I think he can scare Brent a lot more than I can."

He put an index to his temple. "Good thinking, *Mademoiselle*. Good thinking."

In the mirror, she saw the sparkle in his eyes.

For a long time they drove in silence. Her mind drifted as she attempted to put the pieces together. She was following the string she had unraveled, systematically. She needed it to lead her to a conclusion. And she yearned to see it unfold. But she could not see the total picture. Not yet. There were too many blind spots. Something she, as a reporter, was not accustomed to dealing with. There is a certain order, a method, a system for writing articles that worked for her. She always started with interviews, gathered facts, then put the whole thing together, piece-by-piece, interlocking facts and quotes, stacking up her story like a pyramid. Here, there were few facts. Many guesses. And lots of visceral responses. She told herself that she needed to go back to basics. Start from the beginning. Work slowly with the facts then add to them. Build your case.

Right now her mind was in no shape to cooperate. Fatigue, of body and mind, permeated her entirely and she found herself fighting the cobwebs clouding her mind. Finally, she relented and closed her eyes. She immediately fell into a deep slumber.

When she awoke, they had already reached Casablanca. It was only late afternoon, but she felt as if she had been up a long time. Her body ached and all she wanted to do was reach her room and her bed. It had only been three days since she had left the hotel but at this moment, it seemed like an eternity.

They reached her hotel and before she went in, she removed her garment. In her room, she found her telephone lights blinking. She listened to her messages.

"Kennedy, it's me, Harry. Where are you? Call me, I have loads of information for you." Beep.

"Kennedy, this is Martini. Where's the follow I asked for? What's going on over there? Call me. Urgent." Beep.

She listened to the last call.

"Miss Hunter, this is The Torch." The voice was hard and the message curt. "You have betrayed me. You should have known that I would take the necessary precautions before I'd meet with you. I will not trust you again! There will be no negotiating this time." There was a brief pause, then, "the only way you'll get Emily is if you publish my manifesto. Period. And tell that to your chairman!"

She slumped on her bed. Good, she thought, for sure I have managed to anger everybody. An equal opportunity offender.

———— • ◆ • ————

She opened her eyes to a pitch-dark room. For a moment, she forgot where she was and found herself trying to remember the circumstances of her life. She was unable to neither coordinate her movements nor organize her thoughts. Then she remembered.

She had been gone but she was back to where it was safe or at least safer. She was no longer in a jailhouse, this room was her room with her belongings, and all the accoutrements she was accustomed to.

She remained in her bed for a while delaying the inescapable. Accountability to Martini was weighing on her mind. She wished he'd just leave her alone. Let her do her job. Let her follow this story without standing over her shoulder. But then she thought, that's what editors do. Reporters were like kites in the sky and editors were the ones down on the ground, pulling the string, controlling the movement and making sure everyone flew on course.

The lights on her phone were still blinking. Time to face the music.

I'll start with Harry, she thought. It was still early in Virginia Beach. Harry should be home.

"Kennedy, you had me worried! Where were you in the last few days?"

"In jail, Harry."

"You're kidding?"

"No. The detective on this case put me there, Harry. It's a long story, but tell me, Harry, what do you have?"

"I think I have the link to Emily's disappearance."

"Oh. And what's that?"

He explained Porter's love of money, Janet's inheritance.

"So, Harry, it seems to me they have the usual rich people's fight over who is going to inherit what."

"There is more, Ken. They have a horse trainer from Morocco. An Arab."

"Interesting. I'm assuming you think there is a connection there."

"I'm certain there is."

"Don't be so certain, Harry. They could just like Moroccan horse trainers. They are known for their expertise with horses."

"Ken, it's not a coincidence!"

"You mean to tell me that The Torch doesn't have Emily?"

"I'm telling you that there might be another explanation to her disappearance."

"If Porter wanted the money then all he had to do is bump her off—but we don't have a body. So Emily could be alive. And without a body Porter could not get any money."

"What are you saying, Ken?"

"Harry, I'm saying that without a body inheritance is impossible. U.S law says that without a body one has to wait seven years before they can touch any money. Simply put, neither Porter nor Janet can touch the money for seven years."

"So you think it's not Porter."

"Of course not. All Porter had to do was get her killed and produce a body. And he has done neither. That's my logic, Harry."

"Ken, from here things look different, I tell you."

"Maybe. But I feel The Torch has her. I'm certain he has her. Otherwise why would he be pulling these stunts with me?"

"For his cause. You forget he has an agenda. But Porter has all the reasons in the world to get her bumped off. There is so much money involved, you have no idea." He paused briefly. "Ken, my instincts are good about this one. The alliance between Porter and the Arab stinks."

She exhaled heavily. "Harry, I think you're misguided. You might be seeing things that don't exist. True that—"

"True that money is the best reason to kill. Ken, this old dog is sniffing something. Don't discount it."

"I'm not discounting it. I just think that I'm better off pursuing the real culprit. Not an imaginary one."

"Alright. Then, at least look at the picture of the trainer. I'm sending it for you. And, do me a favor, find out who he is and what his connection to Porter is."

"I will, Harry. Soon as I have The Torch off my back. And Martini."

"Apropos, when I'm going to see your byline?"

"When I pen something."

"A little testy, huh?"

"Sorry, Harry. Don't mean to be. I'm very tired, I guess."

"Are you gonna tell me what you did in a Moroccan jail for three days?"

"I taught a scorpion how to do tricks. You know, roll over, turn flips."

"Cute, Ken. I guess I'll hear it all when you get back."

"Ad nauseaum. I promise."

He hung up. On with the show, she thought. Next, Martini's turn. She called the newsroom number.

"Ah! The Princess of the Desert is finally calling! he said. "What took you so long?"

"John, I was incarcerated."

"What laws did you break that you ended up in the slammer?"

"I did not break any laws. I was just doing my job and sometimes doing your job can get you in trouble."

"You care to elaborate, Kennedy?"

"Where do I start?"

"Try the beginning. It always works."

"John, don't be so damn sarcastic. I'm not exactly doing fashion reportage from Paris."

"Alright, alright. Don't be so damn sensitive." He paused. "What do you have for me, anyway?"

"I don't have a story, if that's what you're asking."

"It is what I'm asking. How come you don't have one?"

"I don't have one because I have nothing new to report."

"Then tell me what you have and I'll tell you whether there is a story there or not."

She hated it when he cornered her.

"I had arranged a meeting with The Torch. He was supposed to deliver Emily in exchange for information."

"What kind of information?"

"Skeletons."

"You mean extortion."

"I call it exchange."

"Semantics, Kennedy. Just semantics. It's blackmail any way you slice it."

"Excuse me, John. What do you think he's doing? Playing

hide-and-seek? I went for the exchange and there was an ambush from local authorities. So the exchange did not happen."

"So where do you stand right now?"

"He thinks I set him up. His last communiqué was that he wants his manifesto published."

"Did you set him up?"

"Hell, no, John. I wanted Emily!"

"So, what now, Kennedy? Where does this story go? We are firm on not publishing the manifesto."

"Give me some time, John. I need to re-establish my connection with the man."

"How much time do you need, Kennedy?"

"As long as it takes. People do not hurry in this part of the world. Time is irrelevant to them. I can't ask them to play by my rules, you know that."

"O.K., Kennedy. I'll give you more time but you are going to have to start playing by my rules here."

Without any further explanations, he hung up.

Jerk.

———•◆•———

She turned on her television to CNN International. Christina Riley was filing her story from Casablanca. Oh well, Kennedy thought, the wolf pack is closing in for the kill. She wondered what CNN's sources were and what story they pursued. If Riley was there, then she had a story. Without sources, journalism withered and died. Sources were the spring from which journalism drank.

Instantly, she was filled with doubt and began weighing her decision to withhold information from Martini. Her competitive juices were flowing and she felt a tinge of envy she was unable to suppress. I should have given Martini his thirty or forty inches, she thought.

Finally, she decided that she should not worry about the

competition. She was ahead of the pack. Unless of course, The Torch decided to tell his story to somebody else. Somebody with a higher recognition factor than Kennedy's. Somebody like Riley.

Still, she could not rid herself of the sense of appropriation she had developed towards Emily. And because of it, she felt a rising sentiment of loathing for herself and for falling into the mindset of the competition.

She reminded herself that this was not just a story. This was about Emily. A real person. Not just a story.

She was weary of the paramount importance journalists attributed to a story. It's the story that sold newspapers. The more outrageous the story was, the more it sold. But there always was a person behind that story and the story always trumped the person. But the person often got hurt in the media blitz that followed a story and the public flogging that ensued. But no one stopped and thought about the person. Not even journalists who separate themselves from the person and manage to insulate themselves from the reality. It was always easier to walk away from a story. Easier than walking away from a face.

CHAPTER FORTY-ONE

Twilight blanketed the sky and a gossamer mist floated above the city forecasting a gray and gloomy tomorrow as Kennedy watched from her window a feverish city approach its quotidian night pause.

She listened to the continuous hum seeping through her shutters while pondering the vicissitudes of the past three days. After much reflection, she concluded that tonight she did not possess the visceral fortitude or the appetite to deal with The Torch. His message had been clear but she would make him wait for a response—she was not ready to submit to his predictable tirade.

Instead, she opted for a decidedly more pleasant evening. She hopped in the shower and lingered washing off the unpleasantness of the day. She applied make-up on her face, slipped on baggy pants and an oversized shirt and went down to the bar.

The bar was mostly filled with men. There were few women and Kennedy recognized them as female correspondents with various media outlets.

When she walked in, several heads spun around. Smiles welcomed her as she moved in the room shaking hands with the reporters who had freed her from the nightmare that was Arak.

She heard her name cried aloud and immediately recognized Stone's voice.

He waved her to his post at the counter.

"Kennedy!" He rose from his seat and hugged her. "Glad to see you back. Come and join me for a drink!"

She ordered a pastis, which he found amusing and sat on the stool next to his.

"Well, how was Arak?" His smile was warm and his eyes glimmered in the dim room.

"First, let me thank you for getting me out of that jam. I owe you one."

He nodded then grinned.

"And to answer your question—it would have been a total success if I had achieved my objective."

"Which was?"

"To get Emily, you know that."

"How were you going to do that?"

"I was supposed to meet with The Torch."

He gave her an evasive smile. "You know, everybody is dying to talk or meet with the man and you're the only one who manages to do so." He paused. "What's your secret, Kennedy?"

She chuckled. "Secret? Are you kidding? No secret. We two have a history together as I told you last time. We waltz together, him and I."

"Sometimes when people waltz together they step on each other's toes."

"We've been doing more than that. Sometimes I think I'm going to get trampled on."

"Humm." He leaned over on the counter, his face so close she smelled his Polo aftershave. "Since you owe me one, how do I get an interview?"

She glanced his way and noted he was serious.

He pressed. "I need a contact."

"Stone, I have an adversary relationship with The Torch.

My relationship isn't one of mutual admiration." She leaned back. "In fact, mine is dangerously confrontational."

"I wouldn't mind a little bit of confrontation right now. I might even welcome it—considering that rigor mortis has settled in my writing."

"Rigor mortis?"

"Yeah, dead. Like a stiff."

She guffawed and he joined in. "What's everybody doing?"

"Everybody is scrambling for stories. Even CNN is here."

"What do they have?"

"Nothing. I hear they have more than we do. Of course, sources like talking to them because of their status. They can scoop us all."

"What are they after?"

"They're after anything they can get. You know, The Torch, the girl. Whatever."

"We are all after the same story."

"Of course," he said, "Emily is a *cause célèbre* and you're the woman with the goods."

He raised a glass. "Here is to you Kennedy. For being the woman everybody loves to hate."

She raised her glass. "Cheers."

He brandished an empty glass in the air and flagged a waiter. The waiter sauntered towards them and they waited until he filled their glasses.

"So what do you say, Kennedy. Are you gonna get me that interview?" He grabbed her sleeve and pulled it in a mocking manner. "Come on!"

"Stone, seriously now. I don't even know what I have."

"Can I get something? Just something. Crumbs, any-thing. I love leftovers."

"Stone, you know damn well that this business is all about being first. Being second doesn't count."

"I do have something though." His face turned serious and his tone was no longer playful.

"What do you have?"

"I checked a few of my stateside sources and found out some things about him."

Her eyes flashed. "And what's that?"

"You probably have the same information. I could run with it and see where it takes me."

She did not know if he was bluffing but if he had something and ran with it, she would lose the only bargaining chip she had with The Torch. And with Martini.

"And why don't you?" she said, confidently.

"Because I want to have more. I need quotes. Not just facts. Without quotes from the man, it would make a lousy article." He studied her face. "To be honest, Kennedy, I want the man. Or the girl. Or the manifesto. Very, very badly." He put strong emphasis on the word very. "And you have all three."

She returned his piercing gaze. "I'll make a deal with you, Stone."

He raised an eyebrow quizzically. "Yeah?"

"I'll let you in on all of it when I get the girl. You'll be the first one to know it all. If—"

"If what?"

"If you hold on to what you have on the man." She knew she had asked a nearly impossible thing for a journalist to do. First, he would have to hold back information and second, he would have to trust that she would give him the information he needs.

He paused while considering her offer. And then he said, "Why would I do that?"

"For Emily's sake. And safety."

He cracked a smile. "Social accountability. Practicing your trade with a conscience. Some people would say that that in itself is an oxymoron."

"I hope that I haven't lost my sense of responsibility," she said. "It's been a long time since any of us shoved a microphone in somebody's face and asked, *How do you feel about it, Ma'am.*" Kennedy was referring to the insensitive practice of pursuing victims for a quote. "Stone, I don't want to practice vulture journalism. I would rather give up on the profession than stoop so low."

He nodded imperceptibly. "I understand. So when would I get my cut?"

"Right after my editor gets the first crack. After I publish the whole story. I might even manage to get you an interview with the girl. Exclusive."

"Can I get everything same time your editor does?"

"Are you nuts? Over my dead body!"

"Don't tempt me. I've been getting homicidal since I came here."

He was grinning now, a glimmer in his eyes.

"What else do you want, Stone?"

Immediately, she realized what she said. He burst out in laughter then threw his hands up in the air.

"Your live body!"

"You can't see it in this dark room but I'm blushing."

He reached out and held her hand. She responded with an assenting smile. There was so much static between them, they were like two magnets fighting the natural pull that drew them together.

She eyed him and wondered about him. She realized she knew little about his life. His real life. Not the intellectual world he allowed everyone to see, but his inner core. Was he a passionate participant of life or a mere highbrow observer? Would he jump in with both feet when needed or just dip in his toe to test the temperature? She wondered.

He was a book she wanted to open. She wanted to read the pages as fast as she could and immerse herself in his story wholeheartedly.

"Kennedy?"

"Yeah?"

"How about a stroll down the promenade? The night is beautiful."

She slid out of her chair and brushed him slightly. She felt a frisson travel her body and when their eyes met. She knew that her life would be intrinsically tied to his.

CHAPTER FORTY-TWO

When he returned from his morning classes at the college, Brent Seymour noticed two men in front of his apartment building. Something about cops made them easily identifiable. Their eyes darted, their bodies moved swiftly, and a general nervousness gave them away. They leaned against a wall, their eyes hidden behind wrap-around glasses, scanning the moving crowd while chewing gum. They mirrored each other, even their chewing was in harmony.

Ever since Kennedy Hunter began investigating Emily's disappearance, Brent Seymour felt nothing but a rising sense of apprehension. He knew that eventually they would come for him. He didn't know when but he sensed that Kennedy Hunter was not the kind of woman one could easily dismiss.

There was something about her, he thought, that was unnerving. Perhaps it was the steely eyes, which never blinked when she asked her questions, or the way she held her gaze until he shrunk, but Kennedy Hunter made him feel diminished, small, inconsequential. He understood why she was considered a cracker-jack reporter. She dogged you until you surrendered.

Although he had maintained a detached posture the first time she came questioning him, he was certain that eventually she'd be back. She'd find a way to get under his skin. Strangely, he was more anxious about her than he was about the local cops. They could easily be persuaded or bribed and had no interest in meddling with foreigners who resided in the country.

Kennedy Hunter was, in Brent Seymour's rather inflated opinion, a woman who could move mountains. And if not completely move them, then, surely, she could shake them. He expected to see her at his door anytime now.

Since her last visit, Brent had maintained vigil of his apartment watching carefully for her or detective Ahmed. He needed to avoid both at all cost. Either one will spell nothing but trouble for him.

Now he was rewarded for his prudence.

From across the street, hidden behind the human traffic, he eyed the two men then fled in the opposite direction mingling with pedestrians and disappearing into a sea of bodies.

He walked rapidly, heart pounding, and when his legs began to ache, slowed down to a stroll. At a neighborhood park, he halted his march, his head filled with thoughts that bounced around helter-skelter. Children played noisily but he paid attention to no one. His mind was preoccupied with the events in his life. He needed to think quickly. And act even quicker. There was no going back to his apartment. He knew he should stay away. No good could come out of his encounter with the cops.

He pulled his cell, punched a number and waited nervously.

Morgan Taylor responded. He felt immediate relief.

"Morgan, this is Brent. I need your help."

"Brent, what's happening?" She noted his spasmodic breathing. "Are you in some kind of trouble?"

"Yes and no. No, I'm not in trouble but I have to stay away from my apartment. And I need your help."

"Do you want to stay here?"

"Oh, no, they'll find me. Thanks but I have to find another place. But I need you to do something for me."

"Who are they, Brent?"

"I can't say right now. I think the cops."

"What have you done?"

"Morgan, please just help me right now. In time, you'll know everything. Can you do that?"

"O.K. What do you need?"

"I can't get near my bank. Do you have any money?"

"Yes, of course."

"O.K. This is what I need you to do." He paused. "I need about five hundred dollars. In dirhams. Put them in an envelope, go to the American Express office in town, and submit it to the clerk at the front desk."

"The money is for whom?"

"You write Jamilla on the envelope and that's all."

"Brent," she said, "who is Jamilla?"

He hesitated. "She's a friend."

"Brent, is there anything you need to tell me?"

"No, no, no." He sounded adamant. "You don't need to get concerned with me. By the way, can you drop the money by tomorrow morning?"

"Sure, I can get to my bank this afternoon and go straight from there to the American Express office. Where do I find you if I need to communicate with you?"

"I'll call you. Don't worry." There was a pause. "Morg, thanks. I really appreciate it."

Morgan's hands trembled when she hung up. It was all so unsettling and she did not like any of it. Especially the money part. And who was Jamilla anyway?

Hastily, she slipped on her coat and walked out her door. She needed to get to her bank before they took their mid-afternoon break.

Outside she flagged a taxi and rushed to the bank. She withdrew the money she needed then sped to the American Express office. She made it just before they closed their office.

"Could you remit this to Jamilla when she comes by?"

"Sure," said the clerk. She took the envelope without commenting and placed it behind her in an Outgoing Mail slot.

Morgan flagged another taxi and returned to her apartment. There she paced the floor, too nervous to concentrate on her studies or anything else. Emily was gone and Brent was in trouble. She needed to tell someone. Perhaps, she thought, she could tell the school's director. No, she thought, not a good idea. He would alert the authorities. She was certain of it. She needed somebody to help her. To help Brent. To help Emily. If Emily was still alive.

Suddenly it hit her. *Kennedy Hunter.*

Yes, she was the one. She'd been reporting about Emily all along. She'd know what to do. She glanced at her watch. It was 9:30p.m. Surely, Kennedy would be at her hotel. But she wasn't.

After weighing it all and torturing herself about her role in this drama, Morgan ran out into the night. The night was black and very cold, a January night. She waited anxiously for a taxi. Not one single one showed up. Cars ran past her. Some sounded their horns at her. She was getting impatient and began walking. She knew where Kennedy stayed. At the Riad Salam by the beach where all the reporters stayed. Again, she glanced at her watch. Ten minutes and not one single cab. Damn, she thought, when you don't need them, they're always soliciting aggressively.

She quickened her pace. The more she thought about Emily and Brent the faster she walked. Finally, she ran. A small drizzle fell on the hard and shiny asphalt blinding her and she felt its wetness on her face, arms and legs. But she didn't care. She was remembering her last conversation with Emily and her last conversation with Brent. And somehow both mingled in her mind and fear gripped her realizing that her friends may be in imminent danger.

The rain fell harder and she could see nothing but the

glistening street under her feet. At that hour, there were fewer people on the street. Now and then, someone eyed her suspiciously, wheeled around to watch her run.

She was wet and getting wetter. Her hair was flat on her scalp and rain dribbled down her chin. Finally, she saw the facade of the hotel. She made a final dash across the street and entered the door, soaked and breathless. The concierge glanced at her, nodded, and shrugged.

She dashed to the front desk and asked for Kennedy Hunter. The clerk looked at her disheveled state, a puzzled expression on his face but said nothing.

Finally, he said. "One moment." His voice dripped with condescending hauteur. He rang Kennedy's room as Morgan waited impatiently, her breathing still labored.

"Sorry, no answer in Miss Hunter's room."

"Can I go up to her room? Maybe she's in the shower."

"Sorry, we don't give out room numbers, *Mademoiselle*."

"It's urgent. I need to see her!"

He shrugged then eyed her with the insipid look of a man urinating.

She realized that this amoeba of a clerk was not going to cooperate so she dashed out of the lobby and ran to the lounge where she was certain to find other reporters.

He followed her with his eyes and raised a hand in an attempt to stop her from entering the bar. She spun around, looked him in the eyes, and raised a middle finger.

Inside, the bar was dark and noisy. She examined the room her eyes canvassing the faces of women. Her eyes lit on Christina Riley whom she instantly recognized. She was conducting an animated conversation with a colleague. Then Morgan saw Kennedy. Under the artificial lights, Kennedy's copper hair shone like blazing fire. She held a corner table with a man and their focus seemed firmly fixed on each other.

Morgan stepped inside the bar and neared their table.

"Miss Hunter?" she said hesitantly.

Kennedy looked up not recognizing the drenched woman at her side.

"Yes?"

"I'm Morgan Taylor. Remember me? Emily's roommate."

Kennedy's face lit up. "I'm so sorry! I did not recognize you. You look like you just took one heck of a shower!"

"Yes, I'm sorry. I had to walk, I could't find a taxi." Morgan eyes traveled from Kennedy to Stone. "I need to talk to you."

"Let's go upstairs to my room where you can get dry."

She turned to Stone. "I gotta go. Catch you later."

He nodded as Kennedy whisked Morgan out of the place.

In the elevator, Kennedy noticed that Morgan trembled.

"You need a change of clothes, Morgan."

"Sorry about this," Morgan replied shyly.

Once inside the room, Morgan disrobed, dried out, and wore the bathrobe Kennedy offered her. She combed her hair and walked out from the bathroom.

"Let me call for some tea for you, Morgan. I think you need to warm up."

Morgan's face was ashen but now a faint smile covered her face.

"Sorry to be barging in on you like this."

"Don't concern yourself," said Kennedy. "What's going on Morgan?"

"Remember, you told me to call you if I heard something. Well—"

"What happened?"

"It's about Brent. I'm concerned. I don't—"

Morgan stopped and tears filled her eyes.

"You don't what, Morgan?"

"I don't know what to think. He called this afternoon asking for five hundred dollars to be dropped off at the

American Express office and he's hiding somewhere."

"Why is he hiding?"

"I'm not sure why. He mentioned something about cops. He just said he could not get back to his apartment."

"Where is he hiding?"

"I don't know. He won't say."

"Well, if he is hiding then surely he is going to need some money. Makes sense."

"Except that the money isn't for him. He asked me to address the envelope to Jamilla."

"Jamilla? And who is that?"

"I don't know. Never heard of any Jamilla. It's a mystery to me."

Kennedy was thinking hard. "Morgan, are you afraid?"

"Yes, I'm. I don't know what's going on. Emily is gone and Brent is scared and running. Maybe I'll be next."

"Next what?"

"Next victim. Maybe they'll come after me too."

"Who are they?"

"Whoever is after Emily and Brent."

"Do you believe that somebody is after both?"

"I'm not sure. I'm not sure of anything." She held her head between both hands. "I'm so confused."

Morgan was shaking like a dog after a bath.

"Morgan, listen to me." Kennedy held her hand. "I don't think anybody is after you or Brent. What I think is that Brent is in trouble because of his own doing, she said. "Now, tell me, does Brent deal drugs?"

"Hashish. Here and there. He just smokes once in while, like all of us."

"Yeah, but has he been selling it on campus to other students?"

"Well . . . " Morgan seemed hesitant. "It does seem that lately he's been more selling than just using."

"And why do you think he's been doing that?"

"I guess money."

"Do you have any idea why he needs money now?"

"Not really."

"Can you guess?"

"No."

"Morgan, when did he start selling? Do you remember?"

"Less than a month ago, more or less."

"Does it coincide with Emily's disappearance?"

"Oh my God, yes." Morgan's eyes grew wide. "Come to think of it, right after she disappeared."

"Well, you may have your answer there. I don't believe you have anything to worry about."

"I hope you're right."

"I think The Torch, Emily and Brent are all somewhat intertwined in this story." Kennedy paused. "In what way, I haven't figured it out." She looked over at Morgan who was paying more attention now. "And I bet you I'm right."

"I see, but I'm scared anyway."

"Would you like to stay here tonight? You can have the second bed here."

Morgan looked down, her eyes averting Kennedy. "Yes, thank you. I would really appreciate it. If you don't mind."

"I don't mind at all. Make yourself comfortable."

Kennedy rose. "As a matter of fact, I think you can have the room for yourself tonight. I know a place where I can spend the night."

Kennedy gave a conspiratorial wink to Morgan. "I know somebody who would love to give me shelter tonight," she said and stepped out of the room.

CHAPTER FORTY-THREE

An image filled Kennedy's screen. She stared at the hawk face of Wahid, Janet Carrington's horse trainer, and wondered if there was a connection between him and The Torch. Him and Emily. Him and Porter. Or him and Janet.

She realized the possibilities were endless. The connections could be perceptions. Imagined or real, it warranted her attention.

Wahid possessed the delineated jaws of a man with a steely determination. Angular, gaunt, hard. His piercing eyes shone with brilliance, like those of an eagle.

As she studied his face, she remembered Harry's admonitions and his findings. She could not dismiss his conclusions. He was impartial to The Torch and was not burdened by the emotional baggage she carried.

And then there was Morgan's story.

Could she dismiss her too? Could she continue to ignore those other venues that lead her away from The Torch? She didn't know if she could.

She realized that her possessiveness was perhaps a stubbornness born of a desire to attribute blame. And perhaps, she thought, perhaps there was the infinitesimal possibility that the facts would steer her elsewhere. If so, she concluded, then The Torch and I are both stubborn. He insists on the publication of his manifesto. And I won't let go of the idea that he doesn't have Emily.

To think that she shared anything with him was both repulsing and terrifying.

But could he be that cunning? Could he manipulate her to such degree? Her answer came easily. It was a pure, unqualified, unmitigated yes.

He was capable of just about anything, she thought. And I should never forget it.

Ever.

Kennedy summoned Sami from the hotel lobby. He arrived promptly at her door.

"Sami, I'm going to need you to work alone today."

He eyed her quizzically then raised an eyebrow.

"I need you to go and post yourself in front of the American Express office," she said.

"Who am I looking for?"

"Emily."

He stepped back, startled.

"Emily Carrington," she repeated.

"Emily in Casablanca? Not with The Torch?"

"Maybe. I'm not sure," she said. "She won't look like Emily, I promise you."

"Comment ca? How so?"

"Look for a woman that's about a meter-sixty or sixty-five. She would be wearing a djellabah and a veil. She is fair-skinned and has blue eyes. She goes by the name of Jamilla."

"Jamilla?"

"Sami, you shouldn't have any problems spotting her. There aren't many veiled Arab women going to the Am-Ex office."

"True."

"Generally only foreigners go there."

He acquiesced with a nod. "You're right."

"She would probably go in and out real fast. Don't miss her."

"What do I do once I find her?"

"Trail her to where she goes. Find out her location. Remain unobtrusive. She must not know she's been followed."

"Sure. *Sans probleme, Mademoiselle.*"

He headed to the door.

"Sami?"

He wheeled around.

"Is your allegiance to The Torch stronger than your allegiance to the truth?"

"Pardon?"

She realized he did not understand her language.

"I mean to say, that, are you a Berber first or a cop who seeks justice first?"

"I don't know. I don't know for sure but once a cop, always a cop, Miss Hunter."

She believed him. He smiled showing the toothy grin she had grown to like. In his eyes, she saw the honesty and knew where his allegiance lied.

"Sami, before you go, I need to connect with The Torch. I'll be in my room all day."

He nodded his assent and immediately left the room.

She turned on her laptop, opened the folder with Wahid's picture, and clicked on her Print icon. Then she laid his picture flat on her bed. She added the pictures of Emily, Christine Carter, her son and The Torch side by side. She had no pictures of Porter and Janet Fairfax. Wahid's will do. Then she placed Emily's photo at the top and like a game of Scrabble, she rearranged the pieces making mental connections, constructing different sets, building possible scenarios that did not include The Torch.

Each time, she looked for a motive.

And each time, she concluded that it had to be greed and its incestuous first cousin—-money.

———•◆•———

Sami parked his Renault in front of the Am-Ex office settling in for the long haul. Surveillance, he thought, just like the old days when he was a cop. Boring. Boring. Boring.

He watched as people entered and exited the office for, what seemed to him, an interminable amount of time. He noted how foreigners all looked alike today. He recalled a time when one could distinguish between the French, the Italians, or the Spaniards. Well, he mused, Levi's had, single-handedly turned jeans into the international uniform. It bridged all social barriers. And now no one can tell the difference between the rich and the poor. The highly educated and the barely educated. Ironic, he thought, America, purveyor of capitalism and individualism, exported The Great Equalizer.

———•◆•———

He fell into an almost meditative state and was taking pleasure in the act of observation when he saw the woman. She wore a veil and a djellabah. She hesitated at the door, looked to her left and right, then finally stepped inside the office. Her hesitation betrayed her and Sami knew she was the one. He opened his door and dashed out.

Seconds later, she was out of the office. She melted into the traffic on the sidewalk and Sami fell in line behind her. He remained several feet back not wanting to alert her.

She moved rapidly merging into an ocean of bodies as he tried to keep up with her pace. She neared a bus station and, suddenly, she stopped. Men, women, and children were already in line. She stood behind a woman laden with a cumbersome grocery bag, elbowing and thrusting to make headway.

A bus neared and, en masse, everyone gushed forward. The door yawned and a flood of people moved in blocking its entrance. She was being crushed by the mob but she fought back and made it inside the bus. Good, he thought, she had learned the ways of my country.

The bus at full capacity, Sami wondered if he was going to make it inside. The driver shut the door leaving behind screaming passengers. The bus took off, one man still holding to an outside rail. Sami bolted after the bus. He jumped on the outside platform, grabbed the rail, and pushed the man out of his way. The skinny man fought and yelled never letting go of the rail. The bus sped up but the runt would not cede. Fed up, Sami unhinged his hand prying it open and shoved him into the traffic. The man fell off the bus cursing and brandishing a fist. Sami held on to the rail until the next stop when the driver let out some passengers and let him in.

He moved inside the bus his eyes darting around seeking the woman. A sea of veiled women and dark heads. Inching his way to the back of the bus he positioned himself near the back door. From there he only saw the back of their heads. I would not recognize my own sister, he thought. Frustrated, he moved to the front of the bus. Each time he brushed against an Arab woman, he got a disapproving look. He grabbed the overhead leather straps and scanned the crowd. His eyes traveled the face of each woman landing on passive Arab eyes.

Then a head swung. She was standing a few feet away from him. Her skin was soft and pale. A set of deep blue eyes locked with his.

Suddenly, a flicker of suspicion covered her face and her eyes registered fear. Fear an experienced cop can sense. Like tremors from an earthquake, it traveled the distance between them. He sensed something else too. Her eyes beamed with intelligence and in them, he didn't see the submissiveness of Arab women.

At that moment, she lowered her gaze and turned her head. He did likewise.

For the remainder of the trip he stole furtive glances never wanting to lose her.

They drove through the city's *bidonvilles*—slums—a landscape filled with refuse and wretchedness. Then the bus left the city and drove through the countryside stopping at villages along the way. With each stop the bus lost more of its passengers.

From the corner of his eyes, Sami kept a close watch on her. With many passengers gone, she took a window seat. But she, too, was watching him.

Finally, the bus neared a small remote village. The asphalt road turned into a dirt road as the bus slowed into a market place teeming with shoppers. Vendors of goods, produce and spices lined the main street as donkeys and people mingled.

The bus opened its doors for the final time and heaved its last load on the street. Immediately, she descended amid the new mob that had gathered around the bus.

Sami followed her. She immediately glided into the human mass, at once merging with the crowd.

"Move! Move!" He shoved the pedestrians in front of him making little headway. He peered over the many heads but she had already become one with the crowd. All he saw were dozens of heads covered with dark *djellabahs*. Frantic, he pushed the oncoming traffic out of his way meeting nothing but a barrier of resistance. After several minutes of swimming against the tide, he surrendered and conceded that he had lost her.

Damn! he thought.

She had slipped between his fingers like fine sand running through an hourglass.

CHAPTER FORTY-FOUR

Morning came clear and quiet but Kennedy's night had been neither clear nor quiet. She had awakened early, unsure of whether she had fallen asleep at all and watched the city come to life. She took her time getting ready, lingering in her shower, letting the healing power of water flow on her body.

Sami had come back and his report had been good and bad. Good because he found her. And bad because he lost her.

She turned the TV on and watched CNN. There were no new reports about Emily or The Torch. Riley was still on the beat but she had no more new news than anyone else did. They were all humming the identical tune, the same hackneyed notes. The Torch and Emily were either conspirators, lovers, Bonnie and Clyde. Or he was a Svengali and she suffered from Stockholm Syndrome. The media's fertile imagination ran the gamut between serious news and complete fabrication. The clamor for The Torch's manifesto continued unabated and airtime was filled with speculations and secondary players who claimed to have known Emily, known The Torch, seen Emily, seen The Torch.

She picked up *Le Matin*, the Moroccan paper left at her door, and scoured it. The detective was not figuring anywhere. The axiom, no news was good news, did not apply here. Cops did not feel any compulsion or obligation to share anything with the media. Contrary, they felt that the less the press knew, the better off they were.

She exited her room and went downstairs. There she found a clerk who, at her request, took her behind his desk. He opened a small refrigerator and took out a small plastic bag from the freezer.

She walked to the cafe lobby and found Sami. He was leaning against the counter in front of an espresso. He looked like he had been up for a long time, just like her.

When he saw her, he swallowed his espresso in one big gulp and with an air of conclusiveness, stubbed out his cigarette.

"*Bonjour*," he said. He did not seem overly happy or optimistic and Kennedy knew why. He was still fuming for having lost Emily.

"Good morning, Sami," she replied, "we are going to visit detective Ahmed at the central police station."

His head swung so fast he could have given himself a whiplash. His eyes grew wide and filled with questions.

"I need to involve the detective in some of this stuff," she said, anticipating his questions.

"I see," he said.

He followed her out of the hotel to the street. Casablanca in the morning is a beehive of activity and today was no different.

They left the beach and drove to town. Kennedy was eager to meet the detective. She had not seen him since their contentious encounter in Arak. The last time she saw him, he was standing on a windy sidewalk, raging mad at the foreign press and her for consistently gnawing at his heels.

Now, she needed his cooperation because without it she could not validate or disregard Harry's argument. And she needed the investigative tools he had at his disposal. She knew, however, that she would have to let him in on some of her findings. I would, she thought, up to a certain point.

Again, the press was there. Trucks with antennas jutting out, reporters parked in front of the entrance of the police station and cameras and microphones everywhere.

They parked away from the station and walked to the entrance. The building was modern and they stepped into a large lobby several stories tall. A colossal crystal chandelier hung from its top floor dwarfing all else around. To the right and left of the lobby circular steps led to administrative offices.

The sound of footsteps echoed throughout the building as employees filed in for work. A man in uniform stood behind a desk directing the flow of employees and visitors. Sami waived at him and the man waived back. Kennedy saw a spark of recognition in the man's eyes. This must have been Sami's former station, she thought, as the man waived them in ahead of the ring forming around him.

Kennedy followed Sami to the second floor. He seemed to know the layout and he moved with ease in the building.

Detective Ahmed was talking on the phone when they stepped in. The office held a small battered desk and filing cabinets everywhere Kennedy's eyes lit. Loose files on the desk and many more directly on the floor. The only adjuncts making this office remotely personal were the pictures of Ahmed's wife and daughter on top of a cabinet.

With the wave of a hand, he gestured them in. He eyed Kennedy and cut his conversation short.

"Miss Hunter, ah, *bonjour*," he said extending his hand. She shook it, surprised by his civility. He extended his hand to Sami.

"What can I do for you, Miss Hunter?"

He ran his hand through his dark hair. He wore an oversized white shirt and pleated gray pants. The mustache she had seen him with earlier was gone.

Kennedy opened her bag and retrieved an envelope. She placed the picture of Wahid on the detective's desk.

"Do you know this man?"

He leaned forward, eyed the picture then leaned back and studied Kennedy's face. Poker player, she thought. There was nothing but vacuity on his face.

Finally, "Who is he?" he said.

"If you're asking me who he is, then you don't know his identity."

"Maybe. Maybe not." He picked up a pen on his desk and began playing with the mechanism. "Maybe I should ask you why you want to know."

"I have reason to believe he might be involved in the disappearance of Emily Carrington."

He raised an inquisitive eyebrow. "I see. Where did you get such information?"

"From The United States."

He waited for her to continue. "What do they have in the U.S. that we don't have here?"

"Well, there is a family that's very rich and plenty of motives to eliminate the newest multi-millionaire."

"And who's this man?" he said pointing to the picture. "He looks Moroccan."

"His name is Wahid and he trains horses at the Carringtons in Atlanta. I'm wondering if there's a connection between him and the disappearance of Emily Carrington."

Kennedy saw a flash traverse his eyes. She went on. "Detective Ahmed, The Torch doesn't have Emily Carrington."

"I know that, Miss Hunter."

Her face indicated surprise. "You do?"

"I have known it all along." He smiled confidently. "I just don't know the other half of the story."

He leaned back in his seat. "Miss Hunter, understand that we do not have the resources to conduct overseas investigations."

She opened her bag and retrieved a tightly sealed plastic pouch. "This might help."

He opened it slowly. The frozen ashen ear spilled out. He drew back. Sami stirred uncomfortably in his seat and cleared his throat.

"It's the ear I received from The Torch." She waited for him to regain his footing before she continued. "I don't know whom it belongs to."

"I'm not sure I know either." He quickly closed the plastic pouch. "It's evidence, Miss Hunter. Evidence," he said with reproach.

"You may be able to ascertain who it belongs to with DNA."

A doubting smile covered his face. "Not here. We do not have the sophisticated science you have in America. Not yet." He tilted his head. "Maybe one day."

"Could you ascertain it's not Emily's?"

"Only if we hand it over to your CIA and they would send it back to the United States where it could be analyzed."

"Meanwhile," he reached across his desk and retrieved a file from a pile. He opened it and took out a loose leaf of paper. "Miss Hunter," he said as he handed her the piece of paper, "take a look at this."

She looked closely. It was a ten-digit number divided in three sequences. "It looks like a phone number from the U.S. I mean, the amount of digits corresponds to phone numbers at home."

"Humm," he said, "is it a bank account number?"

"Sure. But this, to me at least, looks similar to a phone number. Bank accounts have longer sequences."

She studied the number and quickly filed it in her memory.

He noticed. "Soon as you find out whom it belongs to, let me know," he said with a knowing nod.

"Sure." She wondered why he couldn't find out on his own. It was a simple thing to do.

She got up to leave. Uncharacteristically, Sami had remained quiet during the whole exchange.

"Miss Hunter, I would be very careful with The Torch. He is not a good loser."

"Thank you for warning me," she said.

She neared the door then spun around. "By the way detective, how did you find out I was in Arak to meet The Torch?"

His response was slow in coming. "Ask him. *Ask The Torch.*"

CHAPTER FORTY-FIVE

Her old story was crumbling and a new story was emerging from the cinders in her mind. The internal turmoil Kennedy felt had crescendoed and reached its climax. She was at crossroads, like the prisoner who must choose between death by injection and death by electrocution. Either way, she knew she would unleash The Torch's wrath and the consequences of her actions would be irreversible.

After she had seen the detective, she had remained all day in her room, preferring the solitude of her room than being with colleagues at the press center or at the bar.

She listened to the sound of ocean waves slam against the promenade and the hissing winds journeying over the waters.

Butterflies filled her stomach and the thoughts in her head leapt like synapses firing uncontrollably. Tonight, keeping herself centered was tantamount to keeping a beach ball under water.

She plugged her iPod and listened to Indian flutes. She needed something soothing, calming. Shortly, she closed her eyes and listened to the haunting notes coming through. She sensed the vibrations of the music travel through her body, echoing like voices in a tunnel.

Soon his image came into focus rising from the depths of her mind, as real and palpable as if he was made of flesh and bones. She saw his face and she saw his bloodied hands. It was the blood of all those who had perished, those he had killed for his blind ambition, those whose life was snuffed out before their time.

She reached out and touched the face that lived in her mind's eye but was jolted by the sound of a ringing phone. She picked it up and heard his voice. Her pulse accelerated.

"Miss Hunter," he said, "this is The Torch." He sounded mellower than he had been.

"Yes," she said, "I have been waiting for your call."

This sudden metamorphosis surprised her, made her feel unsure. Still, she remained cautious. One never lets his guard down in the company of a rattlesnake.

"I'm disappointed, Miss Hunter. I was expecting you to keep your word."

"Sir, this game is over. You set me up in Arak. I went along with your game, but now it's over."

"You alerted the authorities," he said. "You did!"

"Look," she said, "*C'est finis*. It's over. I don't believe a word you say." She paused, the pounding of her heart filling her throat. "Emily isn't with you."

There was no immediate response from him, only a wall of silence.

Finally, he spoke, slow, articulate, pausing after each word. "You . . . are . . . wrong. Very wrong, Miss Hunter. Emily is here. Right here."

"Prove it to me!"

"Haven't I, already?"

"No, you haven't!"

"Then, I'll tell my story to someone else. How about Riley? What do you think of her?"

She froze. Not the way she wanted this to end. She had the big story now and she was going to lose it, lose Emily.

Martini came to mind. He warned me, she thought, he warned me.

"Sir, you are free to tell your story to anyone else. I'm afraid no one will play your games."

She hung up. She was exhausted by words and lies. Lies, she thought, are like invisible jail bars. Eventually, they imprison those who create them and turn against them. Like the pitbull who kills his owner.

Nevertheless, uncertainty gripped her. But there was no turning back. No back-pedaling. It was a done deal. She knew that.

She was so tightly wounded she began pacing her room. She thought of calling Harry but decided against it. His cheerfulness would grate her like sand paper. Right now, solitude felt good. Was good.

Tomorrow, she thought, tomorrow there will be light. And light purifies everything it touches.

CHAPTER FORTY-SIX

"Harry? Harry? If you're home, pick up the phone! It's Kennedy."

Harry reached for the phone by his bedside.

"Damn, Kennedy, what time is it?" His voice was filled with sleep.

"Sorry for waking you up, I've been up for a long time."

"What's going on, Ken?" Harry eyed his clock. "It's four in the morning here." He rubbed his eyes. "Must be something happening."

"Yes, I apologize. I just needed to talk to somebody. I'm going out of my mind here."

"What's up?"

"Harry, I don't think The Torch has Emily. You were right."

Harry's feet hit the barren floor. "How did you find out?"

"We found her right here in Casablanca. She's hiding but she isn't with The Torch."

"Go on."

"She's under disguise, she's hiding from somebody. She's spooked to death right now, I know that."

"Well, wouldn't you? She's just a kid."

"Anyway, I met with the detective in charge and he figured out that The Torch did not have her either. The body found at the dump did not belong to her but you already know that. The ear did not belong to her either."

"Gruesome."

"Wait, it's not all. Brent, her boyfriend, has something to do with her hiding. I figure he helped her go underground with money and all."

"Well, good." Harry walked the length of his bedroom. "I'm trying to figure what are all of the reasons The Torch would go through all of that."

"Harry, I'm going to let you answer your own question. Even at this hour of the morning."

"Yeah, I see the whole picture now. Geez, the S.O.B wanted his manifesto published, so he used her disappearance as a tool."

"He invented a non-existing hostage. Just so that the paper would publish it."

"Bastard."

"I'm mad as hell for falling in his trap. Maybe I was blinded by my past history with him and could not see the holes in the picture."

"Don't blame yourself, Ken. He is a manipulator and an opportunist. You did what every decent reporter would do—you investigated."

"Yes, Harry, but I let him play me like a violin."

"The main thing is that the girl is alive. And he doesn't have her."

"Yeah, I guess so."

"What now, Ken?"

"Well, I'm going to try to reel her in. And find out who really tried to kill her."

"I think I know the culprit, Ken."

"You might be totally right, Harry. Apropos—"

"What? The culprit?"

"Check this number for me. It sounds like a state-side number." She spelled out all the numbers.

"The area code is 770. Well, that's an Atlanta area code. The suburbs." He paused. "What's the rest of that number again?"

She repeated the last seven digits.

"Wait a sec, Ken. Let me check something. Be right back."

He placed the phone down and checked his address book in his cell phone.

"Ken, it's the Carringtons phone number in Atlanta."

"Oh, my God."

"What? Where did you get that number from?"

"The detective gave it to me. He had it."

"Good God. This thing is unfolding the way I thought it would."

"Somehow, this number connects to this whole thing, Harry."

"Easy to connect all the points, Ken."

"What an onion this has been—and each layer is proving to be more intriguing than the last."

"Harry, on another subject—what's the paper like these days? Martini has been tightening his vise since I got here."

"Looks like there's a moratorium on Emily. Bet you that old coot of Martini is lying low until you deliver the big bang."

"He'll get his big bang, in due time. Him and The Torch."

"Talking about killing two birds with one stone."

———•◆•———

Later, she dialed the downstairs lobby and summoned Sami.

When he showed up, he looked rested and ready to tackle anything she threw his way.

"Sami, we are going to the Am-Ex office and I want you

to give this," she handed him an envelope, "to the clerk.
Tell her it's for Jamilla."

His expression indicated surprise. "Is the woman expected to show up?"

"No. But ask the clerk to contact her and tell her she has
something for her."

His eyes widened.

"What, you don't think it's going to work?"

"No. I wonder if she'll suspect something and won't
show up."

"I think she'll show up. It's a chance we take but it's the
only chance we have."

"O.K. I'll give it a try, Mademoiselle."

"Please act as if you know Emily. Like totally natural
and normal."

"Then what do we do afterwards?"

"We wait."

"How long?"

"Until she shows up."

He scowled and shrugged, his bearing telling of his
thinking.

————————•◆•————————

She appeared minutes before the closure of the Am-Ex office just as Kennedy and Sami had decided to abandon their
surveillance.

She walked hastily past pedestrians and entered the office but not before she eyed her surroundings.

"That's it," said Sami, "that's her."

Within minutes, she was out of the office having stayed just
long enough to pick up her envelope. Like the time before, she
walked directly to the bus station and waited in line.

"O.K., let's go" Sami said, "we have plenty of time but,
with this traffic she might make it before we do."

He drove off immediately and merged into the dense traffic.

"Apparently, she hasn't opened her envelope. She isn't in a hurry to see what's in there," she said.

"Good, then. Maybe she won't suspect anything."

He turned around and eyed Kennedy. "What did you put in the envelope?"

"Just money. Same as Brent. He probably adds a message though. She might wonder why there isn't a message from him this time."

"Then it's a good thing she did not open the envelope."

"I didn't think she would. She's too much in a hurry."

He tapped his forehead with a finger as if saying, You clever girl.

"It comes from reporting, Sami. One deals with so many people, you start developing an extra sense about human behavior. Some things are just predictable." She remembered he was a cop and probably a good judge of character too. "It's the same with cops, Sami. Isn't it?"

"Sure is."

"Did you think The Torch had Emily, Sami?"

He paused, holding back. "No. I did not think she was with him."

"You never said anything."

He had his eyes on the traffic and did not look sideways. "You didn't ask."

She sensed a little reproach in his tone. "Sorry. At the beginning of this, I had no idea you were a cop. I should've asked what was your background. It's easy to get all tangled up in a story. I sometimes forget to ask for help from the most obvious people."

"I understand." He managed a smile.

They drove out of the city each lost in their own world. Soon they reached a two-lane road and traffic lightened.

They passed village after village, houses painted in white

and blue, nestled in hills and sprouting from the landscape like an impressionism painting.

"Miss Hunter?" Sami was looking through his rearview mirror. "There's a car that's been with us since we left Casablanca."

She whirled around. "Darn."

"It's a white Ford Escort. There are three men inside. I can't tell who they are."

"Who do you think they are?"

"Guess."

"If I were to guess, I'd say it's The Torch's people."

Kennedy's heart quickened. A confrontation with The Torch was not something she wished for.

"We need to lose them," he said.

Kennedy exhaled. "I leave it up to you. You know the terrain a lot better than I do."

Sami pressed his foot on the accelerator and the small car wheezed before taking off. His eyes still on the vehicle behind, he suddenly pulled the car onto a small dirt road. The car bounced erratically and finally landed under a large olive tree.

"Let's see what they do," he said.

The car sped right past them without slowing down.

"I saw two people in there, Sami."

"I did too. But there are three. I know that, for sure."

"What happened to the third?"

"Probably hiding in the back."

"Let's wait a bit here."

Sami walked out of the vehicle, stretched his legs, and lit a cigarette. Then he walked behind a tree and the next thing she heard was the sound of a trickle. She waited.

"We need to go, otherwise we'll miss the girl," he said as he zipped up his pants.

He climbed back into the car and took off. The road was clear. The Ford was nowhere within sight.

"Think we lost them?" she asked.

"Oh, no. They'll be back."

An overwhelming sense of apprehension gripped Kennedy.

"We'll have to outwit them," he replied. "But we need to reach El Jadida before the girl does."

"Or at least at the same time she does."

El Jadida was located some 100 kilometers south of Casablanca. Kennedy recalled that during her childhood, the town's name had been Mazagan but with the arabization of everything else in Morocco, French names had been dropped in favor of Arabic names. Once a Portuguese enclave along the Atlantic, El Jadida was now a resort area for the many Europeans vacationing in Morocco.

For a while, they drove in silence, both of their minds occupied by The Torch. She was thinking about The Torch's unrelenting pursuit of her and he was thinking about how he could outrun him.

The two-lane road turned narrow and Sami's grip on the wheel tightened. Kennedy glanced at the speedometer and he was doing 130 kilometers per hour—some 80 miles. She marveled at the little car's ability to get up to that speed. But not without effort. It shook as if a seismic event moved under the earth's skin.

Sami glanced at the mirror for the umpteenth time and suddenly his eyes took on an exasperated look.

"They're back," he said. He pushed the vehicle even harder and the little car coughed a billowing dark cloud.

Ahead, a roofless truck with a load of goats was moving at an evolutionary speed. The goats slid all over the truck like ice skaters in a comic bit. Sami nearly ran into the truck and slowed down. His eyes still glued to the mirror, he saw their pursuers near them. He was getting increasingly agitated and irate at the driver of the truck. "*Imshi, imshi!*" he cried and honked furiously but the truck driver seemed comatose.

Abruptly, Sami swerved the car in an attempt to pass the

truck and narrowly escaped a speeding car coming from the opposite direction. Kennedy closed her eyes. She grabbed the door handle and held her breath. When he finally passed, she let out a blast of oxygen.

He drove for a while, his jaws and arms tight. Then, "I think we have lost them. I haven't seen them for few kilometers." He raised a brow and nodded.

Soon, the sienna ramparts of El Jadida appeared between a gathering of gray clouds. At a distance, they saw the harbor and a succession of sardine boats returning from sea.

"This is it," he said, "this is where she's been hiding."

"Pretty remote. I would have thought she would hide in Casablanca. Lord knows there're plenty of places to hide in a large city."

"True. But no one will think of this place. It's close enough to Casablanca in case she needed to come in."

"I wonder where she stayed at."

"Who knows? We'll find out soon."

They entered El Jadida and drove to town. The town bustled with pedestrians, motorists, bicycles, and mules.

"We need to get to the central bus station," he said.

With difficulty, he navigated through the dense crowd. Kennedy wondered if they would have been better off leaving the car parked and tried to make it by foot.

Finally, they reached downtown. A dilapidated lean-to served as a bus stop and a crowd huddled around it.

Sami parked the car across the bus station and glanced at his watch.

"Anytime now," he said, "I timed it last time—it's about an hour's drive."

A rush of anticipation coursed through Kennedy's body. She lowered her window and a gust of dust and emissions filled the vehicle.

Buses came in and out of the station. Sami's eyes were firmly fixed on one area. Kennedy watched him quietly. He lowered his window and lit a cigarette. She did not object preferring to inhale his fumes than interfere with his concentration.

His eyes surveyed the station. A bus arrived and spilled all its passengers on the sidewalk. Immediately, Sami stepped out of the car. Kennedy followed him. He charged across the street merging with the crowd. Kennedy ran behind him. Suddenly, he swung around and motioned Kennedy to follow him.

Amid the many veiled faces and covered heads, Sami had spotted her. She had just stepped out of the bus.

Kennedy caught up with Sami and they both fell in step. They remained at a safe distance certain she had not seen them.

The sky had turned ominously dark and the promise of rain hung in the air. Large billowing clouds blanketed the town and the air smelled of dust and wetness. The crowd had dissipated making easier to keep in step with the woman.

Suddenly, Sami stopped. Behind him, he saw two men walking fast. He grabbed Kennedy by the elbow.

"We are followed," he cried.

"My God, we can't have The Torch's people find out where she's living. She'll get killed!"

Sami pulled Kennedy aside. "Go get her. I'll try to stop these two. Go run!"

Kennedy took off after the woman leaving Sami behind.

They entered the Mellah, the old Jewish quarters. Bougainvillea scaled the walls and roofs of whitewashed houses with doors painted in bright yellows and aquas. There were few cars and mostly pedestrians. Kennedy saw the woman a few yards ahead. She dashed and grabbed her arm.

"Emily! Emily!"

She swung, eyes wide and immediately unlocked herself from Kennedy's grasp.

Kennedy ran after her.

"Emily! Listen! I'm here to help you!"

Again, Emily broke away from Kennedy and took off running.

Kennedy followed. Emily could not outrun her, her djellabah restricted her walk.

Breathless, Kennedy caught up with her grabbing her by the arm.

"Emily! Listen, I'm here to help you! You need to trust me!"

Emily halted. "Who are you, anyway?"

"I'm Kennedy Hunter, the reporter. I've been covering your story!"

"Oh, my God!" Disbelief registered on her face. She raised the veil from her face.

"I can't let them see me," she said, panic in her voice. "I can't!"

"Who are they?"

"Whoever wants to kill me, I don't know. Please let me go. I need to go."

"Let me help you."

"What can you do for me? They'll get me." She walked away.

Kennedy pursued her. "They won't if you come out of your hiding."

Suddenly, Kennedy heard the roar of a car and sudden brakes. Dust rose in a cloud as the car halted and a door flung wide open. The car blocked both Kennedy and Emily cornering them against the wall of a building.

A man leaped out of the car. Emily's eyes turned like those of a hunted animal.

"Miss Hunter, glad to see you again," the man said. Kennedy blinked in disbelief.

"Detective! What are you doing here?"

He grabbed her and Emily by the arm. "Doing the same thing you're doing, Miss Hunter. You two come along."

"You've been following me all along!"

"Of course." He smiled.

Neither Emily nor Kennedy was smiling.

He opened the passenger door and motioned them to get in.

Emily resisted. "Get in," he said in a commanding tone. She remained standing still. "Get in voluntarily—or would you prefer my assistance?" She lifted her djellabah and got in.

He slid into the driver's seat. "We have some talking to do, all three of us." He took off.

"Where are we going?" Kennedy asked.

"To a police station." He glanced at Emily. "Miss Emily, please place your veil back on. I don't want the media to hear of this. Not now. Not yet."

"What about my driver?" Kennedy asked.

"He's in safe hands, your driver."

They drove through a few blocks to the nearest police station. Ahmed parked on the sidewalk near the entrance. They got out and Kennedy got a whiff of something rank.

"What am I smelling?"

"Oh, *that*. Yeah, this station is called Dar El Bouala." He chuckled.

"What does it mean?" Kennedy asked.

"It means the Urinal House. See, next door is a public urinal."

"Is this your idea of torture?"

"It is one way of torturing people," he replied. "They say that smells evoke memories. Pleasant and unpleasant ones, *Mademoiselle*."

"Have you ever smelled death, Detective?"

"Of course," he replied, "just like you." He paused briefly, then said, "it never leaves your nostrils." He eyed Emily. "The last time I smelled death was the day Emily died."

Emily flinched. She stood by Ahmed's side and hearing her name in the same breath as her death had jolted her.

"Anyway," he said wanting to change the subject, "you wouldn't want to be imprisoned here."

"I don't see how it would differ from the one you put me in," she said in a crisp tone.

"Oh yes, it would. Arak is like a five-star hotel compared to this one."

"*Vive la différence,*" she said.

He ignored her sarcasm and walked inside the small station. The cop shop was an old building in need of a painting job. A cop sat at a small wooden desk and upon seeing the detective rose.

"*Ya' habibi,* detective," he said bowing. Ahmed raised his right hand and saluted him military style. Kennedy and Emily followed him inside a back room.

They found Sami in a barren room flanked by two other cops. There were several metal chairs around. A dusky light filtered through a bare window and a naked bulb hung down from the ceiling.

Sami looked exasperated and bored.

"Sami!" Kennedy cried. He raised his hand as if saying everything is alright.

"Everybody sit down," said the detective. "Emily, tell us what happened."

Emily lowered her veil and her head wrap. She was on the verge of tears. "Where do I begin?"

"Tell us everything," interjected Kennedy.

"I don't know what to think. I'm so afraid."

"You have nothing to be afraid of. From now on," Ahmed said "Go ahead."

"I went to Marrakesh for a weekend. I was taking photos of the Gnaouas and Berbers when I was accosted by two men who said they were guides." She stopped and wiped a tear from the corner of her eye.

"Go on," said Kennedy. She touched her lightly in a comforting gesture.

"They were supposed to show me around."

"Then what happened?" Ahmed said.

"Well . . . I don't know. I was knocked unconscious. After that, I think I was drugged. I remember little—it sounded as if I was out in some village or in the desert. Somebody removed my clothes and my jewelry."

"How did you escape?"

"I was taken in the back seat of a car. I woke up—I guess I was not supposed to. When they stopped for gas, I ran out of the car. I called Brent and I stayed hidden in Marrakesh for few days then I traveled to El Jadida."

"Brent has been the one helping you," Kennedy said.

"Yes, I could not have done it without him."

"Why did you stay in hiding?"

"Well, I overheard a conversation between the two men. I understood them to say they were going to get rid of me. They were debating where to do it."

"You must have been scared," Kennedy said.

"Of course. I did not know who wanted to get rid of me."

"I understand," said Ahmed

"I could not trust anybody." She sniffed. "I'm so tired of running. Then there were all the stories about me. And The Torch got involved. I didn't think I could ever come out."

"Did you ever have anything to do with The Torch?" Kennedy asked.

"Never. Never met the man."

"Where have you been all this time?"

"Right here in El Jadida. In the Mellah. There is an old Jewish woman I knew. I had interviewed her for one of my research papers and I stayed with her. I don't think she ever read the papers or knew exactly who I was. After a few days with her, I moved to a local hotel." She looked around the room, her eyes filled with apprehension. "What will happen to me now?"

Ahmed responded. "You are under my protection until we know more about this."

"Who do you think is after me?"

The detective eyed Kennedy. "Well, it isn't The Torch. He was using you to advance his cause." He glanced at Kennedy. "He was using the press to get some publicity for himself."

Kennedy looked at Emily. Emily's composure was dissolving.

"My Mom died," she uttered. "I could not even go her funeral." She blew her nose.

"Emily," said Kennedy, "I'm going to ask you something relevant to all this."

"Yeah?"

"Did you stand to inherit something once your mother died?"

Emily recoiled. She looked around the room, first at Kennedy then at the detective.

"What are you saying?"

"I'm not saying anything. I'm trying to find out who would want you dead and one cannot discount anything."

"Well? You mean Janet, my sister? Oh my God, no!"

"No, not your sister. How about Porter?"

"How do you know about Porter?"

"I have been checking up on him."

"And?"

"He has all the reasons in the world to want you dead."

Emily's face was falling apart. "I can't take this," she said and hid her face in her hands. She began sobbing.

Kennedy reached out and squeezed her hand. "Do you know Wahid?"

"Who is Wahid?"

"The horse trainer at your sister's."

"Oh, him. Porter hired him when he was here. I knew of him but don't know him personally. What did he have to do with me?"

Ahmed interjected. "We think he was the one organizing this thing. Porter's orders, of course."

In between sobs, Emily said, "I can't believe Porter would do anything like this. I love him. He's like my dad to me."

"People will do many things for money," Kennedy replied.

"What about my sister?"

"It doesn't seem to be your sister's idea. Janet really loves you."

Emily glanced at Kennedy. "You know Janet?"

"No. But a good friend of mine does. He says she's a very fine person. And she's really concerned about you."

Kennedy eyed Ahmed. "Detective, I think we need to go. I wouldn't mind harboring Emily until this is over."

"Everybody stays right here," he said. With his hands, he motioned Kennedy to rise. "Miss Hunter and I will be next door," he said to Emily and Sami.

He grabbed Kennedy by the elbow and led her out. They walked out to a patio filled wild with evergreens and palm trees.

"Miss Hunter, this is the end of your search," he said, "but not mine."

"Perhaps. I'm afraid Emily isn't any safer now than she was before."

"The phone numbers?" he asked.

"Atlanta. The phone number of Emily's relatives. Porter Fairfax," she said reluctantly.

He bowed his head down and nodded. "I suspected."

"Is it Porter and Wahid?"

"Yes. Wahid, probably is the one who set it all up. He was associated with the two who got rid of the Arab girl."

"Why kill the girl, detective?"

"Covering up a botched job. They were supposed to get rid of Emily and they lost her. Killing the girl would have achieved two things. Temporarely, of course. First, please

Porter, second the police. Probably stalling for time until they recovered Emily and got rid of her."

"So…"

"So they picked up the Arab girl, put her in Emily's clothes and threw her in the dump knowing that one of the kids at the dump would find her and take the jewelry. After that, it was easy for The Torch's goons to find out who had the jewelry."

"It was all The Torch needed to convince me."

"And the ear, detective, whose ear was that?"

"Goons have a way of being creative, who knows?"

"And I have put an arrest out for Wahid. As soon as he puts his feet back in Morocco."

"Is Brent going to be O.K?"

"Oh, yeah, we'll just ship him home."

"What about Porter?"

"Porter is an American problem. I can only alert the authorities. I have no jurisdiction over him."

"It's easy to bump off somebody overseas."

"Bump off?"

"I mean, kill."

"Indeed."

"What now, detective?"

"I'm going to keep Emily under surveillance until further development. And you, *Mademoiselle*?"

"I have some accounts to settle, detective."

He raised a brow.

"The Torch and I.

CHAPTER FORTY-SEVEN

Kennedy entered her darkened room. Instantly, a spot-light flashed over her head leaving the rest of the room bathed in darkness. Pupils dilated, hair on end, she halted. From the corner of her eyes, she caught a fleeting shadow and sensed a presence in the room. A scent she was not accustomed to lingered in the air. She focused on the blackness of the room and saw, in the far right corner, a dark silhouette seated in a chair.

Startled, she halted her walk.

"Who are you?"

The door slammed behind her.

Dressed in suit and tie, he sat legs crossed, hands folded in his lap.

"Miss Hunter," he said, "it's a pleasure seeing you again."

His voice, his pitch, the sarcasm that dripped from his tone.

"How did you get in my room?"

"Oh, it's not that difficult," he replied casually

She hardly heard his answer for the pounding of her heart. She pressed herself against the door behind her. "What are you doing here, anyway?"

"Miss Hunter," he said, "you and I have some issues to settle."

Kennedy wheeled around to open the door.

"No point in trying to get out. The door is locked from the outside," he cackled.

"What do you want?"

"A little intellectual debate. I enjoy intellectual debates, you know that."

"The best thing you can do is leave right now."

A tinny sound like that of metal came out of his throat. "Not so soon," he said, "you know I enjoy feisty women. Like American women. Our women are obsequious, servile. They obey us too much."

"Get up and leave right now!"

He ignored her demand. "Wouldn't you enjoy a little *tête-à-tête*? Please, don't disappoint me. I came from the desert to see you."

"I need to get back downstairs. My friends are waiting for me."

"Miss Hunter, don't you see that our destinies are weaved together. That my destiny has been your destiny."

"You're controlled by your ancestry whereas I make my own destiny," she replied.

"See, you're not as enlightened as you presume to be. Can't you see that the world has been bringing us together, repeatedly? We are repeating certain patterns in our lives. You cannot ignore them. You should not ignore them"

"You're undeserving of the attention I've been giving you. You are undeserving of any attention *anybody* is giving you."

"Miss Hunter, we're more alike than not, you and I. We're both users of this medium called the press. We are manipulators. I manipulate it for my benefit and you manipulate your subjects, extracting from them information. It's all about selling papers, isn't it?" He paused. "So you see, we are not that much different from each other."

"Please don't put me in your category. I'm a seeker of

truth, whereas you are a master at obfuscating the truth. We are anything but alike. Perhaps in your mind. But not in mine."

"Ah, you're fighting the forces that have brought us together. You need to surrender to them. Accept them, embrace them."

He rose from his seat.

"Stay there, don't move and don't you even think of getting close to me!"

He stopped as if suspended in mid-air. "No need to be frightened by me. I'm not the enemy. The enemy is your mind."

"Stay where you are!"

He sat back down. He reached for the lamp beside him and turned it on. A dim light shone on him casting shadows on his face.

"You're all grown up," he said. "More mature, more beautiful than the young woman you used to be."

She ignored his comment. "I'm asking you to leave."

Once more, he ignored her. He rose from his seat again, removed his jacket, folded it neatly over the armchair, and sat back down. He wore a crisp white shirt and a red tie. Sharply tailored pants. He looked like a Wall Street banker.

Her mind wandered briefly. She was hoping for some godly intervention.

Suddenly, the phone rang.

"Don't answer it!" he ordered.

She moved towards the phone.

"I said, don't!"

She halted. The phone rang several times filling the room with earsplitting sounds. When it stopped the room was plunged into an eerie silence.

She looked beyond him and into the balcony. The dark was so black. Palm trees loomed like giant behemoth and the moon hung pale, casting little luminosity on the roofs around the hotel. On her balcony, she hadn't noticed two silhouettes standing. Her heart leaped and her throat tightened.

"Who are these men outside?"

"My guards."

"You mean your goons."

"You wouldn't expect me to show up without guards, would you?"

"I don't feel comfortable with them over there. Can you ask them to leave?"

He chuckled. "I don't feel comfortable *without* them."

"What is it that you want anyway?"

"A meeting of minds, if you will."

Her heart skipped a beat and her hand tightened on the chair she held. "How about if you get rid of those two guys outside before we talk. They make me nervous."

"O.K., I'll agree—if it makes you feel better."

He wheeled around and knocked on the window glass behind him. Immediately, the two leaped out of the balcony.

"*Voila!* Just the two of us. Cozy."

Not exactly what she had in mind.

Her eyes probed the room. Her mind was reeling so much, she found it impossible to think of anything else other than his threatening presence.

"Can I sit down?" she asked.

"Sure, make yourself at home." He chuckled at his own joke.

She faced him. A thin smile graced his lips.

"So," he said, "I've been reading your articles for the past fifteen years. I must say you have matured into quite a reporter."

"I'm not here to discuss my career with you. Just answer this. Why Emily?"

"Oh, *that* girl. Because she's the heiress to a media empire. And I would have used her if I had found her. Except, of course that she's been hiding."

"You never had her."

"She's quite clever your Emily. Clever young woman, indeed."

"The whole thing was about the manifesto, wasn't it?"

"The whole thing is about my *vision* and about *you*," he hissed.

"Myopic vision."

"Don't insult me!" he sprung to his feet. "I won't tolerate it!" He made two steps forward then sat back down.

"You could have given your manifesto to any other reporter. Why me?"

"Ah." He paused, looked away, then returned his gaze on her. "You're special. We have a unique relationship." His eyes pierced her, an arrow piercing her soul. "Remember the night we spent together on the rooftop?"

She bristled at the thought.

"I don't recall ever spending a night with you. *Ever*."

"Oh, yes, you did. You just don't remember. You don't know we were together."

She could feel the hair on the back of her neck stand. "What do you mean?"

"The day of the locusts."

She swallowed hard. "I remember that day. What about it?"

"I spent the night with you. I kept vigil all night."

"You mean to say that you spent all night watching me?"

"I spent the whole night with you." He was slow, deliberate. "I realized then that I did not want you to die. I just wanted you punished. And I wanted you to remember."

She closed her eyes not wanting to look at him. "Did you do anything to me?"

He did not respond.

"Did you?"

Still, no response.

Floodgates of anger opened in her chest and she struggled to maintain her composure. He had just tightened a vise around her heart.

"You have a sick and twisted mind," she said, "and a distorted way of looking at life."

He ignored her comments and went on. "It was quite a night. You were delirious."

"Why are you telling me all of this right now? What's your point? Because, I know you have one."

"Getting acquainted with you again. It's been many years, Kennedy." He brought his hand to his face and stroked his beard. "Kennedy," he said softly, "you're Kennedy for me, never Miss Hunter."

"Spare me the patronizing. What is it that you want from me right now?"

Suddenly, he rose and came forward. Few steps and he covered the distance between them.

She was already on her feet. He grabbed her by the wrist. "We are going for a ride in the desert."

"Hell if we are!"

"Keep quiet! Don't make me angry." He hissed in her ear while holding her in a tight embrace.

She attempted to unhinge herself from him.

"Get away from me!" She screamed louder.

Unexpectedly, there was a knock at the door, then several more. She heard her name called.

"Kennedy, Kennedy! Are you alright. Open! Open! This is Sami."

She cried, "Sami, help me! Help me!"

The Torch was still attempting to subdue her.

Suddenly, she saw something flash in his hand. A glimmering silver stiletto pierced her arm. She felt a sharp pain traverse her arm and then something thick, red, unctuous, trickle down her hand. She cried from the pain as he thrust her toward the balcony. Still holding on to her, he attempted to open the door.

She suddenly remembered she had her hotel key in her pocket. The key dangled on a plastic holder with sharp corners.

She pulled it and with one sharp movement thrusted it in his face. Instantly, he pulled back and as he did, the sharp edge of the key slid over his left eye.

Blinded, he screamed then grabbed his face.

The pounding on the door grew louder and more forceful and she heard voices down the hall. At once, there was a loud crash. The door came tumbling down and Sami tore in.

Instantly, The Torch released her. He opened the door to the balcony and leaped out. She rushed behind him, her open wound burning like embers under her hide. Sami dashed to the balcony and stopped short of leaping out. She spotted the indecision in his eyes, a moment of uncertainty she had not noticed till now. He did not utter any words but his eyes told her he would not, could not go after The Torch.

"It's O.K. Sami, let him go." She leaned over the balcony and peered in the dark but the night, thick, heavy, had already swallowed him.

CHAPTER FORTY-EIGHT

Casablanca—Emily Carrington, heir to the Coca-Cola fortune has been found, unharmed, after a long and arduous search. In a complicated plot worthy of Hollywood central casting involving plenty of bad guys, money and intrigue, the suspect allegedly responsible of the attempt on Emily Carrington's life is none other than a family member—Porter Fairfax—the greedy brother-in-law eager to cash in on an inheritance.

The Torch, who all along had claimed to hold her as a hostage, admitted fabricating the story in an attempt to manipulate the media. He had asked for his manifesto to be published by the international press in exchange for Emily's release.

Educated in the United States, The Torch was married to Christine Carter, an American and non-Moslem who bore him a son in Santa Monica, California. The Torch's son is being raised as a Christian and he has been making child custody payments since.

Ever since his return to Morocco more than fifteen years ago, he had been rallying North African Berbers in an attempt to kindle a nationalist movement and a return to strict Islamic rules. His forces had been concentrating mostly in Berber territory— namely south central Morocco, the Atlas Mountains and the sub-Sahara.

———•◆•———

She wrote an extended account of The Torch's life in the United States followed with a story about Emily's kidnapping and survival. Then she wrote how The Torch had manipulated her and the media.

She pounded on her laptop for several hours, her fingers flying over the keys like naked feet over hot asphalt. The words came fast. She did not have to think them or manipulate them. They were there, gushing from within, a volcano spewing lava.

When she finished she felt spent. Again, she was exhausted by words. She loved words but this time she had used them like a weapon, doing as much damage as if she had loaded a gun and fired it.

She read her copy one last time then, without hesitation, pressed the Send button. She added photos of The Torch, Christine Carter and her son. This, she thought, should make Martini happy. Then she climbed into her bed, turned off her lights, and closed her eyes. Tonight, she thought, I will not dream of Emily. Or The Torch. Or Africa. I will dream of golden beaches. Of curling waves. Of empty highways and vast expanses. Tonight, she thought, I will dream of America.

———•◆•———

Sometime during the night, the phone rang startling Kennedy.

"Kennedy! It's me!"

"Geez, Harry. You scared me!"

"Well, I know it's the middle of the night there, but I just could not stand it anymore. Your article. Wow, what a story!"

"You liked it?"

"You're kidding? It's all over the place. Picked up by the wires. I read it in *The Washington Post* too."

"Where is it in the paper?"

"Front page. Above the fold. What was it?"

"Oh, you mean size? The whole front page.

"Should make Martini happy."

"Hope so. You know anything about Porter and Janet?"

"Yeah, that's the reason I'm calling."

"So—what's happening?"

"I guess Janet heard from her sister last night. Then things started to happen very fast. Almost too fast."

"Well, are you going to tell me or just string me along?"

"Well, there was a little accident in the barn. I think things got hot between Porter and Wahid and there was a physical altercation."

"And?"

"One of the horses got excited and kicked Porter real bad."

"That's awful."

"Yeah. Guess which horse it was?"

"The one that belonged to—"

"Emily. The one named Maroc."

"Oh, really. How's Porter doing?"

"Not good. Doesn't look like he's gonna make it."

"That's too bad. I guess the universe has a way of settling things sometimes."

"Call it karma or poetic justice, whichever. If he makes it, he's gonna have to consider a different career other than playboy or gold-digger."

"What happened to Wahid?"

"He fled."

"Well, Harry, if he comes back to this country there's an arrest warrant out for him. He isn't going to get a wonderful reception here either."

"Hope not."

"Alright, Harry, I better get ready for the airport. I'm leaving this morning before all hell breaks loose."

"See you soon, Ken. I'll be glad to see you back here."

"Yeah, I'll be glad to get home. How cold is it in Virginia Beach?"

"As cold as a witch's tit," he chuckled.

"You always turn me on when you talk like a drunken sailor, Harry. You know that."

He guffawed aloud and hung up.

———————•◆•———————

The Royal Air Maroc counter was under siege. Passengers crammed the terminal as Sami navigated through and past the hordes. Finally, he walked her to the tarmac and watched her board the plane. He had kept quiet during the trip to the airport but now and then she had glanced at him and when their eyes met, he had averted her gaze.

"Good bye, Sami. Thank you for everything." She held her hand out and he took it.

"*Au revoir*, Kennedy," he said, then held his thumb up, "I'll remember you." He walked away.

Inside the plane, she viewed the terminal and beyond. She watched him from her window as passengers filed in. He was leaning against his little car, a cigarette dangling from his mouth, kicking dirt with his shoe, just like the first time she had seen him.

She raised a hand and waved and just at that moment, he lifted his eyes and saw her. He raised his right hand, and like a marathon runner brandished a hand in the air forming a V with two fingers. She waived and returned the gesture.

The plane was filling quickly. She hoped the seat near her would remain vacant.

Instantly, Kennedy's phone rang.

"Congratulations, Kennedy!" Ah, Martini. "Great job. I have another assignment for you."

"Think I can take a few days off?"

"Well, yeah, I suppose. Not for too long though. You might get rusty."

"Not a chance. What's the destination?"

"Oh, I'll tell you about it when you get home."

She listened to the roar of the plane and as they lifted, she kept her eyes on the city below her. The plane rose above the Atlantic then veered south towards the Sahara. Soon, there were only golden stretches below her, vast, barren, unforgiving. Instinctively, she reached as if to touch the sand. It glided between her fingers, turned to shimmering dust and vanished in the Saharan sky like ghosts in the night.

ABOUT THE AUTHOR

Monique Williams was a journalist at The Virginian Pilot and wrote for The Atlanta Journal Constitution, The Richmond Times and many more publications. She has also served as a Communications and Public Relations expert at various companies.

She currently lives in a suburb of Atlanta, GA.

20552992R00232

Made in the USA
Charleston, SC
16 July 2013